2003

Four Mothers

our Mothers

Shifra Horn

Translated from the Hebrew
by Dalya Bilu

ST. MARTIN'S PRESS
NEW YORK

Book design by Ellen R. Sasahara

Library of Congress Cataloging-in-Publication Data

Horn, Shifra.
    [Arba imahot. English]
    Four mothers / Shifra Horn ; translated from the Hebrew by
Dalya Bilu.
        p.   cm.
    ISBN 0-312-20547-3
    I. Bilu, Dalya.   II. Title.
PJ5055.23.O75A7313   1999
892.4'36—dc21   99-17448
                                                              CIP

First published in Israel by Sifriat Ma'ariv, 1996

First U.S. Edition: May 1999

10   9   8   7   6   5   4   3   2   1

To my son Gilad

Four Mothers

Chapter One

I was born in my great-grandmother Sara's brass bed in the summer of 1948. Salvos from the Jordanian cannons saluted the dramatic event with suitable noises in the background. Shells cleaved the whitening sky of the city of Jerusalem, seeking the addresses of those with whom destiny had made a bloody appointment. On that day I joined my voice to theirs and screamed my first scream. I was told this by the three women who greeted me in the outside world. We'll begin with my mother, Geula, whose expression of horror at the sight of the red creature emerging from her womb was the first image imprinted on the cells of my brain. To this day, even as I write these lines, she has not succeeded in recovering from what she calls the "humiliating" experience of giving birth to me. My grandmother, Pnina-Mazal, was the one who bent over the bed, smiled at me, and cooed the first words that shook the delicate membrane of my eardrums: "It's a girl, it's a girl. . . ." My great-grandmother, Sara, whose fresh scent of roses filled my nose, was the midwife, and when I grew up she told me that my birth had been a particularly easy one. No man was on hand to receive the news of my birth joyfully, and on my birth certificate, under "Father's Name," is written in round letters: "Unknown."

My story begins because of my father. I never met him and his name was never mentioned at home. I began my investigation into the question of my paternity after discovering the facts of life in a book that we would read furtively under the stairs leading to the grade three classroom in the Lady Meyuhas School for Girls. Since I was brought up by three women, I was sure that the role of the men I met in the homes of my friends was confined to earning a living for the members of their households and mumbling the Kiddush on Friday nights. In my family there was no man, I thought, because my mother and my two grandmothers did not need a breadwinner, and when they felt like having Kiddush, they knew how to do it themselves. The book that came into my hands threw my mind into a turmoil and shattered all my previous beliefs. My friends, who had read it before me, repeatedly assured me that it was impossible for a baby to be born without the participation of a man in the act of creation. This fact was written there in explicit, vowel-pointed words, accompanied by graphic illustrations that gave me a funny feeling in the pit of my stomach when I looked at them, and led me to the gloomy conclusion that in my family too there were men who had participated in bringing the women of the family, including me, into the world.

From then until the writing of these lines I have known no peace. Without beating about the bush I immediately commenced my investigations and inquiries into my mother's partner in the act of conception, the man called "my father." In reply to my questions my mother would shrug her shoulders and turn her back to me, revealing the nape of her stiff and wrinkled neck, from which hard, wiry red hairs sprouted together with soft, curly white ones, as if the years had softened her wayward hair as they turned it white. To this movement was usually added the word "pest" and the sentence "Who the hell cares!" which was repeated whenever I asked the question. These words were hissed at me between clenched and pointed teeth, which according to my grandmother had been like that ever since my mother was born.

I received no cooperation either from my grandmother Pnina-Mazal, who wandered round the town with her battalions of cats like a queen walking among her humble subjects. She had entered into a conspiracy of silence with my mother and adamantly refused to tell me anything about the fathers of our family in general and my father in particular, even during those hours of grace when she agreed to receive me in her house, which was steeped in the strong smells of tomcats in heat. Then she would dish up my lunch on a battered tin plate, exactly like the ones scattered throughout her large, spacious house and containing delicacies reserved for cats: chicken heads and the quivering intestines of creatures into whose identity I had no wish to inquire more closely. When I put my list of questions to her and tried to coax her to talk to me about my father, she would clear her throat, sum up her childhood in two sentences, and launch into detailed stories about the ones really close to her, her cats. And again I would try to turn things round and catch her out in a slip of the tongue, but she would extricate herself like a cat with nine lives, elegantly evading any pitfalls in its path.

Of her brother Yitzhak, who lived with her under the same roof, I had long despaired. Like a tree that had taken root he would sit all day long in an ancient armchair with bits of straw sticking out all over its shabby red upholstery. His flabby stomach descended in degrees from his many double chins to his always wet groin, and his bald head festooned with residual yellow moss gleamed at me.

Today I think that Pnina-Mazal agreed to keep him in her house because he served as a private playground for her cats. They would climb up his paunch with their curved claws hidden in their velvety paws, reach his ears, which were blocked with yellow wax, and cautiously taste with their jagged tongues. Then they would tickle the caves of his nose with their whiskers, elicit a sneeze, lightly bite his swollen cheeks, climb onto his head, and stand erect on its polished dome. When they tired they would leap straight into his capacious lap, where they would snuggle up like kittens and purr contentedly. Others would butt his calves, polish their nails on the thick material of his trousers, rub themselves against his thighs, sprinkle them with the marks of a strong male smell, and annex the pillars of his legs to their own private domain. During the afternoon nap Yitzhak's "regulars" would snooze cradled in his plump lap, their ears pricked, keeping a wary eye out for intruders.

In the course of one of my interrogations about the men in the family, Pnina-Mazal told me irrelevantly about how, a few years before, the tabby cat, the strongest and boldest of the tribe, hissing like a snake, had chased the "regulars" from Yitzhak's lap. Pushing down with her paws, the tabby leveled out a protected area, waited until she was alone, and then gave birth effortlessly to four multicolored kittens, over which she then kept guard fiercely, forbidding anyone to approach him, her, or them. When Yitzhak uttered his traditional cry of "Food," the women watered him through the long copper pipe normally used by

Sara, my great-grandmother, to distill rose water, inserting one end in his mouth and plunging the other into the clay jar of cold water in the kitchen. When his hunger grew they borrowed the long, charred wooden baker's peel from Abu Yussuf's pita bakery and served him his meals from a safe distance, for fear of the spitting and scratching of the new mother. Only twenty-four hours later, and after much coaxing, lip-smacking, promises, and soft, wheedling words showered on her by Pnina-Mazal, did the cat agree to move, leaving a souvenir on Yitzhak's fly in the form of a moist, red-rimmed stain festooned with the remains of four afterbirths, soft and quivering as purple jellies.

Such were the stories I succeeded in eliciting from Pnina-Mazal in reply to my questions about my family and my father. And if she preferred to talk about her cats, whose number was beyond my reckoning, it must have meant that in the course of time they had acquired the status of family relations, which the men had not.

*   *   *

The only one who agreed to cooperate and offer cautious replies to a few of my questions was my great-grandmother Sara. To this day, whenever I mention her name, I can smell the fresh scent of plucked roses that wafted from her and clung to her clothes, to her dishes, to the air in her stuffy room, and to me whenever I came to visit her. When I took the number 15 bus from her house to my mother's house in Talbiyeh, the sweet smell of roses would mount the steps with me, sit down on the hard wooden bench with me, and accompany me to school the next day.

Everyone agreed that my great-grandmother Sara was the most beautiful old woman they had ever seen. It was said that in her youth she had been the most beautiful woman in the world. From the day she was born, her admirers claimed, her beauty had been unrivaled. And if there had been competitions for beauty queens then, they added, Sara undoubtedly would have walked off with all the prizes year after year.

It was no easy matter to gain an interview with my great-grandmother Sara. In order to see her I had to wait my turn in the long line of grave, expressionless women huddled outside her door under the faded khaki canvas awning. This shelter had been put up for their benefit and tied to the top of the great mulberry tree, whose roots cracked the courtyard tiles, in order to protect them from the furious rains of the

Jerusalem winter and the blazing sun of the dry *hamseen* days that hung over the town in the summer. For hours they would stand under the awning, determined, patient, and silent, until crazy Dvora, who took care of my great-grandmother devotedly, parted on the doorstep from the happy supplicant who had emerged from her audience beaming with the grace bestowed on her and smelling sweetly of roses. Only then would Dvora invite the next woman to enter. Sometimes she would come out to the mute crowd and announce that Sara was tired and tell them to come again tomorrow. And they would disperse, quiet and obedient, and come back the next day to take their places in a new group of dull-eyed women. Thus I would stand there for hours in the line, until Dvora came out and ushered me in.

My great-grandmother Sara would receive me in her brass bed, leaning against starched pillows that sprouted flowers of *broderie anglaise,* and her white hair would surround her head in a ring of pure radiance and illuminate the faces of those sitting opposite her. The color of her hair was the whitest I had ever seen in my life. Perhaps it could be compared to the gleaming white of the highest mountaintops in the world, covered with a snow that no human foot has dirtied, no speck of dust has touched, and no human eye has beheld. For if that white penetrated your eyes they would be blinded and black spots would dance before them.

Her long white hair and her eyes glowing with the sweetness of honey would illuminate the dimness of the room for me. After asking me how I was getting on at school and work, she would respond to my inquiries and tell me about her childhood, her mother, her children and grandchildren. But when she came to her granddaughter, my mother, she would stop talking, close her eyes wearily, and ask me to come again tomorrow for the end of the story. The next day, after a long wait, she would tell me new stories about rose water, about horses whose manure was fragrant, and about a comet that cleaved the sky, but when the conversation turned to my father, she would tire and ask me to leave. This went on for years.

How old was she? No one spoke of this for fear of the evil eye. To me she revealed in a whisper that she was "a day and a night old" without explaining what she meant. It often seemed to me—and my grandmother Pnina-Mazal and my mother Geula hinted this too—that Sara was waiting to receive the sign to close her eyes forever from me, of all people. Something special was supposed to happen to me in order for her to yield her body to death, and this premonition prevented me from doing anything out of the ordinary. I was careful to keep to as regular a daily schedule as possible and I imposed a tedious routine on myself, from which I never strayed to the left or the right. I tried not to move the furniture in my room unnecessarily, refrained from stepping on the lines dividing the floor tiles from each other, and followed exactly the same path to school every day. I even refrained from abandoning the neighborhood grocery store, where Haim the grocer cheated on the weight of the sliced yellow cheese, and taking my custom to the gleaming new supermarket that had opened near our house, in case this move should prove to be the act in which Sara would find a pretext for responding to death's invitation.

I imagined death as a man dressed in a tailcoat and top hat, just like the figure I had seen in the picture on display in the dusty window of "Rahamim & Sons, Photographers." This elegantly dressed gentleman had passed over Sara all this time, as if he was stricken by her beauty and dazzled by the radiance of her hair whenever he tried to visit her and take her away with him.

❈   ❈   ❈

This terrifying responsibility for the longevity of my great-grandmother, which was irrevocably tied to my future actions, was conveyed to me by the women of my family indirectly and without words. Perhaps this explains my late marriage. When I decided to get married, in willful opposition to my mother, who did not believe in the institution, I prepared to announce my intention to Sara in fear and trembling, lest it provide her with the excuse to die at last.

To my surprise, on the day I had chosen to make my announcement I was not obliged to wait with the other women. As soon as I joined the end of the line under the mulberry tree, crazy Dvora came running up to me as if she didn't have a moment to lose and told me that Sara was waiting for me and that I was to go in to her immediately.

Weak at the knees I entered the room, afraid of her reaction to this significant change in my life, a change that was liable to shorten her own life. Contrary to my expectations, she greeted me with a smile. After congratulating me, she asked me for a picture of my husband-to-be and laid down its measurements: forty centimeters by thirty. When I returned with the picture she gave it to Dvora and magisterially instructed her to take it to David the framer in the nearby neighborhood of Zichron Moshe: "He'll know what to do with it." And when Dvora returned with the picture in a heavy frame surrounded by gray passe-partout, Sara asked her to hang the new male addition to the family at the end of the ruler-straight row, where the faces of three men trapped in identical frames hung side by side at regular intervals, like beads lined up on an abacus. The picture of my future husband Sara ordered to be hung exactly over the dark rectangular stain on the wall, and the nail that had once held the portrait banished from its place in the distant past easily bore the weight of the new picture. As I contemplated the exhibition on the wall, the four men surveying me mercilessly with their mocking eyes looked like a collection of trophies gathered by headhunters.

At this moment of grace, with the picture of my husband-to-be hanging over her head, I asked her to tell me about the fathers of the family. She began with Yitzhak, the husband of her mother Mazal, continued with her own Avraham, and concluded with my grandfather David. There she stopped, because when she reached my father her lids drooped and she intimated that she wanted to rest. When crazy Dvora accompanied me to the door she muttered, as if to herself, that now that my husband's picture was hanging there on the wall with all the rest, the minute I gave birth to our first offspring he would leave me. She added that it was the curse with which the women of my family were blessed.

At the time I failed to understand how a curse could bless, and since Dvora had lost her wits a long time before, I didn't attach any importance to her words. I remembered them ten months later, the day after my son was born, when my husband slammed the door behind him, never to return.

*   *   *

My great-grandmother Sara did not depart this world immediately after my marriage. On the contrary, it seemed to me that she was waiting, with renewed strength, for the next change in me before she could close her eyes in peace. Dvora, who knew her better than any of us, would say, "So that she can be reincarnated in a new baby, which will never be as beautiful as her, because Sara in her present life has used up all the beauty due to her in all her incarnations, past and future." Even after the wedding, which was certainly a dramatic and unusual event in my life, the elegant gentleman in the top hat and tails did not succeed in visiting Sara and taking her away from me.

Now full of hope that my great-grandmother would live forever, I would go to her house once a week and wait my turn among the silent women. When I sat down next to her I could feel her eyes gazing intently and expectantly at my still-flat stomach. At the end of each visit I would leave with a pain in my gut, as if her eyes had succeeded in penetrating my stomach, delving into my intestines, invading my womb, and making as free with my body as if it were her own.

Three weeks after the wedding the thing happened that we had been trying as hard as we could to prevent. In spite of all the precautions we had taken, and against all odds, the sperm hit the egg.

From that moment I remember nights of weeping and desperate attempts on my part to explain to my new husband that it wasn't my fault I had become pregnant. I tried to explain to him that Sara had done it to me, just as she had done it to all the women who waited for her in the cold and the heat under the canvas awning. My husband would wound me with a disbelieving look and mutter something about the hereditary insanity of the women in my family that had now clearly affected me too.

Now I would wait patiently in the line with the flat-bellied women for an audience with my great-grandmother, painfully aware of their sidelong looks piercing my rounding stomach like daggers. I would enter her presence stabbed by looks that tore the sides of my stomach, wounded my heart, and roamed enviously and yearningly in the darkness of my expanding womb.

Sara would receive me with her honey eyes glowing, slide her sweet look over my belly, and murmur as if to herself, "Blessed be the Lord, a son, a male child."

"How do you know I'm going to have a boy?" I would ask her repeatedly, and receive the reply, "Because of your stomach, which comes to a point in the front."

Later on I dared to ask her about the curse hinted at by crazy Dvora and about my husband who would leave me after the birth; Sara would shrink at the question, pretend to be deaf, survey my belly with eager eyes, and ask me to leave the room because she was tired.

I became afraid of her, as if my beloved great-grandmother had turned into the Lilith who kills fetuses in the womb and steals babies from their cradles, and I would try to hold my swollen belly in and make it smaller whenever I visited her.

The day I left the hospital with my son in my arms I went straight to Sara. She looked at my sleeping baby, whose pursed lips were busy reconstructing the taste of my milk, whose mind was busy dreaming about the protective walls of my womb, and whose ears were full of the sounds of the warm, soothing waters in which he had been swimming for nine long months, and asked me to give her the diapered bundle.

With weak, gnarled hands whose taut skin revealed a network of pulsing blue veins she received her great-great-grandson, and immediately dropped him again. The baby fell softly onto the starched bedcovers.

"Is it a boy or a girl?" she asked, as if she needed to hear the answer from my own lips, even though she had already heard the news from her daughter and granddaughter.

"A boy," I replied.

"Undo the swaddling clothes!" she commanded in her flowery Hebrew. "I want to behold him with my own eyes."

With the clumsy fingers of a new mother I undid the urine-soaked diaper and waved the lower half of the baby's body in front of her.

Her myopic eyes armed with spectacles whose thick lenses looked like the bottoms of transparent wine bottles focused on the foreskin-covered little protuberance sticking up before her.

"A son," she said as if to herself. "The curse is over." And she closed her eyes and asked me to leave the room, as she was tired.

If I had expected to be asked to call the child after his grandfather or great-grandfather, I was wrong. Sara made no such request.

I left her on her smooth, spotless white bed with her eyes closed and her hair shining radiantly around her head.

✴　✴　✴

Dvora accompanied me to the door and told me that my grandmother was very happy now. "A son has been born and the chain has been broken."

When I asked her what she meant, she said that if I investigated my family history I would understand, and the first fact I should take into account was that my husband had left me the day after I gave birth, never to return.

When I looked deeply into her demented eyes she suddenly seemed completely sane, and the seriousness of her words made my skin prickle in fear.

"You're lucky, a son at the first birth, and you have no husband now to force you to give birth to a daughter who will bear the curse," she said.

The next day she called me and told me in tears that when she got up in the morning and went into the old lady's room to make her bed and wake her up for her morning coffee, she found that she had died in her sleep. "But she had the same smile on her face as when she saw your baby," she added as if to console me.

When I reached my great-grandmother's house that morning I was greeted by a strong smell of dying roses. I found her on the brass bed—more beautiful than ever. She was lying on her back, her face radiant as if she had just received glad tidings, and her hair, which Dvora had combed, covering her entire body like a white silk sheet. When I went home after making the funeral arrangements I was accompanied all the way there by the smell of wilted roses, which clung to my body, my clothes, and the baby at my breast, and refused to go away for many days afterward. The smell would steal into my nostrils at unexpected hours and inappropriate moments, squeezing jets of tears from my eyes and convulsing my body with sobs whose meaning I did not always understand. Sometimes I felt in them the grief at the death of my great-grandmother, sometimes I was sure that they stemmed from the post-partum crisis against which I had been warned, and sometimes I wept for my husband's desertion.

⁕   ⁕   ⁕

My great-grandmother Sara left me three things: her brass bed, in whose softness I had been born and on which I loved to jump, as if on a trampoline, when I was small; the gold napoleon that she always wore round her neck on a black velvet ribbon, even in the bath; and the *sandouk*—the hooped dowry chest made of rusted metal that looked like a pirate's treasure chest, which stood at the foot of her bed and upon which she would grandly lay her dressing gown. The enormous brass bed and the *sandouk,* which was heavy and full of treasures I could as yet only imagine, were transported by Haleb, the porter I hired next to the Damascus Gate. The bed and the *sandouk* swayed on the ramshackle van bearing the blue license plate of the occupied territories and attracted curious looks from the passersby.

I sold the napoleon the same month, being short of cash, to Zion, the goldsmith from Geula. He was glad to buy it from me for two thousand shekels, its value by weight. At the same time he was honest enough to tell me that his price did not include its value as a two-hundred-year-old coin, and that if I wanted to get more money for it, I should look for a coin collector, who would undoubtedly pay me more, while he could pay me only its weight in gold. But upon closer examination he told me that I would not find a collector who would pay me more, since the coin had been cut in two and joined later by the hand of a master craftsman. He pointed to an almost invisible scratch on the gold coin, which he had been able to discern only with the help of a magnifying glass. After a long and thorough examination he added that only his grandfather Yihiye, once the neighborhood goldsmith, would have been capable of making the join.

He called his mother from the upstairs apartment, and she glanced at the coin through the magnifying glass and told us about the beautiful woman holding two halves of a coin in her hand who had illuminated her father's dark little shop with her golden hair. "My father, a very pious man, refused to look at her. All the time she was talking to him he sat opposite her with his eyes closed. As a child I thought that he was dazzled by the radiance of her hair and afraid of being blinded and rendered incapable of pursuing his profession. Today I'm convinced that he was afraid to look at her lest she bewitch him by her beauty, cause him to lose his wits and bring down trouble on his head."

Thus I heard the first story about my great-grandmother Sara. In the course of time, as I collected more and more stories about my family, I came to realize that within the radius of the neighborhoods of Zichron Moshe, Ohel Moshe, and Geula there was hardly a single soul who had not known her, seen her, met her, or heard about her.

As for the *sandouk,* it remained locked and unopened for an entire month. Whenever I approached it I shrank from opening the lid, afraid of confronting the dark and terrible secret that I both longed and feared to know.

Until one evening when I put my baby to bed after the ritual of the bath and the broken television set transmitted nothing but hypnotic flickering lines and shining stars to my tired eyes. That evening I went apprehensively up to the chest and lifted the heavy lid quickly, before I could have second thoughts. The lid rose with difficulty, with the discordant creak of rusty iron, and a silvery flock of pale, soft-bodied, short-winged moths rose in its wake, sprinkling me with dust, like stardust from a fairy's wand. I watched the moths as they sailed suicidally toward the swaying naked bulb, and then changed their minds and settled haphazardly on the walls of the room. With a sense of doom I peeped inside the chest, expecting the worst.

The chest was full of tin boxes of different sizes, some of them round English shortbread tins with a picture of a sentry in a bearskin hat on their lids. There were also coffee tins with Arabic writing on them, tins for cocoa imported from Holland, and many other, unidentifiable tins, piled one on top of the other. All the tins I opened contained pictures, masses of pictures, which rose into a great, yellowing pile on the bed. Some of them were brown, some crudely colored, and nearly all of them were eaten into by tiny insects whose like I had never seen before and whose name I did not know. Judging by the inroads they had made in the apparel of the figures in the photographs, their gastronomic preference appeared to be for clothing. When they wanted to vary the menu, they devoured the hand-painted snowy mountains appearing on the backdrop of the photographs, and the long hair crowning the heads of the women. Occasionally they enjoyed nibbling the eyes, leaving an expression of hollow-eyed panic in the wake of their jaws.

On the backs of those photographs in which steep mountains rose behind photographed figures whose cheeks had been reddened, whose hair had been yellowed, and whose eyes had been painted bright blue by the hand of the photographer was a round purple stamp bearing the legend "Photographic Studio of Rahamim Cohen—Ohel Moshe." And underneath the words in the circle was a picture of a delicate gazelle.

Other photographs looked like the pathetic attempts of an amateur journalist who had carefully posed battalions of soldiers in front of him and ordered them to hold their stomachs in and their heads up and clean the specks of dust off their breeches or their tartan kilts. And others documented gleaming, heavy cannons loaded with the help of a long rod, squares, horses, foreign landscapes, and portraits of men and women who had departed this world long ago. These photographs were stamped in red with the initials "EG." The stamp looked new, as if it had been impressed only a few hours before. The letters were surrounded by an oval frame and decorated with curlicues, like Gothic letters.

At the bottom of the chest the last box waited to be opened. It was wrapped in tulle, which disintegrated at my touch and left a little heap of yellow dust behind it. The edges of the box, which had become stuck together during the course of the years, refused to open and reveal their secret. I pulled a hairpin out of my hair, inserted it beneath the rim of the lid, and loosened the thin tin a little. The lid opened timidly and reluctantly.

A pile of pictures spilled onto the bed. At the sight of them I felt my heart literally skip a beat. And when I recovered I looked to see what was written on the backs of the photographs. They too bore the red stamp with the initials "EG." From the subjects of the photographs it was clear that the photographer had been very close to my great-grandmother Sara.

Her glowing eyes, which gazed at me from the moment immortalized by the photograph, glittered with the look of a woman in the afterglow of the act of love. Her naked body was shamelessly arched, her breasts defiant and her chin held high. With my skin prickling into gooseflesh I knew that this photographer, whose name had never been mentioned at home, had been closer to her than any other man.

And thus, cradled in her brass bed that sucked me into its lap with the gentle insistence of silent, discreet old mattresses, which have suffocated the sighs of people long gone, and swallowed the passionate cries of those who drowned in their softness, I dived into the mountain of photographs. During those sleepless nights, between changing diapers and breast-feeding, I made up my mind to embark on a journey in search of my family.

Chapter Two

When I was born, so I was told, my mother decided to call me Amal (which means "labor" or "travail" in Hebrew and "hope" in Arabic), a pure socialist name with profound class symbolism, one that sounds good in both Hebrew and Arabic. Not everyone applauded her decision. I remember incidents in which my mother would encounter raised eyebrows in reaction to my name, which in those days was considered unusual and strange. Gleefully she would pounce on the eyebrow-raiser and wither him with one of her harder looks, scornfully remarking that it was "disgraceful to expose such ignorance." She would ask: "How could you fail to recognize that my daughter is called by a pure biblical name?" And when she saw the puzzled look on her interlocutor's face she would quote chapter and verse from the Book of Job: "For man is born unto travail."

At the Lady Meyuhas School for Girls, too, which I attended in my early years, my name proved controversial. The headmistress claimed that it was unbecoming for a pretty little girl to be called by such a charged, portentous, and foreign-sounding name. So they decided to add the letters "y" and "a" to my name and called me Amalya. In the first term of my studies in grade one I was called Amalya at school and Amal at home. This custom came to an end when my quick-tempered mother discovered the appending of the holy letters "y" and "a" to my name on my end-of-term report; the very next day, after shouts and protests clearly audible from the headmistress's room, she was promised that from then on I would be called by my original name.

Since I was only too well aware of my mother's belligerent nature, I never told her that at school they continued to call me Amalya and only used my original name, Amal, on official documents and end-of-term reports, as if for form's sake, to mollify and appease her. My close friends were allowed to call me Mali for short, but with one reservation: when they were at my house they had to address me by my official name as it appeared on my ID card—Amal.

The problem of my name became particularly difficult from the moment I was discovered by boys, worsened when the boys grew into youths, and caused irrevocable damage when men appeared in my life. The name Amal was ground like gravel in their mouths, and led them all, as if they had agreed in advance, to call me Mali for short, a non-committal, amiable name with a romantic sound. For how could anyone love a girl called Amal, however attractive she might be, how could anyone groaning in the heat of passion call out this name, whose very sound was enough to cause the stiffest member to dwindle? Accordingly, all the youths and men who came into my life called me Mali, and all my attempts to explain to them that in my house I had to be called Amal fell on deaf ears. When they phoned me at home and asked to speak to Mali, my mother would slam the phone down, though not before announcing in her hard, official voice that no one by that name lived in her house.

To this day, when I have to introduce myself, I become confused. Sometimes I introduce myself as Amal and sometimes as Amalya. And sometimes, when I'm particularly flustered, I introduce myself as Amalya-Amal, and they're all sure that Amal is my surname and they admire the originality of the combination.

✳   ✳   ✳

Questions about my father became particularly important to me during my school days, when I had to fill in forms from the Education Ministry at the beginning of every year. I had no trouble filling in my mother's name and occupation—Geula, lawyer—but when I came to my father's name I hesitated between Moshe and Ya'akov. I decided on Moshe, and as his occupation I chose policeman. All the children in my class wanted their father to be a policeman, but only I could permit myself to proudly write it down. I would boast of my policeman father and talk about his peaked cap and pistol and handcuffs, and how all the crooks in town trembled at the mention of his name. I explained his absence by saying that he was busy chasing burglars all day and only came home late at night. Only my two best friends, Dafna and Na'ama, knew that I didn't have a father—or, more precisely, that I once had a father and now I didn't.

My father the policeman played a starring role in my life until the third grade, until the moment when the homeroom teacher asked me to bring him to class so that he could tell us about his work. When I evaded the issue with all kinds of excuses, she phoned my mother. That evening, sitting across from me at the kitchen table, over our omelettes and salad, she told me that from now on, when I had to give my father's name, I should write "Unknown."

"He's known to you," I retorted, "and I'm his daughter, and I deserve to know his name and occupation too."

"It's none of my business and none of yours," she replied, shrugging her shoulders and waving her hand in the familiar gesture of dismissal.

"And if I haven't got a father, why don't you get married so I can have a new father?" I insisted.

Her reaction astonished me. She burst into wild laughter, wiping the tears bursting from her eyes with her sleeve.

"What for?" she asked. "What do we need someone hanging around the house and dishing out orders for? For me to have to wash his socks and listen to him snoring at night? We're better off alone," she added, and uncharacteristically put her arm round my shoulders and hugged me affectionately. The smell of naphthalene clinging to her pinched my nose and made me sneeze.

⁎   ⁎   ⁎

The hug she gave me then was rare. Strain my memory as I will, no pictures of tenderness and closeness between me and my mother come to mind. My mother was an advocate of strictness in education. In body language and without words she expressed the feeling that this was not the child she had wished for, and that she would have gotten along just fine if I had never been born.

In general, whatever I did in my life I felt that I was disappointing my mother.

The first bone of contention between us was my hair. She wanted me cropped and I wanted to grow my hair long. My mother had an inexplicable objection to long hair; to be more precise, she hated long hair. Whenever my hair passed the ear line she would seat me on the tall stool in the kitchen and chop it off with hatred, her teeth clenched in rage. For years I went about with a boy's cropped haircut, until the day I stood my ground and prevented her by force from shearing my locks. After that she would try to persuade me to do her will with the legal tactics she had adopted in daily life as well as in court. For hours she would prove to me with cold logic that short hair was both healthier and more beautiful. When her words had no effect, she would draw my attention to the plumbing, and threaten that my long hair would clog up the pipes and cause a flood. When logic failed, she would raise her voice. Despite the psychological warfare she waged against me I clung to my long hair and prevented her from wreaking vengeance on it with her ruthless scissors.

I shall never forget her satisfaction upon discovering lice eggs in my hair. Resolutely she seized hold of my arm, led me to the kitchen stool, and with hands reeking of naphthalene ruthlessly chopped off my locks, repeating through pursed lips: "I told you so, long hair brings nothing but trouble."

And there were quarrels about clothes too. Even though I asked her to buy me dresses and skirts, she would return from the shops with a pair of short gathered bloomers in summer and long flannel trousers in winter.

My grandmother Pnina-Mazal, who saw my suffering, would surprise me from time to time with the gift of a dress. I couldn't take the dress home with me, and I would wear it clandestinely, far from my mother's watchful eyes, when I went to visit my friends and on the days I spent at my grandmother's house because of my mother's long working hours.

On account of the gnarled mulberry tree growing in my great-grandmother's yard too I aroused my mother's wrath. I refused adamantly to climb it despite my mother's announcements that the best mulberries grew at the top of the tree. When I wanted to enjoy its fruit,

I would set a stool below a low branch, stretch my body, and pluck the juicy fruit carefully so as not to stain myself.

My mother would watch my efforts scornfully, twist her mouth in contempt, and retire to the house in order to avoid witnessing the shameful spectacle.

The summer I turned eight our relations reached a severe crisis, and all because of the tree. That year thousands of cardboard boxes swarmed with life in houses all over the country, boxes that once had held shoes and were now home to soft-bodied silkworms, whose thin gray skins were grooved and marked with delicate folds. I hid my box under the gas stove in Sara's kitchen. It had made its way from my house to my great-grandmother's because of my mother's hysterical reaction to the sight of the tiny, delicate, touchingly innocent-looking and completely harmless caterpillars. Screaming with a shrillness that was utterly at odds with her cool, reserved image, she threw me and my silkworms out of the house. My scientific explanations about the fine silk blouse she wore to court, which owed its existence to these same little caterpillars, fell on deaf ears.

The permanent heat in Sara's kitchen and the freshness of the mulberry leaves, which I took care to pick every day from the tree in the courtyard for the soft-bodied little guzzlers, accelerated their growth. They swelled and thickened, and the steady rustling of their jaws as they munched the crisp leaves was music to my ears.

My silkworms might have spun their cocoons in peace and turned into glorious moths if not for the constant rustling noise they made with their jaws, and it was this that caused my mother to bend down by the stove, holding a dustpan in one hand and a rolling pin in the other, an expression of brave determination on her face, ready and willing to wage war to the bitter end against the mouse she knew lurked underneath. Her screams when her groping hands encountered my box of silkworms and crushed a few, squirting green worm juice in all directions, brought crazy Dvora running with a pail full of dirty water, which she proceeded to pour over my fainting mother. Anticipating the trouble about to descend on my head, I jumped over my mother, who was lying on the floor with an expression of disgust on her face, and crawled under the cooker.

I picked up the box of plump silkworms and hurried to the mulberry tree. I pulled up the stool, placed the box on a broad bough above my head, and hung suspended from the bough. For the first time in my life I found myself climbing the tree, ascending from branch to branch with the swarming shoebox squashed under my arm. At a height that made me giddy I removed my plump, well-fed protégés one by one from the box and set them down carefully on the dusty leaves. The silkworms swayed on the broad leaves, slipped, strengthened their grip with the help of their slimy secretions, and began to eat with dedication. Only after making sure that they were acclimatized on the leaves did I climb down, ignoring the astonished looks of my mother, sitting under the mulberry tree to recover in the fresh air.

"Where are they?" she asked, the expression of disgust still on her face.

"They're all on the tree," I replied, the toe of my left shoe tracing semicircles on the ground. The picture was spoiled when her hand landed on my cheek in the first slap I had ever received from her in my life.

"And what do you think will happen on the tree?" she asked, a threatening note in her voice. "They'll be fruitful and multiply there and we'll never be able to get rid of them, and you can say good-bye to Grandmother's tree."

I didn't really understand why I had to say good-bye to the tree, but since she was so angry I did as she bade me and waved good-bye to the crest of the tree.

A second slap, more painful than the first, landed on my cheek. "Don't you dare be smart with me," she snapped through her jagged teeth, but she stopped when she saw Sara standing in the door, staring at her furiously.

"Don't touch the child," Sara said in a voice whose softness was in shocking contrast to the fury on her face.

All that summer my mother refrained from sitting under the mulberry tree lest one of the loathsome creatures, as she called them, should fall on her and be impaled on her bristling hair. If she was obliged to cross the yard, she would make a wide detour round the tree swarming with caterpillars and inspect the ground carefully before she put her foot down, lest she squash a fat silkworm with her shoe.

At the end of summer the tree was decorated with scores of shiny, rough, yellow cocoons, as if long, ripe, silken fruit had grown on it. A few days later there were already pairs of clumsy white moths fluttering heavily on its branches, stuck to each other by their tails, in an endless dance of love that brought them closer to their deaths.

The summer after that my mother's prophecy was not fulfilled: The mulberry tree was not covered with caterpillars, and when shoeboxes full of silkworms were distributed at school I refused to accept one.

*   *   *

As a rule my mother was very busy. As an advocate she defended the underdogs, especially the Arabs, who she told me had been robbed of their land by the state to build railways and roads that bisected their villages and cut through their fields, and whom she helped even when the authorities suspected them of nefarious deeds. She took no money from them, and was compensated for her work when they arrived at our door with heavy wicker baskets full of grapes, peaches, or broody hens, which she would make haste to transfer in disgust to my great-grandmother's house. Sara knew exactly what to do with the hens, and how to make chicken soup with delicate beads of fat floating on its surface.

When I was a child I thought that my mother was the most elegant woman in Jerusalem. She was apparently very different in her childhood and youth. Then, according to my grandmother Pnina-Mazal, my mother dressed exclusively in boys' clothes, and if she bought her a dress as a present, my mother would cut it to pieces with scissors. Now that she was a lawyer, she would leave the house dressed in a tight black skirt and a white silk blouse.

For her appearances in court she would remove from the wardrobe—without taking into account the season of the year or the opinion of the judge—her fox fur. Smelling strongly of naphthalene, the fox would slumber on her shoulders, its tail stuck in its mouth and fastened with a rusty metal clip, and its fur decorated with round bald spots produced by the jaws of generations of moths. The circle of fur would dig its claws into her shoulders as if afraid of falling, look straight into the judge's face with its amber eyes, and prick up its cardboard-stiffened ears, as if determined not to miss a word of the proceedings.

When my mother was angry in court her hard red hair would bristle, and her upper lip would rise in a snarl, exposing a row of pointed teeth. Afterward the accused would say that the fox's fur bristled too, and that they had heard it growl threateningly at the judge. Under these circumstances the toughest and strictest judge would quail, and she always won her cases. "Vixen" they called her in the courthouse corridors, because of her red hair, because of the malevolent expression on her face, because of her teeth, or perhaps because of the fox that had been cruelly slaughtered in order to provide a faithful companion for her neck. Both of them, the fox and the neck, grew shabbier in the course of the years, but they never deserted each other.

* * *

During these years of my childhood, when my mother was busy with endless litigation in the courts of the town, I was lovingly brought up by my grandmother Pnina-Mazal. Every day after school I would walk to her house, which was close to the school, a spacious house in the neighborhood of Rehavia purchased with the compensation she had received from the British army.

Together with me dozens of cats in all the colors of the rainbow grew up in that house. It all began with a pampered English cat my grandmother received from her commanding officer in the British staff headquarters. Before he left the country he begged her to give it a home, because it was forbidden to bring animals into England, and if he had insisted on gaining entry for his pet, it would have had to spend six months in the solitary confinement of quarantine. My grandmother, who had never touched the fur of a cat in her life and whose sole verbal contact with hairy quadrupeds consisted of the word "scat," could not withstand his pleading eyes and agreed to give the aristocratic cat a home.

A month later the cat began to utter deep throaty sounds, to arch its back, to lie on the floor and wriggle from side to side, and altogether to behave in a suspicious manner. My grandmother, inexperienced in the rearing of cats, could not understand why all the mangy cats of the neighborhood, to which she referred slightingly as "catos vulgaris," were besieging her front door, scratching themselves nervously and giving off a sharp smell that made people keep their distance from her.

At the end of two and a half months there were already six varicolored little balls of fur growing up in her house, fighting with dainty claws for every teat. Pnina-Mazal, a kindhearted woman, loved them all. She gave them names and decided to keep them at home. Thus it happened that a year after she had been presented with the English cat there were thirteen cats in her house, and they too were fruitful and multiplied. During the course of the years her house filled with cats of every hue. Sometimes, when she served me my lunch on a chipped tin plate, I was obliged to fight off impertinent cats climbing onto my lap and from there to the table and straight to my plate, where they tried to compare the food I had been given with that dished up to them.

*   *   *

On weekends my grandmother was visited by Yiftah, who lived on kibbutz Givat Hagefanim, not far from Jerusalem. Yiftah, who was my own age, was the son of Avraham, whose father, Yitzhak, had been planted motionless in the armchair in Pnina-Mazal's house from the day I first met him.

Yiftah and I had a lot in common. I had no father and Yiftah had no mother. Actually he had a mother, but she left him when she found herself an American millionaire who came to plant a tree in Israel. Pnina-Mazal told me that Flora, Yiftah's mother, met the millionaire when she served him supper in the kibbutz dining room, and won his heart with the tanned legs covered in soft golden fuzz exposed by her short pants. He took her with him to America, and from there she would send Yiftah colored postcards, Crayola crayons, and jeans, which were then hard to come by in Israel. In spite of all this, Yiftah used to say that for him she didn't exist, she wasn't with him here, and as far as he was concerned he didn't have a mother.

His father Avraham remarried, a young girl from the kibbutz, who gave him four children in six years. But she too could not be a mother to Yiftah, and he called her a "phony mother." The kibbutz children called Yiftah a "son of a whore" and I could never work out if they called him this because of his American mother or because of the one on the kibbutz.

When Yiftah arrived to visit Pnina-Mazal and his motionless grandfather Yitzhak, we would shut ourselves up in one of the rooms of the house—not before emptying it of all the cats, which hissed and spat disapprovingly in our faces and threatened us with their claws. There, in the room smelling of cats in heat, we would play at mothers and fathers. Since we had never actually seen a mother and father in action, the game took on a character all its own, and it would always end with desertion by the father or abandonment by the mother.

The game went something like this:

Yiftah: "Perhaps you'll do my kitchen duty tonight. I've been working all day in the cowshed and my back's broken."

Me: "I've been in court all day and I'm just as tired as you are."

Yiftah: "And where did you put my Sabbath trousers?"

Me: "I don't know. Look for them yourself."

Yiftah: "I'm fed up. I'm going to look for another wife."

And so the game was over in a flash. Then we played the version where the mother leaves, and this time it was over even more quickly.

In those days we both felt very special and different from all the other children. I often envied my friends, whose fathers came home from work, gave them presents, swung them in the air, and took an interest in how they were getting on at school. With me there was nobody to take an interest. My mother was busy with her work, Pnina-Mazal with her cats, and my great-grandmother Sara with the women coming to petition her from all over the country. My feeling of deprivation disappeared when I discovered that things could have been far worse. This happened when my mother traveled out of town to attend a course, and Pnina-Mazal informed her that she was expecting three births over the weekend, and she would therefore not be able to look after me or have Yiftah to stay. It was decided that I should go to Givat Hagefanim and spend the Sabbath with Yiftah there.

Excited and spick and span, his Sabbath shirt gleaming with whiteness and his fair hair wet and precisely parted, Yiftah met me at the kibbutz gate and led me proudly along the narrow paths, pointing out the one-storied little houses surrounded by flower beds and green lawns. At that moment Yiftah looked to me like a king showing off his private kingdom to his queen. In the evening he took me to a building whose rooms were crowded with beds covered with brightly colored bedspreads and showed me my bed.

"And where are you going to sleep?" I asked.

"Right here, next to you."

"And who's going to sleep in the other beds?"

"The kibbutz children."

"Don't they have a mother or a father either?" I asked, pleased that we all shared a common fate.

"They do, but their parents sleep in their own houses and they sleep here."

I tried to take in this new information. There were fathers and mothers, but the children didn't stay at home and they slept together far from their parents. In other words, their parents weren't interested in them, and this meant that the children of kibbutz Givat Hagefanim were abandoned children. I considered the pros and cons, and came to the conclusion that my situation could have been a lot worse. I had been abandoned by my father, and Yiftah had been abandoned by his mother, but here on the kibbutz the children had been abandoned by both their parents. I fell asleep with a feeling of relief, knowing that fate had been kind to me.

Chapter Three

As mentioned above, my mother did not believe in the institution of marriage and took every opportunity to denounce it as fossilized and obsolete. At the same time, she failed to understand why I took an interest in boys, or what all the excitement was about. Apparently she assumed that if she herself took no interest in men, it was a foregone conclusion that her daughter, flesh of her flesh and bone of her bone, would follow in her footsteps.

The tension at home reached a climax when boys began to show an interest in me. They would hang around outside our house, closed and barred to them, dense with the smell of naphthalene, and my mother would go out and chase them away with her bristling hair and the noises she made though her clenched teeth. When they grew a little older, they would wait for me on the corner on my way to school, far from my mother's watchful eye, and cast lots to decide who would have the good fortune to carry my heavy cowhide bag to the gates of the Lady Meyuhas School for Girls. The bolder ones would wait for me after school and try to kiss me under the purple bougainvillea that covered the walls of the school. When these boys became youths they would interrupt my mother's afternoon nap with their telephone calls, asking to speak to Mali. The taller they grew, the more their voices deepened and their muscles swelled, the more self-confident they became, and they mounted a frontal assault on my heart. The bolder among them would advance right to the threshold of the house and wait for me to come out, and the moment the door opened grudgingly they would insert the toe of their shoe between it and the doorpost, to prevent my mother from slamming it in their faces.

When the youths grew into men the situation worsened. At this stage my mother installed a security chain on the door and declared war on them, obliging them to mount a counterattack. The more belligerent among them adopted the tactics of a blitzkrieg. They took no notice of the chain on the half-open door and broke through it with a force that almost tore the door from its hinges, slamming my mother against the wall, crushing her, and pushing their way roughly into my room. Others developed more sophisticated tactics. They went in for a war of words, using their tongues as weapons. They would address her politely, ask after her health, sniff the smell of naphthalene she exuded as if they enjoyed it, admire her mangy fox fur, and show a sincere interest in her latest appeal to the High Court of Justice. The more imaginative warriors adopted guerilla tactics. They would invade the house disguised as tradesmen, florists' delivery boys, or mailmen with a registered letter to be handed over to the addressee in person, and would finally reach my room after various demands, cross-examinations, and other delays thought up by my mother. Others, who went in for a war of nerves, would disturb her afternoon nap with dozens of phone calls, slamming the phone down as soon as she picked up the receiver and snapped "Hello" in a loud and threatening tone. The more argumentative suitors would engage her in polemics and try to make her tell them what she had against them and why she was placing obstacles in the way of her daughter's happiness.

In these wars my mother made no distinction among her opponents. She fought them all to the bitter end, and emerged victorious from every battle, routing all my heroes and sending them running for their lives.

Filled with a desire for revenge, I decided to go to the aid of my defeated heroes by mounting a cold war on my mother. I declined to answer her questions, refused to wash the dishes, and spent most of the time shut up in my room, planning acts of vengeance that would hurt her in the most sensitive spot. Indifferent to my efforts, my mother would pace the rooms of the house, full of the spirit of battle, devising new strategies for fighting the fresh recruits who had reached the battlefield after the regular troops had retreated.

"Just like my mother's tomcats in heat," she would say as if to herself, but loudly enough for her words to impress me behind my closed door. "One goes, and ten more come to take its place."

* * *

Despite the anxieties instilled in me by the women of the family with regard to my great-grandmother Sara, and the fear that any change in my life would cut short her own, in my revenge against my mother I was obliged reluctantly to deviate from the daily routine that up to now had preserved my great-grandmother's life. I had made up my mind to deliver my mother a crushing blow, and follow it up with another, which would finally detach me from her and leave her helpless and utterly defeated—by getting married.

As the first stage in my plan I rented a dark, windowless den in the neighborhood of Nahlaot in Jerusalem. I was sure that her witch's broomstick would not carry her so far, and she would not be able to sweep my suitors away or chase them from my door. As the second stage I planned to register for the kindergarten teachers course at the religious seminary for girls, Yesurei Rachel. This female institution of so-called higher learning was particularly hateful to her. Whenever she wanted an example of an institution that was completely beyond the pale, that in addition to all its other failings was also religious, she would mention its name and list its shortcomings. According to her, the place was notorious for its foolish and ignorant students, for its bigoted teachers, and for its academic standards, which were the lowest of the low. Its name was mentioned frequently in our house, usually as a threat. At the end of every term, when she examined my report with an eagle eye, making venomous comments on this or that mark, she would repeat that if I failed to improve my marks by the end of the year, I would end up in Yesurei Rachel learning to be a kindergarten teacher. When I went there to register as a student, I knew that I had shattered all her sweet dreams, all the plans she had made for my future, and all her confident assumptions that I would follow in her footsteps. At every opportunity she would drum it into my head that I was duty bound to study law, and when the time came I would inherit her office and defend all the miserable wretches who besieged her door.

During the course of the long years she spent in court, my mother had perfected an inscrutable expression that she wore like a mask, at first only in her court appearances, but that was later assimilated into her skin so that she came home with it, did her shopping with it, and went to the movies with it. When I informed her of my new plans I was horrified by the sight of her reaction. The mask she maintained with such stubborn determination was suddenly stripped from her face, slid down her fox fur, and shattered on the floor at her feet. On her face appeared a mixture of revulsion, bewilderment, astonishment, and fear. The same expression accompanied me as I packed my bags. In a rare gesture she agreed to drive me and my entire past life bundled into my bags to the room I had rented, and then, when she walked through the door, her expression changed to one of pity. In the weak light of the single bulb her hands groped over the walls to find an opening to the air. When she examined her hands afterward she found a mixture of flaking whitewash and black mold under her well-manicured nails.

"This place is unhealthy. You'll get sick," she informed me unequivocally, slammed the door behind her, and left me there in the middle of the domed room with all my belongings scattered round me.

The next day I registered at the Yesurei Rachel teachers seminary, where they promised to find me a suitable match. After that I invited Amitai, one of my most persistent suitors, to visit me in my room.

*   *   *

My marriage was a failure known in advance. Known to everyone but me, that is. A conspiracy of silence united the women of my family against me. Everyone expected the marriage to fail, as if by a divine sentence that no mortal could change. Only crazy Dvora, who took such devoted care of my great-grandmother, actually said this to me in so many words, after hanging my husband's picture in the row of male portraits in my great-grandmother's gallery. At the time I refused to pay any attention to her words, which sounded senseless to me. Today I know that she was right.

On second thought, I'm sure that even if I had been told before the wedding that my marriage would end up on the rocks, I wouldn't have believed it, and I would have married my chosen mate despite all the prophecies of doom. Nevertheless sometimes I am assailed by doubts. Especially on sleepless nights when I wake every half hour from an exhausting, hallucinatory sleep, tossing and turning on the thick down mattress framed in the brass bed and full of Sara's memories. On these nights I am consumed by the question that gives me no rest, and gnawed by the suspicion that even if I had married some other man and given birth to his child, I would still have been abandoned.

If this question had been put to Sara, to Pnina-Mazal, or to my mother, and if they had agreed to answer it honestly, their answer would almost certainly have been affirmative. They were sincerely convinced that any man I married and had a child with would desert me forthwith, owing to circumstances that had nothing to do with me but belonged to the cycle of life whose meaning I was never able to discover. They made me feel like a puppet in the hands of fate, which I imagined as a short, fat, red-faced man, standing high above me, baring his teeth in a yellow, tobacco-stained smile while his orange-tipped fingers pulled the strings.

At moments when I felt trapped and suffocated by the walls around me, I would reconstruct my life from the point in time where it had frozen, making it impossible to go forward. From this point I would go step by step backward down the dark corridor of my memories, reexamining the doors I had irrevocably locked behind me and those that had been slammed in my face.

From behind every door voices arose. Each door and its voice. The strains of music and laughter from one, from another the sounds of lovemaking and groans of pleasure. From some of the doors I heard the sounds of strange, distant places that I had never visited and never would visit in my life. One heavy door embellished with carvings resounded with soft, inviting murmurs, while from the one next to it came the piping cries of the babies I had never given birth to. As I stood outside each locked door with my ears pricked, listening avidly to what was happening inside and trying to break through, the smells of the interior would succeed in reaching me through the keyhole. From one came the appetizing smells of dishes whose like I had never tasted, from another the heavy fragrance of flowers and perfumes I had never smelled. Some of the doors permeated the air with the complex molecules of strange love juices, making my head spin, and others exuded the smells of babies fresh from the bath combined with the sweet smell of milk and the faint odor of wet diapers. Sometimes, as if in obedience to a secret command, the doors would irradiate me with all the lights stored up behind them. The lights would filter through to me in a glorious rainbow from the cracks under the doors and from the keyholes, bathing me in a kaleidoscope of colors such as my eyes had never beheld in the world outside.

Slowly and despairingly I would make my way backward from door to door, pounding the locked doors with my fists in the hope that someone inside would hear me and open up. In vain I would try to turn the door handles, and when the doors refused to open I would throw myself against them and try to break them down like a detective in a movie. Despite all my efforts and pleas, and my attempts at physical force, the doors continued to bar my entry, confronting me blankly and uninvitingly. At those moments, breathing heavily and shedding tears for the life I might have had, I would hear the mocking laughter of the yellow-toothed dwarf at the end of the corridor. Then I would strain my eyes in the darkness illuminated by the colors filtering through the cracks beneath the doors, and look at him waving his nicotine-stained hands at me in contempt and pulling the invisible strings of my fate.

During those sleepless nights the hurt, anguished faces of all the men who had loved me and wanted to open all the doors to me would rise before my eyes. The men I had not married because of the laughter of fate and because of the divine decree that had made me fall in love with my husband's feet.

*   *   *

Of all the men who loved me I'll never forget Amitai. Amitai, kibbutz-born, with his mop of curls and handsome face, would display his sensitivity and his love for me in moist, tearful looks, which penetrated deeply into my eyes, ran through my body like electric currents, and melted my heart. For two years we lived together in the neighborhood of Nahlaot in the airless, sunless apartment that my mother called a rabbit warren, and that was permeated by the smell of our love juices. My own smell and that of Amitai were compounded by the act of love into a unique and complex chemical formula. The heavy odors, which to us were as fragrant as perfume, clung to the peeling walls with their vari-colored coats of paint, saturated the mattress on the floor, and refused to leave the towels and sheets even after they had been through the ordeal of washing, boiling, and drying in the neighborhood laundromat.

Wrapped in our scents we would cuddle up on the mattress, listen to the Tchaikovsky violin concerto, gaze into each other's eyes, and sniff like rutting dogs the smells we exuded, which united when we coupled into a new aroma of desire. Sometimes a spirit of mischief would descend on Amitai and he would pick the roses from the vine covering the entrance to the house, and sit patiently pulling the petals from the heads. Then he would approach me, holding the fragrant handfuls, and scatter my naked body with the velvety red petals. They would flutter in the air, cover my eyes, my breasts, and my navel, and collect in the hollow of my stomach. During the act of love, when I rubbed my body against his, our bodies would be stained crimson, and the scent of roses would mingle with the smells of our love.

Everything was wonderful until Amitai received a scholarship to study in Japan. He was a student at the medical faculty in Ein Karem, and his dearest wish was to study Chinese herbal medicine under the great master Van-yan III, who was third in an illustrious line of Chinese herbal doctors. This master was now in Japan, teaching at the school of medicine in Tokyo. Amitai took care of the tickets, went into the details of the scholarship, and told me optimistically that according to his friends I would be able to supplement our income by selling pictures in the street. My girlfriends told me that I would be able to work as a hostess in a bar, but this he would not countenance. "My future wife," I heard him tell them, "will never work in a bar even if we're starving." This was the first time he had ever hinted at marriage. When it was too late I discovered that he had begun preparations for the wedding behind my back. The week he arrived in Tokyo he phoned to tell me that he had found us a small apartment whose floors were covered with rice-straw mats, and that he was waiting impatiently for my arrival.

At this stage fate stepped in, pulled the strings, played a joke at my expense, and threw me far from the loving arms of Amitai. His plans were never carried out. It would be possible, of course, to lay the blame on Air Egypt, which offered the cheapest flight, including a stopover in Bangkok. If I had bought my ticket from a different airline, my flight would have taken me straight to Tokyo, and I have no doubt that today I would be with him. On the Egyptian plane, full of excited youngsters exchanging information on the wonders of the East, it was impressed upon me that it would be a sin to fly directly to Tokyo without visiting Bangkok, tantamount to breaking the rules of the game. They told me the island of Japan was always the last stop on the journey; first one should taste the East with all one's senses. I took their advice, and spent the three most magical days of my life in Bangkok, in a steamy tropical climate full of the heavy scents of flowers.

And because of those three days I didn't marry Amitai. Afterward I discovered that he had planned a surprise wedding. Carrying a bag containing a wedding dress and pair of white shoes he had bought for me in Israel, he waited at the airport for the flight on which I failed to arrive. From the airport we were supposed to drive in a fancy limousine he had hired with the last of his money to the offices of the Jewish congregation, where about two hundred members of the community were waiting for us with kosher food and a wedding cake. When I walked into the room they were all supposed to shout "Surprise!" Then Amitai would lead me to the wedding canopy where the rabbi was waiting to conduct the ceremony.

Three days after the wedding that never took place Amitai met me at the Tokyo airport, and the liquid, loving look had disappeared from his eyes. After a week of sleeping on the fragrant rice-straw mats, which confused and changed the chemical formula of our love smells, I decided to leave. I said good-bye to Amitai and flew to Thailand. I retired with a few hundred other Israeli youngsters to the dreamy tropical island of Kosmoi, sipped coconut milk straight from the shell, abandoned my body to the sun and the hands of the local masseuses, and tormented myself with my thoughts.

Amitai disappeared from my life. Today I read about him and his method in the newspapers, and I even saw him once on a television program. His look, which penetrated me through the television screen, was blank. But the pain I had seen in his eyes when he met me in Tokyo was still there.

⁕ ⁕ ⁕

In the same past that became the known-in-advance and doomed-to-failure future, I met Ya'akov, who became my husband, the father of my son, and—the day after the boy was born—my ex-husband. If you asked me what I saw in him, the man with whom I shared about ten months of my life, I wouldn't be able to tell you. Actually, I suppose I could explain, but I don't think you would accept the explanation or understand the reason why I fell in love with this man. I fell in love with him on our first date, when we went to the beach. The minute he removed his shoes and socks I knew that I would marry him. To the question of how anyone could possibly fall in love with a man because of his bare feet I have no satisfactory answer, and so I had better confine myself to the facts.

The Saturday of our first date was the hottest Jerusalem had ever known. In an attempt to appear spontaneous, Ya'akov suggested driving down to the beach in Tel Aviv, and without waiting for my reply he opened the door of his car with a courtly flourish that was in stark contrast to the battered Volkswagen he drove.

Dazzled by the glare of the water and the white sand, we ran hand in hand, like the heroes of a romantic movie, toward the waves wetting the sand and darkening its color. We hired two deck chairs and I began to peel off my clothes, exposing my white Jerusalem skin to the longing looks of the dark-skinned boys lounging on brightly colored towels and soaking up the hot rays of the sun. Ya'akov sat down heavily on the deck chair and hesitated. Today, with the intimate knowledge of hindsight, I can guess that he was making up his mind which article of clothing to remove first. This hesitation, which amused me during the first weeks of our lives together, drove me crazy later, when he would sit on the bed and deliberate at length as to which shoe to take off first—the left, which he had put on first in the morning, or the right, which had been relegated to second place then and should be compensated now.

Since this was our first date and he wanted to impress me, he acted with relative speed. After cutting his soul-searching to a minimum, he decided to tackle his right shoe first. With slow and concentrated movements, to which he appeared to devote a great deal of thought, he undid the laces. After neatly setting aside his gleaming shoes, to which not a single grain of sand had stuck, he turned his attention to his socks. If you were to ask me their color, I would not know the answer, since I was too riveted to his actions to trouble myself about trifles. First he removed the left sock as carefully as if his life depended on it, or as if he were about to reveal a long-buried treasure to the world. With deliberate slowness he rolled the sock down his calf in small, careful movements like a snake trying to shed its skin. Once the ankle of his left foot was exposed he pulled the sock off with one brisk, decisive gesture, shook it lightly in the air, lifted it to his nose, sniffed it with open enjoyment, and then folded it carefully as if it were a precious article of clothing liable to crease. After a moment of vacillation he laid it in his left shoe, which was waiting under the deck chair with commendable patience to receive it. His right sock was awarded similar treatment. I lowered my eyes to his feet. The ritual that had just laid bare these innocent extremities revealed a pair of touching ankles, slender, white, and hairless. The hair began to grow sparsely again beyond the shallow depression halfway up his calves, where the elasticized tops of his socks had left their mark. At precisely that moment I knew that I had fallen in love with him.

After my divorce, when I went out with other men and followed with interest the ritual of their sock removal, I reached the conclusion that the man had not been born who could move me once more by the baring of his feet. Most of them employed only a small part of the actions performed by Ya'akov, and I missed the integrity of all the movements as a whole. A few of them did indeed sniff with relish the socks they removed from their feet after a long day of sweaty service, others carefully folded their socks, but hardly any of them knew how to concentrate properly on the act of removing the sock itself. Sacrilegiously they would pull it off and then dismiss it with a callous wave of the hand, throwing it under the bed like a stinking little ball.

*　　*　　*

Two months after the episode of the socks we got married. Under the wedding canopy I was the happiest of women. In my imagination I reviewed the moving sock-stripping ritual awaiting me that night, and I knew that from this day forth I would be able to witness it every night of my life. In the throes of my excitement I heard the rabbi asking me to hold out my finger for the ring. I had bought this ring with my own money, after my beloved had refused to buy it for me on the grounds that he was broke. I did not know then that according to the Jewish religion this was forbidden. After our divorce, looking back on the marriage ceremony, I remembered the inquiry to which the rabbi had subjected my husband, and how Ya'akov had lied and declared out loud, without turning a hair, that the ring had been purchased with his money. If you like, this was the first sign of the preordained failure of my marriage, that my husband bought me with my own money.

Beside myself with happiness on the night of my wedding, I buried my face in the bouquet of white gladiola in my hands, and while everyone was admiring my beauty, which could almost compare with that of my great-grandmother, or so they said to flatter me, I averted my face and spat discreetly into the dusty dwarf palm standing in the corner of the hall. But even this precaution against the evil eye was powerless to prevent the failure.

And perhaps a premonition of failure could also be found in the wedding pictures that were taken and didn't come out. The photographer hired by Ya'akov was the cheapest in town, and after exhausting negotiations he agreed to photograph the wedding for "the cost of the materials," as he explained through clenched teeth. A week later we arrived at his shop with an empty photograph album, which was just as empty when we left. It turned out that the film he had used dated from the previous decade. "Sorry, the pictures didn't come out," he informed us with barely disguised satisfaction. We left the shop empty-handed, and the sentence pronounced by my ex-husband still rings in my ears whenever I open the desolate album and think of the pictures that never came out: "At least we didn't have to pay him for the materials."

❊   ❊   ❊

And if only I'd had eyes in my head, I might have been able to see the signs on the eve of the wedding when I went with my grandmother Pnina-Mazal to the mikvah for the prescribed ritual bath. Not with my mother, who despised all those "black-coated idol-worshipers" and who greeted the news of my coming marriage with the announcement: "As far as I'm concerned you can live in sin for the rest of your life and you needn't get married at all."

I set out with my grandmother to look for the mikvah at the address given me by the woman at the rabbinate offices, who had taken me aside when we went to register our marriage and tried to explain the menstrual cycle and the way of a man with a maid. We arrived at the building but were unable to find the door. An ultra-Orthodox woman with a shaved head and a fresh face saved us from circling the sealed building for the seventh time by pointing out a half-hidden door with "Women" written on it, where she left us with a little smile and a whispered "Mazal tov."

In the waiting room a handful of women with kerchiefs bound tightly round their shaved heads were sitting and leafing through prayer books and psalms, avoiding each other's eyes. The place looked like a gynecologist's waiting room. When my turn came I was received by the bath attendant, who was wearing a loose, gaudy cotton rag that looked like a dressing gown or else a shapeless dress. Her genial expression did not change even after she had shamelessly examined my bare arms and the length of my miniskirt. She led me down a dark, narrow corridor, which smelled strongly of dankness and mold, into a huge hall. And there they were. Women, more women, and only women, wearing ragged, faded dressing gowns and, on their swollen feet, colored plastic clogs. They milled about like sleepwalkers with shaved heads and stern expressions in the weak light afforded by the single naked bulb. Some of them rummaged between their toes, others poked little sticks covered with cotton wool into their ears, while others openly picked their noses, in order to remove any speck of dirt that might separate them from the holy water, as the bath attendant explained. She asked me to take off my clothes and pushed up one of the peeling, painted wooden chairs that in the course of the years had accommodated the bare backsides of hundreds of women coming to purify themselves.

At her request I too cleaned my ears, picked my nose, combed my hair, and used dental floss to remove any leftover food from the spaces between my teeth. When I was finished, she sat down opposite me on an identical chair, asked me to give her my feet, took my right foot, and grounded it firmly in her lap. Then she began to examine my toes, whose nails I had cut the evening before, as if she were studying a complicated road map. At the sight of my toes she clucked her tongue and drew a large, rusty nail-clipper from her pocket. My toenails were cut again, until the pink skin was exposed and sharp, thin half-moons of nail fell onto the horny snippets that already covered the floor, piercing my bare feet, in the area she jokingly referred to as the "pedicure salon." When she had completed her handiwork she surveyed my body and smoothly combed hair with satisfaction, and stealthily pressed a little piece of white gauze into my hand.

"And now you must go behind the screen and examine yourself," she whispered into my ear, as if confiding a state secret.

"What am I supposed to examine?" I asked.

"Yourself," she repeated.

I retired behind the screen she opened for me, examined my arms, my legs, and my groin, and returned to the attendant.

"And now give it to me," she said.

"What?"

"The cloth I gave you, of course."

I handed her the little piece of gauze, which I had been holding in my fist.

She examined it with her shortsighted eyes, and it seemed to me that she was trying to inhale its smell.

"You didn't do it," she said in a tone of rebuke. "You're supposed to push it inside you and check to see if it comes out stained. And if you want your husband never to leave you and to give you beautiful children, you must do it every month," she explained to me, and added: "It's like a chicken; just as you don't cook a chicken with blood on it and you have to clean it before putting it into the pot, in the same way there must be no sign of blood before intercourse."

She went on to explain that after the first intercourse, with the letting of the virgin blood, I had to keep away from my husband and go on examining myself every day until the gauze came out clean, and then return to her at the mikvah.

Obediently I retired behind the screen and pushed the bit of cloth deep up inside me. A dark red stain appeared reproachfully on the white cloth when I pulled it out. I approached her anxiously, but she was already busy with another woman, whose thick-soled feet lay in her broad lap waiting for the nail-clipper. I tried to tell her what had happened, but she was busy talking and waved me away dismissively, with instructions to proceed in the direction of the bath, from which a skinny woman with flabby breasts had just emerged under the vigilant eyes of the rabbi's wife.

"Have you been taken care of?" the latter inquired, inspecting me sternly through her water-spattered spectacles.

I nodded.

"Have you examined yourself and did the cloth emerge from inside you as white as snow?" she asked, and before I had time to reply she pushed me lightly toward the steps that led deep down into the black water, which gave off a smell of acid rain and had bits of frothy green slime floating on its surface. My feet fumbled on the slimy, slippery floor and I did everything she told me to.

With wet hair I joined Pnina-Mazal, who was waiting for me in the waiting room.

"How was it? I see you survived." She smiled at me.

"I'm not sure that I should get married today," I said, thinking of the crimson stain I had discovered on the white gauze and the possibility that my husband would leave me because of it.

*   *   *

Even if I ignore the ring bought with my money and the matter of the mikvah, with the help of hindsight I can try to explain the reasons why my husband left home only one day after the birth of our son. His work might provide a clue. Ya'akov was a zoologist who specialized in the ibex, or to be more precise in the reproduction of these animals or their love life, if their coupling could be defined as an act of love. For days at a time during the mating season of the ibex, he would be away from home, busy with his work in the wilderness round the Dead Sea. During the period when he courted me he gave in to my pleas and took me there in his noisy, smoky Volkswagen, affording me a glimpse of the mating rituals of the male ibex. I witnessed this spectacle through field glasses, and felt a sensation of déjà vu as events similar to those that had happened in the past and would happen in the future unfolded before my eyes.

In the evenings we returned to Ya'akov's steamy caravan, where even the air conditioner that had been on all day during this blazing season had not succeeded in cooling the air. We lay down naked on the bed, lacking all desire to touch each other because of the heat, and then my husband would hold forth on the wisdom of the ibex. The male ibex, he informed me, like many other animals, had an erotic strategy that was suitable for us humans too, even though for thousands of years religion, culture, and morality had tried to suppress it. He had formulated a personal creed, observing the laws of reproduction in nature and applying them to ourselves, which he was in the habit of reciting at every possible opportunity. "As a student of the ibex," he opened his speech, "I take my cue from them. I, as a strong and healthy male, am duty bound to fertilize females, a lot of females, as many females as possible. Every female I fertilize will bear one healthy child, to whom she will be able to devote the maximum attention. Since I will not be by her side, the mother will be able to invest all her resources of energy in her only child. When I have accomplished my purpose with one I shall go on to the next, and when she gives birth I'll continue my search for new females to fertilize. And if everyone follows my example the world will be full of the offspring of the strongest and most fertile men and single mothers devoting themselves to the care of healthy, robust only children."

At the time, lying naked and exhausted on the joined iron beds, listening to the desperate sawing of the cicadas searching for a mate, I didn't take his words too seriously. Nor did I pay attention to the warning signals when he stroked my body conciliatorily and said that I had to understand that the phrase "till death do us part" contradicted the laws of nature in general and of human nature in particular, and that it should be eradicated from the collective memory of the race.

No red lights went on in me even when I discovered that before meeting me Ya'akov had already been diligently putting his beliefs into practice. He had been married twice before, and he had two children, one each from these two wives. One of the women lived in New York, and from time to time she would phone and upbraid him angrily for his steady refusal to pay alimony for his son. His relationship with his son was confined to the sending of one cheap greeting card on the boy's birthday. His other son grew up on the kibbutz Givat Regavim. The mother was a girl from the kibbutz who had knocked on the door of his caravan, told him that she was interested in the sex life of the ibex, and landed up in the middle of his bed with his penis deep inside her.

Ya'akov lived with me for ten months. The first quarrel to disturb the tranquillity of our life took place when I came home with the results of a pregnancy test, which were positive in spite of the precautions we had taken. He accused me of tricking him, cheating him, and stealing his sperm. Today, looking back on his angry reaction, I would like to believe that he loved me so much that he was unwilling to leave me, but knew that he would be obliged to do so after fulfilling his genetic role in my life, an outcome that he wanted to postpone for as long as possible.

*   *   *

The bill of divorcement he dropped into my lap was awarded with a speed uncharacteristic of the rabbinical courts, thanks to his confession that the ring he had placed on my finger had been purchased not with his money but with mine. Two weeks later he found another woman, married her in a posh wedding at a Jerusalem hotel, and took her down to his caravan in the wilderness. In spite of the weekly visitation rights to which he was entitled by the terms of our divorce, my ex-husband remained loyal to the child-rearing practices of the ibex and refrained from any contact with his son. And while the father was busy pursuing his sacred vocation of reproduction, the son grew up without a father figure.

Every evening, in a ritual whose rules he had dictated to me, and from which I was forbidden to deviate in the slightest degree, my little son would ask me to tell him the story of Bambi. Then I would tell him about the tender little Bambi who grew up with his mother in the parched desert and on the rocky hills, and about the father busy locking horns with other ibexes, and looking for a new female ibex who would give birth to a new little Bambi. And I told him, too, about the female ibexes who lived together in big herds and brought up their little Bambis alone. "And this is the way all the ibexes live," he would say, repeating the concluding sentence with me, as proud and happy as a little hawker advertising his wares. Afterward we would recite together: "Great-great-great-grandmother Mazal brought up Great-great-grandmother Sara by herself. Sara brought up Great-grandmother Pnina-Mazal by herself. Pnina-Mazal brought up Grandmother Geula by herself. Geula brought up Mother Amal by herself, and now Amal is bringing up her little Bambi all by herself." I would conclude the procedure with a good-night kiss by rubbing noses like the mother ibexes with my own fawn. And then my son would blow a kiss to the picture of the Walt Disney Bambi on the wall above his bed, and ask me to kiss it with my lips. At the end of the kissing ritual he would repeat the unchanging formula: "And that's why Bambi has such sad eyes." And when he went to make weewee before getting into bed, he would go up to the bathroom mirror in order to contemplate and reappraise the depth of sadness in his eyes.

Chapter Four

 My son's birth established new rules in the game of fate and broke a link in the chain of the family dynasty, which up to then had been exclusively female. The game began with Mazal, Sara's mother, the head of the dynasty and the earliest woman to surface in my great-grandmother's memory. I know of no other woman before her. The only fact that Sara was able to tell me about the period preceding her mother's existence was that her grandmother, Mazal's mother, had been called Sara, and she had been named after her. When I pressed her to tell me more about her grandmother, she insisted that she knew nothing about her, since she had departed this world before she herself was born, when her mother was still a child of tender years. This leaves Mazal as the original matriarch who began the chain of divinely ordained events that ended in my ex-husband slamming the door behind him forever the day after the birth of our son.

In the moments of grace I had with Sara she claimed that it had all started about a hundred years ago, perhaps because of the brown stains that appeared on her mother's panties on her thirteenth birthday. Like a dog scenting blood the matchmaker Shulamith turned up in her Aunt Miriam's house as soon as the first drops of blood appeared.

When she arrived Mazal was busy washing the stone floors, a blood-stained rag pushed between her legs and fastened with pins. With her bare feet she felt the grains of dust that had collected on the flagstones and in the cracks between them. With her eyes she searched out the long fair hairs covered in fluffy gray dust, waiting to be swept out of their hiding places under the furniture and in the dark corners of the room. She polished each stone separately, as if it were the only one, rubbing the surface devotedly with a wet cloth and trying not to step on the cracks between the stones. In five years of polishing she had come to know every flagstone in the vaulted room intimately. She could tell her charges apart with her eyes closed, by their setting, their size, and their degree of coolness. Mazal even knew where each stone had come from, and where it had been dressed. When she walked through the ruined houses of the old Jewish quarter she could point to the naked skeletons of the hovels, their walls as full of gaps as an old lady's gums, and recount the history of each and every stone on the floor of her aunt's house—which building it had been taken from and where it had been laid. Some of them were pink, like the house itself; some were white and flat and gave rise when they were polished to powdery drifts of chalk. There were also three lemon-yellow flagstones, and one dark brown one. The latter she loathed. The more she scoured and polished it, the darker it became, and when it came into contact with water it gleamed blackly and stood out horribly among all the other paving stones. Most of the stones were smooth from years of rubbing, polishing, and the tread of feet. Others, under the table, were rough, and one stone, hidden under the sideboard, boasted a carved hump, as if it had once been part of a fortified wall.

While the two women whispered in the sooty alcove of the kitchen, Mazal was absorbed in polishing the pink stone embedded with white veins crossing and recrossing its surface with endless slanting lines. When she had finished with this stone and turned her attention to the porous yellow stone that was covered with tiny indentations that dammed the murky water like miniature puddles of black rain, she was summoned to the kitchen. With lowered eyes she walked toward the smoky little room.

Her honey-colored hair, which had escaped from its braids, curled wildly round her head in a thousand glints of radiance, and as she stood in the doorway it was touched by a ray of twilight coming through the window, and she looked as if she were surrounded by a halo of light, like one of the saints in a Christian church.

The women conferring confidentially as they bent over the black kettle streaked with soot and grease instantly fell silent. Mazal approached them, wiping her wet hands, which were red with the cold mopping water, on her soiled apron. As she stood before them the halo of light stopped playing with her hair. Her amber eyes, speckled with pinpoints of brown, rounded in a question. Her Aunt Miriam asked her to come and stand beside her. Without any preamble she rolled up the sleeve of Mazal's gray dress with her shriveled, rheumatic hands and exposed her white arm to Shulamith's inquiring eyes.

"As I told you," she said after pinches and palpations that reddened Mazal's skin and printed it with the marks of her crooked nails, "she's white. There isn't a superfluous hair on her body and her flesh is soft."

Shulamith fixed Mazal with her eyes, which were framed in a thick layer of kohl. The girl lowered her eyes, revealing heavy lids fringed with long, thick, shiny black lashes.

"Mazal," began her aunt with the sigh that always preceded bad news. "You are an orphan without a father or a mother. Your parents, may they rest in peace, left you no property when they perished in the great plague. I cannot support you. You are a grown woman now. Our neighbor Yitzhak, the haberdashery merchant from the market, has singled you out. The engagement is tomorrow. He is an orphan like you, his parents too died in the great plague, and God willing the two of you will found a new family in Israel. You're a lucky girl." (*Mazal* means "lucky" in Hebrew.) "With God's help Yitzhak will become a great merchant and a wealthy man, and you will wear silk and be waited on by servants."

Mazal bowed her head, excused herself to the women, and escaped to the outhouse in the yard. There she removed the warm cloth from between her legs and examined the findings that had brought the matchmaker down on her. Then she put it back and ran to Geula, the neighbor's daughter, to tell her the double news.

"I told you it would come," whispered the corpulent Geula, whose hair was red and whose face, legs, and arms were dotted with faded spots of rust. She raised her eyes from the black iron pots standing over the fire, tiny drops of sweat making their way between the freckles adorning her flushed face. "And now you have to get married," she added compassionately. "Couldn't they have waited a while? You're a child. What does that Yitzhak want of you?" she asked, nervously prodding and pinching Mazal's budding breasts.

"He saw me in the shop. I should never have gone there," Mazal replied, a deathly fear creeping into the pit of her stomach.

No bridegroom had been found for the eighteen-year-old Geula. Nobody wanted her red hair, her freckled white body, and her sharp tongue. Everyone tricked into coming to the house preferred her younger sister, Rachel.

"Until Geula gets married, we won't give Rachel," her father, the ritual slaughterer of the neighborhood, would say. And so both sisters remained virgins, content with their lot and secretly thanking their lucky stars and Geula's bridegroom-repellent red hair.

"Listen carefully to what I have to say to you," Geula whispered to Mazal, whose body had turned to a lump of ice despite the heat in the kitchen, and she dragged her into the yard. There, in the outhouse, she asked her to show her the brown spots on the cloth.

"If he wants to get inside you, say you have to go to the outhouse, and when you return tell him you found blood. If he insists two weeks later, push a piece of cotton wool dipped in olive oil deep inside you," she said, and she pushed the cotton wool she had brought with her into the blackness of Mazal's insides. "Do this whenever he wants to be intimate with you. Otherwise children will start coming, and you're still a child yourself," she said, inspecting with undisguised satisfaction the orange spots on her hands that had saved her from a similar fate. "And if nothing helps and you get pregnant against your will, I'll find a solution for that too. Just don't tell your aunt," she warned, making her swear.

The next day the bridegroom's presents arrived: embroidered sheets, silk ribbons of the kind Mazal had seen and yearned for in his shop, a gold bracelet, and paper cones of sugar crystallized into thick, transparent cubes.

From the day her engagement to Yitzhak was announced, Mazal was careful to keep away from the market. Only when her aunt insisted, scolding her, and raising her voice, did Mazal do as she was told, doing her best to make a wide detour round her fiancé's shop. She felt as if she were walking down the street naked, with only her long hair covering her nakedness. And as she walked with her head lowered toward the dusty alleys of the marketplace, she felt the men's eyes stabbing her like knives, and her back, covered in the thin wool of her shabby dress, reddened under their lecherous looks. She blocked her ears, but could not help hearing the whispers of the hawkers, avidly describing the wedding night awaiting her fiancé on her smooth white body.

The obscene cries and male whispers sent her running breathless and flushed to her aunt's house, and as she ran her virginal breasts shook and brought all the shopkeepers out of their holes. The rumor of Mazal's running spread through the market like wildfire, from shop to shop and alcove to alcove, and to an observer it might have seemed that a guard of honor of men in fezzes, with ragged clothes and fallen paunches, were lining the pavements, raising their flies in a manly salute to the princess galloping down the street like a noble steed. Only one door was deserted—the door to the haberdashery, where Yitzhak had taken cover in the dark recesses of his shop.

Not only the hawkers and their intrusive looks vexed Mazal then. Her playmates too, pious Miriam and black Nehama, gave her no rest.

"Lie on your back and part your legs," ordered Miriam, who had been given the epithet "pious" in a spirit of irony. When Mazal obeyed, Miriam threw herself between her friend's parted legs and began raising and lowering her hips to the shrill, gleeful giggles of the watching girls.

"And tell us what he does to you and what side he mounts you from," they demanded, rubbing her flat stomach with hands chapped by the cold water with which they washed the floors. And Mazal nodded her head, trying to appease her playmates and make them let her be.

At that moment a warning cry was heard in the distance: "Leave her alone!" Geula came running up like a red, menacing ball of fire. Like a flock of chicks alarmed by the shadow of a hawk in the sky the girls ran off with little cries of glee and fear, leaving the bride sprawled on the ground behind them, her head covered in white dust like the neighborhood keeners.

"What happened? Have you taken leave of your senses? Why do you let them do this to you?" Geula scolded, swallowing the sob that began in her throat and threatened to spread to the rest of her body, shaking her friend's dusty clothes and dragging the frightened little girl into her house. There she put the big copper kettle on to boil, fanning the fire by blowing fiercely on the coals, and with a face flushed from effort poured the water into the tub. "Get undressed," she commanded without looking at her, pouring cold water into the hot and testing the temperature with her elbow. Hesitantly Mazal took off her dusty clothes. Before allowing Geula to insert the cotton wool between her legs she had never exposed her nakedness to a stranger's eyes.

"Hurry up. The water's getting cold," the redhead urged.

Naked in the tub, with only her long hair covering her and reaching all the way to her vulva, Mazal surrendered herself to Geula's hands. The yellow cube of soap roamed and slithered over her silky white body, giving rise in its wake to transparent little bubbles of pleasure. With her eyes closed Mazal yielded to the new sensation making her insides contract. Delightful, ticklish feelings crept up from her feet to her thighs, stiffened her nipples, and concentrated in her vagina. With her head light and free of troublesome thoughts she felt the circles of pleasure spreading all over her body, like the ripples from a stone thrown into a pool. Circle after circle the pleasure spread through her until the great, strong wave that made her vagina contract and her body shudder as groans escaped her lips. Afterward, with a sweet fog filling every cell of her body, she let Geula shampoo her long hair, as the water in the tub turned a murky brown. It was a sunny day, and they went out into the yard. Mazal, her body limp, her thighs weak, her head giddy, felt a joyful sweetness spreading through her limbs as she laid her head in Geula's lap and let her friend comb her long, clean hair glinting in the light of the sky.

On her wedding day she asked to go to the mikvah with Geula. Perhaps as she bathed in the water there she would experience the same bodily sensations again.

"Today you must go with your aunt," Geula said gently and kissed her on her forehead. "And I wish you good luck."

The smell of mold assailed her nose as she took off her clothes and stored them rolled up in a ragged ball in the alcove next to the baths. The walls were covered with black spots of mold, and bits of painted plaster dropped from the ceiling into the stagnant water. With timid steps she descended the slippery steps, which felt as if they were covered with a layer of invisible mucus, into the pool of black water, which gave off gray smells of rain. Batya the daughter of Mushun the Turk, who was in charge of the women's wing, explained how she was to hold her breath and immerse her whole body in the water. Mazal plunged into the deep pool. Her loose hair refused to sink along with her body, and floated on the surface of the murky pool like water lilies.

"Sink, sink," Batya scolded.

Mazal rose to the surface, filled her cheeks with air, and sank again until her feet squelched in the soft slime at the bottom of the pool. But this time too her hair, as if it had a will of its own, refused to immerse itself in the dark rainwater.

"Hold your hair in your hands and sink," Batya screamed.

Mazal tried, she tried with all her might, and her hair, to spite her, rose and floated as if it was full of air bubbles.

"A bad omen," spat Batya the daughter of Mushun the Turk, and told her to get out.

* * *

Wearing the white silk dress she had received from the charity to help poor brides, as befitted an orphan, and accompanied by the mocking looks of pious Miriam, Mazal peeped at her bridegroom standing by her side. She had seen him a few times before, standing in the entrance to his shop and stealing shy, sidelong looks at her. Occasionally she had bought items of haberdashery from him, with lowered eyes, on her aunt's orders. But now she could feast her eyes on him to her heart's content. When she saw his face under the bridal canopy through her veil, she felt a frisson of delight. Until this very moment she had not paid any attention to the skin on his face. And now she saw that it was a patchwork of pimples, a veritable treasure trove of poxlike little pustules. They proliferated on his forehead, spread over his cheeks, spotted his chin, and covered his fleshy nose. Between the lumps grew soft shadowy wisps of sparse, boyish hair.

As the rabbi sanctified their union in a low, unintelligible mutter, she was seized by a passionate desire to take Yitzhak's head between her hands and squeeze the sticky contents from his pimples. When the groom placed the ring on her finger, she imagined herself examining the results of her labors. And when he stamped on the glass, to cries of "Mazal tov!" and the ululations of the women, she continued in her imagination the work of cleaning the hidden pimples nestling behind his ears, like a stork pecking between the feathers of her mate.

There's a lot of work in store for me, she thought. I only hope he'll agree to let me deal with his pimples.

As her pleasure grew more intense she closed her eyes, praying that her bridegroom would not guess the nature of the passionate desire bursting from every pore of her skin.

That night Yitzhak took her to his parents' house. Before Mazal had a chance to inspect the floor and compare it to the one in her aunt's house, and before she could imagine herself polishing it, her husband quickly covered the mezuzah on the doorpost and the copper mirror on the wall and blew out the flame in the oil lamp. Then he threw her on the bed, hitched the skirt of her dress up over her head as if he was ashamed to look at her face, and came at her from behind like a rooster. Mazal was surprised to hear the heavy sighs he breathed into her ear. These ceased abruptly. As soon as the deed was done, he got up, washed his hands, tugged at the wisps of his beard, made his bed on the floor, and fell asleep. The creaking of the bed went on echoing in her ears long after he had had his way with her. The next morning, while he was sleeping, she inspected his face in the light of the rising sun. The pimples on his chin had disappeared during the night, and smooth pink skin greeted her eyes in their place.

The first person to arrive at the house in the morning was Geula.

"I knew you wouldn't do what I told you to," she whispered in her ear in a corner of the room, far from Yitzhak who was busy saying the morning prayer, inspecting with an eagle eye the stained, crumpled sheet on the bed. "Perhaps you were lucky this time and you didn't get pregnant. Be careful," she added with a grave expression on her face, "because what's done is hard to undo. And now come with me to the market," she commanded. "You have to organize your household, and whether you like it or not you have to cook for your husband."

"If I come with you everyone will know what happened to me last night," Mazal replied with downcast eyes.

"Everyone knows why a bride gets married. And if you come with me they won't dare to open their mouths," Geula said confidently. And the two girls, one tall, hefty, and redheaded, the other pale and golden-haired, went out into the alley.

The stares fixed on Mazal were lowered before the fierce look in Geula's eyes, and the terror of her sharp tongue choked the lecherous cries before they were uttered.

"Will you always come with me to the market?" Mazal asked in a faint voice. "When you're with me they keep quiet."

Her new husband Yitzhak was not to be seen in the entrance to his shop, as if he were ashamed of the night of pleasure he had enjoyed.

Ten days after her wounds were healed, he came to her again, and this time he remained with her on the bed. The next day the pimples on his face had disappeared again. The same thing happened each morning after he had visited her bed the night before, until the day when her bleeding stopped. That same month, when he came to her every night with no fear of blood, her husband's face grew smooth and free of pimples and pustules, which vanished without a trace.

⁂ ⁂ ⁂

After Mazal learned that she was with child, she tried to get rid of the fetus in her womb. First, in her nausea, she tried to vomit it up, until she felt as if her insides were hollow and empty. When there was nothing left inside her, she spat out the dregs of her stomach, a black-green bile that splashed in all directions and filled the vaulted room with a sour stench. When her husband was out of the way she put the huge kettle on the coals to boil, immersed herself in the copper tub, and scalded her skin in the boiling water until it turned scarlet. She lifted the heavy *sandouk* again and again, stood holding it in the middle of the room, closed her eyes, and enjoyed a sense of lightness as her head spun giddily. When nothing helped, she forced herself on her husband night after night and morning after morning. And with the first light of day he would stumble to the synagogue, weak-kneed, bleary-eyed, and with a dryness in his mouth that even his morning tea failed to quench. As her desperation grew, she pummeled her still-flat stomach with the rolling pin and skipped rope secretly with her playmates, pious Miriam and black Nehama, far from inquisitive eyes and gossiping tongues.

"You're pregnant," Geula said to her one day, after scrutinizing her face and reading the signs, and she took her to Ibrahim, the Muslim barber, who concocted a mixture of wormwood and the juice and seeds of the squirting cucumber for women who shared her plight.

"When they're watered by the magic potion the intestines boil over and turn upside down," the women whispered on their doorsteps.

When the potions failed, Mazal imagined that if she held her breath the fetus would suffocate and vanish without a trace. She would lie for hours on her embroidered sheets, holding her breath and stopping her nose with her thumbs, until her face turned blue and her lips grew cold. And the fetus, to spite her, kicked and screamed in her stomach, beat at the walls of her womb with its little fists, and struggled like a caged bird in the prison of her swollen belly.

And where would the fetus emerge when its time was up? She inspected her navel and rummaged inside it to see if the fetus would come out there. When she failed to find an opening, she began to examine herself in the mirror she removed from the wall. And once, when her husband came home unexpectedly early, he found her sprawled on the bed with her legs open and her fingers probing her tangled, golden pubic hair, while the mirror displayed the slit to her eyes and to his. Red-faced, he fled from the room. All that evening he avoided looking into her shining eyes, which were full of the joy of discovery.

As she thickened and swelled, and all her attempts to get rid of the fetus failed, she resigned herself to her fate, and at night she lay awake in bed and consoled herself with thoughts of the pretty doll she would soon have. Mazal would take her for walks in the neighborhood streets, and her skin would gleam in the sunshine and dazzle the sky. She would have hair like silk, and Mazal would braid her silky hair, and all who saw her would smile with joy.

As the fetus ripened inside her the pious neighborhood women came secretly to her house bearing gifts for the baby to be born: little cotton dresses worn ragged with washing, gray gauze diapers that had served dozens of infants, and tiny bootees tied with new white ribbons. She accepted them all and put them away in the *sandouk* between her mother's moth-eaten bridal gown and her father's cracked and travel-weary shoes. The princess who emerged from her womb would be dressed in robes of the finest silk, she promised herself at the sight of the wretched gifts. Bonnets knitted of silken thread would adorn her head, and her feet would be shod in kidskin shoes. The fleece of black lambs slaughtered while still in their mothers' wombs would pad her bed. As the rumors of the child's beauty spread far and wide, Mazal would adorn her wrists with golden chains and hang heavy, ancient amulets around her neck. They would banish the baby-murdering Lilith, the evil eye, and all the devils and demons from her presence. Sara, she would call her, like the first Hebrew matriarch and like her own mother, who did not live to hold her granddaughter in her arms.

When her belly grew so big that it was hard for her to walk, Geula came to her aid again.

"Your hair is so greasy and dirty that you can't see its color anymore. I'll wash it for you," she offered, and before Mazal had a chance to reply she had already put the big kettle on to boil and prepared the copper tub.

Mazal sat in the middle of the pool of hot water surrounded by low copper walls, her gleaming stomach thrust defiantly in front of her, her swollen breasts upright, marbled with blue veins and armed with dark, prickly nipples. And once more the transparent bubbles of delight invaded her flesh as her friend soaped her, accompanied by sensations that spread through her body giving rise to involuntary shudders and uncontrollable moans of pleasure.

After getting out of the bath, wrapped in a sheet torn from the bed, Mazal lay on her back, her eyes glittering, while Geula bustled about her noisily and clattered the dishes in the kitchen.

That night she was possessed by the dybbuk of cleanliness. She lit the lamp and shook Yitzhak till he woke. In a daze he turned toward the door to fetch Fahima the midwife.

"I'm not ready yet," Mazal said, laughter gurgling in her throat. "Come and help me to move the bed and the wardrobe, we have to make room for the baby." Silently and obediently Yitzhak complied with her caprices, and the shadow cast by his body in its long nightgown looked stooped and miserable. When dawn broke and he returned wearily to bed, Mazal decided that it was time to wash the floors. She washed each flagstone separately, just as she had done in her aunt's house, and her heavy belly pulled her down, splashing in the murky water covering the floor. The coldness of the water seeped into her body, and a dull pain pierced her and felled her to the floor with a scream that sent Yitzhak running to fetch the midwife.

From then on, so people say, none of the neighbors had a moment's sleep. The sound of her screams maddened the muezzins reading verses from the Qur'an on the minarets and drowned out their voices. Women went into her room and emerged with their hair on end, covering their faces with their aprons and sticking their fingers in their ears. Even Ibrahim the barber, who was summoned urgently to her bedside, fled from the terrible shrieks that penetrated every crack. Lock their doors and shutter their windows as they might, the voice reached the neighbors besieged in their houses as if erupting from the bowels of the earth. It climbed the stairs to the uppermost stories, rose echoing from the wells, invaded the synagogues, and disturbed the children at their Torah lessons. Even the cotton wool that people stuffed in their ears in the dead of night could not keep out the voice, which was great and terrible and grew louder from minute to minute. Only Fahima the midwife, after pressing the mother's bursting stomach and dancing on it, fell peacefully asleep by her side, and some of the neighbors were prepared to swear that they heard her snoring between the screams. Women experienced in childbirth told those about to give birth for the first time that Fahima was deaf to the screams of the woman in labor and only heard the cries of the fetus in the womb.

On the seventh day, when the clock in the Ashkenazim's houses chimed five times, Mazal's womb opened and brought forth her daughter, first her buttocks and then her flattened head, which emerged at last to the sound of deafening yells. It was said that Mazal gave birth on her fourteenth birthday, but whether it was the actual day itself or the day before or after it, no one could confirm or deny. Her parents had taken the date of her birth with them to the grave.

*   *   *

When Mazal woke up and received the baby, wrapped in an old sheet, in her arms, a scream escaped her lips. The child was black and ugly as a monkey—like the one she had seen in the book of Bible illustrations she had found in a shop, the monkey standing on the shoulder of the Queen of Sheba when she came to pay her respects to the wisest of men. The baby's nose was flat, her ears stuck out, as big as pillowcases flapping in the wind, and her face and back were covered with shiny black hair. When Mazal removed the sheet she exposed thin, bandy legs, and above them a gray stomach, swollen and creased as a cracked water gourd. When the baby cried her face turned yellow and her navel stuck out. Her voice was loud and screeching and her fists punched the air as if she wanted to hit out at the world and everything in it. When she suckled she pinched her mother's nipple between her strong, toothless gums and made rude, impertinent burping noises. After every feeding Mazal would inspect her nipple with an eagle eye, swearing that she had felt two tiny teeth gnawing at her flesh.

Her neighbors whispered in the marketplace that even though the baby had no teeth, they had seen tooth marks on the breast with their own eyes. Some even swore that they had seen two drops of blood, one drop for each tooth, glistening on the pink of Mazal's nipple. The stained and ragged nightgowns covering the baby's skinny nakedness added nothing to her charms, but rather underlined her ugliness in the sight of God and man. Thus she lay, bundled up in her rags, giving voice to loud cries of protest and waving her fists threateningly at invisible enemies.

After Mazal had kept the baby hidden in her dark house for five months, her husband Yitzhak muttered one steamy summer night that the baby's legs were growing bandier and her chest more sunken.

"If you don't take her out into the sun," he said, "she'll shrivel up and fade away, her hair will fall out, her teeth won't grow, and everyone who sees her will scorn her."

Geula, who came every morning to help her bathe the baby and clean the house, repeated Yitzhak's warnings. "You have to take her out into the sun," she said, after worriedly inspecting the baby's bandy legs.

One morning, after her husband had left for the shop, Mazal took a long look at the screaming, nightmarish lump whose scalp had begun to shed yellow scabs. From her late mother's sewing basket she removed the thick black thread used by the women of the neighborhood before celebrating weddings and betrothals. She placed one end of the thread between her strong white teeth, and twisted the other end round her thumb and forefinger. Stealthily she plucked the baby from her cradle and placed her frizzy head between her strong thighs. Rolling the thread expertly between her fingers she uprooted the coarse black hair growing on her offspring's face. The baby screamed and choked, tried to catch her breath, and fainted between her mother's thighs, but Mazal didn't stop until she had plucked the last bristle of hair from her ear. Then she took a handful of flour from the glazed clay jar in the pantry and sprinkled it over the baby's flaming scarlet face. She bundled the horrid, screaming bundle in the torn sheet and went out with her baby into the sun.

The little mite's beady black eyes closed in the glare of the light, which she had never seen since the day she was born. Her face wrinkled up in a worried expression and her fists waved in the hot air spiced with the smells of the market. Mazal walked between the stalls with the living bundle clutched to her chest. She sniffed the spices in Mussa's shop, tasted the ground cinnamon on the tip of her moistened finger, inspected the cabbage leaves and smelled a bunch of mint at the greengrocer's. In the butchers' alley she hastened her steps and averted her eyes from the decapitated sheep with their hairless red flesh hanging from the hooks by their tails, while their blood dripped into the square kerosene tins standing beneath them. The head of a ram with a baleful look in its eyes sent her running to the perfume market, where she strolled at her leisure, disregarding the bundle in her arms, devouring with wide, quivering nostrils the perfumed air enveloping her and making her dizzy.

As Mazal strolled round the alleys of the marketplace the drops of water in the air joined with the flour on the baby's face to form a sticky, doughy mask. At midday, as the heat increased, little bubbles of salty sweat broke out on the baby's face and trickled down from her plucked forehead to her chin, leaving furrows of dark skin that had never been touched by the sun. As the flour was washed away in the tide of sweat, little lumps of dough were left behind in the open pores that had recently hosted bristles of hard black hair. The pox spread over the baby's black face in a sickly white rash. At that moment pious Miriam and black Nehama came strolling toward Mazal in the perfume market, looking for a victim to tease.

"Show us your little beauty," said pious Miriam sweetly, and without waiting for a reply she turned down the cover of the sheet. At the sight of the baby's face she recoiled in alarm.

"She's a leper," she whispered in horror, and turned on her heel and ran without waiting for black Nehama.

"A leper, a leper!" The cry rose in the air, passing from stall to stall, reverberating among the hawkers and rolling down to Yitzhak's haberdashery shop.

Mazal covered the baby's face with the gray sheet and ran all the way home, swearing that the sun would never touch her daughter's face again until her skin grew white and fair. Having been failed by the flour, she consulted her aunt Miriam, of the pale complexion and pure white hands, and heard her secret:

"There's nothing like lemon juice for whitening the skin."

Geula confirmed the remedial qualities of the lemon. "They told me too to rub my face and hands with a wedge of lemon in order to make the freckles fade," she said with a smile, exposing her arms covered with freckles to the elbows and examining them affectionately. "As you can imagine I didn't do it, for if I had they would have hurried to find me a husband, and who needs a nuisance like that in her house."

From then on Mazal rubbed the baby's face regularly with the sour yellow liquid. Bit by bit she worked on the skin, and examined the results. The dark skin grew a little fairer but darkened again the next day. When she saw that the lemon juice was of no use she attacked the baby's nose. While she breast-fed her she would pinch her flat nose between her thumb and finger, and she didn't let go even when strange wheezes escaped the baby's mouth. Every night she tied her loosely flapping ears to her skull with strips of cloth she tore off the old sheet. She bound the baby's horrifying bandy legs up in a diaper, and every day she increased the pressure, and she wrapped a thick bandage tightly round her swollen stomach, like one of the stiff corsets worn by rich women that she had seen in Fruma's shop in the Ashkenazic neighborhood.

*   *   *

During this whole period Mazal kept away from her husband's bed. She laid her bedding next to the baby's iron cradle, and thrust her husband away when he tried to approach the warmth of her body and the smoothness of her flesh. Nor could the neighbor women who came to the house at her husband's bidding make her change her mind.

"Even though I know I can't get pregnant as long as I'm breast-feeding the baby, I won't let him touch me, not until I come to him and tell him I'm ready," she said to her husband's emissaries.

Geula welcomed her decision, and came to visit her friend every morning, examined her face, sniffed the sheet, and searched anxiously for signs of her activities during the previous night. When she found nothing, she would press Mazal to her bosom, stroke her cheek and the inside of her arm, and gently kiss her ripe breasts with their milky smell.

"Don't let him come near you," she counseled her for the umpteenth time. "Wait. Let him control himself."

To Mazal's surprise, her husband's face began to blossom with a radiant new crop of pimples. The pimples spread over his forehead, crept down his cheeks, struck out at his nose, and came to rest on his chin. Mazal knew that if she slid her hand down his back she would find fresh new colonies of pustules there too.

Soon enough wicked tongues made haste to bring her the news. Her husband had been seen leaping like a calf onto the fat, kohl-painted Arab whore Fatima, whose house, like that of her ancient predecessor Rahab, adjoined the city walls. Mazal answered the slanderers, "I hope he enjoys himself," and continued her labors with the child. Her husband's pimples, which had blossomed due to his banishment from her bed, began to shrivel and shrink, and once again his fresh, pink skin was revealed.

When her daughter turned one, on Mazal's fifteenth birthday, as she believed, she entered her husband's bed. He stiffened immediately and without any preliminaries penetrated her body. The moment he was inside her he froze, then withdrew in alarm.

"There are no walls," he mumbled fearfully.

The next day he tried his luck again, and again his member shrank and emerged from her body small, limp, and unsatisfied. The same thing happened a few nights in succession. And again his face was resplendent with pimples, and again Mazal heard of his visits to the prostitute.

Fahima the midwife, who had stood by her bed and delivered her daughter, was summoned to the house by Mazal's husband, and was rewarded handsomely for her pains. At her command Mazal removed her underclothes, opened her legs, and allowed her to probe into her private parts in the faint light of the setting sun filtering through the window. Fahima's filthy, black-nailed hands rummaged inside Mazal at length, leaving an unpleasant burning sensation in her flesh.

"Your husband says you have no walls and no bottom, and he's right," the midwife said after completing her examination. "The baby's backside, which emerged before the head, made a great tear inside you, and there is no cure," she informed Mazal. "You will be able to have children," she added, pronouncing Mazal's sentence, "but you will never be pleasured by your husband again." And she went out to Yitzhak, who was waiting outside biting his nails in suspense.

Yitzhak went back inside dragging his feet heavily. All that night he did not dare look into his wife's amber eyes. In the morning, when the cock crowed, he mounted her, pressed himself against her naked flesh, beat his member on her belly, and rubbed it on the entrance to her body. At last he gained his satisfaction, but not before drenching Mazal's body with rivers of sweat, which soaked the sheets and dripped onto the floor through the heavy down mattress. All this time her husband wept in her arms while the baby laughed loudly and refused to go to sleep.

The next day he took her to the rabbis and presented her with a bill of divorcement. Before parting from her he broke a gold napoleon in two. He gave her one half, and promised to send her the other if he made his fortune in foreign lands. That same night he set out for Jaffa with the caravan of mules, and from there, so she heard, he embarked on a ship and sailed over the sea.

In the days to come Mazal tried to conjure up the vision of his pimples, which she knew intimately one by one. As time went by the vision faded from her eyes and the pimples disappeared without a trace.

Chapter Five

That year, so they said in the neighborhood, the great miracle occurred. One morning the baby woke up from her sleep and she was bald as an eagle. On the little pillow of her bed Mazal found all the dark, hard hair of her head lying like a round halo of black sheep's fleece. The next day Mazal saw that silky golden hair like a chick's down was covering the baby's scalp. Every day the hair thickened and grew. Every morning Mazal would hurry to her daughter's cradle to witness the wonder, and the hair rapidly grew longer until it reached the baby's ankles, so that she tripped over it when she took her first steps. Her feet were ensnared in the golden tangle, and she fell flat on her face, crying heartrendingly.

Everybody praised and extolled the baby's hair so much that Mazal decided never to cut it, and she let it grow and lengthen, until at night it covered the child's body like a silken blanket, whose color was like that of the garments of the emperor of faraway China. Mazal never ate the fresh eggs sold her by the Arab peasant women in the market, but kept them in a little wicker basket in the corner of the kitchen. When the basket was full she broke them all very carefully, lifted out the yolks, mixed them with olive oil, and beat the mixture lightly with a wooden spoon until it was airy and pale. Then she took the child, put her in the wooden tub, and shampooed her hair for hours with the mixture she had prepared. To rinse the hair she used the rainwater she collected in the wooden barrel standing outside, and finished off the treatment with an infusion of camomile flowers. Every day she would roam the fields, spying out the tiny flowers and snipping off their yellow heads carefully, so as not to squeeze them between her fingers and crumble them to dust.

"There's nothing like camomile tea for lightening the hair," said the neighbors who came to see the golden-haired little girl. When Mazal finished shampooing the golden hair, she dried it carefully with a big sheet and sat with the child outside, combing her hair, until she succeeded in separating each hair. So that the long hair would not sweep up the dust on the floors of the house, Mazal plaited her daughter's hair into two thick braids and wound them many times around her head.

When Mazal walked with her at dusk in the streets of the market and the fields of the town, the child looked as if a huge ball of white radiance sat heavily on her head. So heavy was the burden of her hair that it was hard for her to hold the stem of her neck straight and her head high, and she would walk heavily, with her head tilted forward, like a fat goose. As her hair grew lighter, so did her two beady little black eyes, until they took on the golden honey of her mother's and matched the color of her hair. Later on her eyes became speckled like her mother's eyes with tiny brown spots, which danced and played hide-and-seek with the sunbeams. The color of her skin, which from the day of her birth was hardly ever exposed to the burning sun, was pure as the ivory imported from India. Her flat nose, tirelessy pinched by her mother's fingers, grew straight and delicate. Even when her face grew, her nose remained tiny, refusing to keep up with the rate of growth of the rest of her body.

* * *

Sara had two mothers, or, if you like, a mother and a father, both women, so they said in the neighborhood. For the day Yitzhak left home Geula occupied his empty bed. One day, the story went, she set out for Mazal's house, with Yussuf the Kurdish porter striding behind her. Under his arms he carried eiderdowns and pillows, on his head he bore a copper basin, and in his broad sash were stuck household utensils, pots and pans, which made a loud noise and rang out with every step he took. Without a word, as if it were self-evident, Mazal cleared a space in her wardrobe for Geula's things, and she gave her half her empty bed too. Together they shared the household chores, the task of selling in the shop, and the burden of bringing up Sara. In the evening hours it was possible to see them cooking together, and Mazal never set out for the market alone. Geula would accompany her there, bully the hawkers, and walk away with the fresh produce she had bought for a song. Only the washing of the floors Mazal did not share with Geula. That task was hers alone. When she washed the floors she would close her eyes, feel the stones with her sensitive hands, try to guess which stone she was scrubbing, and delight in the act of washing and the game of hide-and-seek she was playing with the paving stones. While Mazal was washing the floor, Geula, who had studied for a few years at the dressmaking school next to the Siftai Hakhamim synagogue and was considered a learned woman, would play counting games with Sara, improve her writing, and practice thinking games with her.

In the long days they spent together they would go for twilight walks in the fields surrounding the town. Sara would walk between them, clinging to their hands and sailing through the air with little shrieks of joy whenever she asked them to swing her. In the fields the women would pick flowers, anemones and cyclamens, and weave them into garlands for Sara's fair head. Sometimes Mazal would leave them to amuse themselves and wander farther afield to pick the camomile flowers. When she returned with the straw basket in her hand full of tiny fragrant golden blooms and marjoram and sage leaves, they would lie under the ancient olive tree in the valley at the foot of the wall. The head of one resting on the belly of the other, they would stroke each other on the head and the cheek. Sara would run about near them, disturbing their tranquillity and filling their laps with bunches of flowers she had picked, red beetles with black-spotted wings, and glittering stones she had found.

One day they were disturbed by an Arab shepherd from the village in the wadi. He chased away the sheep that surrounded him on every side, and unhesitatingly he approached the women sprawled under the ancient olive tree, fixed his smouldering dark eyes on Mazal's spotted eyes, weighed her breasts in his imagination, and let his eyes wander to Geula's red hair. Before he decided what to do with the double prize that had fallen to his lot, Geula scowled at him, stuck out her tongue, opened her eyes wide, and waved her thick hands in front of his face.

The shepherd did not move. He stood before her as if paralyzed, as if he were carved in rock. When Geula saw that he had no intention of going away, she ruffled her red hair and screamed at him with loud, discordant sounds.

Only then did the poor man flee panic-stricken back to his village, with stories of the white she-devil and the red-haired she-devil he had found in the field, their breasts exposed, their genitals dripping, fornicating and caressing each other, and between their loins the little girl they had given birth to, her body covered with a cascade of golden hair reaching to her ankles.

When they returned to the field a week later they found the shepherd with a few dozen youths from his village waiting in tense expectation. When they saw the women and the little girl walking between them they made excited snorting noises, like stallions scenting a mare in heat. Geula examined the men through the slits of her eyes and whispered to Mazal, "Take the child and run for your life." Then she walked up to them, rumpled her hair wildly, smeared her face with earth, exposed her immense breasts, which were covered with dark spots and armed with pointed orange nipples, and laughed loudly in their faces. With shrieks of fear like the squawking of abandoned chicks the youths fled to their village, looking over their shoulders at the bare-breasted red she-devil, who threw clods of earth and stones after them as they ran.

A week later, when the women came back, there was no one waiting for them. Years after the incident, in the twilight hours of the short winter days, the shepherds would sit with their families in their narrow stone huts, listening to the bleating of the sheep, and tell of the crazy she-devil with the red hair and the giant breasts, who boded ill to men. Of the white she-devil, they said that when the sheep looked at her their babies dropped out of their wombs, and of the golden-haired child of the she-devils, they said that anyone who looked at her would be blinded and would never be able to look at another woman as long as he lived.

❊ ❊ ❊

Sara grew up and her beauty was so great that its fame spread beyond the sea, and the pilgrims who came to see the holy places of Jerusalem made a habit of stopping at Yitzhak's tiny shop, where Mazal now stood

with the girl at her side, to feast their eyes on the great wonder. They
came from many distant lands, some of them simple folk who came to
worship at the graves of the saints, some of them wealthy men from
rich countries who lodged in inns and were accompanied by guides.
Like the waves of a stormy black river were the pilgrims from Russia:
clad in black, felt boots on their feet, and in their mouths hymns of
praise to their Lord Jesus Christ. Ship after ship anchored in the waters
of the port of Jaffa and disgorged their human freight. Singing, the
pilgrims marched through the fragrant orange groves of Jaffa, and glasses
of tea poured from giant samovars cheered them on their way. The
columns of dust raised by their feet brought all the beggars of the town
running to meet them. They streamed in en masse, proudly exposing
the deformities of their birth and the ravages left by the mutilations of
leprosy. And the pilgrims would put their hands in their pockets and
bring out small coins and loaves of black bread to revive the wretched
creatures who fought like famished puppies over every crust thrown
their way.

After prostrating themselves on the graves of the saints and crawling
on their bellies, crowned with crowns of thorns, on the last road of their
beloved Jesus, they ascended in waves to Mazal's shop to feast their eyes
on the beauty of the Jewish madonna. Equipped with cameras standing
on tripods and many photographic plates, and hidden beneath their black
tents, the wealthy among them sought to capture her face in photographs. Those with no money in their pockets took out paper and quill,
dipped the quill in ink, and sought to immortalize her radiant beauty
on paper, in order to take the icon of the most beautiful of the daughters
of Zion back with them to their homes. Others streamed to the shop
of Rahamim the photographer. There, said the rumor that spread by
word of mouth, her picture could be seen. It was a tradition that a
picture of Sara on her last birthday hung in the window of his shop.
Rahamim, smelling fat profits to be made, allowed them to look at her
picture and draw her face for a fee. Like a policeman guarding a prisoner
in his cell, he stood before them with his back hiding the picture, until
they opened their bundles of money and dropped a coin in his hand.
After they had finished drawing the picture, hands trembling with suppressed desire, he took them into the shop, opened a long wooden box,
and sold them pictures of the Stations of the Cross. And when they had
completed their purchases he guided them to the darkest corner in the

depths of the shop, and fished from a painted tin zbox photographs of the most beautiful of women on her last birthday. In some of the pictures she was wearing a Bedouin robe and a chain of gold coins on her forehead; in others she appeared in her Sabbath best with her luxuriant hair falling loose around her and illuminating the whole picture in a halo of light. Then the purses would open again and many coins would drop into his hands.

Because of the hunters of beauty who came to feast their eyes, Mazal's business prospered and flourished. Those who failed to immortalize a touch of the beauty's loveliness in drawings or photographs bought at her mother's shop, while their eyes stared deep into Sara's speckled eyes and glided secretly over her golden hair. When they returned to their countries of origin they told of the place of Christ's birth, of his grave, of the shrines of the saints, and also of the girl whose mother never had to light a lamp in the darkness. All that was necessary was for her daughter to undo her braids and let down her hair for the whole house to be bathed in golden light. And in her sleep, so they said, her mother covered her hair with a dark blanket lest the light penetrate her eyes and keep her awake.

And the child was not only beautiful. She was also very clever. In her mother's shop she knew how to calculate large sums in her head, to give the exact change, to speak sensibly; and she even read books, so it was said. Sara learned the art of reading from the packages of haberdashery in the shop, poring over the words that described the contents of the package and learning the letters by heart. People said too that they had seen her peeping into the infants' class of Menahem the melamed. And the little ones themselves described a radiance of gold suddenly bursting forth behind the windowsill, illuminating the dark classroom and dazzling their eyes with its brilliance. So Sara learned to read the Pentateuch from behind the windowpane, which was greasy from the foreheads of the infants pressed against it to see the street outside. When she finished the Pentateuch she climbed up the drainpipe to the second floor, and there she studied the Mishnah and the Talmud with the young boys. As incriminating evidence they found tangled knots of long golden hair wound around the rusty nails attaching the pipe to the wall.

"If she continues like this," people predicted, "she'll end up in the opening of the chimney, like Hillel the Righteous."

On the day Sara celebrated her fourteenth birthday, Mazal shampooed her hair with the mixture of eggs and oil she had previously prepared, rinsed it in the infusion of camomile, and sat outside with her, combing her hair and plaiting red silk ribbons into the halo of gold encircling her and enveloping her body. Then she busied herself with ironing her best dress with a coal iron and polishing her red Sabbath shoes, and they set out in all their finery for the photographer's shop, where Rahamim was waiting impatiently to take the birthday photograph. Posed against the background of a painted curtain depicting foreign scenes of mountains and waterfalls, Sara was photographed by Rahamim every year, and the new picture was displayed in his window. "And since then they've never stopped coming to the shop," he would say to anyone who asked the meaning of the custom. Every year, on Sara's birthday, as if the rumor had spread through the town, dozens of young men and yeshiva students would gather round the shop and wait quietly and patiently to feast their eyes on the most beautiful of Jerusalem's daughters. Every year they waited for her arrival, and when she appeared they crowded around her with bated breath, then cleared a path for her, and she would pass between the rows like a queen reviewing her guard of honor.

Her fourteenth birthday was engraved in her memory because of the foreigner. Scores of yeshiva students in their black suits waited patiently for her arrival. Suddenly one young man detached himself from the press of bodies silently besieging her. He stood out among them, with his fair hair, his khaki suit, the puttees on his legs and the new pith helmet on his head. Excitedly he signaled her to stop, set up his tripod and camera opposite her, and asked her with gestures of his hands to stand still. Sara obeyed. The stranger wasted no time: He tucked his head under the black cloth and took a photograph. Quickly he extracted the plate, inserted another in its place, signaled her with his hand again, his head still under the curtain, and took another one. When he was done he bowed deeply, smiled his thanks, and his eyes caught hers. Sara was swallowed up in his blue eyes and refused to emerge from their warm lair. She bathed in the blue, drowned in it, drank it down in mouthfuls, wound it round her body like a sheet of silk, and snuggled into the tenderness of his gaze, as if he were enveloping her in a thick, airy down quilt. As the warmth spread through her body she felt her mother's elbow digging into her, propelling her step by step into Rahamim's shop, while her head turned back and her eyes remained fixed in the brilliant blue facing her.

For a long time Rahamim photographed her, loading and unloading the plates upon which her features were engraved forever, and all this time the eyes of the stranger danced before her. For many days afterward his image disturbed her waking hours. She tried to conjure up other images, of green fields and red roofs, but to no avail. His gaze would return to invade her eyes and paint the scenes she saw in a deep blue.

* * *

When Sara came of age deputations of matchmakers came knocking at her mother's door, but they were all turned away.

"Sara will marry whomever she pleases," said Mazal expressionlessly to the matchmakers, and the news spread through the town like fire through a field of thorns.

"What can that Mazal be thinking of?" people said in surprise. "The most eligible bachelors of the town are interested in her daughter, and offers have even come from matchmakers beyond the sea. Why is she so stubborn?"

* * *

The answer to these questions Mazal locked in her heart, and it acted inside her like poison consuming her body. The more the girl grew and bloomed the more her mother wilted and withered, as if a worm were gnawing at her body and devouring her flesh. A terrible secret gave her no rest, and she tossed and turned on her bed at night and groaned in her sleep. Only she knew the secret: The inside of her daughter Sara did not match the outside. One day she found her bathing in the tub, and discovered to her horror a patch of black hair growing on her groin. And with the passing of the days the patch grew larger, blacker and denser; it grew like a wild bushy plant, it grew like a weed. And the infusion of camomile flowers Mazal gave her to make the hair lighter did no good. Sara's pubic hair remained dark, glossy, and tangled, a memorial to the dark, black days of her infancy.

"This is my punishment for defying fate," Mazal said to herself, tortured with bitter thoughts. "And if she marries, her husband will see black, and know that the gold of her hair is a deception, and divorce her, and her end will be like mine." Therefore she decided that Sara would choose her own husband; please God she would be lucky in her choice, and her husband would pay no heed to the blackness of her mound.

Sara had no girlfriends, and her mother discouraged any attempts on her part to approach the neighbors' daughters.

"All you need is here in the house with me. I forbid you to make friends with unsuitable girls, for no good will come of it," she would say to her, afraid of the evil eye of her neighbors and of the discovery of the secret she was at such pains to keep. And the obedient little girl submitted willingly to her mother's wishes and did not protest.

One day, when Mazal was washing herself in the tub and Geula was helping her and scrubbing her back with the loofah, Sara noticed the gold half napoleon hanging round her mother's neck on a black velvet ribbon.

"One day I'll tell you about it," Mazal promised her, "and the day this napoleon finds its twin brother and unites with my half coin will be the happiest day of your life and perhaps of my life too. Pray God I live to see that day," she added, lowering her eyes before Geula's penetrating gaze. Sara had never seen her mother's face so radiant as when she told her about the coin.

"And who has the other half?" she pressed her.

"The man who will make you happy," she answered enigmatically.

"And how will that other half be found?" she asked again.

"It will find us even though we hide at the bottom of the sea," she replied. "Harder with the loofah! Don't spare me! I want you to peel my skin," Mazal said to Geula, who scrubbed at her skin. Sara looked at the half coin dangling between her mother's breasts, and she tried to imagine the happiness that would flood her if its twin half were found, but she was unable to imagine anything.

✳   ✳   ✳

Until the arrival of the winter that was recorded in the annals of the town as the winter when the sky split open, Sara never heard a man's name mentioned in the house. That winter the rain fell without stopping on the town and the mud houses of the Arab quarters almost dissolved. The houses of the Jewish quarter leaked burning tears of lime, and the householders were obliged to walk between buckets full of the muddy rainwater that penetrated the domed ceilings and formed shapes of damp roses on the walls. After the rain came the snow, and after the snow hail, and the sun was not seen in the town for two or three months. That same year, even before the coming of the spring, the roses of dampness on the walls turned into black roses of mold. Their smell wafted into the distance and penetrated every corner, afflicted the clothes stored in chests and wardrobes with black spots of old age, greedily devoured the leather shoes, and damaged the joints of men, women, and children. The whitewash peeled off the walls, exposing layers of paint in all the colors of the rainbow.

That year brought death to the homes of the Jews. First it smote the babies and the toothless old. Then it struck at the young and the mature in years. The first to fall ill was oddly the strapping, sturdy Geula, though it seemed as if the Angel of Death himself would shrink from visiting her, with her red hair and her sharp tongue. Her flesh dwindled, her face fell, and all the rusty freckles covering her body faded and turned into white spots dotting her gray skin. Mazal never left her bedside, and she fed her, washed her, and begged her in an imploring voice to get well, "for without you my life means nothing to me."

From the day Geula fell ill Mazal would ask Sara to bring her bunches of fragrant sage from the fields. She would lay the leaves in rows on an iron tray, which she placed on the tin of smouldering embers in the room, in order to warm the flesh of the dying woman. The perfumed smell would spread through the room and somewhat dispel the stink of approaching death. She was afraid to fall asleep beside the patient's bed, lest death should come and take her unawares, and when her weariness increased she would put wet compresses on her head, to keep her eyes open and her mind clear.

One morning her weariness overcame her and her head dropped on her chest. She woke up suddenly because of the glaring white light penetrating her eyelids. Alarmed, she sought the source of the light. The blinds were closed and the door was shut, and the room was shrouded in darkness again. She went up to straighten Geula's bedclothes and when she plumped up the pillow the sick woman's head wobbled like a heavy flower on a slender, fragile stem. Mazal tucked the blankets round her body and went to the kitchen to brew tea. At noon Sara arrived with a fresh bunch of sage leaves, and food and medicines. She went up to Mazal's bed to greet her and recoiled. The sick woman's eyes were open; her dry mouth gaped, surrounded by a narrow band of spittle upon which rested the messenger of death, a green fly washing his hairy feet.

"Mother, Geula is no longer with us," said Sara gently to her mother who was busy in the kitchen.

Mazal did not react, as if she were deaf. She went on cooling the tea she had brewed for the sick woman by stirring it briskly with a spoon, and when she put the cup to her lips and found that it was still hot, she poured the tea from one cup to another and from time to time she tested the temperature of the liquid. When it had cooled down she went up to the bed. First, with an expression of hatred, she chased away the fly, which ignored the energetic waving of her hand and returned to the band of spittle that had dribbled out of Geula's mouth. Defeated, she stared at the winged creature that clung with all six hairy legs, and stubbornly she began to pour the tea into the gaping mouth, wiping away the drops of spit and tea with a white handkerchief.

"Mother," Sara repeated loudly, "Geula's dead. Leave the tea alone."

Mazal took no notice and went on pouring the tea into the dead woman's mouth and trying to chase away the fly.

"Today she drank a whole cup," she said proudly when she had finished.

"Mother, touch her, she's cold. She's dead. What are you doing?" Sara cried in horror.

"It's time to wash her," Mazal said. "Come and help me. I'll get the water ready and you watch her in the meantime, so that the Angel of Death won't come and take her soul behind my back."

Mazal hurried to the kitchen and put the big kettle on to boil. Afterward she poured the hot water into the tub and threw in a few heads of camomile flowers and a bunch of sage leaves, which floated like green boats on the water. She breathed in the scented vapors with satisfaction. The strong smells seared her lungs, her head spun enjoyably, and she felt her strength coming back to her. On her return to the room she began to undress Geula with brisk movements. A naked arm dangled from its sleeve like a branch in the wind, and Geula's flesh, which had begun to turn cold, was stiff to her touch. Mazal stepped back in horror and examined the body lying limply on the bed like a rag doll.

"What have you done?" she shrieked. "I turned my back and you let Geula die." She sat down on the floor, exposed her breasts, and beat them with her hands. Then she let down her hair, pulled out clumps of it, and scratched her face.

Sara tried to stop her, but her mother's madness grew.

Sara ran screaming out of the house and summoned the neighbors. They covered Geula with a sheet and gave Mazal sugar water and smelling salts to revive her. Dissolving in tears and leaning on her neighbor Rivka, Mazal swayed from side to side and mumbled unintelligibly. When they came to take the body away to wash it she refused to part from it. With her hands she clung to the slowly cooling body, digging her nails into the dead flesh and refusing to let the women take it away.

Itzik, the massive, stammering attendant at the men's ritual baths, was summoned to the dead woman's house. Gently he loosened Mazal's grip, bending her fingers back and drawing her nails out of Geula's body. No sooner had he succeeded in freeing one hand than the other dug its nails into the shriveled body, leaving deep crescent moons imprinted in the stiff dead flesh.

Only after Haim the grocer and Moussa the carter had been summoned, too, and with their strong arms restrained the screaming and kicking woman, did the undertakers succeed in removing the body and taking it away for purification.

⁕ ⁕ ⁕

Bowed under Geula's weight and struggling to lift their feet from the mire of brown mud clutching at their ankles and threatening to suck them and their silent burden with greedy squelching noises into the bowels of the earth, the stretcher bearers made their way to the cemetery. Puffing and panting, their heads covered with heavy, soaking gray sacks, beneath a barrage of hail the size of cannonballs raining down from the sky, they advanced to the hastily dug grave. They found it as full of water as a small ritual bath. As fast as they bailed it out with pails and pots, the water kept rising in the open grave, brimming over and flooding the surrounding ground and the mounds of smooth, shining mud that covered the fresh graves around it. Exhausted, they stood at the graveside, and as one man they tipped their burden into it. The body of the redheaded Geula, wrapped in a shroud of icicles, slid rapidly into the dark, foaming water, sinking and disappearing into the pit and giving rise to a trail of air bubbles in its wake. When the grave diggers began throwing lumps of mud and stones into the little pool, a cry of alarm went up from the handful of people standing round the grave. Geula was floating on the surface of the water like a cork, refusing to sink to the depths and leave the land of the living.

"Sink, sink," the rabbi implored, flinging clods of earth and stones at the body floating in the pit, which gaped like a wound in the ground. The body refused to sink. Mazal let out a grievous cry and ripped the collar of her coat. At that very moment, as if the dead woman had taken fright at her friend's scream, Geula sank, making a little wave in the water, which rose above the pit and splashed the shoes of the people standing round the grave. Then the mourners began to pelt the grave with lumps of wet earth and stones. Sara refused to watch the stoning, and Mazal looked at the open grave with ravaged eyes.

"You must say Kaddish," Mazal ordered her daughter. "She was like a father to you."

In order not to upset her mother, who seemed to have gone out of her mind, Sara whispered the Aramaic words with the young yeshiva student who had been hired to say the Kaddish. After the grave had been covered with heavy red mud and the people had withdrawn, Mazal began digging with her nails in the sodden covering of soil.

"Leave me here. I want to be buried with her," she screamed at Sara, who tried to pry her fingers away from the blanket of ground covering her friend, and her wet hair, heavy with the mud sticking to it, slapped at Sara's face. But Sara would not let go, tightening her grip until she dragged her mother off the grave.

For the first time in her life Mazal raised her hand to her daughter, scratching and furrowing her face with grooves of mud smeared with blood. Sara screamed for help, startling the people walking away from the grave, and Itzik the bath attendant hurried up in response to her cry. With practiced hands he gently bent her arms and hoisted her swooning onto his back like an empty sack of grain. He opened the door of the house with a light kick from his boot, soiled with the mud of the graveyard, and threw the trembling Mazal on the bed, whose sheets were still soaked with Geula's sweat and still bore her smell.

From the moment Mazal was thrown onto her bed she never got off it again. At first she burned with fever and her eyes rolled up to the mold-blackened ceiling until the eyeballs were revealed, yellow as the yoke of an egg. She cried out for Yitzhak, whose name Sara heard in the house for the first time, and demanded that she hurry up and bring him to her bedside. None of the doctors' medicines helped. Her flesh dwindled away and her skin hung on her fragile bones in folds as yellow as old Torah scrolls. Her honey-colored hair turned white and her teeth began to wobble and fall out. She was confused and tossed and turned in her bed, which was wet and stinking with salty sweat.

All this time Sara did not leave her side. When she had to go to the market to buy food she asked a neighbor to look after her mother, making her swear not to leave her for a moment, lest the Angel of Death steal into the room and take the sick woman's soul in her absence. She tried to sweeten her mother's restless sleep with the lullabies Mazal had sung to her when she was a baby. She cooked her gruel from semolina, and Mazal vomited it up again, mixed with black bile.

All that winter Mazal faded away, growing thinner and thinner, until Sara was afraid that one morning she would look at her bed and find her embroidered nightgown empty of her body and her bed-socks bereft of her skeletal feet with their crooked toenails.

On the eve of Passover, when the spring sun came out to illuminate the world long deprived of its light, Sara scoured the house, trying to rid it of the pervasive smell of death. A ray of light filtered through the curtains and danced on the walls, flickered on the ceiling, and played between the flagstones, emphasizing their colors and the lines between them. When it had finished playing with the flagstones the sunbeam stole silently and stealthily toward the sick woman's bed. First it touched her long-nailed toes, then it warmed the wilted flesh of her feet, lingered on her decrepit vulva, latched onto her flabby breasts, tickled her nipples, and climbed slowly up the creases of her neck. When it had finished roaming over her body it leaped into her gaping, toothless, wheezing mouth, penetrated the darkness of her nostrils, and inspected her nasal passages, illuminating them from within and making delicate, transparent threads of blood stand out on her nose. Then it leaped out again, straight into her dull, lifeless eyes.

Mazal woke up at once, calling out Yitzhak's name in a voice so terrible that her startled neighbors came running, under the impression that her long-lost husband had come home at last. With the cry of

"Yitzhak" on her lips the sick woman sat up in bed and ordered Sara to bring her the mirror hanging on the kitchen wall.

"He's coming," she whispered. "I must make myself beautiful in his honor. Give me the kohl and the rouge, quickly," she demanded.

Sara stared at the sunbeam playing on the ceiling and opened the windows and the curtains wide. The sunbeam disappeared. For the first time in her life Sara refused to obey her mother, supported by the neighbors' opinion that there was no point in upsetting the sick woman with her moribund appearance. When she failed to obtain her wish, Mazal began to scream and curse her daughter in front of everybody for all the troubles that had descended on her head. Sara fled the house, sat down on the doorstep, and stopped her ears with her fingers against her mother's dreadful screams.

"Yitzhak's coming, and I want a mirror. I want a mirror, a mirror," her mother wailed. "And that wicked girl won't bring me one. All my troubles are her fault. I wish she had never been born. She's the devil's daughter, a Lilith come to steal my soul. It's a pity she never died at birth, the accursed girl."

Sara went back into the house, tore the burnished copper mirror from the wall together with the nail, covered her eyes so as not to see the horrified expression on her mother's face, and took it to her bed. With her yellow-skinned, skeletal hands her mother took the mirror, but immediately dropped it again.

"The mirror is too heavy for me," she whispered to Sara. "Hold it in your hands, Lilith, and bring it close to my face."

Sara did as her mother bade her.

"I can't see. Bring it closer," repeated Mazal, and Sara brought the mirror closer until the dying woman's beaky nose touched it and her breath condensed into tiny drops on its surface.

Mazal strained her purblind eyes in vain. "Open the curtains. It's dark in the house and I can't see," she scolded her daughter.

Sara pretended to open the already open curtains.

The mirror reflected a toothless, shriveled skull with wild white hair and rolling, upturned eyes whose whites had turned a murky brown.

"Lilith," moaned Mazal. "Lilith has bewitched me," she whispered and breathed her last.

Even when they lowered her mother's body into the grave, a bag of skin covering a pile of hollow bones, her screams and the name she had given her, Lilith, went on ringing in Sara's ears and distressing her mind. And she did not know what she had done to make her mother hate her in her dying days.

Chapter Six

Throughout the seven days of mourning for her mother Sara sat in the house and with her fingers felt the gold half coin hanging round her neck. The women who had purified her mother's body gave it to her, baffled as to what it might mean. Neighbors offering condolence came and went, bearing various foodstuffs and murmuring words of consolation. But Sara paid no attention. Her eyes roamed the room and discovered dirt and neglect. Dust covered the floor, the walls were black and peeling, and the smell of her dead mother's soiled sheets still lingered in her nostrils. While they murmured condolences in her ears she was busy planning and scheming: When the last of the visitors left she would clean and polish the house, wash every flagstone till it gleamed, launder the filthy curtains and give them back their original color, throw out her mother's stinking sheets and spread new ones on the brass bed, which was now hers. She would paint the walls white and plant herbs in the yard. In this way she would wipe out her mother's memory and banish the shadows of death, and only then would she be able to fill the house with a man's voice and the sounds of childish laughter.

When the last of the people left she set to work. With clenched teeth and full of fury she scrubbed the walls of the room, tore down the curtains and sewed new ones in their place, plastered the peeling walls and painted them white, burned the sheets with the smell of death clinging to them in the yard and spread new ones on the bed. Then she went out into the little garden in front of the house, pulled out the weeds with hatred in her heart and planted a little bed of herbs, with mint, parsley, hyssop, and rue, and jasmine for its sweet scent. Day and night she worked at cleaning the house, and when she was done she returned the few pieces of furniture she had put out in the street, boiled a kettleful of water, and poured the boiling water into the tub. With slow movements she began to wash herself, scrubbing away the memories of death and bringing calm and consolation to her body. Her hair, which reached her ankles, she shampooed in rainwater, and wound it wet and shining several times around her head.

When she had finished washing herself her eye fell on the rusty *sandouk,* her mother's dowry chest. Wondering why she had never noticed it before, she went up to the iron trunk and tried to imagine what she would find inside it when she opened the lid. She lifted it cautiously, as if afraid her mother's ghost might pop out of the chest, white-haired and toothless in her stinking nightgown, and seize her by the neck.

A flock of fleeing moths and a cloud of suffocating dust greeted her and covered her shampooed hair in a layer of white swarming with silver-winged moths. At the top of the chest, neatly folded, she found a silken wedding dress, moth-eaten and yellow with age. When she tried to spread it out the dress disintegrated at her touch and turned into a pile of yellow dust dotted with rusty little hooks. Underneath it she found a pair of shabby leather boots, and utensils such as she had never seen in her mother's house. As she removed the objects, her fingers encountered a roll of stiff paper wrapped up like a mummy in several layers of crumbling, yellowing tulle. Carefully she unwrapped the tulle, feeling as if she were removing the moldy winding sheet from a corpse in its grave. Inside the paper shroud she found a tattered brown photograph, spotted with wormholes the size of a pinhead. In the photograph she saw the image of herself in a bridal gown, and next to her a young man in an oversized wedding suit whose face was covered with a rash of pimples. Sara strained her memory. She was sure that she herself had never been photographed in a bridal gown, or with a strange man at her side.

All that night Sara hardly slept a wink and she wore her brain out with thoughts. That night, and all the nights that followed, the image of the blue-eyed stranger who had taken her photograph rose before her eyes. His fair hair and blue eyes overshadowed the image of the pimply youth in the picture. In the morning, when she woke from her troubled sleep to the sound of the cock's crow, she looked at the picture again. It's a prophecy about my future husband, she thought. If I'm photographed in a bridal gown with a young man by my side, it means that he is to be my husband and I his wife. This is a picture of the future.

From that day on she would open the *sandouk* stealthily, as if she were afraid of her mother's ghost hovering in the air and catching her in a forbidden act. With the curtains drawn she would take out the picture and in a long, slow ritual she would remove its shroudlike wrappings. After the picture was exposed she would commune at length with pimply-faced youth, her future mate, and think loving thoughts about him. She imagined the children she would have with him, the Sabbath evenings in her new house, and the kitchen where she would cook his meals. Sara prayed that he would bring his books with him, so that she could read until it was time for the morning prayers while her husband lay sleeping in his bed. The more she looked at the picture, the more the face of the blue-eyed stranger faded, until he disappeared from her life and the picture of her future husband was so clearly engraved in her heart that she could draw his likeness in her head and she no longer needed to look at the photograph.

Thirty days after her mother's death Sara returned to the shop. Never had the pokey little shop been frequented by such an abundance of yeshiva students—all of them set on buying silk ribbons and buttons, mumbling their requests in blushing embarrassment, and explaining that they were buying these feminine articles for their mothers or their sisters. Her hands were full of work and money, and she began to think of buying a new shop in a new quarter of the town, a sunny shop with big windows and flowery curtains. That year she was also sought out by many matchmakers in the wake of the youths, but she rejected them all.

"You're no longer a girl. You're a grown woman, and if you don't hurry up and get married you'll go to your grave a virgin with no one to say Kaddish for you," the matchmakers would threaten when their hopes of a commission were dashed by her stubbornness.

But Sara stood her ground. She was sure that the bridegroom fate had chosen for her, the man in the photograph, would knock on her door one day and ask to come in. Gradually the stream of young men stopped coming to the shop and the matchmakers stopped visiting her house, and she remained alone, clasping the picture of her bridegroom, blurred by her tears, to her bosom.

And perhaps he'll never come, the heretical thought stole into her heart. But she shook it off like a scarecrow banishing the pesky birds pecking at its garden.

When the matchmakers despaired of Sara, the pregnant women came to feast their eyes on her beauty. For hours they would bargain with her about the price of a velvet ribbon that cost no more than a penny, sucking in her beauty and assimilating it into themselves, swallowing the gold of her hair and the sparkle of her eyes and storing their magic properties in the dark chambers of their wombs. And indeed it was said that the girls born to these women came into the world endowed with a measure of Sara's beauty.

But the rejected yeshiva students would cover their eyes at the sight of her dazzling hair, lest she steal into their fantasies at night and rob them of their moonstruck souls. Then they would struggle with her on their stinking mattresses and sheets soaked with sweat and stained with the sperm they ejected in their dreams, sperm that was collected and hoarded drop by drop in the womb of the demon- and devil-spawning Lilith. And they would be ashamed to tell their dreams the next day when she visited them again as they pored over the pages of the Gemara and caused their members to stiffen oppressively on their loins. Even when they tried to banish her with oaths and excommunications, with execrations and curses, she would come back to haunt them, clinging to the pages of the Gemara, swaying before their eyes red with hallucinatory nights, and her dazzling smile would whisper to them in words of flattery and seduction.

And when they could not overcome her, they went to the rabbi and asked him to speak to her and request her not to walk in the lane leading to the beth-midrash. And when she complied with the rabbi's request and even covered her hair lest any of them be led into temptation, even then her image continued to dance before their eyes made bleary by nights that shook both body and soul, and some say that in those days the study of a single tractate took months to complete, because of the phantasmagoric sights whirling giddily before the eyes of the students.

Those unable to banish the sights would fan the flames of the hunger inside them and follow her wherever she went. The bolder among them would lurk outside her door, and at night, when the light went off in the window, they would pounce with trembling fingers on the washing lines, where bodiless garments swayed like ghosts waiting for their victims. Their palms clammy with lust, they would tear the flapping garments from the line. Then they would bundle their treasure under their coats, where it burned like the embers of an alien fire whispering words of temptation, and carry it off to a hiding place. There, far from prying eyes, they would feast their eyes on the curves conjured up by the clothes, grope with trembling fingers to feel the smoothness of her body, and dazzled by the gleam of her skin they would sniff with flaring nostrils the scents of her naked limbs as their hands pawed the stiffly laundered fabric. When the clothes on the washing lines dwindled, the boldest of them penetrated the secrets of the house itself, and returned with rare and precious loot, a pair of panties gray with washing, redolent of her smell and the memory of her private parts.

And in the neighborhood they told of all the stoop-shouldered and hollow-chested youths who lined up to pay the robber for a sniff of his booty. The same student, they added, abandoned his studies, and with the money he collected from the sniffers and pawers he opened a small lingerie, brassiere, and corset shop in the new quarter of the town.

⁎   ⁎   ⁎

Sara knew that her waiting was over on the day she saw her bridegroom enter the shop and walk down the stairs toward her. His foreign clothes were torn and dusty, his sparse beard was dry and stiff with sweat mixed with red desert dust. Without a word she welcomed the wayfarer with whose picture she spent her sleepless nights. After giving him hot water to wash his face and setting a dish of lentils before him she asked him his name.

"Avraham," he replied.

Playfully she whispered his name and tried out a variety of nicknames in her heart: Avraham, Avram, Avreimele, Avroom, Avi. Avraham our Father and Sara our Mother.

Apart from his name she asked him nothing, but he told her about his family abroad. He was the only son of his father, a wealthy carpet merchant.

"My father sent me to the Holy Land to seek fortune. So he said and that is why I have come."

"Let us set a date for the betrothal," she said suddenly. "I have no relatives and your parents are far away. We have no need of consultations. It has been determined by heaven. Your fortune is right here with me," she added as she saw the pallor spreading over his face.

When he recovered his spirits his happiness knew no bounds. His father had been right. Fortune had smiled on him. He, Avraham, with his meager body and sparse beard, would marry the most beautiful of women.

A month later they were married.

*   *   *

On the eve of her wedding Sara went for the first time to the neighborhood mikvah. The rumor that the beautiful Sara was going to the mikvah spread from house to house and brought all the women of the neighborhood to the dank, moldy building. That day was recorded in the annals of the mikvah as "the great day of the bathing of the beautiful Sara." The brawny, red-calved bath attendants said there never had been and never would be such a day in the entire history of the mikvah, and that the place had never been visited by so many women at once.

To the mikvah streamed women whose menstrual period was not yet over, and women who had been there only a day or two before and did not need to come again for another month. Sara stepped between the women clustering and buzzing with excitement as if oblivious to their presence. A circle of half-naked women formed unconsciously around her, some of them in shabby petticoats, others hiding their thick legs mottled black and blue in brown stockings, and others whose fleshy thighs were encased in wide, faded bloomers while the nipples of their immense, wobbling breasts ploughed into their groins. And the circle of half-naked women expanded and swelled.

And order reigned in the mikvah. The short or shortsighted women took up their positions in the front row of the circle, with the tall and sharp-sighted standing behind them. Sara stood in the middle of the circle closing in around her, under the air vent in the vaulted roof. In normal times the vent let the light from outside into the dark room, where it poured down in a narrow golden shaft speckled with dust motes. The radiant motes whirled upward in an endless dance. Each speck of dust shone and glittered as it spiraled eternally upward in its predetermined dance, carrying the sights of the place with it into the streets of the town: bare female feet, flabby breasts with empty nipples, bellies shrunken as an empty gourd, cropped and shaved heads, hands laced with green rivers, knotted thighs, and crooked nails on fleshy toes.

The sunbeam dancing round her touched her hair. Thunderstruck the women gazed at the resulting radiance and stifled a cry. Flashes of golden light spun round her head, shooting out sparks of alien fire that threatened to burn anyone who touched her. The phantasmagoric dance of radiance igniting her hair was sucked up through the vent, taking with it the fiery golden sparks that burned as quick and hot as flames in a field of thorns.

Shooting sparks of fire around her, Sara stood on the wet spot of light, splashing sparkling drops of rainwater onto the concrete floor. Two long hands lit by the silvery light rose slowly and dreamily to the golden head. Long, transparent fingers groped in the cascades of hair and emerged from the tangle bearing the hard metal clips that fastened the roll of braids around her head. A pair of braids thick as a ship's rope, freed from the grip of the clips, fell down her back. Sara took one of them and slowly unplaited it. Three snakes of wavy hair plunged down her back and lapped her ankles. With her eyes fixed on a secret point somewhere on the wall, piercing the bodies of the women surrounding her and passing through them, Sara unraveled the second braid. Covered by a thick, wavy cloak of hair she began to take off her clothes. First, standing in the pool of light, she removed her shoes. When she felt the wetness of the illuminated water lapping at her stockinged feet, she slowly and meticulously peeled off the thick black stockings, exposing a pair of vulnerable, white, slender-ankled feet. Then she turned her attention to her dress. Carefully she undid the buttons. The women, breathing heavily as they watched her, counted them one by one. In days to come they would say that the dress had twenty buttons. When the days turned to years, they would say that the dress had exactly one hundred buttons. The eyewitnesses added that Sara's long white fingers undid the buttons, twenty in number, or if you will exactly one hundred, with irritating slowness. They dawdled provocatively between one button and the next, lingering, feeling and caressing each button and buttonhole as if uncertain whether to undo them all.

Like the curtain of the Ark of the Law the dress parted and with a shake of her shoulders Sara shed it like a snake shedding its skin. Barefoot she stood on the cold gray concrete floor, dressed only in her hair and her underwear, shivering all over. The women devouring her with their eyes let out a sigh as her smooth white arms were revealed. Slowly she pulled her woolen undershirt over her shoulders, exposing a pair of doelike breasts threaded with delicate blue veins. Her pink nipples stiffened in the cold room, stabbing the eyes of the beholders and drawing a sudden uncontrollable cry of admiration from their lips.

As if her audience did not exist, she took off her panties with her back to them and revealed her ripe, firm buttocks to their eyes. When she turned around in order to make her way to the ritual bath she noticed the scores of prying eyes fixed on her pubic hair. At that moment a cry of dismay broke from the lips of the spectators. On the smooth white flesh of the most beautiful of women they saw the black curls of her nether hair, coiling and glistening, covering and revealing.

"Her hair is black." The whispers rose on every side, piercing the thick gray walls and penetrating the innermost rooms of the men's mikvah. "She's a fraud." The whispers echoed through the rooms, broke through the walls, burst out of the heavy stone domes and rolled down the alleys of the marketplace. The voices went to war with the flashes of golden light rising from the vent, climbed up the fiery sparks and escaped into the air bearing the tidings of Sara's black hair to the world.

And Sara herself, as if none of it had anything to do with her, stepped out of the pool of light, walked slowly toward the place of purification, and dipped her body into the murky rainwater, where her golden hair floated on the surface like a tangle of swamp lilies and refused to sink.

⁎ ⁎ ⁎

Like a pair of orphans, without mother or father, Avraham and Sara were married with only a minyan of beggars for an audience. In the town they said that the moment the groom lifted the veil from the face of the bride in order to give her the Kiddush wine to drink, his face was bathed in a luminous light and all his pimples were exposed. The only one of Sara's acquaintances invited to the wedding was the photographer Rahamim, whose lips never ceased praising the bride's beauty and extolling the good fortune of the groom. After the ceremony was over he took the couple to his shop and immortalized them against a backdrop of rocky mountains and waterfalls. This time Sara asked him not to embellish the picture with the colors of his paintbrush. The picture of the couple on their wedding day remained hanging in Rahamim's shop even after his demise. His sons refused to take it down, and even when years passed and color photographs crowded the old pictures off the walls, it remained in its place, brown with age, and people would come into the shop to ask about the bride and her fate.

The night after the wedding her husband never left her side. Even after performing his conjugal duty he went on holding her in his arms until dawn, and her golden hair covered both their bodies like a thick warm blanket of silk. The next morning she lifted the blanket covering her beloved to see his nakedness. On his chest, which was still as smooth as a boy's, glittered half a gold napoleon threaded onto a slender golden chain. Sara removed her own half from her neck, where it had been hidden all this time under her clothes, and pieced the two halves together. Before her startled eyes the pieces united into one perfectly matched whole. Her cry of astonishment woke her husband. Without a word she showed him the united napoleon.

"Our match was made in heaven," he said with a radiant smile. "It was no coincidence, but determined from on high."

Nine months later she gave birth to her son. The pregnancy was easy and so was the birth. When the midwife gave her the baby, he opened his great blue eyes wide, as if he didn't want to miss a single ray of sun. The baby was as beautiful as his mother and his head was crowned with silky golden hair.

"We'll call him Yitzhak," said her husband, "after my father, may he live long."

Because of the baby's beauty, which was the talk of the town, Sara tied an amulet to his clothes. She took the two halves of the gold coin to Zion, the Yemenite goldsmith, and he joined them artfully together, as if they had never been split. Only an eye assisted by a magnifying glass could make out the join between the two halves. Sara would take Yitzhak, dressed like a prince, protected by the coin, and armed against the envious by the amulet, for walks in the parks and the marketplace so that passersby could feast their eyes on his beauty and sing his praises. The baby's eyes devoured the scenes, his ears absorbed the sounds, and all who saw him marveled at the sight.

⁂ ⁂ ⁂

When the child was six months old Sara noticed that he was late in developing. When she approached his cradle in the morning he never smiled at her, and when she sang to him he did not seem to hear. And when the other babies began to take their first steps he went on lying in his cradle, his blue eyes staring at the ceiling as if he saw something there that was hidden from her eyes. Then she began to take him to the sages and the kabbalists, to collect amulets, charms, hamsas to ward of the evil eye, bits of blue glass, bells, and parchment scrolls bearing magic spells. All these she sewed onto the serious baby's white coat, until it was completely covered and not a trace of its original color was left. When the child waved his hands the amulets tinkled and rattled with a loud, alarming noise. Then his face would fall, his nose would wrinkle, and a piercing wail would erupt from the little body encased in its motley armor of metallic objects glittering in the sun.

As the child grew so the charms and amulets multiplied, and when she bought him a new coat she would sit up at night to undo the amulets attached to the old garment and sew them onto the new one. And as the coats grew bigger and heavier the child grew stiller, lest his movements rattle his armor and terrify him with the noise. And he looked like the statues of the Virgin's plump son in the churches, with his body covered in coins, charms, and amulets offered up by the faithful. All this time the baby did not utter a word or direct a glance at his mother, and she was sure that he had a mission to perform on earth. One day he would open his mouth and utter words of wisdom, and Jews and gentiles alike would flock to him, for he was the King Messiah. In order to prepare him for his pure messianic life Sara would wash her hands whenever she breast-fed him, and wash his hands before his mouth clamped round her nipple and after he did his business in his diaper.

Sara did not dare to share her thoughts with her husband. Even when the child refused to look her in the eye, never uttered a word or smiled at what he saw, even then she did not abandon hope. When he grew older and went outside in his heavy, amulet-covered coat, he looked like a battle-weary warrior wearing his medals on his chest, with his head poking out like that of an old tortoise and his yellow crest of hair glittering in the sun.

The children teased him, poked sticks between his legs to make him stumble and fall flat on his face, and mimicked the grunting noises he made. "Here comes the amulet" would pass from courtyard to courtyard, mustering and uniting rival camps of neighborhood children. Ashkenazim joined forces with Sephardim, Yemenites with Kurds, Jews with Arabs, Armenians with Muslims. They all surrounded Yitzhak, wrapped like a mummy in his amulet-armored coat, plucking at the amulets, hitting him, pulling out fistfuls of his fair hair, and pinching his fat flesh until it bled. And the child did not cry. The more they tormented him the tighter he closed his mouth, and only strangled grunts escaped his lips.

The noise brought Sara running, armed with a thick stick. She waved it over the heads of his tormentors, yelling at them, her eyes wet, her face flushed with anger. Like a swarm of bees fleeing from a cloud of smoke the bullies ran from her dark rage, peeping pitilessly through the cracks in the fence at the weeping mother leading the "King Messiah" back home.

All the visits to the kabbalists, sages, and seers were in vain. Every visit emptied Sara's purse and burdened her son's coat, with more and more charms and amulets sewn on to "banish the evil eye afflicting him because of his beauty." When the amulets did no good, the fear crept into her heart that all was not as it should be. She sat with the child for hours, gripping his waist between her legs to stop him escaping, and holding his head straight between her hands. Then she would try to look directly into his eyes, blue as bottomless pools, and make them meet hers. But the child gazed ahead as if through a glass wall. After failing to catch his eye, she tried to catch his tongue between her fingers and manipulate it in the cavity of his mouth to make him say something. And the boy would mumble unintelligible syllables, grunt at her, and bite her fingers thrust into his throat. He gnawed the paintbrush she placed in his hand for him to copy the letters she drew, and tore to pieces the little picture book she gave him, cramming the pages into his mouth without even looking at them.

When she lost patience and slapped him, he didn't blink an eye or shed a tear. He was absorbed in a world of his own. At meals he polished off his food, devouring it straight from the plate like a wild animal and stretching out his hands to snatch more from his parents' plates. In bed at night he would roll his head and bang it ceaselessly against the wall. Anyone passing by late at night would hear a rhythmic thudding as if someone were beating a drum. After first stopping their ears, Sara and Avraham grew accustomed to the noise in the end, and could not fall asleep without it. As soon as Yitzhak started his drumming Sara's eyes would grow heavy and she would fall asleep, worn out by the labors of the day, and when the banging stopped she would wake up and hurry to his room to see what was wrong.

When all the boys his age were going to heder to study the Torah, Yitzhak roamed the house like a wounded animal, beat his head on the walls, defecated in the corners of the rooms, and stained his amulet coat with the spittle dribbling from his mouth. And Sara stayed at home with him instead of working in the shop with her husband. From the day she left the shop Avraham failed to prosper. New businesses were opened in the town and the customers stopped coming to their shop.

✻   ✻   ✻

"We're going home, to my father," Avraham announced one day. "Over there, in the big city, we'll find a cure for the child." For a week they packed their belongings, sold the house and the shop, and prepared themselves for the journey. Early in the morning, under cover of darkness, and far from the prying eyes of their neighbors, they set out for the port.

The journey over sea and land lasted many days. Sara thought it would never end. Yitzhak with his amulets was a favorite of the sailors on the ship and the stevedores at the ports. They would throw him from hand to hand like a ball, play with his amulets, knead his flesh, and comb his hair. Sara, laid low by the swaying of the waves, watched the sailors amusing themselves with her grunting son, and believed with all her heart that in the foreign city the miracle would take place and her son would become the King Messiah.

During the journey her bleeding stopped, and she was sure that it was because of her excitement about meeting her husband's parents. To this same excitement she attributed her lack of appetite, since in any case she had never liked the herrings and potatoes that were the staple diet on the ship. When the nausea and vomiting began, she told her husband that they were due to the motion of the waves and the storms at sea.

The gleaming white Salonika, city of her husband's birth, they saw from the deck of the ship. Carrying their bundles they descended the swaying ramp to the dock, searching for Avraham's family. The docks were deserted.

"Perhaps they never received my telegram," Avraham said in disappointment.

When they entered the strange streets Sara found herself in the heart of a bustling city, surrounded by carriages, horses, and tall buildings. Worn out by the journey, dragging Yitzhak, stunned by the noise of the crowds and the traffic behind them, they set out for Avraham's parents' home. The house that greeted her eyes was large and spacious, surrounded by a garden of fruit trees. All the windows were draped with white crocheted curtains, and smoke rose from the broad chimney on the red roof, together with subtle smells of cooking.

"Don't worry," Avraham said to his pale wife, "my parents will love you for your beauty too," and he knocked softly on the big wooden door. An elderly maid in a starched apron opened the door and fell upon Avraham's neck with loud shouts of joy. When she saw Sara and the child clasped in her arms, she recoiled and hurried off to summon her masters. A thin woman with her hair rolled into a silken snood dangling down her back, and several rows of little pearls around her neck, came hurrying to greet them. She pecked Avraham lightly on the cheek, and the huge bunch of keys attached to the broad leather belt round her waist made a loud rattling noise. When her eyes fell on Sara they rounded in surprise at the sight of the beautiful woman clasping the fat child to her breast.

"This is my mother, Pnina," Avraham said, introducing his mother to his wife.

Suddenly a heartbreaking cry rose from inside the house: "Mazal!"

A stooped, gray-haired old man burst out of the door and gathered his daughter-in-law into his arms without noticing his son standing by her side as if nailed to the spot.

"This is my wife, Sara," Avraham tried to explain to his father, who was clinging to Sara like a drowning man, feasting his eyes on her beauty and seeking her lips with his.

The father let go at once, his eyes rolling in their sockets.

"Who are you and what is your name, my daughter?" he asked as if he didn't believe the words of his son.

"I'm Sara, your daughter-in-law, and this is my son Yitzhak," she said faintly, trembling all over.

"And where is the half medallion I gave you?" The father turned to Avraham.

Avraham took hold of Yitzhak's lapel and groped for the coin among all the amulets and bits of glass sewn to his coat. "Here it is, whole again, sewn to your grandson's coat," he replied in a weak voice, holding the coin between his fingers.

At that moment the father's eyes bulged out of their sockets; he turned red and his face contorted. White foam dripped from his mouth, and the words that came out of it were as slurred and broken as the words of a baby trying to speak for the first time in its life. Only when his father fell fainting on the doorstep did Avraham overcome his paralysis and burst into the house, shouting for help.

The joy of the meeting turned into grieving. Dr. Ben-Maior, the Jewish doctor summoned to the house, examined the paralyzed patient with all kinds of instruments and then took Avraham into a corner, where he conferred with him at length. His face downcast, Avraham returned and announced that his father would not recover. He would be paralyzed in half his body and dependent on other people for the rest of his life.

"You should never have come without informing us in advance," hissed Pnina, the elder Yitzhak's wife, after they had put the paralyzed father to bed. "All you've brought me is trouble. And who's going to work in the shop now that your father is sick?" she demanded, and looked with hard eyes at her beautiful daughter-in-law and her grandson.

The next morning Avraham went with his mother to the shop, and Sara soon found herself alone in the big house, looking after Yitzhak her son and Yitzhak her husband's father. When she fed Yitzhak senior the dishes she cooked for him and wiped the spilled soup from his chin, the sick man did his best to avoid looking into her speckled eyes. And when he could not resist the temptation, he asked her in his slurred speech questions she could not understand. When her belly swelled, he would stretch out his good hand covered with dark liver spots and stroke it lingeringly. Sara did not scold him. Sometimes, when he had a nightmare, she would hurry to his room as he called out "Mazal!"

"Mazal," he addressed her when he woke bathed in sweat from such a dream.

"I'm Sara," she said gently.

"Mazal," he repeated like a stubborn child.

Chapter Seven

From the day he arrived at his father's house Avraham stopped visiting Sara's bed. Even when she was aroused and tried to stroke his face and whisper words of love in his ear, he pushed her away with both hands, as if she were polluted and it was forbidden to touch her. At night she would creep into his bed, reach for his groin, and grope in the darkness. His member, which in normal times would leap up and shoot out to meet her, was now limp and still, a useless appendage of flabby, excess flesh. He would push her massaging hands away, and she would retire to her own bed, her body burning with desire. On those nights she would secretly rub herself under the blanket until her body convulsed and she relaxed.

There was no one so beautiful as Sara in her pregnancy. The rumor of her beauty spread through Salonika, and people came to the house to peep through the slits in the blinds, to feast their eyes on her abundant yellow hair and try to catch her honey-colored eye. Even when her body thickened and swelled, she was more beautiful than all the girls of the town. Her mother-in-law Pnina hated her for her beauty and for the excitement that seized her husband whenever Sara came near him. Not only did she make her take care of her crippled husband, she also ordered her to work with the maid. Thus Sara found herself drawing water from the kitchen pump, cleaning the floors, cooking the family's meals, and washing their clothes in the tub. Even when her stomach swelled and dragged her body down, her mother-in-law kept her busy from morning to night. And little Yitzhak roamed the rooms of the house, banged his head on the walls, and soiled the floors his mother had just cleaned with the excrement trickling down his legs.

One day Dr. Ben-Maior, who paid frequent visits to Yitzhak senior and prescribed medicines for him, looked at the child.

"What ails him?" he asked Avraham.

"He's been like this since the day he was born," Avraham replied. "He doesn't understand, he doesn't talk, he doesn't smile."

The doctor seized the child with both hands and held the little body in a firm grip. Yitzhak averted his eyes from the doctor's penetrating gaze.

"This boy of yours will grow up like a wild animal," he said sternly to Avraham after examining the child. "He'll never communicate with you. All his life he'll be absorbed in a world of his own. He won't be able to talk or to understand what's said to him." Then he prescribed a drug to make him sleep quietly at night without disturbing them by his head-banging.

As soon as Sara heard the news about her son Yitzhak, she was seized by severe pains. Although the fetus in her womb was not yet ready, she found herself in a pool of warm, clear water, which ran down her legs, wet her dress, and stained the carpet where she stood.

"You must take her to the hospital at once," Pnina said. "The baby isn't ready."

They had to take her to the hospital almost by force. "All the modern women give birth here," her husband told her. "They'll know how to take care of you here," he added and went to the shop to help his mother.

Sara lay on the white iron bed, wrapped in starched sheets and surrounded by doctors in white coats whose language she didn't understand. When the pain grew more severe and she felt a pressure in her loins, she didn't know how to tell them what was happening. And the doctors made their rounds of the women writhing and screaming in a foreign language, armed with wooden ear trumpets through which they listened to the sounds made by the babies imprisoned in their mountainous bellies.

After a few hours they laid Sara on a narrow bed, put her legs in stirrups, and pressed her stomach. The baby slid out, weak and tiny. When the doctor separated her from her body Sara noticed her blue color and miniature fists. She waited for the baby's cry, and instead she heard a wheeze like an old man struggling for breath.

∗　∗　∗

The next morning Avraham came to visit her. "The doctors said that the baby will probably die tonight, and if not tonight, then in a few days' time," he said, looking at the floor.

Through the veil of her tears Sara saw that her husband didn't look sorrowful or grieving.

"It's better this way," he said impatiently when he noticed her tears. "Imagine if you had to look after another cripple, in addition to the two you've already got at home," he added and walked out of the room.

A few days later she came home, with a baby the size of two fists joined together nestled in the cleavage between her bursting breasts, bundled inside her dress. Pnina looked scornfully at the tiny head poking out of the top of Sara's dress and whispered, "She won't last the night. Put her in the attic and don't go to her even if she cries. It's better this way. Otherwise we'll have another defective child on our hands."

Sara sought Avraham's eyes, but they remained directed at the floor as if searching for a lost coin. She looked at her mother-in-law, who pointed to the attic. Slowly Sara climbed the wooden stairs in the direction shown by the index finger, which went on pointing firmly at the sky, and in the silence that had fallen on the house the creaking of her footsteps on the stairs echoed in her ears like thunder. With every step she took she felt the fluttering of the unripe baby on her breasts, like a weak little fish drawn up from the depths. She looked sorrowfully at the perfect little face and stroked the bald head in farewell. At that moment it seemed to her that she saw a shadow of a smile flitting over her baby's face.

She ran down the stairs and declared: "I won't let her die. My baby will live."

Pnina and Avraham tried to bar her way, but she hurried to the kitchen, where Victoria the cook, as if she had been expecting her, bustled up and removed the whimpering bundle from between her breasts. She laid it on the chipped wooden table and looked compassionately at the face crumpled in soundless weeping in front of her.

Victoria lit the little oil burner used for the slow heating of the Sabbath cholent. A faint smell of kerosene spread through the kitchen. She lowered the flame to the minimum, took a big tin of olive oil, emptied it, made a hole in the side, washed out the dregs of the olive oil, and padded it with cotton wool. Then she took the baby and laid her carefully in the tin, wrapping her snugly in a new woolen cloth. The tin with the baby inside it she placed on the burner over the little flame. When she was finished she turned to Sara and asked her to expose her breasts. Sara's milk-swollen breasts, freed from the constraint of her dress, began to secrete white drops, which collected on the kitchen floor. With light milking movements Victoria squeezed a little milk from the swollen breast into a glass cup. She held the cup up to the light as if to inspect its color, stuck her finger into the liquid, stirred it round, and then put it in her mouth. With a satisfied smack of her lips she dipped a little piece of cotton wool into the white liquid and pushed it into the baby's tiny mouth. The baby latched onto the cotton wool and with greedy gums and lips began to suck the milk.

That night Sara moved her bedding into the kitchen. Smells of kerosene, fried onions, crushed garlic, and milk mixed with the sweet scents of a new baby filled the air. During all the days and nights that the baby cooked on the little flame she did not leave her side. She checked the heat of the tin lest the baby be roasted, God forbid, and turned up the flame in the cold nights. Whenever the baby whimpered she pushed a piece of cotton wool dipped in milk into her mouth, and cleaned her red, crumpled skin with a soft cotton cloth soaked in olive oil. All that month Avraham did not come down to the kitchen, and Pnina too kept away and gave the cook her instructions in the sitting room. All that month no cholent graced the family table on the Sabbath day, and during all that time they refrained from mentioning Sara and the flawed, unripe baby to which she had given birth. So the days passed, until Sara emerged from the kitchen with a rosy-faced, plump-cheeked baby clasped to her breast.

At the sight of the tiny baby the mother-in-law's face softened. She fussed round her daughter-in-law and danced attendance on her, urging her to go to bed and forbidding her to do even the easiest housework. The vacant eyes of the paralyzed Yitzhak widened at the sight of the baby. With his good hand he tried to stroke her bald head, and he made obscure sounds of joy. And Sara was happy and contented, embracing the baby, who never budged from her breast. Even when the baby was finished feeding and her mother tried to detach her, she refused to let go of the nipple, as if she were afraid that she would not find her food when she grew hungry again. At night too, when Sara fell asleep, the baby went on sucking at her nipple, and even when she needed to relieve herself she was unable to detach the mite from her breast.

The firm grip of the toothless mouth on the mother's breast did not relax even to burp after feeding. As soon as she had drunk her fill she would fall asleep, with the nipple clamped between her naked gums. Since all her needs were met, and the supply of milk was plentiful, and her mouth was gagged by the nipple, the baby never cried, and she was quiet, placid, and good-natured. The doctors whom Sara consulted tried to squeeze the baby's cheeks, to pinch her legs, and to shake her head, but to no avail. The baby's mouth gripped her mother's breast as tightly as a drowning man hanging on for dear life to his rescuer.

When she grew bigger she weighed heavily on Sara's breast, pulling it down until the pink nipple between her gums grew as long as a cow's teat. In order to make things easier for Sara and her baby, Pnina sewed her a kind of pouch, tied it round her body, and slung the baby's bottom in it; the little legs, which had already put on flesh stuck out on either side of the mother's body.

When the baby was three months old they realized that they had forgotten to give her a name. The name Mazal, Sara's late mother's name, Pnina forbade to be spoken in the house. "It's bad luck for a baby to be called after a dead person," she argued. In order to please his mother, Avraham decided to call the child Pnina. But Sara, in her heart, called her Mazal.

One day, when Sara was wondering how long the baby would remain stuck to her body, she felt a sharp pain, like the stab of a dagger. With a scream of pain she shook the baby off her body and dislodged her from her breast. The constant stream of milk trickling into the baby's mouth was suddenly cut off, and the soothing sound of her mother's heart stopped beating in her ears. The baby opened her mouth wide, displaying a small, sharp tooth, and for the first time in her life she began to cry. Everyone laughed at the sound of her crying, which was as soft and gentle as the bleating of a lost lamb.

✳ ✳ ✳

At night Sara fell asleep, with a feeling of relief, on her stomach. The baby lay in a cradle next to her bed, trying out her voice in the new sounds she was learning to produce. Ever since the nipple had been dislodged from her mouth, leaving it wide open, she was in no hurry to close it. By the time she turned one she was already wearing out the members of the household with her never-ending chatter in the language of her parents, of her grandparents, and of Victoria in the kitchen. She soon learned to compose sentences, and was able to explain herself and make her wishes known in three languages.

In the evening, when the family gathered for dinner, little Pnina-Mazal would sit between Yitzhak senior, whose head lay slumped on his chest, and Yitzhak junior, encased in his amulets, and speak for them.

"Big Yitzhak wants you to wipe his chin," she would say to Sara. And when Sara looked at him she saw that his chin was indeed festooned with the remains of the meal.

"Little Yitzhak wants more soup," she would say to Pnina. And when Pnina gave him another plate of soup he would quickly polish it off.

"Little Yitzhak says he's cold and he wants you to light the stove," she would report.

As soon as Sara became aware of her daughter's gifts, she began to use her as an intermediary between herself and her son. "Ask little Yitzhak if he needs to go to the lavatory," she would say to her daughter, and indeed, the little girl knew exactly when her brother had to go. Soon he no longer needed diapers, and most of the time he was dry. From the moment he found himself a mouth, little Yitzhak stuck to Pnina-Mazal, following her around, sitting next to her, looking deep into her eyes, reading her lips, and expressing his wishes without the need for words.

"How do you know what big Yitzhak and little Yitzhak want?" they would ask her.

"They speak to me," she said simply.

One day Pnina-Mazal tugged at Sara's skirt and announced: "Little Yitzhak says he wants to go home."

"This is our home," said Avraham.

"Little Yitzhak says that it isn't his home. He wants to return to the home where he was born."

Avraham and Sara looked at her in amazement. They had never told her of their lives in another country, and how could she know? When little Yitzhak's wishes were repeated via his sister's mouth, Sara knew that the time had come. They had to go back. That night, after she had whispered words of love in her husband's ear and begged him to visit her thirsty body, as she did every night, and after he had rejected her as usual, she asked him to take them back to the land of her birth.

"You go back with the children," he replied. "I can't leave my father and mother in their present state, and I have to take care of the shop. I'll send you money, and very soon, when things improve, I'll join you."

* * *

When Pnina-Mazal turned three Sara packed her bags. On the eve of the journey she forced herself on her husband, whispering words that in days gone by would have sufficed to make him stiffen and penetrate her with no more ado. Now she touched his groin. He averted his face and removed her hand from the flabby piece of flesh that refused to stiffen. With tears in her eyes she returned to her bed. Early in the morning, enflamed by lust, she got into his bed again and took hold of his private parts as he slept. To her surprise she found herself with a stiff, erect member in her hands. Unhesitatingly she mounted him and pushed it inside her. As soon as she felt his flesh in hers she began to ride him as if he were a galloping horse, raising and lowering her backside. He reached his climax at once in a strong stream, saturating her groin with a milky liquid. Carefully she dismounted, pressing her legs together to prevent the precious liquid from escaping, and returned to her bed.

Avraham turned his face to the wall.

In the morning she tried to look him in the eye and spoke to him in terms of endearment, but he pretended not to hear, averting his eyes from her calm and radiant look.

* * *

Seen off by her husband and her weeping mother-in-law, Sara embarked on the ship with her children. When she looked at little Yitzhak it seemed to her that she could see a hint of a smile in his eyes. Pnina-Mazal held his hand and explained to him where they were going: "Home, we're going to our home."

On the quay Sara offered her yearning lips to her husband. Unlike his habit in recent years Avraham did not turn his face away, and he gave her a light peck on the lips as a farewell kiss.

"I'll send you money. Don't worry. When things improve I'll come back," he promised again. Then he kissed the children and walked away.

The way back seemed to Sara to pass too quickly. She stood on the deck and looked at the black, rocky outcrops of land suddenly looming up from the sea. Their names in the mouths of the sailors sounded like a soft, melodious love song in her ears: Khios, Sámos, Patmos, Kos, Rhodos, Mersin, and Alexandretta in the Gulf of Iskenderun. Every morning of the voyage she made it a habit to go up to the deck and bask in the warm rays of the sun. Whenever she did so, the passengers would gather round her and feast their eyes on the golden hair tumbling down her back like tumultuous waves. When the sun vanished from the spot where she was sitting and twilight shadows took its place, she went up to the higher deck in order to absorb the last rays of the sun, her children clinging to her sides.

On the third day of the voyage a young man followed her. Elegantly dressed and flourishing a cane decorated with a bronze knob, he accompanied her as she pursued the sun from deck to deck. The next morning he preceded her and usurped her regular daily seat on the lower deck, stationing a black camera stand next to him. The surprised Sara looked about for an alternative seat, but the stranger stood up and offered her his place, and when she sat down he made haste to sit down beside her. He took off his pith helmet and introduced himself with a smile as Edward. Sara looked into his eyes and was caught in the soft blue sparks radiating from them. Weakness spread through her limbs. She had seen those eyes before. Blushing she told him her name and explained with her hands that she did not understand a word he said.

Pnina-Mazal came to her rescue. "He's talking English," she said to her mother, "and he says that he's already photographed you once when you were a girl, and with your permission, he would like to photograph you again."

Sara was prevented from replying to his request by the friendly conversation into which he immediately entered with her daughter, in a language Sara did not understand.

At the end of the conversation, Pnina-Mazal informed her mother: "Edward loves you."

"Did he tell you to tell me that?" Sara asked, a blush spreading over her face and a feeling of warmth through her body.

"He didn't tell me," the little girl replied, "but he loves you."

From that day on Edward accompanied Sara like a shadow. He followed in her footsteps, looked deep into her amber eyes, and in his imagination stroked her long golden hair. Then they no longer needed Pnina-Mazal's mediation: when they looked into the fathomless depths of each other's eyes they knew and sensed everything they needed to know.

From the moment her mother no longer needed her services, Pnina-Mazal was free to amuse herself, and she ran about the deck, engaging the passengers in conversation and learning new languages and old dialects. She spoke Russian to the pilgrims embarking at Odessa, Turkish to the government officials who came aboard at Constantinople, Greek to the passengers who embarked with them at Salonika, Ladino with the old Sephardic Jews making the voyage to die on the soil of the Holy Land, German to the representatives of the Austrian-Palestine Bank, and English to Edward, who never left her mother's side. And when she caught a Hungarian in her net, she wore her mother's ears out at night by endlessly repeating the unpronounceable new words he taught her. "A language collector" Sara called her in her heart, wondering what profit the child would derive from the knowledge of so many tongues, and afraid they would scramble her brain and lead her to speak Turkish to the Englishman, Greek to the Hungarian, and German to the Jews. But Pnina-Mazal did not become confused, and she spoke to each one in his own language, as fluently as if she had spent all her short life in the city of his birth.

Her brother Yitzhak clung to her skirts and tagged along behind her, and while she was busy learning a new language he would express his wordless wishes and requests, which she would translate to the passengers in their languages. Sometimes Sara suspected that some of the wishes Pnina-Mazal expressed in her brother's name she had made up herself. Every evening when Sara put the children to bed their pockets would spill forth treasures of chocolate, pistachio nuts, sugared almonds, silver coins from remote countries, and brightly colored packets of sweets.

Night brought Sara's finest hours. She waited for nightfall with an expectation that sent sweet shivers through her flesh and turned her knees to water. As soon as she had put the children to bed and sent them to sleep with her mother's lullaby, she would loosen her hair, comb it, enjoying the feel of the brush on her locks, tie a kerchief round her head to dim the radiance of her hair, dress herself in her best clothes, and slip out of the cabin to the lower deck. There, between sea and sky, waited the boat suspended from great iron hooks, with the rope ladder dangling down to it from the deck. Once she was safely inside it, she undid her kerchief, took off her shoes, and spread the scratchy woolen blanket she had hidden underneath the wooden bench. With a sigh of relief she lay down on her back, spread-eagled her limbs, and looked up at the stars, her luminous eyes shining with expectation in the dark like those of a suddenly dazzled cat.

Edward would lie in wait for her like a nocturnal bird of prey. Stealthily he would descend the rope ladder, and like a thief in the night he would leap into her, encouraged by her cries of fear and delight, rocking the little boat as if it were being tossed on a stormy sea. Afterward Sara would gather up her hair and make room for him, and he would lie down beside her, his hands under his head, and count the stars with her and tell her about the signs of the zodiac in a language she did not understand. And when the air grew chilly and little drops of water formed on the sides of the boat and in Sara's hair, frizzing it slightly, he would tell her of his love for her in a language she understood. Then the storm would break and the boat would rock above the calm water, threatening to fling the lovers into the sea. When the sun rose and the storm in their bodies subsided the boat would steady. With weary limbs Sara would tidy her clothes and slip into her cabin without a backward glance.

☆   ☆   ☆

On their last night the boat rocked as it never had before, not even in the worst storms at sea. It creaked and shuddered under their writhing, sweating bodies until it seemed that the strong iron hooks were about to straighten and drop the little boat into the calm water below. And when it steadied, their tousled heads peeped over its side. The lights of Jaffa port twinkled at them in the distance and the sea was as smooth as a mirror.

"Where were you?" demanded Pnina-Mazal. "Yitzhak woke up and asked for you," she added rebukingly.

Sara did not answer her question. "Come up on deck with me, the shore is in view," she said and pulled Yitzhak out of bed, draping his amulet coat over his shoulders.

Swaying like drunks the passengers disembarked at Jaffa port, where the air was thick with the smell of donkey and camel turds and the commotion of the Arab stevedores. Edward accompanied Sara and her children with his eyes and walked toward the magnificent carriage awaiting him at the exit from the port. A woman with short red hair was sitting inside it, and when she saw Edward approaching she jumped out and fell upon his neck as if she hadn't seen him for years.

"That's his wife," Pnina-Mazal explained to her mother. "But it's you he loves," she added, catching Edward's eye through the glass of the carriage window.

The stevedores unloaded her baggage, and Sara stood on the quay, with all her belongings scattered round her and her two children holding her hands. A skinny Arab boy suddenly put his hand on one of her iron trunks. Sara pulled it away from him in alarm.

"Hotel?" he asked.

Sara nodded, and the boy stuck two fingers in his mouth and whistled. Three more ragged boys popped up as if from the bowels of the earth. Weighed down by her trunks and carrying her bundles on their heads, their backs, and under their arms, they led Sara and her children out of the port. Sara hurried in the wake of Edward's receding carriage, dragging her children behind her, and the Arab boys laden with her luggage ran panting in the rear. In the back window of the carriage she saw Edward's face, entwined in the thick arms of the redhead, and his eyes were fixed on Sara's eyes. The carriage disappeared round a bend in the road, and Sara sat down panting for breath on a stone.

The Arab boy said something and Pnina-Mazal made haste to translate. "He said that the yellow-haired foreigner lives in the American quarter," she said to her mother. Sara straightened her back and stood up, shook out her clothes, and asked Pnina-Mazal to tell the boy to take them quickly to the nearest hotel, since evening had already fallen and they needed to rest before the long journey to Jerusalem.

The hotel manager received them draped in a black velvet dress ornamented with tassles and fastened round her waist by a purple sash, a felt hat boasting a moth-eaten peacock feather perched on her abundant, piled-up black hair. Her eyes opened wide in surprise at the sight of the beautiful Jewess in foreign clothes holding a fat little boy encased in amulets by one hand and a skinny little girl by the other. Plump women in fancy dresses decked with frills and furbelows, their breasts half-exposed, waited in the lobby, exchanging admiring whispers at the sight of the strange woman coming to join them.

"I have a room for you," said the hotel manager with a wink, "but not for the children."

"The children will share my bed," replied Sara.

"You won't like the room I have to offer you," said the manager, inspecting Yitzhak's amulets and Sara's luggage and appraising the curves of her body beneath her rich attire with an eagle eye.

"I have nowhere to lay my head," said Sara humbly. "We're tired, and we only need the room for one night."

At the sight of the weary children the woman took pity on them at last, and led them to a room.

"This is a place where bad women stay," said Pnina-Mazal to Sara.

"We have nowhere else to go, and we're staying here," Sara said firmly.

A small, stinking room greeted them. In their exhaustion they fell on the bed with its stained sheets and were soon sound asleep.

*   *   *

The next morning Sara woke up with an unpleasant itching in her scalp. When she combed her hair next to the open window she tried to get rid of the itch with the help of the close-set teeth of the comb. She looked at the comb in the faint light coming through the window and felt faint. It was full of gray lice caught between the teeth and swarming all over them. When the itch grew worse she went to the nearby public baths to wash her hair with boiling water, but to no avail. It seemed to her that the itching was getting worse.

Her long hair clean but swarming with lice, she went into the Arab barber's shop next to the hotel.

"Shave it all off," she requested.

The barber, who had a dirty apron round his waist, recoiled. The handful of effendis waiting to be shaved held their breath.

"Heaven forbid that you should shave off such hair. It's a gift from God," they chorused.

But Sara stood her ground. "Cut it first and then shave it, and if not, I'll go to another barber," she said.

Pale-faced, the barber tied a long sheet round her neck and brought his scissors to her head with trembling hands. He tried to open the blades of the scissors with his right hand but it was trembling so much that he failed to do so. Then he transferred the scissors to his left hand and held them next to Sara's hair. The scissors made a snipping noise, but when the customers and Sara looked at the floor they saw not a single lock of hair.

"I can't do it," said the barber at last, and buried his face in his hands as if to shield his eyes from the light shining from her hair. The effendis waiting to be shaved breathed again when he put the scissors down and removed the sheet from Sara's neck. At home they would tell their black-haired wives about the crazy Jewess with the golden hair who asked the barber to shave it off.

Sara did not give up. Dragging Yitzhak and Pnina-Mazal behind her she went into the next barbershop. This time the barber was ready and willing to shear off her locks, and even gave her a price. He plaited her hair into a thick braid and tried to lop it off with his scissors. The thick braid resisted his attempts. When he exerted all his strength, the blades of the scissors bent out of shape. For a moment or two he stood and stared in confusion at the braid in front of him, but immediately recovered and began to sharpen the razor on the leather strap attached to the chair. He tested the edge of the blade on his finger and brought it to her hair. A few strands of hair fell off her braid. But the braid was as thick and as strong as a sailor's rope, and before he managed to shear off more of her hair the razor blade blunted and he was unable to continue cutting. Then he undid the braid he had plaited and the silken waves of gold released from the confines of the braid flooded her nape and poured down her back, covered her waist and her thighs, flowed down her legs, and coiled tightly round her ankles, as if refusing to part from her. Then the barber took fine tresses of her hair between his thick fingers and passed them under the razor one by one. Soon the filthy floor of the barbershop was covered with piles of golden silk. Strand by strand Sara's shorn hair surrounded her. With every tress of hair she shed Sara felt as if a weight had fallen from her head and her heart. After laboring long and hard the barber concluded his work, leaving Sara's head covered by a stubble as hard as the bristles of a brush.

"And now shave it off," she demanded.

The barber soaped her head, sharpened his razor, and shaved her round head, stretching the skin and passing the blade over it as carefully as if he were shaving the cheeks of a man. With a sigh of relief Sara passed her hand over her smooth, shining scalp. The lice had vanished without a trace, the itching had stopped, and a pleasant coolness spread through her from her head right down to her toes.

"Bring me a mirror," she commanded.

A piece of broken mirror spotted with black mold was hesitantly offered her.

Sara stared at her new image. Her head was smooth and gleaming and her eyes swam large and prominent in the nakedness of her face.

Yitzhak, who had been busy all this time banging his head against the peeling blue wall, stopped abruptly. He looked at her as if he were suddenly seeing her for the first time in his life. Sara felt his gaze sliding over her bald head and penetrating her eyes. For the first time in her life she was able to look straight into the eyes of her son, which rounded in surprise.

"Yitzhak says that you're much more beautiful now," Pnina-Mazal suddenly said, after standing by her mother's side without saying a word during the entire operation.

"And what do you think?" asked Sara.

"I think so too," lied the child. "You're more beautiful without your hair."

Laughing, Sara embraced her children, paid the barber, and with a light heart and a hairless head hurried out of the shop. A cool wind blowing from the sea chilled her shaved scalp and sent an agreeable frisson through her body.

The barber closed the door behind her, pulled down the blinds, and like a thief in the night began collecting the shorn hair from the filthy floor of his shop. Strand by golden strand he gathered up the hair covering the floor, tied it up with a white ribbon, and plaited it into a long, thick braid. Weighing the braid in his hands he looked round for a place to hide the unexpected bounty that had fallen to his lot. When he found a loose tile in the floor he dug a deep hollow with his scissors, wrapped the heavy braid in a cotton cloth, coiled it like a snake, and buried it in the ground. Then he replaced the tile, covered up the traces of his work, raised the blinds, and opened the door, rubbing his black-nailed hands together in satisfaction.

❄   ❄   ❄

Bald as an egg Sara hurried back to the hotel. As if in anticipation of her arrival, the lobby was full of men with double chins and fezzes, rolling dark amber prayer beads in their fleshy hands in concentrated expectation. Their eyes were fixed on the door, waiting to be dazzled by the radiance of Sara's hair. The hotel manager who hurried to meet her clapped her hands at the sight of the catastrophe.

"How could you? How could you do such a dreadful thing?" she mumbled in horror. When she recovered from the shocking sight she asked: "And the hair? Where is it?"

"At the barber's," replied Sara faintly.

"What barber?" asked the manager in a choked voice.

"The one next to the Turkish baths," replied Sara.

The men waiting in the lobby twirled the tips of their mustaches, whistled in admiration, and caressed the shining bald head with moist, lustful looks. Sara fled their looks in horror, rushed upstairs, and packed her belongings. A gleeful gleam appeared in the eye of the hotel manager as she contemplated a golden treasure in her imagination. She turned to the boy slouching at the entrance, took out a leather purse full of silver coins, and whispered something in his ear. The lad leaped from his place and hurried off in the direction of the barbershop.

Under the ogling eyes of the men crowding the lobby Sara descended the stairs and walked down the street, accompanied by the porters carrying her luggage and gripping the hands of her children so tightly that she left white pressure marks on their palms. At twelve o'clock the train left Jaffa for Jerusalem. Pnina-Mazal and Yitzhak ran about among the passengers, one learning new languages and the other filling his pockets with candies and nuts. Sara sat on her seat in the coach looking through the window and smoothing her hands over her hairless head, preoccupied by the slight feeling of nausea in her stomach, as if she were still on the ship, and the dull pain piercing her breasts, which had grown heavier overnight.

In the afternoon they reached their destination. Jerusalem welcomed them with a cold rainstorm, which sent shivers down their spines and soaked their light summer clothes. Sara felt as if the hair she didn't have was standing on end. Now she missed the warm, heavy pelt that had covered her head since the day she remembered herself. Absentmindedly she ran her parted fingers through her imaginary hair, only to realize that she was bald. When the cold sharpened, and entered her exposed ears, she wrapped her naked head in a colored scarf, like Ashkenazic women on the day after they lost their virginity. The carriage that bounced over the pits in the road and jolted the passengers and their luggage took Sara to an inn on the outskirts of town, where she knocked on the door like a travel-weary wayfarer coming home at last.

The hostile gaze of the elderly innkeeper turned quickly from astonishment to undisguised delight.

"Sara's come home," announced Rachel, the red-haired Geula's younger sister, to the deserted parlor. "You can stay with me until you find a house," she said, clasping Yitzhak and Pnina-Mazal to her bosom. "Where did you go? Where's Avraham? What happened? Who's the little girl? And what have you done to your hair?" she asked, her voice turning into a shriek as she suddenly realized the hairless state of Sara's head under the tightly bound scarf.

"It's better this way," Sara replied shortly, ignoring the rest of the questions. She asked to see her room.

The next day she left the children with Rachel and went to look for a house to stay in. Her feet led her to the new neighborhood of Ohel Moshe. The new houses were spacious and had flat ceilings supported on thick iron bars, like the rails for some great train to ride on. The floor tiles were square and smooth, colored and patterned like a carpet that would never wear out, and all the houses boasted red-tiled roofs, as if they had fezzes perched on their heads. Next to each house two sturdy trees were planted, and between them lay beds of flowers, fragrant herbs, and vegetables.

With the money she had brought Sara purchased a house with a red-tiled roof, a spacious veranda, and three big, light rooms. The next day she went to town and bought a big brass bed, iron beds for the children, and a dining table big enough for her to feed a regiment of soldiers, or so the furniture seller promised her with a wink that was not at all to her liking. Within the space of a few days she organized her new household and left the inn.

Chapter Eight

The day Sara moved into her new house she went to the Arab village next to the spring of Shiloh and returned with vegetable seedlings and the shoot of a mulberry tree in a round kerosene tin. The neighor women cast sidelong looks at her as she walked past and as she dug a pit and planted the sapling in it. The next day her neighbor Esther went to the same village and returned with a similar mulberry shoot and planted it in her yard. A year later the fresh young tree in Sara's yard produced plump purple fruits that filled the mouth with sweet, dense juice. Esther's tree was bare, a target for the scorn and derision of the neighbors. They would look at it and compare it to a barren woman with an unfruitful womb. Then Esther would go up to her empty tree, fix it with a baleful eye, and curse it for its stubborn barrenness. Every year she would threaten her tree that if it failed to bring her fruit she would chop it down and turn it into firewood. But Esther's barren tree remained planted in her yard opposite Sara's abundantly fruitful one, mocking the threats of its planter. The sentence was postponed from year to year, and the tree grew stronger, spreading its boughs and sheltering Sara's fruitful tree in its shade.

Life in the new house was quiet and good. Pnina-Mazal played with the neighbors' children and went on learning new languages, and Yitzhak, who spent most of his time eating and drinking, grew and swelled and thickened. His red cheeks rounded and his blue eyes sank deeply into the fat surrounding them until they looked like two slits painted blue. When he wasn't busy grinding food between his strong teeth he would follow his sister like a shadow, voicelessly expressing his requests for new kinds of food and demanding sweetmeats from passersby and neighbors. Sara did not go out to work, since a sum of money reached her every month, accompanied by a short letter from Avraham. The sum grew larger and the letters grew shorter, until one month the money arrived without a letter, and this happened the next month too and in all the months that followed it.

⁎   ⁎   ⁎

Exactly nine months after leaving Salonika, she gave birth to a son. Her neighbor Esther ran to fetch the midwife, and when they returned they found her with a big baby lying by her side, its blue eyes wide open.

"I'll call him Ben-Ami," she said to Esther and asked her to send a telegram to Avraham informing him of the birth of her child.

That month the sum of money was doubled and redoubled. Sara turned the envelope upside down and inside out, but there was no note to be found. Tight-lipped she went to Esther and asked her to donate the money to the charity for poor brides, to the fund for the destitute, and to yeshiva scholars. "Give it to whomever you like. I don't want it." Esther quickly buried the money in the deep cleavage between her breasts. The envious neighbors told Sara that she had hidden the money behind the stove and given not a penny to charity.

"She too is needy," said Sara quietly. "Let her enjoy the money. If she took it for herself, it means that she needs it."

The rabbi performed the brith as if for an orphan and blessed the big healthy baby.

"The child will grow to be tall and broad-shouldered," said the doctor who examined him in the hospital. And the baby grew as if of its own accord. It needed nothing but food and for its diapers to be changed. And every morning, when she went up to its cradle, it would look at her with its blue eyes and smile, revealing two tiny teeth growing from its lower gum.

From the day the baby was born Pnina-Mazal neglected her older brother Yitzhak. Now she had a new toy to enjoy and to play with. The baby was quiet, and Pnina-Mazal took the credit. She always knew when to feed it, when to change its diaper, when to turn it on its stomach, when to burp it, and when to put it down to sleep. And most of the time the baby smiled, happy and content and with no need to cry in order to express its wishes.

*   *   *

A few months after the birth Sara's neighbor Dina, daughter of pious Miriam, came and told her that while she was shopping in the market a yellow-haired stranger had approached her with a picture in his hand. "And as I live and breathe, the picture was of you. And when he saw that I was on the point of fainting, he asked me where he could find you."

Sara's knees turned to water and a deep blush spread over her cheeks. "What did the stranger look like?" she asked in a trembling voice.

"Tall and blue-eyed, and he spoke English," Dina replied, with her eyes boring into Sara's.

"And what did you tell him?" Sara asked, trying in vain to hide the tremor in her voice.

"He looked to me like a drowning man, so I brought him to your house and showed him where you live. He looked at the diapers hanging on the line and asked me if you had given birth to a baby," Dina replied. Then she went home, closed the shutters, and peeped through the slats at Sara, who went on standing rooted to the spot.

After a moment Sara hurried into the house. She pulled the kerchief off her head and examined her hair. Since it had been shaved off the year before it had grown and now reached her ears. The new hair was darker in color, a light brown mingled with strands of white. After putting the children to bed she swept the floor and lit the oil lamp. Then she combed her hair, washed herself, changed her clothes, and waited in the dark, her eyes, smouldering like those of a cat in heat, fixed on the window. She fell asleep sitting on the chair and woke at dawn, her limbs stiff and her bones aching.

The next day she put the children to bed early, put on her best dress, and waited. A thud startled her from her light sleep on the chair, and she ran to open the door. Darkness greeted her and the doorstep was deserted. With her body aching she got into bed and fell into a restless sleep. She dreamed of the boat swaying above the dark water and felt the coarse woolen blanket pricking her naked flesh.

For a number of days she waited for the yellow-haired foreigner, and when he did not come she was afraid that she would never see him again. She began to neglect her appearance, and Pnina-Mazal had to remind her that she hadn't washed for a week. Her hair was matted and greasy and stuck to her scalp. The festive attire in which she fallen asleep waiting at the window hung on her like a dirty rag. She would lose her temper with the children and scold them for trifles. She was especially impatient with Yitzhak, and she pinched him mercilessly when he stretched out his hands to take food from her plate or Pnina-Mazal's. She didn't even have the strength to cook and bake, and she would buy fresh pitas from the Arabs and stuff them with goat cheese and olives for the children to eat. Yitzhak had never been so hungry as he was during this time, and he would visit the neighbors at mealtimes, staring at the food on their tables and waiting for them to feed him.

Departing from her usual habits, Sara stopped sweeping and washing the floor, and there were muddy footprints everywhere. Filth covered the carpets, the colored bedspreads, and the linen. Piles of dirty washing and soiled diapers rose in the sitting room, moldy and stinking. Nor did she take care of the garden, and couch grass and thorns attacked the coriander, the basil, and the parsley she had lovingly cultivated, stole their water and choked them with the offshoots of their hard, murderous roots. Pnina-Mazal and Yitzhak roamed the streets dirty and hungry, and the neighbors could not understand what had happened to Sara, who had always been so scrupulous about her own and her children's appearance.

During this time she hardly bothered to get out of bed. She lay in her stinking bed shivering with cold, her hair tousled and her eyes dull and red. Esther took the baby Ben-Ami to her bosom and cared for him until his mother should recover, and Pnina-Mazal with Yitzhak sticking to her like a leech spent all day on the street, stealing back at dark and tiptoeing round the house in order not to bring their mother's wrath down on their heads. Then the little girl would share a supper of hard pitas with her brother and put him to bed. After that she would stand by her mother's bed, offer a cup of sweet tea and a crumbling biscuit to her dry lips, and tell her to get up, eat, and wash herself. When Sara did not respond, Pnina-Mazal demanded that she get out of bed so that she could change the linen. But her mother clung to the sheets until her knuckles whitened and refused to get up.

✿ ✿ ✿

One night there was a knock at the door. Sara, restless in her expectation of the yellow-haired foreigner, was the first to wake. With her hair tousled and her nightgown stinking and sticky with sweat, she opened the door. Edward stood before her, and she fell into his outstretched arms, murmuring his name. He examined her face in the moonlight, wonderingly touched her short, dirty hair, and recoiled at the strong smell her body exuded. Mumbling to himself in his own language he turned away abruptly, and she followed him with her arms stretched out before her like a sleepwalker. Edward picked up his hat, which had fallen off his head, muttered something, and fled. Sara tried to run after him, but her feet caught in the hem of her nightgown, and she was thrown to the ground.

At the sound of the fall Pnina-Mazal woke and found her mother lying weeping in the yard, her body as cold as ice. She helped her up and led her back to bed, and then ran to Esther's house to call for help.

"First we must change her bedclothes and wash her foul-smelling body," determined the bleary-eyed neighbors who had been woken from their sleep.

Pnina-Mazal lit the lamp and the neighbors lined up on either side of the bed. Taking hold of Sara's sobbing, emaciated body they lifted her up in the air to enable Pnina-Mazal to change the bedclothes. Then they carried her to the kitchen, put the kettle on to boil, and washed her weakly resisting body and shampooed her hair. As she sat wrapped in a big sheet, with her clean hair falling on either side of her thin face, the women forced a little soup through her clenched lips, and put her to bed.

The next morning the children woke to smells of baking. Sara, washed and dressed in a clean frock, with Ben-Ami on her hip, was standing smiling in the kitchen and baking the children's favorite biscuits. When they went out to play she began to scrub the house and remove the layers of dirt clinging to it. Then she put the kettle on to boil and washed the piles of dirty clothes, rubbing and beating them furiously, and when she had finished hanging out the washing she knelt down in the garden and angrily uprooted the couch grass choking her beloved plants.

She tried to wipe Edward's memory from her heart, and whenever she thought of him and of the rocking boat she would quickly conjure up the sight of his horrified face as he looked at her in the moonlight and his panic-stricken flight from her house, and her composure would return.

❋ ❋ ❋

The year that Yitzhak approached his bar mitzvah Sara went with him from one rabbi to another looking for someone who would agree to teach her son.

"If he hasn't learned his letters till today, he won't learn them tomorrow either," they told her, and added another amulet to his already overburdened coat.

"Your son is exempt from becoming a bar mitzvah," she was told by others.

"Even if he says one word on the day of his celebration it will be enough for me, just tell me your fee and I'll pay it," she told the teachers.

Lame Menashe agreed to teach him when he saw the bag of coins jangling in Sara's hands. Night and day he sat with the boy, trying his best to teach him, but in vain. Yitzhak would come home gray-faced and covered in shame. At night he banged his head on the wall so hard that all the neighbors heard the thuds. Soon his head was covered with swollen blue bruises.

"He doesn't want to go to the melamed," said Pnina-Mazal one morning. "Lame Menashe hits him on his hands," she added.

"His bar mitzvah is approaching," said Sara. "Who will teach him? He has to learn to say at least one word."

"I'll teach him," the little girl volunteered.

"If the melamed has failed, how will you succeed?" Sara said with doubt in her voice.

"I can talk to him. The melamed doesn't know how to do it," the child replied.

"Do as you wish," said Sara in despair.

❋ ❋ ❋

From that day on Pnina-Mazal shut herself up with her brother from morning to night. She tempted him with food and sugar lumps and pressed pastries into his mouth for every effort he made. The friends who came to ask her to play with them were turned away.

"After Yitzhak's bar mitzvah I'll come out to play," she promised.

Sara looked at her daughter's thin face, and her heart ached for the little girl shut up in the dark house instead of playing outside with her friends. Sometimes she tried to listen to what was happening in the closed room, but she couldn't hear anything. Once, when her curiosity got the better of her, she peeped in at the children. She saw Pnina-Mazal holding her brother's hands and looking deep into his eyes. Yitzhak, his eyes fixed on hers, sat still, as if hypnotized. For almost an hour the children sat there in silence, until Sara tired of looking at them and left the room.

"Why don't I hear you teaching him?" Sara asked Pnina-Mazal the next day.

"We're studying," the child replied shortly.

"But why in silence?"

"That's the way I talk to him," Pnina-Mazal said, and refused to elaborate.

A week before the day of the bar mitzvah, the children took their places at the supper table with gleeful, mischievous faces, looking as if they had something up their sleeves.

"Food," suddenly cried the deep, cracked voice of an adolescent boy.

Sara, who did not know the voice, went on busying herself at the stove.

"Mother, Yitzhak asked for food," said Pnina-Mazal with a beaming face, continuing in her role as her brother's translator.

"Food," Yitzhak repeated.

The plate fell from Sara's hand and smashed into a hundred pieces on the floor. The lump that had choked her throat since the day her son was born dissolved at last, flooding her face and clothes in salty streams. Wordlessly, with her back to them and her shoulders shaking, she went on deliberately dishing up the food, placing a double portion on Yitzhak's plate. And Yitzhak, whose appetite had been increased by the exhausting lessons, polished it off, put his plate down on the table, and repeated, "Food." And again Sara gave him food, this time from her own plate, and again he polished it off and repeated his cry. While she was busy preparing yet another portion at the stove, she noticed Pnina-Mazal stealthily passing him food from her plate.

Usually Sara forbade her to do this. For the more Yitzhak grew and swelled, the thinner and paler his sister became, and even the freckles on the tip of her tilted nose seemed to shrink and fade. Pnina-Mazal took every opportunity to empty her plate onto her brother's and relieve herself of the punishment of eating, and her mother watched her with an eagle eye. But today, in honor of Yitzhak's first word, Sara decided to let her get away with it.

Encouraged by his success Yitzhak would do the rounds of the neighbors' houses, repeating the word he had learned to say, and go to bed at night with his belly swollen and his pockets full of drumsticks, meatballs, fresh bread, pastries, and sweets. People appeared to have found a new interest in playing with him and talking to him. "Food, food," the neighbors would cry, and Yitzhak would hurry round to join them at the table, and to the giggles of the children he would stuff himself with food in quantities that just to look at were enough to make a person sick to the stomach. And when he came home, full and satisfied, he sat down at the table and demanded his due, and Sara hurried to place his favorite foods before him.

⁕ ⁕ ⁕

In honor of his big day Sara sewed him a white silk coat from quantities of cloth sufficient to cover his immense bulk.

"Yitzhak doesn't want you to sew on the amulets," said Pnina-Mazal to her mother as she removed the amulets from the old coat.

Sara nodded her head, went to the corner of the kitchen, emptied the sugar tin with its picture of a fat farmer brandishing his scythe over a field of wheat, and put the amulets away in it, except for one. The gold napoleon she hung round her own neck on a black velvet ribbon.

When Yitzhak tried on his new silk coat he seemed to grow taller—the oppressive burden of the amulets had been lifted from his shoulders. That Saturday, free of amulets, wrapped in a prayer shawl, the beaming boy was taken to the Maoz Hadalim synagogue in the center of the neighborhood. Ezra Ben-Zion, the synagogue rabbi, refused at first to hear of a bar mitzvah for Yitzhak.

"I told you before, the child is exempt. The Lord of the Universe will not be angry if he doesn't read the Haftarah and if he doesn't pray to Him every morning."

Sara insisted. First she begged, then she tried to explain that the ceremony was important not only to her as his mother, but also to the boy himself, and perhaps the Holy One—blessed be He—would perform a miracle and open Yitzhak's mouth on the pulpit. And when nothing helped, she opened a bag full of money before the rabbi's eyes and said shortly, "Tell me your fee."

Anyone visiting the synagogue to this day will find the wooden bench dedicated to Yitzhak son of Sara and Avraham, and the heavy velvet curtain on the Ark of the Law, its color the blue of the sky, embroidered in gold and silver and dedicated to Yitzhak and his parents, who had made a generous donation to the synagogue.

At Pnina-Mazal's command, Yitzhak mounted the rostrum with a heavy tread, and the rabbi unrolled the Torah scroll before him. Yitzhak stared at the letters and scratched his head, as if trying to make up his mind where he was supposed to begin reading. After long moments went by and no words of wisdom passed his lips, the women crowding the women's gallery began to giggle and the rabbi began to read the weekly portion himself. Sara sat paralyzed in the gallery. Now their shame would be made public, and perhaps the Greek doctor had been right in the harsh things he had said about Yitzhak.

"Do something," she hissed at Pnina-Mazal. "Make him talk!"

Pnina-Mazal rose from her place and climbed onto the bench, trying to catch Yitzhak's eye as it wandered round the hall. When her eyes met his she looked deeply into them. Yitzhak stood up straight, puffed out his chest, pushed his fair hair off his forehead, looked at the scroll, and opened his mouth. There was a tense silence, as if the entire congregation were holding their breath, and the rustle of the ladies' fans stopped abruptly.

"Food," cried Yitzhak in his cracked voice.

The members of the congregation turned their faces toward the ground, avoiding each other's eyes lest they burst out laughing.

The first sound rose from the women's gallery, a little shriek erupting from clenched lips. The laughter rolled from bench to bench, infecting all the women and sweeping them up in its gales. Some of them bellowed like cows through the hands covering their mouths, others cackled like geese behind the fans hiding their faces. Fat women with double chins brayed like donkeys, tears pouring down their mountainous cheeks. Pregnant women spread their hands over their swollen bellies, as if afraid they might miscarry their babies, and writhed in laughter that shook their stomachs up and down.

And the laughter swept down the stairs to where the men were sitting. First it spread to the youths, who bellowed like calves led to the slaughter; from there it spread to their fathers, who barked as if they had succumbed to a sudden attack of asthma, while tears streamed down the furrows in their faces. After that it took hold of the old men, who wheezed and choked before breaking into short, dry coughs, and in the end it hit the rabbi, who covered his head and shaking body with his prayer shawl, and rocked himself to and fro as if absorbed in praying devoutly to his maker.

Sara, with Ben-Ami on her lap and Pnina-Mazal by her side, sat proudly in her new red velvet dress, trying in vain to suppress the tears of happiness choking her. And the tears gathered in her throat, rose in her nose, and flowed like a fountain from her eyes, falling onto the fair head of Ben-Ami, who chortled and chuckled with the rest of the congregation. Her Yitzhak had not let her down. She was impervious to the gales of laughter assailing her from every side. In days to come, when she remembered the occasion, she saw before her eyes her pale, overgrown son, wrapped in a prayer shawl, standing on the rostrum in all his glory and pronouncing the one and only word he knew how to say: "Food."

Hoarse and limp with laughter, the congregation arrived at Sara's house to partake of the festive meal she had laid on in honor of the occasion. The tables groaned under the weight of the sweetmeats and delicacies she had prepared with the help of her neighbors. There were pigeons stuffed with rice and raisins, pastries filled with meat, clear soup with egg noodles, mountains of rice studded with almonds, raisins, prunes, and sweet grated carrots. On the dessert table there awaited the guests almond cakes that melted in the mouth, sugar-coated almonds, sweets made of sesame seeds and honey, bagels smeared with sugar water and sprinkled with sesame seeds, crystallized quinces, hills of marzipan decorated with almonds, and mountains of figs and dates. While the guests shoveled the food into their mouths, groaning and holding their swelling stomachs, Yitzhak circulated among them like a bridegroom on his wedding day. With his eyes and mouth, he devoured the food that had been prepared especially for him, tirelessly repeating the word he had learned, while his cheeks, swollen with food and fat, grew red from the affectionate pinches of the guests.

✻   ✻   ✻

Life returned to normal. Pnina-Mazal played with her friends and conducted conversations in foreign languages with strangers passing through the neighborhood. Ben-Ami began to attend heder, Yitzhak went on guzzling, swelling, and following his sister round like a shadow, and Sara busied herself about the house. Everything could have gone smoothly but for the disaster that began to develop in the fly of Yitzhak's trousers. The calamity that overtook them began in the hard protuberance that grew and swelled of its own accord when he was playing with his sister. Sara was the first to notice it. When she was washing him one day in the tub she noticed the member sticking out of the fair hair curling on his groin. Her heart contracted in pity at the sight of her son's great member, which would not bring her grandchildren, and as she washed him with the rough loofah she took care to avoid touching the ill-omened place and arousing it.

Catastrophe descended soon enough, on a day never to be forgotten in the neighborhood. Sara was working in the garden, hoeing the herb beds, examining the poor harvest of celery, and strewing salt to kill the worms that nibbled the cabbage leaves. She had a splendid vegetable garden. Every morning she visited her neighbor Esther and raked up the droppings of her plump chickens. She spread the still-warm manure on her cherished beds, and then picked the fruit of her labors. In those days Sara turned a blind eye to the fat, clucking chickens that invaded her garden to vary their diet with the leaves of parsley and celery she lovingly grew on their excrement.

That afternoon, while she was busy in the garden, Pnina-Mazal was playing outside with her friends and Yitzhak was with her. The voices of the little girls interspersed with Yitzhak's hoarse grunts rang in Sara's ears like a sweet melody. Suddenly the voices stopped and an ill-omened silence filled the air. And then the shrill shrieks of frightened little girls scattering in all directions broke the silence. Sara stood up and strained her eyes to see what had happened. Before she could make anything out, Pnina-Mazal burst into the yard, pale and wild-haired, trampling the vegetable beds and crushing them mercilessly. With one foot treading on the wormy cabbage leaves and the other crushing the parsley, she buried her head in Sara's apron. Yitzhak waddled behind her, his arms strenuously rowing the air, and the swelling in his trousers sticking out in front of him, as if to announce the arrival of its master.

Sara stared numbly at her flushed, agitated son. His lolling tongue dribbled transparent saliva onto his bar mitzvah coat, which he had refused to take off after the ceremony. Yitzhak approached Pnina-Mazal with a hurried step, his eyes fixed on her face, and she began to scream, burying her face in her mother's apron and banishing the sight of her brother from her eyes.

While she was skipping rope with her friends, Pnina-Mazal tearfully told her mother later, Yitzhak suddenly seized hold of her, pressed the front of his body to her back, and moved his loins backward and forward straight into her buttocks. "I told him to stop, but suddenly he didn't understand me. He tried to do the same thing to Rivka and Shula and Rachel, but they ran away," she added.

Sara washed her daughter's face and revived her with sugar water. Before an hour had passed a deputation of anxious mothers arrived. With grave faces they secluded themselves with Sara in the kitchen. Pnina-Mazal tried to eavesdrop on their conversation but all she succeeded in hearing was the agitated voice of Rachel's mother, Esther, repeating, "It's forbidden, it's forbidden," over and over again. Her own mother's voice sounded quiet and conciliatory, soft and apologetic, but the agitated women interrupted her and refused to listen to her words. When they were finished they left the house with pursed lips, united and determined, and Sara dissolved in tears. During the entire discussion Yitzhak had shut himself up in the children's room and refrained from banging his head on the wall, as if waiting for his sentence to be pronounced.

From the moment the deputation left the house Sara began to watch Yitzhak with an eagle eye.

"He's forbidden to leave the house," she instructed Pnina-Mazal, "and you must stop talking to him."

"And what if he starts talking to me?" asked the child.

"You must explain to him that what he did was wrong and he must never do it again."

When Pnina-Mazal went out to play with her friends Sara struggled with Yitzhak at the door and prevented him by force from leaving the house. In spite of his great bulk and the fact that he was a head taller than she was, she succeeded in slamming the door against him and locking it. Furiously Yitzhak banged his head against the door, like a battering ram trying to breach the defenses of a besieged city. When he failed to break down the door, he pressed himself against the bars of the window overlooking the yard and roared unintelligibly at the little girls playing outside. That evening, Sara took Pnina-Mazal's bed out of the children's room and put it in her own room. When they retired for the night, she barricaded the door with the heavy linen chest. Yitzhak pounded on it with his thick fists and banged his head on the doorposts, and when he tired he sat down opposite the door and waited quietly for them to come out.

The next day, when Pnina-Mazal went out into the yard, he struggled with his mother again next to the open door, and Sara barred his way with her hand. Yitzhak grabbed hold of her outstretched hand and bent her arm backward, to the dull crack of breaking bones. With a cry of pain Sara clasped her dangling arm with her other hand. Yitzhak broke out of the open door and like a stumbling bull charged into the yard. The little girls skipping rope scattered with shrieks of fear. Pnina-Mazal was left alone, the skipping-rope in her hands, staring with paralyzing fear at her advancing brother.

"Go home," she screamed at him as he drew nearer, the bulge in his trousers growing apace.

Yitzhak took no notice and went on advancing with a heavy tread. At that moment Sara burst into the yard, holding her hurt arm with one hand and screaming for help. The men were at work and only the women and children peeped at her through the shutters. As soon as Yitzhak caught hold of his sister's waist and began rubbing his loins against her body Sara cried in a terrible voice: "Food!" Instantly Yitzhak froze, the bulge in his trousers disappeared, and he began walking clumsily toward the house. Sara hurried after him and piled the food she had prepared for the whole week in front of him, and while he was busy polishing it off, she slipped out of the house with Pnina-Mazal and Ben-Ami and locked the door behind her.

All the way to the Tomech Dalim hospital Pnina-Mazal supported her mother and tried to calm her. A scream of pain escaped Sara's lips when the doctor took hold of her red, swollen arm to try to assess the damage. After setting the broken bones and wrapping her arm in a thick bandage, he asked her gently, "How did it happen?"

"I fell in the yard," she lied.

"That's not true." Pnina-Mazal quickly intervened to set the record straight. "My brother Yitzhak broke her arm."

The doctor bent over the little girl and asked her kindly to tell him how it happened.

Pnina-Mazal began to tell the whole story from the beginning, despite Sara's vigorous protests.

"You have to send him away from home," the doctor pronounced. "He's dangerous to himself and others and the sooner you remove him from harm's way the better, or I won't be responsible for the consequences."

"But where will I send him?" whispered Sara faintly. "Who will agree to have him?"

The doctor gave her the address of Pesiah-Leah, who kept a special home for children like Yitzhak. "It's the only place in Jerusalem that accepts children like him. You could also send him to the monastery in Ein Karem, but it's far, the roads are in poor condition, and it's better for him to be taken care of by Jews."

✴   ✴   ✴

The next day two burly men arrived at Sara's house to take Yitzhak to the home.

"Go with them," said Pnina-Mazal gently to her brother. "You'll be happy there. Go with them."

Yitzhak, with the look of a trapped animal in his eyes, dragged his feet helplessly and unresistingly between the two toughs in white coats so filthy that they looked as if they belonged behind a butcher's counter. Sara opened the door for them and embraced her son with her good arm. At the sight of the open door the overgrown boy broke into a lurching run, dragging the two toughs behind him.

"Tell him that we'll come to visit him every day and bring him food," Sara said to Pnina-Mazal. At the sound of the word "food" Yitzhak pricked up his ears, dug in his heels, and refused to move. Sara took a few biscuits, sweets, and sugar cubes and gave him some of the treats with every step he took, until there were none left. The toughs hurried him up and he lumbered heavily between them until they put him onto the cart. When he tried to jump off, they tied his hands and feet with rope. Bound and bellowing Yitzhak lay on the wooden floor of the cart and rode through the neighborhood, while the neighbor women and the children sheltered under their aprons accompanied him with stares and clucking behind the half-open shutters of their houses.

The next day Sara baked his favorite sugar cookies and roasted chicken legs, bundled them all into a cloth bag, and set out. Pesiah-Leah's children's home lay outside the town between the ruins of the Arab village and the broad fields surrounding the town. When she reached the environs of the home she heard the grunts and growls of the inmates. The children were locked up in abandoned old chicken runs, clinging to the fences dotted with brown chicken feathers. A strong smell of chicken droppings, rotting vegetables, and sour urine assailed her nostrils as she approached Yitzhak's cage. Pesiah-Leah's charges shared their cages in pairs. As she hurried past she saw squat children with straight hair, lolling tongues, and slanting eyes. They lumbered back and forth in their narrow cages, waving long arms with stubby fingers and making strangled sounds. Some of the children lay on mattresses reeking of urine, their bodies convulsed and twitching in an endless dance. In one of the cages was a boy with a gray face, a flat nose, and a dwarfish body. Compared to these children her Yitzhak looked like a prince. He was handsome, his blue eyes sparkled in his white face, and he was as tall as a nobleman. In return for a few coins she had previously slipped into Pesiah-Leah's hand he had received a cage to himself and a moldy kapok mattress covered with a prickly blanket.

She found him lying curled up on the floor of trodden earth, his bar mitzvah coat stained with dry chicken droppings, and his hair full of the feathers and dark down of fowls no longer among the living. From the moment he arrived in the home he had refused to eat, and he rejected the food his mother brought him too. He turned his face away from her and huddled up on the ground littered with scraps of food. Sara gave the food she had brought to Yitzhak's neighbors grunting in the adjacent cages, and they scratched and fought bitterly over every scrap of food thrown to them through the wire fences.

The next day Sara returned with Pnina-Mazal. "Ask him how he is," she requested.

Pnina-Mazal gripped the wire fence and stared at her brother in dismay, but Yitzhak avoided her eyes. When she found an angle at which she could look straight into his eyes, he covered them with a black-nailed hand.

"He doesn't want to talk to me," she said to Sara in a whisper.

The sweets she threw him through the fence remained untouched on the filthy floor. Yitzhak refused to look at the colored sweets rolling toward him with a merry clatter.

"Food," said Pnina-Mazal softly. A spark of life flashed in his eyes and immediately died down again, and he went on lying on the floor with his face buried in the ground.

A week later Sara removed him from the home and led him outside to the sound of the grunts of the inmates, who stretched their black hands through their cages in a demand for sweets. As he stumbled down the streets with her his stench spread through the air and people recoiled from them as they made their way home. Indifferent to the stares of the neighbors shaking their heads and clapping their hands in dismay, Sara opened the door and led him into the kitchen. There she set the big kettle on the stove, boiled water, and filled the tub. The soiled garments she peeled off the body of her son, which was covered with little bite marks, she asked Pnina-Mazal to burn in the yard. Naked, helpless, and humble, the boy sat in the tub, and Sara soaped his dwindled body and scrubbed it with the loofah, peeling off solid layers of black filth and kneading his flesh until it turned red. She cut his hair, which was swarming with lice, and shaved his scalp, and when he was clean all over she soaked bay leaves in lukewarm water and laid them like little bandages on his oozing sores.

The next morning Yitzhak woke up in his gleaming room and his white bed. "Food," he demanded, and began to swallow the delicacies she placed before him.

At night she locked him in his room and kept him away from his sister, but it appeared that all these preventive measures were superfluous. The bulge in his trousers disappeared and did not return even when Pnina-Mazal was standing next to him, even when she was trying to read his thoughts with her eyes fixed on his. Yitzhak no longer wanted to go outside, and when strangers came to the house he fled to his room and huddled up under the bed, holding his breath and waiting for them to leave.

* * *

Since Sara could not leave Yitzhak alone in the house, she hired the services of a young yeshiva student, David, to stay with him when she was busy shopping in the market or doing chores in the town. She also asked him to sleep in the house and watch over Yitzhak at night, and he agreed willingly. David, a penniless scholar, was glad of the opportunity to earn a little money, to enjoy a hot meal every day and a soft bed on which to lay his body after a long day's study. He was thin and lanky, his clothes were shabby, and his hat was squashed.

When he arrived at their house at the bidding of the head of the yeshiva, she thought to herself, what good will this creature do us? She took him to the kitchen and gave him a cup of tea and soft sesame cakes fresh from the oven, and he bit into them absentmindedly and looked deep into her eyes, appraising the curves of her body and measuring the weight of the breasts under her dress.

When David entered the house Yitzhak did not run to his room to hide under the bed as usual. As soon as he heard the stranger's voice he emerged timidly from his bedroom and came into the kitchen.

"Food," he said when he saw the cookies.

Sara pushed a cookie into his hands and he swallowed it immediately, with his eyes fixed on David's sparse beard.

From then on Yitzhak followed David like a shadow wherever he went. Even when the young man had to relieve himself Yitzhak accompanied him and watched him closely. At night, when David spread out his bedding, Yitzhak would remain on his bed, staring at the ceiling and waiting for David to join him. When David read his books in the light of the oil lamp Yitzhak would watch with interest as he turned the pages. Pnina-Mazal swore that once she had seen him pick up a book, open it, and pretend to read.

David would take him for short walks. At first Yitzhak clung to him fearfully, but later he calmed down and let David lead him through the vineyards and fields. They would pass the Arab villages and walk along the prickly pear hedges. There David would take the tin cup he had borrowed from Sara's kitchen, put it over the fruit growing on the fleshy thorn-covered leaves, and pluck the fruit with a twist of his hand. With one hand wrapped in a cloth he would slit the thick, prickly skin with a knife, carefully free the sweet, pip-filled fruit, and push it into Yitzhak's gaping mouth. After that they would pass fig trees, and there he would set a big stone under a tree, climb onto it, and feel the heavy fruit hanging before his eyes with his fingers. The hard fruit he would leave on the tree and the soft fruit he would pick with a jerk of his arm, split it open with his fingers, and examine the juicy contents closely. If he saw no worms stirring in the red flesh, he would drop it into Yitzhak's mouth opened wide beneath him. Yitzhak's head would gradually be covered with the white milk dripping from the wounds on the branches bereft of their first fruits. Sometimes the two would come across carob trees on their way and they would gather up the hard brown fruit from the ground, bite into it, and relish the honeyed sweetness trickling down their throats.

There in the fields, in the shade of a carob tree, David would pore over his books and recite his lessons aloud to himself, and Yitzhak would watch the movement of his lips and move his own lips soundlessly. For these walks Sara would pack a cloth bag with fresh, warm pitas, olives, and a hunk of fine goat cheese. David would break the bread and say a blessing over it, and Yitzhak would fall on it with grunts of hunger.

"Not like that." David tried to teach him table manners, and he would eat his pita slowly and delicately, collecting the crumbs and distributing them to the sparrows that gathered round them. Sometimes he would seek and find a nest of busy ants, scatter the remaining crumbs around it, and show Yitzhak how each ant carried a crumb that weighed more than it did. For a long time the two of them would sit and watch until all the crumbs had disappeared into the darkness of the nest. Early in the evening, when the western sky was covered with fiery red clouds, they would walk home across the fields, their eyes shining. Yitzhak fell asleep peacefully at night, and no longer banged his head against the wall.

On the cold winter evenings, when they could not go out into the fields, they would sit in the warm kitchen, steeped in cooking aromas and the faint smell of kerosene. David would pore over his books, with the two children snuggling up to him, Yitzhak imitating the movement of his lips and Pnina-Mazal sitting on his knee and following his finger as it slid over the words in the book, comparing the sound to the letters on the page. She enjoyed the new game so much that she abandoned her playmates and neglected her household chores.

One day Sara found her absorbed in a thick book, studiously twisting a curl round her finger and soundlessly forming the words with her lips.

"What are you doing?" she asked her.

"Reading," replied Pnina-Mazal shortly.

"Who taught you?" Sara asked with a smile.

"I taught myself," the little girl replied without raising her eyes from the book.

"Read it aloud," requested Sara.

And Pnina-Mazal read aloud from the Talmud in her hands, explaining the Aramaic words to her mother.

Sara remembered her own childhood. How she would press herself against the window of the heder and learn the Pentateuch with the infants and the Mishnah and Gemara with the older boys. She had to find books for her daughter, she thought, and began to make inquiries as to where to obtain them. Rumors reached her ears about the lending library at the Ashkenazi orphanage. In exchange for a small deposit it was permitted to borrow one book a day. She took Pnina-Mazal there, and the child stood before the shelves beside herself with excitement, pulling down one book after the other and paging through them avidly. There were books in Hebrew, English, and German—*Little Red Riding Hood, Uncle Tom's Cabin, Memoirs of the House of David, The History of the Jews in America, The Love of Zion,* and a lot of books about physics and mathematics. Pnina-Mazal stood there overcome with confusion, not knowing what to choose.

"Why don't you begin with the bottom shelf and take a new book from it every day. When you finish reading the books on the bottom shelf, you can go up to the next shelf, and so on," suggested Sara at the sight of her daughter's confusion.

Pnina-Mazal did as her mother advised. When she came to the end of the first shelf, she realized that if she read during meals and when she was supposed to be sleeping, she would be able to read two books a day. Since it was only permitted to take out one book a day, she asked her mother to take one out under her name too. When Sara was unable to accompany her, she went to the library with David—and Yitzhak dogging his heels—and took out three books at a time. Her nights grew short. She ate her meals without paying attention to her food and never went out to play with her friends. When Sara saw how thin and pale she was and how red her eyes were, she forbade her to read more than two books a week. Little by little the color returned to her cheeks and she began to go out to play with her friends again.

One day David looked at Pnina-Mazal devouring a new book. He looked at Sara too, as she busied herself about the kitchen, cleared his throat, and said, "I think you should send her to school; the child has the makings of a great scholar."

"What good will it do her?" Sara replied with a question. "The main thing is for her to find a good husband and bear him children. I too went to school, and look where it got me."

"Times are changing," pronounced David.

Chapter Nine

Sara pondered his words in her heart, and when she was finished with her housework, she went out to look for a suitable school for her daughter. Her inquiries led her to the Baroness Sarita Cassuto School for Girls. Many girls attended this establishment. Ashkenazic and Sephardic, Persian and Bukharan, girls from the diasporas of Salonika and Turkey, Yemenites and Georgians, all of them with their hair in braids of different colors and all of them wearing blue skirts and white blouses. And most important of all, all the subjects were taught in English, but time was also allocated for the study of the Hebrew language and for prayers. The school was situated outside the walls of the Old City and surrounded by a spacious garden. Pink-cheeked girls were busy planting radishes and harvesting onions, and an old maid by the name of Miss Lizzie Farkash from distant London directed the school with a high hand and a strong arm.

Sara took Pnina-Mazal, scrubbed and excited, her hair plaited in two braids and tied with red ribbons, to meet Miss Farkash.

"Do you know how to count?" the headmistress asked Pnina-Mazal in her office, giving her a stern, penetrating look through her glasses.

"I do."

"And do you know how to read?"

"I do," Pnina-Mazal replied in a soft, barely audible voice.

Miss Farkash opened a thick, illustrated book and placed it before the little girl, who read in a voice trembling with excitement.

"And do you know English?"

"I do," she replied.

Miss Farkash began to talk to her, at first in simple, easy words, about the weather, the neighborhood she lived in, what she did in her spare time, and then in more difficult, complicated language. Her strict, serious expression softened as the conversation proceeded. Pnina-Mazal, her confidence growing, began to list the languages she spoke. Miss Farkash's eyes rounded in astonishment and she called Miss Laniado to test the child in Spanish, Miss Mansoor to test her in Arabic, and Madame Motzkin to test her in French. Since there were no speakers of German, Russian, or Greek available she was obliged to take Pnina-Mazal's word for it that she spoke these languages too.

"We have a problem," said Miss Farkash to Sara. "The child knows more than girls of her own age, and she will have to study in a class with much older girls."

The next morning, accompanied by Miss Farkash, scrubbed and festive, Pnina-Mazal joined the class of the older girls. They looked at her curiously, struggling to suppress their laughter. In the morning assembly Pnina-Mazal was swallowed up in the mass of thick-thighed and heavy-breasted girls, like a skinny child who had landed by mistake among buxom brides preparing for their wedding. Her classmates decided to take her to their collective bosom, included her in their conversations about periods and matchmaking, and invited her to the engagement parties at their houses. Pnina-Mazal, in her childish dress and thin braids, became one of them, and as a sign of her gratitude she helped them with their homework and taught them to chat in English and French.

She shared a bench with Shulamith Abulaffia, who had black braids circling her head, laughing brown almond-shaped eyes, and dimples in her cheeks. Shulamith was famed for her beauty, and every morning she was followed to school by the boys of the town, who feasted their eyes on her curves and tried in vain to catch her eye.

One of her suitors, Yonatan Ben-Ari, whose learned father was the editor of the Hebrew newspaper *Halevona,* was the most persistent of them all. Every morning, her girlfriends would surround her, avidly drinking in her beauty, and Shulamith would tell them of her adventures with Yonatan. One day he paid court to her with a flower, one day he lay in wait for her with a handful of sugar-coated almonds, once he pressed upon her a novel about King David's love for Batsheva, and when these gifts were favorably received he timidly handed her poems and reflections he had written himself, describing his love for her. His father with his modern views refused to send matchmakers to the home of the girl, who had been promised by her father to her cousin who lived in Turkey. Yonatan suffered the pangs of his love and Shulamith accepted the charming lad's gifts, and tossed and turned in her bed at night.

Pnina-Mazal listened to the stories and examined her face in the bathroom mirror. The thin, transparent face of a little girl looked back at her. Her tilted nose was covered with pale freckles, and her pale brown eyes were flecked with little spots of light. She was not beautiful like her mother, and what boy would want a woman like her? So she thought, and buried her nose in her books.

* * *

One day she came home unexpectedly at noon. Sara was busy cooking for Yitzhak in the kitchen and the odors rising from the pots were making him jiggle his legs impatiently.

"Miss Farkash said I can't come to school for a week," Pnina-Mazal said.

"What did you do?" Sara asked, clasping the weeping girl to her bosom.

"She asked me to tell you to come to the school tomorrow to talk to her."

The next morning Sara hurried anxiously to present herself in Miss Farkash's wood-paneled office.

"Your daughter is a clever girl who outshines even the girls in the senior class," Miss Farkash opened immediately, without the customary civilities. "But there is a problem. She refuses to take part in the sewing and cooking classes on the grounds that we are wasting her time, and that she could put those hours to better use in pursuing her studies of languages and geography. She simply refuses to attend those classes; she spends her time in the library instead, and worst of all, her classmates have decided to follow her lead and they too have begun to boycott the sewing and cookery classes. Such a thing has never been heard of in this school before. I told her in so many words to go back to her classes, and she refused. She even had the impudence to remark that in the boys' schools there are no lessons in sewing and cooking and that we should learn from them." Upon concluding her speech Miss Farkash gathered up the train of her long dress and made a dignified exit from the room. Outside the door two little girls were waiting, quarreling as to which of them should have the honor of carrying her train.

"I'm not going back to school," repeated Pnina-Mazal. "I won't learn sewing and cooking. I'll learn what I want to learn," she said resolutely to her mother, who stood before her in silence.

From that day forth Pnina-Mazal no longer went to school. A deputation of students headed by Shulamith came to the house. After tasting Sara's refreshments, they tried to persuade Pnina-Mazal to return to school. "Without you school is boring and tedious. Sit with us in the cookery classes and pretend to be learning, and in the sewing classes you can prick your finger with the needle, stain the cloth, and be excused from the lesson," they advised her.

But Pnina-Mazal stood her ground and refused to listen to their advice.

At that moment David and Yitzhak came into the kitchen. The girls stared at Yitzhak. "This is my brother Yitzhak, and this is his teacher David," said Pnina-Mazal weakly, praying that David would notice her discomfort and take Yitzhak away.

"You never told us you had such a big, handsome brother," the skinny Davida whispered in her ear, lustfully examining Yitzhak's fair hair and trying to penetrate his blue eyes.

Sara came into the kitchen and quickly whispered something to David, who left the room with Yitzhak trailing behind him.

"The fewer people who know about Yitzhak's condition the better," she said to Pnina-Mazal when the two of them were alone. "When you grow up he'll frighten off your suitors, and we have to be careful of him," she added.

The next day Davida came to visit Pnina-Mazal.

"Where's Yitzhak?" she asked, her eyes prying into the corners of the house.

"Gone for a walk with David," Pnina-Mazal replied.

Davida refused to give up and remained until it grew dark, regaling her friend with tales of the pranks of the girls at school and stories about Miss Farkash, and how the train of her dress had been caught up in the banister and three girls had come running to disentangle it. And how with one girl pulling in one direction and the other in another direction while the third supervised their efforts, the train had torn with a loud rip, and how Miss Farkash had ordered a carriage and driven home in disgrace, like a poor peacock that had lost its tail. And how it was about time that Miss Farkash started coming to school in a normal dress, instead of risking her life and the lives of others with superfluous appendages that added nothing to her beauty, charm, or dignity, and caused unnecessary conflict and fighting among the girls, who were prepared to scratch each other's eyes out for the honor of carrying the train like the train of a bride being led to the marriage canopy, whereas Miss Farkash was an old maid who had never known a man and whose time to marry had long passed.

And Davida told her about Miss Mansoor, the Arabic teacher, who taught the girls the Egyptian pronunciation, so that when they went to the market and tried to show off their Arabic, the hawkers would split their sides laughing at their accents and mockingly call them Gamilla instead of Jamilla, in the local pronunciation.

And Pnina-Mazal listened to her stories and felt no nostalgia for the school, for the morning prayers, for Miss Farkash's parades, and especially not for the sewing and cooking lessons she hated.

In the evening Davida departed disconsolately, having failed to catch a glimpse of the resplendent Yitzhak, whom David had smuggled into his room through the back door.

❖   ❖   ❖

Having once tasted the delights of learning, Pnina-Mazal could no longer do without them, and she decided to develop her linguistic skills. A French tutor, Jean-Louis, was soon found for her. By day he worked as a clerk in the French Post Office, and in the evening he sat in the coffeehouses and ogled the girls of easy virtue with his roving eye, his oiled and parted hair, his waxed mustache, and his smooth talk. At the request of Sara, whose honey-colored eyes had pierced his heart, he agreed to come to her house once a week and teach her fair daughter the language of the aristocrats.

To procure a Russian teacher, Sara went all the way to the Russian compound, where she found Father Nikodeem. With his eyes boring into hers he agreed to come to her house and instruct her daughter, and

herself if she so desired, in the Russian language and the works of Tol-
stoy. "I am honored, Madam, that your daughter wishes to learn our
language," he said with flashing eyes.

For instruction in the Greek language, Sara brought the novice
monk Cyprianos to their house. Every Monday afternoon, before he set
out, he would curl his mustache and oil his long hair and gather it into
a neat bun on the nape of his neck. And when he sat with Pnina-Mazal
in the sitting room and practiced Greek verbs with her, his eyes would
wander over Sara's curves, invade the neck of her blouse, and encircle
her breasts.

Miss Mansoor, the Arabic teacher at the Baroness Sarita Cassuto
School for Girls, gladly agreed to Sara's request to teach her most gifted
pupil, but on condition that no hint of the arrangement should reach
Miss Farkash's ears.

Now all that remained was for Sara to find an English teacher, a
teacher whose knowledge of the language would be superior to her
daughter's. On Jean-Louis's advice she went to the American colony
and made inquiries about an English teacher there. Everyone she asked
recommended Mrs. Rachel Godwin, who taught both Jewish and Arab
children with excellent results. The next day Rachel came to Sara's
house. Her round face was encircled by a reddish plait coiled around
her head. She was wearing a gleaming white lace dress, and a dainty
parasol of the same stuff protected her fresh complexion from the blazing
sun of the Jerusalem summer. Her hands were encased in white cotton
gloves, and her whole appearance bespoke authority.

Pnina-Mazal was summoned from the yard and stood in front of the
English teacher with her cheeks flushed. "I know you," the little girl
suddenly announced joyfully, as if she had discovered a long-lost relative.

"Where from?" Rachel asked her with chilly reserve.

"We met once, many years ago," stated Pnina-Mazal confidently.

Rachel smothered a little laugh with her white gloves. "I don't remember," she said politely to the adamant child.

"I remember you," repeated Pnina-Mazal, "but you had short hair
then."

"True, I only started growing my hair a few years ago, at my husband's request. After he returned from his travels he decided that I had
to grow my hair long. And it's a great nuisance," she added compla-
cently, touching her braid and wondering whether there was any truth

in the child's words. "But when my hair was short you were a baby," she added, and put an end to the conversation.

After that Rachel's carriage drew up at their house twice a week. She would step out of the carriage with a dignified bearing and enter the house with the white-robed Sudanese driver in his red fez bringing up the rear, her books under his arm. With every visit the books grew heavier and thicker, and Pnina-Mazal would pounce on them gleefully. Rachel worked hard on Pnina-Mazal's accent, which was too British for her taste, and taught her to speak like a young lady from the Southern states, tittering discreetly at the rapid Texan drawl emerging with youthful charm from her pupil's mouth.

"If I took you with me to America nobody would guess that you came from here," she said, smiling at her as they conversed in English.

"I have a daughter of your age," she told Pnina-Mazal one day. "I would be happy if you came to our house and talked to her. Her legs are paralyzed and she can't walk," she said sadly, "and she lacks friends of her own age." Rachel asked Sara's permission. Sara gave it after some hesitation, on condition that Pnina-Mazal be given nothing to eat but fruit, and she told the child herself that she was to stop her ears if anybody tried to talk to her about the Christian Messiah and his virgin mother.

The next day the carriage drove up, and the driver opened the door for Pnina-Mazal as if she were a fine lady. The women of the neighborhood gathered in the yard, excited by the rumors about Pnina-Mazal, the Christian woman's carriage, the Sudanese driver, and the American girl with the paralyzed legs.

*   *   *

In the evening Pnina-Mazal came home in a new ruffled dress and a straw hat decorated with a bunch of dried flowers; she was laden with books and full of stories about the beautiful house, or palace, as she called it, the splendor and luxury surrounding Rachel's daughter Elizabeth, and how sweet and kind the girl was.

Sara was soon obliged to resign herself to Pnina-Mazal's weekly visits to the Americans' home.

"She's learning spoken English there," she said to her neighbor Esther, who cross-examined her on the subject, "and besides, she doesn't taste a crumb of food in their house and she doesn't talk to them about religion."

Pnina-Mazal returned from her weekly visits full of stories. First she told them what Elizabeth did on the days when she wasn't studying. "The servant carries her to the fields surrounding the big house. She points to the wildflowers she wants him to pick for her, and they're always the smallest, tiniest flowers, so small I don't see them when I walk through the fields and sometimes I even trample them under my feet. And she always comes back from the fields with a big bunch of little flowers. And at home she had two boards of wood joined together with a big screw. And she lays the flowers one by one between two pieces of paper, separating the petals from each other, and pushes them between the two boards of wood. Then she tightens the big screw, waits a few days, and the flower comes out completely flat and dry, as if a heavy foot has trodden on it."

"And what does she do with the flowers?"

"She sticks them on thick paper or on album covers and they sell them in their big shop next to their house. Elizabeth showed me herself. They call them 'Flowers from the Holy Land.' And to think that I tread on flowers like that almost every day." Pnina-Mazal giggled.

"And who buys them?"

"The Christians who come here, of course," replied Pnina-Mazal. "Everything that belongs to our country is holy to them. The water, the soil, the air, and even the flowers."

"And what does her father do?"

"I've never seen him, because he's hardly ever at home. Elizabeth told me that he's a photographer, and the pictures he takes here in the town are sold in their shop and even appear in newspapers all over the world. And when there's nothing special happening in Jerusalem he travels all over the country and photographs the pioneers and the landscapes, and sometimes he gets on a ship and sails to other countries and takes photographs there. He hasn't been home for nearly six months and Elizabeth misses him very much," she added, hesitating as to whether she should ask her mother the painful question about her own father and when he would come to Jerusalem and be united with them.

∗　∗　∗

One day Pnina-Mazal came home in great excitement and told Sara that next week Elizabeth's father would return from abroad and bring Elizabeth a lot of presents. Both of them were invited to visit the Godwin family. "The only refreshments they'll serve us will be fruit, and tea in glass cups, and you'll come with me," she added.

On Tuesday afternoon the carriage stopped at the gate and the Sudanese driver opened the door for them. The carriage drawn by two horses raced through the streets of the town to the ringing of the bells round the horses' necks. In the end they stopped outside a house that looked like a palace. It had three stories and a large garden surrounded by pines and cypresses, the rustling of whose branches in the breeze clouded Sara's eyes with an inexplicable sadness. A Sudanese servant in a snowy robe, his white teeth gleaming in his dark face, opened the heavy wooden door for them. A red carpet led them to the drawing room, whose high, flat ceiling was decorated with pictures of plump pink angels blowing trumpets. The glowing light of the summer twilight streamed into the house from the huge windows set in all the walls.

Sara and Pnina-Mazal sank into a sofa covered with crimson velvet and decorated with heavy silk tassels. Then Rachel entered the room, pushing a wooden bath chair holding Elizabeth, a slender little girl whose bright red cheeks and fair hair and dark blue eyes looked artificial, as if they had been painted by a photographer. Pnina-Mazal ran to meet her, kissed her on both cheeks, and engaged her in animated conversation. Rachel turned to Sara and made a few pleasant remarks, after which she rang the silver bell lying at her side. The Sudanese servant entered the room carrying a copper tray holding glasses of tea, cakes, and a bowl piled with fruit, nuts, and raisins. Pnina-Mazal swallowed her saliva at the sight of the soft butter cookies, the crumpets soaked in honey, and the walnut cakes, which she was forbidden to touch.

"My husband will join us shortly," said Rachel to Sara. "He has just returned from a long journey," she added apologetically. "In the meantime you can look at his photograph albums." And she pointed delicately at the stack of albums piled on the footstool in front of her.

Sara picked up a heavy album bound with soft yellow leather. She lingered before opening it, breathing in the smell of the fine leather and feeling its softness with her fingertips. The pictures in the album were not foreign to her. Jews, Muslims, Christians, and Bedouin crowded the pages. She put the album down and picked up another. She paged through it absentmindedly and suddenly froze. The cover dropped from her hand and fell onto the thick pages filled with photographs held in place by black corners, raising a little cloud of dust that dispersed before her eyes.

At that moment the heavy oak door opened and the tall figure of a man entered the room. Sara, whose eyes were fixed on the cover of the album lying closed on her lap, turned to look at him. Through the mist filming her eyes she perceived only the silhouette of the man, who stopped dead in his tracks.

"Sara, this is my husband, Edward," Rachel said, breaking the oppressive silence.

Pnina-Mazal looked into Edward's eyes, then into her mother's, and her merry chatter with Elizabeth stopped abruptly.

Edward froze for a moment, then he smiled, greeted Sara and Pnina-Mazal politely, and went up to his daughter, whose thick curls he rumpled affectionately.

"And how are we today?" he asked her, looking over her head at Sara, his gaze transfixed by the sparks of light flashing from her eyes.

"I'm afraid we have to leave, Yitzhak and Ben-Ami are waiting for their supper," said Sara suddenly, gathering her skirt and beckoning Pnina-Mazal to stand up with her.

"But you've only just arrived," Rachel said. She hurried up to Sara, taking her hands in hers and looking at her appealingly.

"Mother, Mrs. Godwin's right, let's stay a little longer."

"You can stay and play with Elizabeth," Sara snapped. "I'm going home."

Edward accompanied her to the gate and helped her mount the carriage step. "I want to see you," he whispered in Hebrew in his Anglo-Saxon accent.

"Don't come to me," she warned. "You mustn't."

Edward took her hands, just as his wife had done a few minutes before, enclosing them in his big hands.

"Tonight," he whispered.

"Don't come," she replied, feeling the same weakness in her knees and butterflies in her stomach as she did whenever she thought of him. The Sudanese driver, with his back to them, pricked up his ears. Only then did Edward let go of her, and he stood watching the carriage as it drove away.

* * *

That evening Sara burned the food. The rissoles turned black, and when she slapped them down on the plates with a loud clatter they looked like shapeless lumps of coal. The lentils stuck to the bottom of the pot, and the bean soup evaporated on the stove. Yitzhak devoured his supper as voraciously as usual, demanding "food," but Pnina-Mazal looked askance at the food in her plate, and avoided her mother's eyes.

Before she went to bed Sara told David explicitly not to open the door to anyone, even if someone pounded on it with his fists. After she had washed the dishes and the house was still, she turned the wick down in the oil lamp, blew out the flame, and retired to bed. As soon as her head touched the pillow, the storm broke. The rise and fall of choppy ocean waves rocked her bed and turned her stomach upside down. Afraid she'd fall, she held on tight to the mattress, her nails digging into the kapok padding until her knuckles whitened. Her giddiness increased as the rocking grew more violent. Swaying like a sailor too long at sea she got out of bed and walked unsteadily to the kitchen, her knees like water and her stomach churning.

Then she heard the knock at the door and Edward's authoritative voice commanding her in his strange accent, "Open the door."

"Go away," she hissed at him. "You're waking the children."

"Only for a minute," he begged. "I want to talk to you."

Sara dropped to her knees at the door, clinging to the handle, with her body pressed against the cold metal.

"Get out of my life, go away," she hissed at him through the keyhole.

The sound of Edward's receding footsteps echoed loudly in Sara's ears as he walked away, followed by malevolent stares from dimly lit windows behind half-closed shutters. When she rose heavily to her feet she sensed eyes fixed on her back. David stood there, looking at her pityingly with his hands clasped behind his back.

"Go to bed, why are you standing there staring at me with calf's eyes?" she snapped, with a hatred not intended for him.

All that night she battled the ocean waves in the worst storm she had ever experienced in her life. Struggling for breath as she rose to the surface, she felt as if the waves were dragging her down to the bottom of the sea. In the morning she made haste to wake the children, the black rings around her eyes emphasizing the lightness of their color. David avoided her eyes, but while she was busy at the stove he stole a worried look in her direction. Her eyes met his, and she gave him a warning glance.

Later that morning Esther came hurrying round. "We heard that he came last night," she said, waiting to hear the details.

"Who are you talking about?" Sara said with pretended innocence.

"Him, the goy with the yellow hair."

"I don't know what you're talking about. I didn't hear or see anything," Sara replied angrily, and turned her back to her.

When Sara left the house to do her shopping at the market, she felt the eyes of the men penetrating the thin stuff of her dress, burning and consuming every inch of her body. She ran the gauntlet of their looks, reached her house panting for breath, and slammed the door shut behind her.

⁕ ⁕ ⁕

"You won't be having any more English lessons from Mrs. Godwin," Sara said grimly to Pnina-Mazal.

The child turned pale and even the freckles on her nose whitened. "Why?" she succeeded in blurting out after a long silence.

"They're not for us," Sara answered shortly.

"But I love her lessons," Pnina-Mazal whispered. "English is my favorite language. I'm prepared to give up French," she announced bravely.

"You're not having any more lessons from Mrs. Godwin," Sara repeated.

"I'm prepared to give up my Arabic lessons too," Pnina-Mazal tried to bargain.

"That's it. I've had my say. You're not going there anymore, it will only end badly."

Pnina-Mazal burst into heartbroken tears, shut herself in her room, and remained there for hours, sobbing intermittently. Sara pretended to be busy, clattering pots and pans loudly in the kitchen. Early that evening, as she laid the table, she called her to come and have her supper. Loud sobs and shouts of refusal rose from behind the closed door. The food on Pnina-Mazal's plate was devoured by Yitzhak. Without asking permission David entered the little girl's room. Sara strained her ears, trying to overhear their conversation through the lip-smacking and loud belches that accompanied Yitzhak as he ate.

After a long time David emerged from the room, and with an expression on his face that she had never seen before said accusingly, "You can't punish the child for your sins."

Sara's face turned white and she swallowed her saliva. "The impudence, I'll teach her a lesson. And you, who set you up in judgment?" she said, looking at him scornfully through narrowed eyes. "Don't you dare interfere in my affairs again, or you'll find yourself outside the door."

David went red and tried to efface himself. Pnina-Mazal, who heard them through her sobs, emerged red-eyed from her room and announced defiantly: "I'm going to Mrs. Godwin." She walked out of the house and slammed the door behind her.

✻　✻　✻

That night Sara woke from a light sleep to the sound of loud banging on the door. She knew that she would be the talk of the neighborhood if she let Edward go on standing there, beating on the door with his fists and waking everyone up, and so she reluctantly opened the door. He confronted her, angry and determined.

"You can't forbid her to come to us," he said. "She and Elizabeth are friends, she's a good student, why are you punishing her?" And without waiting for a reply he gathered her up in his warm arms and clasped her to his chest in a desperate embrace, seeking her grimly pursed lips with his.

Sara extricated herself from his embrace and escaped into the house, leaving the door open. He walked straight into her bedroom as if he owned the place, and closed the door gently behind him. In the light of the oil lamp Edward examined her face earnestly, and began delicately brushing her brow, her eyelids, and her cheeks with his lips. When his tongue probed her ear he felt her body trembling and pressed his mouth to her eagerly parted lips. Her knees gave way beneath her and he seated her on the bed and slowly undressed her, kissing her bare body as he did so. When his lips reached her breasts he clamped his mouth around her nipple and sucked like a hungry baby, and when he entered her she clenched her teeth and suppressed the groan threatening to burst from her depths and wake the household.

Before he left he asked if he could see the little boy. Gently he removed the blanket and lightly touched his cheeks. Ben-Ami woke up and sent a dazzling smile in the direction of the strange face he was seeing for the first time. Edward stepped back.

"Mine," he murmured as if to himself and turned toward the door.

"Only mine," she responded and pushed him lightly out of her house. Then she quickly shut the door behind him, as if afraid he might change his mind and demand to come back in. Breathlessly she pressed her back against the door and found herself looking straight into David's eyes. "I'm leaving tomorrow," he said shortly, turned his back to her, and returned to Yitzhak's room.

The next morning he packed his few belongings and vanished from her house.

*   *   *

The day David left Yitzhak began banging his head on the wall again. His trousers wet and sour with urine, he roamed the house like a sleep-walker, looking for David and grunting obscurely. Pnina-Mazal, in defiance of the whole world, stopped talking to him and disappeared from the house for days at a time. When Sara questioned her friends, they told her that she spent her time at Rachel Godwin's house. When Rachel was busy, Pnina-Mazal would play with Elizabeth, look at Edward's photograph albums, and dream of distant worlds. And when Rachel invited her one day to join them for supper she did so without hesitation, and sat down in the big dining room at the long, dark table whose carved legs ended in the shape of a lion's paw holding a ball.

"What will you eat?" Rachel asked her tactfully. "Would you like me to order special food for you?"

"I'll eat what you eat," she said defiantly, as if her mother and not Rachel Godwin were standing before her.

She gobbled down the meat placed before her and finished off with a glass of milk and melt-in-the-mouth butter cookies. A feeling of ease and relief spread through her, and she exchanged glances and giggles with Elizabeth.

While Pnina-Mazal was enjoying herself at Rachel's house, Sara struggled with the burden of caring for Yitzhak. Every day she sent messengers to David to entreat him to return, and she even promised that she would give him a weekly salary for looking after Yitzhak. David turned her down. On the seventh day of his absence from the house, Sara went to see him at the yeshiva, dragging Yitzhak behind her. She found him, thinner and shabbier than ever, sitting with his friends studying the Gemara. Yitzhak roared with joy at the sight of him, hurried toward him with his clumsy, lumbering gait, seized him under the armpits, and tried to raise him to his feet. A shadow of a smile appeared on David's austere face.

"We want you to come back to us," Sara said humbly.

"You know my conditions for staying at your house," he replied.

"I'll pay you a salary," she offered.

"I won't take a penny from you," he said. "You know my conditions."

Sara nodded her head reluctantly and David promised to return that evening.

And so he did, his meager bundle in his hands, and Yitzhak fell upon his skinny, stalklike neck with its goiter as thick as a turkey's, and refused to leave his side. Sara served him his supper and avoided his eyes. Late at night, when Edward knocked discreetly at the door, she went out and spoke to him in a whisper. Edward dropped his eyes and returned to the carriage waiting a few streets from her house.

Chapter Ten

One day Rachel called Pnina-Mazal as she was playing with Elizabeth and said to her, "As you know, Elizabeth is very sick, and I have to take her back home to America. Perhaps we will find a doctor there to operate on her legs and alleviate the pains from which she suffers."

Pnina-Mazal stammered, forgetting her fluent English, "And I won't see you anymore?"

"Edward is staying here, and you're invited to visit whenever you like. He has promised to read with you so your English won't grow rusty," Rachel said, trying to evade the question.

Only shame prevented Pnina-Mazal from bursting into tears and throwing herself at Mrs. Godwin's feet, hugging her knees and imploring her not to go away and leave her alone.

"I'm coming with you," she said finally, after much hesitation.

"I would be very glad if you could," replied Rachel. "You would be a great help with Elizabeth. When she's with you she forgets all her pains. But you have to think of your mother."

That evening Pnina-Mazal was particularly nice to her mother, cleared the table and washed the dishes without being asked, played with Ben-Ami and made him laugh out loud, and conversed at length with Yitzhak with her eyes.

"What do you want this time, what new language have you discovered that you want to learn?" asked Sara in an appeased tone of voice.

"I don't want to learn another language."

"In that case, what would you like me to do for you?"

"I want to go away with Mrs. Godwin and Elizabeth," Pnina–Mazal said firmly.

"Where are they going, if I may ask?" asked Sara, numb with dread.

"Elizabeth is very ill and she needs an operation, and they're going to look for a good doctor."

"And where is this doctor?" Sara asked, rehearsing her refusal in her mind.

"In America," the girl replied.

Sara didn't even bother to answer her.

"Mother, I'm going with them. They'll come back after the treatment. I have to go," she said with the tears welling up in her throat.

Sara maintained her silence.

"I'll go even without your permission." Pnina–Mazal mustered her courage and confronted her mother's frozen face. "And you had better agree, because if I leave without your blessing I won't come back," she declared, and shut herself up in her room.

Numb and rigid with pain Sara began making preparations for her daughter's journey. She sewed new dresses for her, bought her a large traveling bag made of yellow camel hide, and showered her with advice, warnings, prohibitions, and oaths.

On the day of the departure the grand carriage arrived, and the driver opened the door for the excited girl and her mother, who could not hold back her tears. The views on the way to the railway station blurred before Sara's eyes. At the station she felt detached from the shouts, the crowds, and the people milling around her. Porters quickly surrounded them, took their bags, ran along the platform, burst into the open door of the coach, and sat down on the seats upholstered in green velvet to keep their places for them. Sara got in after them and smoothed the seats reserved for herself and her daughter with her tear-soaked handkerchief, as if to wipe out all traces of the backsides that had sat there before them and efface the sight of the ragged, mean-faced porters who had preceded them. Rachel and Edward, who sat opposite them in the coach, avoided her eyes. The hooting of the locomotive, the smell of the burning coal, and the pungent scent of the sage growing along the tracks penetrated the open window of the slowly moving train, made her skin bristle with a sense of foreboding, and reminded her of forgotten sights from her previous journey.

A few hours later she set foot on the platform in Jaffa, faltering and breathing in the sweat of the porters and the steamy air that enveloped her and covered her skin in little beads of perspiration.

Leaning on Pnina-Mazal's slender body, Sara was taken by an unfamiliar route to the Jaffa port, to the foot of the great ship with the name *Margaretta* emblazoned in black letters on its side. There on the quay Rachel turned to her for the first time and promised her that she would watch over Pnina-Mazal and look after her as if she were her own daughter. This promise brought a fresh wave of tears to Sara's eyes and she wordlessly embraced her daughter. Pnina-Mazal, the freckles on her nose pale with excitement, kissed Sara and promised to write to her every day and to obey Rachel.

Chattering and laughing, the little girls settled down on the deck, and Sara examined the lifeboats through the veil of her tears. Suddenly she felt the rocking of the waves on her flesh, seeing and not seeing Edward as he embraced his daughter and kissed his wife lightly on the cheek.

"Promise me you'll look after each other," Rachel said to her husband as they turned toward the ramp.

"Gladly," Edward replied, and waved good-bye.

Supported by his strong arm, her legs failing, Sara left the port area.

"Hotel, you want a hotel?" demanded an Arab urchin whose feet had grown thick black soles as a result of years of running about barefoot.

"I know a hotel," said Sara, and she showed Edward the way.

∗　∗　∗

When she entered the stinking little room she felt as if it were only yesterday that she had lodged there with her children. Pale with the seasickness that had suddenly overcome her, she sat down on the bed, and the sordid room spun round her like a merry-go-round.

Blind to his miserable surroundings Edward began taking off his clothes impatiently, throwing trousers, jacket, shirt, and socks in all directions. When he was naked he began unbuttoning Sara's dress while she sat pale and motionless on the bed.

"So many buttons," he complained, "a hundred at least."

Sara seized his hands hurrying over her breasts and the buttons of her dress, pressed them to her body, and began slowly undoing the buttons while he watched. With every button Edward breathed a sigh of relief, until she reached the last one. Impatiently he pushed her hands away and grabbed hold of the button as if his whole life depended on the thread connecting it to the dress. Under the pressure of his demanding fingers the thread snapped and the button fell off the dress and rolled under the bed with a little clatter, like a hard pea falling on the kitchen floor.

Sara hurried after it, pushing her head under the bed and exposing her gleaming white buttocks. Before she could get up Edward seized her from behind and threw her onto the soiled sheets of the bed.

Much later, when she was lying by his side with her head on his shoulder, the button was still clasped in her fist, printing her pink palm with a round mark like that of a coin with two tiny holes in it.

❖ ❖ ❖

From then on Sara waited in suspense every day for Pnina-Mazal's letters and Edward's visits. They would meet in the mornings, when everyone else was busy shopping and cooking. David was with Yitzhak, and Ben-Ami was at the heder, after which he went to Sara's neighbor Esther, who gave him lunch in exchange for a handsome fee. Then Sara would cover her hair, raise her collar, and make her way by a circuitous route to the carriage that waited for her every day in a different place, agreed upon between them the day before. Pierced by the blank, shuttered eyes of the windows staring at her in dumb rebuke, averting her eyes from the houses bowed beneath the weight of their stone domes and tiles, which closed in on her threateningly as she hurried past, she mounted the carriage with a faltering step. Only when she was safely ensconced in the red velvet seat with her hands on the armrests did her heart stop beating wildly and begin to whisper to her reassuringly again.

They made love in a large, spacious room, on a huge bed covered with embroidered, lace-trimmed sheets that was reflected in the polished mirror of the dark wardrobe, which boasted a carved pediment as magnificent as that of a temple. The first time she saw their naked bodies reflected in the mirror she giggled and buried her eyes shyly in Edward's neck. Gently he raised her head and turned it toward the mirror and the sight of their bodies tenderly twined about each other like a pair of supple, loving snakes. Again she averted her eyes, and again Edward turned her head, until she grew accustomed to the sight, and she would gaze at the joined limbs twisting and twining and dissolving into each other, and delight in the "game of limbs" she invented on the brass bed opposite the mirror.

"Who does this leg belong to?" she asked Edward and pointed to the mirror.

"And who does this nipple belong to?" he replied, pinching it lightly and making her squeal and giggle like a little girl.

When they finished making love, and she lay replete on the embroidered sheets with her limbs outspread, Edward would bring his camera and set it on its stand. "You're so beautiful," he whispered ardently, and drew aside the heavy curtains protecting the sights of the room from the world outside. "I have to photograph you. Such beauty cannot be allowed to vanish from the world."

Sprawled in the pool of light entering through the drawn curtains she looked languidly at the round black eye flickering opposite her, worshiping her body with its wide-open lens. Sara looked straight into it, following with interest its blinks and winks, which were accompanied by a faint clicking sound. Obediently she followed the muffled instructions shot at her through the heavy black cloth, staring impudently at the single eye that gazed without shame at her nakedness.

"And now raise your arms above your head," Edward instructed, and she obeyed, stretching her breasts as she did so, and her nipples instantly stiffened and rose toward the ceiling, which was decorated with paintings of fruit and flowers and plump pink angels, whose tiny pointed members seemed to stiffen in response.

With his head thrust beneath the black cloth covering the camera, Edward clucked his tongue in satisfaction and with the tip of his finger issued his commands to the open eye. The eye looked at the beautiful woman lying before it, uttered a tiny cry of admiration, winked, and engraved the sight forever on its heart. With eager fingers the headless hand removed the plate engraved with the dazzling beauty, and planted a new one on the side of the black box, whose Cyclops eye widened in wonder, as if afraid of missing a single second of that beauty. After immortalizing the crown of creation from a new angle, he asked her to turn over on her stomach, and photographed her round, plump buttocks. Only after he had photographed her naked body from every possible angle did he allow her to get up and put on her clothes.

Late in the evening, when the darkness waited impatiently for the plates engraved with the memory of that peerless beauty, he arranged the three basins in the kitchen and poured the water, the fixative, and the developing solution into them. Carefully he dipped the plates into the stinking fluids and tortured them into giving up their secrets. With a pounding heart, his fingertips branded by the real and solid touch of her beauty, he sailed the plates in the water, and the smell made him pleasantly giddy. Shining white shapes appeared before his eyes. At the third basin his eyes were greeted by the sweet sights that melted the lump in his throat. The drops rolled down his cheeks and set a stamp of salt on the naked glory lying wet and shining on the kitchen table, where it was spread out to dry. Replete with carnal pleasure she flaunted her beauty at the illuminated darkness.

When the work of developing was done he prepared the photographic paper. A pile of gleaming white eggs waited for him in the corner of the little room. Like an expert cook he broke the eggshells and separated the yolks from the whites, which he collected on a flat tray. The yolks he threw casually into a glass bowl, where they peeped at him like yellow-amber eyes. With a practiced gesture Edward gripped the thick paper and dipped it several times into the egg whites, which he had previously mixed with salt. After the paper was coated with the stuff he dipped it in a solution of silver nitrate and hung it up to dry. Soon the line was covered with dripping sheets of paper waiting impatiently to be exposed to the light.

The next day she asked to see the pictures he had taken.

"They didn't come out," he lied. "The pictures got burned and I'll have to take new ones." He took the new ones that same day, after saturating his body with hers, and the flashing of her eyes penetrated the polished lens and was reflected like a flickering flame in the picture, splashing in the chemical fluids of Edward's laboratory.

❖   ❖   ❖

The more time went by the more worried and anxious Sara grew. No letter had yet arrived from Pnina-Mazal, and she was not comforted by Edward's reassurances and explanations that many days would pass before she could expect a sign of life. It was already two months since she had parted from her daughter, and Sara could not sleep at night. She tossed and turned on her bed, pining away in agonies of body and conscience. Even her stolen meetings with Edward ceased to bring her pleasure.

Every day she walked to the Austrian Post Office and asked if there was a letter from her daughter. The postal clerk, an elegantly dressed Jew who always wore a red tie shaped like a butterfly without feelers around his neck, which was as rough and coarse as orange peel, would hurry toward her.

"It hasn't arrived yet," he would murmur apologetically in his slow, heavy accent, looking straight into her eyes. "Come again tomorrow," he always added invitingly, whispering into her blushing ear, as if he didn't want anyone else to hear.

"I haven't received a letter either, and I'm not worried," Edward said as he studied the fingernails on her right hand, which were bitten to the quick.

"If anything bad happens to my daughter, her blood is on your head," she said in a sudden burst of hostility.

Edward took her rigid body in his arms and rocked her gently, like a father calming his baby daughter.

The next day the clerk was waiting for her in a state of solemn excitement. Sara stared at him. It seemed to her that the butterfly clinging to his throat was spreading its red wings dotted with yellow pollen, about to flap them in the air, take flight from the clerk's coarse neck, and wrap itself about her own. As she went on gazing at the spotted wings she felt the pollen penetrating her mouth and blocking her throat.

Before her eyes filled with the butterfly's wings the envelope waved. A refined white envelope, embellished with pink foreign stamps. Abruptly she detached herself from the sight of the butterfly, and with a hoarse cry tore the envelope open, tearing a bit of the letter too in her impatience. Overcome by weakness she leaned against the post office wall, ignoring the commotion of the hawkers and the noise around her as she read. The clerk glided back to the counter with his butterfly and watched her furtively out of the corner of his eye.

The voyage had been difficult for all of them, wrote Pnina-Mazal. Elizabeth and Rachel were very sick, their faces had turned green, and she had looked after them until the storms abated and the sea grew smooth as a mirror again. She had met interesting people who spoke foreign languages on the ship, and enjoyed talking to each of them in his own language. Elizabeth was jealous and asked her to teach her new languages too. About America and the city of New York Pnina-Mazal wrote things that Sara found it hard to believe. She wrote of buildings dozens of stories high, where in order to get to the top you walked into a little room in the entrance, closed the door, and it took you to whichever story you desired, with no need to wear yourself out climbing the stairs. She wrote too of a train that drove right through the city; of women teetering on shoes like stilts, who wrapped their bodies in the fur of unclean animals; of places where people went just to eat; and of elegantly dressed men who served the food and asked the diners if it was to their taste. And music played in these places from great metal ears attached to a box whose single hand impaled a round black disk placed upon it. Sara laughed out loud in the face of the butterfly, whose wings wilted before her eyes, and she nodded her head in farewell and hurried out of the building.

Edward was waiting for her at home with a letter stamped just like hers.

"This arrived from Rachel this morning," he said with a frozen face. "The doctors have refused to operate on Elizabeth, on the grounds that there is no chance of her ever walking again. They haven't told her anything yet, for she is full of hope of a cure. Rachel writes that Pnina-Mazal is settling down nicely; she already has a lot of friends and she's learning new things every day."

"When are they coming home?" Sara interrupted.

"Rachel didn't say. But since they aren't going to operate on Elizabeth, I assume they'll come back soon, within a year or two."

With a sigh of relief Sara sank into the armchair.

*   *   *

Pnina-Mazal's absence was felt everywhere. Yitzhak seemed to miss their eye-conversations, Ben-Ami needed her, and David prowled the house like a sleepwalker, with nobody to talk to. Her friend Davida was a frequent visitor, timing her visits to coincide with the return of David and Yitzhak from their walks in the fields. Then she would sit in the kitchen with Sara, making pointless conversation of no interest to anyone and looking at Yitzhak out of the corner of her eye. Even though Davida was already aware of his condition and had never exchanged a single word with him, Sara sensed that she was attracted to him like a magnet.

Sara received frequent letters from Pnina-Mazal, full of her life in new, strange worlds. Sara's pockets were crammed with rustling papers, and when she met her neighbors she would put her hand in her pocket and rustle the pages of the new letter, until her interlocutor gave in and asked her to read the latest stories of America. When she stood in the public square next to the neighborhood pump holding the pages in front of her eyes, the destitute street urchins would gather round her too, opening their eyes wide in wonder at the marvels they contained. And when she went about her business in the neighborhood they would run after her, tug at her skirt, peep into her crammed pockets, and ask for "America." Glad of any opportunity to read her daughter's letters again, she would abandon her business and read them out loud to anyone who asked her to. To herself she admitted that she had done well to send Pnina-Mazal to that distant land. Like a grand lady in all her finery she would return to Jerusalem, where she would have her pick of the best boys in the town, marry a rich husband who would keep her in style, and spend the rest of her life bringing up her children and learning foreign languages.

Every Tuesday Sara made her way to the Austrian Post Office. When she arrived there she would stretch out her hand and open her fingers to receive the white envelope sliding across the counter. After she had finished reading the new letter she would add it to her swollen pockets and a few days later she would lay it on top of the growing pile of letters in her bedroom. Then too she began numbering them according to the date of their arrival, lest she grow confused and read the first ones last and the last ones first. The one-hundred-and-fifty-eighth letter brought the great news.

Pnina-Mazal was coming home.

She was homesick and Mrs. Godwin had already purchased her ticket for the ship. When Sara read the letter out loud in the neighborhood square to her regular audience, she saw David looking out of the window of her house, his eyes shining with a new light.

Immediately after the letter with the great news she began to receive postcards with views of distant lands that Pnina-Mazal had visited on her way home: a picture of a tower leaning to its side, threatening to fall on the heads of the people looking up at it admiringly from the ground; a picture of great ruined buildings with triangular pediments and broken marble pillars. And more ruins, and more rubble, until it seemed to Sara that her daughter was touring a continent where a terrible war had raged or a great earthquake had taken place and ruthlessly smashed all its houses and palaces. After these postcards had arrived, Sara did not hear from her for a month. She went to the post office every day and stretched her open-fingered hands out blindly. When nothing landed in her palm, she would open her eyes as if in shame, withdraw her hands, curl up her fingers, and emerge from the building with her head bowed to the waiting crowd with their eternal refrain of "America, America, America. . . ." In order not to disappoint them Sara would rummage in her pockets, pull out a previous letter, and read it in a choked voice to her audience, who followed her lips with their eyes and finished her sentences for her.

❊ ❊ ❊

One day after she had returned empty-handed from the post office, the door opened and Pnina-Mazal fell into her arms.

She was taller, dressed in a blue velvet traveling suit, and her long hair fell in soft brown waves to her knees. Sara held her at arm's length and looked emotionally at her face. The little summer freckles on her nose danced before Sara's damp eyes.

The driver carried in three iron trunks, which blocked the entrance to the house. After he had been paid he was obliged to jump over them one by one, his paunch quivering, his greasy fez teetering on his bald head, and the concentrated expression of a boy surmounting an obstacle course on his face. The mother and daughter looked at each other, trying to stifle their laughter, but it burst out in loud peals in spite of their efforts, causing the fat driver to jump over the third trunk with unseemly haste and fall on his moutainous belly. Sara hurried up to him with an expression of concern on her face, evoking a renewed burst of laughter from Pnina-Mazal.

As soon as the driver left the house, Sara put the kettle on to boil and settled down for a long talk with her daughter over a hot cup of tea. So absorbed were they in their conversation that they failed to notice David returning from his daily walk with Yitzhak. They came in at the kitchen door and stood stock still at the sight of the two women sitting at the table with their heads together. David's face turned scarlet and he rushed out of the room, while Yitzhak stared into his sister's eyes and uttered a choked cry. So loud was his cry that it brought the neighbors running to the open, trunk-blocked door, where they stood chanting the one-word refrain of "America, America, America, Ameri—" and hurried to add: "Welcome home." Pnina-Mazal waved weakly at the crowd besieging the door.

It was late at night before they began to unpack the trunks.

"Books," sighed Sara. "What will you do with so many books? And where will we put them?"

When they opened the third trunk she uttered a cry of admiration. It was full of fine silks and lace, flowery parasols, silk ribbons in all the colors of the rainbow, hand-embroidered linen, high-heeled shoes made of soft kidskin, cutlery, and china crockery rimmed with bell-shaped pink flowers, the likes of which Sara had never seen in her life. When Sara pounced on a hard black cardboard box, Pnina-Mazal tried to prevent her from opening it.

"Later," she wheedled. But the box was already open on Sara's knees as she scanned its contents.

A magnificent bridal gown made of silk and trimmed with lace and pearls lay there on a bed of green velvet.

Sara paled. "Are you planning a marriage of which I know nothing?" she asked when she recovered her breath.

"Rachel bought it for me. It was on sale for a reduced price. Rachel said that in the end I would get married like everybody else, and I might as well have a gown ready for the occasion. I objected, but both Rachel and Elizabeth insisted. They said that in any case they would not be able to come to my wedding when it took place, and this was their wedding gift."

"You're tempting fate," said Sara, and she felt a pang of dread in her heart. "A woman who prepares her wedding gown before she finds a husband will end up an old maid."

Pnina-Mazal bowed her head. "I'll find a husband," she said, "and I'll marry him in this dress."

With her throat choked by fear and in the wish to conciliate her mother, who was looking at her with a hard face, Pnina-Mazal opened the parcel of gifts. Sara received checked woolen material, Yitzhak a pair of long trousers and a jacket of suitably vast dimensions, and Ben-Ami a case full of wooden blocks painted with pictures of animals such as Sara had never seen in her life.

"I saw them all," Pnina-Mazal told her. "The gentiles collect the animals in great parks with high fences, and there you can go and look at them while they eat, play, and even copulate," she whispered in her mother's ear in order to change the subject.

Sara was astonished. "And did you see the animal with the long neck and the spots too? And the one with the long nose and the floppy ears?"

Pnina-Mazal laughed. "They call this place a zoo. On Sundays, their Sabbath, the park is full of thousands of couples with their children coming to look at the animals."

The next day Sara hurried to her meeting with Edward. "Pnina-Mazal is back," she announced in excitement, overjoyed at her daughter's return.

"I know. My driver saw her in a carriage on her way home."

"And today is our last meeting," Sara blurted out quickly, before she could change her mind.

"I wanted to tell you that in a few days' time I'm leaving to visit Rachel and Elizabeth. I don't know when I'll be back," he said and averted his eyes from her inquiring gaze.

"It's better this way," she said, swallowing her tears. "People are talking about us, and God forbid the rumor should reach Pnina-Mazal's ears."

*   *   *

When she came home, her eyes red with weeping, her cheeks seared by the stubble of Edward's beard, which had ploughed them with fine furrows of love, and her lips swollen and scratched by his farewell kisses, she found Pnina-Mazal and David conferring over the kitchen table. Her daughter's tear-filled eyes were looking deeply into the eyes of the young scholar, and she did not notice her mother standing at the door. The first to see her was David. He started back with a clumsy movement that overturned the wooden stool on which he was sitting.

Pnina-Mazal turned to face her. A cold shiver ran down Sara's spine as she felt her daughter's eyes staring at her unseeingly, fixed on some invisible point in the distance. Without a word the girl got up and followed David out of the kitchen.

Sara hurried after her. "What did he tell you?" she asked hoarsely. "Don't believe him, whatever he told you. He's trying to make trouble between us. There was nothing between me and Edward. It's all a pack of lies."

A shock passed through Pnina-Mazal's body. Sara saw the blood draining from her face and the little freckles turning white on the tip of her nose. The girl her mother a cold, contemptuous look. Sara tried to look into her eyes, but to her horror Pnina-Mazal looked right through her, as if she were transparent.

"If he told you stories about me, don't believe him. It's all lies. Gossip and slander," she tried again.

Pnina-Mazal maintained her silence.

"If he told you lies he won't stay under my roof any longer," she said quickly, before she had time to regret it.

Pnina-Mazal narrowed her eyes in pain and said nothing.

"Answer me," Sara screamed at her, shaking her thin shoulders violently. The girl's slender body swayed limply between her hands like that of a rag doll. When she continued shaking her, her body shrank in pain. All this time she kept staring fixedly at the invisible point on the wall. Suddenly red finger marks appeared on her pale face. Sara looked at her hand as if refusing to believe that she had slapped her daughter.

Tears flowed soundlessly down Pnina-Mazal's cheeks. She stared blankly over Sara's shoulder without moving a muscle.

Sara turned on her heel and found herself looking into David's flashing eyes.

"Don't you dare raise your hand to her," he whispered and took the silent girl into his arms.

Sara tried to tear her daughter from his grasp, but his hands protecting the weeping Pnina-Mazal were too strong for her. He led her gently from the room, and she looked as fragile as a pale butterfly fluttering in his arms.

Sara remained alone, refusing to believe the evidence of her eyes. With an anguished cry she burst into her daughter's room. She was lying calmly on her bed, with David sitting beside her and holding her slender hand.

"Go away," he hissed. "She doesn't want to see you now."

"How dare you!" Sara replied in a whisper full of hate. "Pack your bags and leave this house tonight."

"I'll leave," he said, "but Pnina-Mazal will come with me. We're engaged and we'll be married soon."

Waves of cold ran through Sara's body and made her hair stand on end. Her daughter deserved the best, not some skinny, penniless yeshiva student dependent on her for his keep. Swaying like a drunk she left the room and closed the door quietly behind her.

✿   ✿   ✿

David spent the night at Pnina-Mazal's side, holding her hand, gazing at her transparent eyelids with their delicate tracery of veins, and counting her freckles. Sara paced her room like a caged lion, unable to decide which to mourn first—Edward's departure or her daughter's unexpected wedding. She opened and shut the wardrobe's doors and pulled out its contents, emptied chests and packed them again with sheets and towels, household wares and clothing. The next morning she stole into Pnina-Mazal's room and found David there, wide awake and holding her daughter's hand.

"I give you my blessing," she said in a trembling voice, "on condition that you don't leave the house. Yitzhak needs you both, and I couldn't endure another parting from my daughter."

David smiled at her conciliatorily and let go of Pnina-Mazal's hand. The girl woke up suddenly and at the sight of her mother standing over her she buried her face in her pillow.

Sara sat down beside her. "Make all the necessary preparations for your wedding," she said gently. "I'll telegraph your father. Perhaps he'll be willing to make the effort to come to his daughter's wedding."

A faint smile illuminated Pnina-Mazal's face. Slowly she tried to get out of bed, only to fall back on the pillow again, overcome with giddiness. As the first rays of sun penetrated the shutters Sara saw to her horror that the marks of her fingers from the night before were still stamped on her daughter's face.

✿   ✿   ✿

Sara led her daughter discreetly to the mikvah. When Pnina-Mazal took her clothes off she looked at the skinny girl standing in front of her like a snail that had lost its shell. Her little breasts peeped impudently through the hair falling round her body. In the dim light coming through the air vent in the ceiling she looked at her childish, bony knees and then at the down covering her thin freckled legs like a halo of yellow fur.

Sara tried to banish the picture of her daugher crushed under David's body from her mind's eye, but the picture grew sharper. Her ears heard the moans and her nostrils filled with the smells of their lust. Ashamed of her thoughts, she led Pnina-Mazal to the pool of black rainwater, holding her hand and supporting her down the slippery steps.

Pnina-Mazal's hair refused to sink with her body into the water, and it spread out around her head like the long roots of weeds choking the wellsprings of life and sucking the sap out of them.

"Sink, sink, sink," the voice of the rabbi's wife hammered in Sara's ears, rousing her from the visions of her daughter's carnal lust swaying before her eyes and from the cries of passion ringing in her ears and covering her face in a deep blush.

As if waking from a dream she looked at her daughter ducking her head in the black liquid, her water-darkened hair floating around her like a creature with a life of its own, threatening to strangle her stalklike neck. It seemed to Sara that a long time had passed since her daughter had sunk her head in the water.

"Tell her to take her head out," she ordered the rabbi's wife.

"Get out," said the latter, but the girl's head remained still in the water, surrounded by floating hair.

"Get out," screamed Sara, but there was no response. When the head refused to rise, Sara jumped into the water in her clothes and pulled Pnina-Mazal out, her eyes closed and her lips blue. She dragged her up the steps with superhuman strength, crouched down beside her, and shook her still body. A strong jet of water burst out of her throat and nose and wet the feet of the rabbi's wife, who was standing nailed to the spot. Sara turned her daughter onto her stomach and slapped her cheeks to revive her.

Pnina-Mazal opened her eyes and a violent fit of coughing racked her thin body, which went on vomiting quantities of stagnant water, as if she had swallowed the entire contents of the pool.

"Now she's clean on the inside too," mumbled the rabbi's wife in an awed voice. "Not only from without but also from within," she repeated to herself incredulously.

"The girl's a saint," the rabbi's wife proclaimed, summarizing the events of the day for the benefit of the women who streamed to the mikvah in the wake of the rumors.

Chapter Eleven

The wedding Sara laid on for her daughter would long be remembered in the neighborhood. It was a large and sumptuous affair, attended by all the students and teachers from David's yeshiva, all the inhabitants of the neighborhood down to the last of the beggars, Pnina-Mazal's school friends, the librarians from all the libraries where she had borrowed books, her language teachers, and even the residents of the American colony. Until the last minute the mother and daughter entertained the hope that the father of the bride would arrive. A telegram of congratulations had announced that he was preparing for the journey and had every intention of attending the wedding. But on the great day Pnina-Mazal stood beneath the wedding canopy, dressed in the magnificent bridal gown that Rachel had bought for her in America, with only her mother by her side. Afterward she heard from their neighbor Esther that she had heard from Ya'akov the barber, who had heard it from Shimon the butcher, who had heard it from Theodosios the Greek monk, that a man matching Avraham's description had been seen on board a ship sailing for Palestine, but he had disappeared without a trace the moment he set foot on the filthy, sinful soil of Jaffa.

But why had Avraham failed to attend his daughter's wedding? Theodosios the monk described how Avraham had mounted the ramp of the ship in the port of Salonika, accompanied by three iron trunks encircled by hoops and reinforced by thick leather straps, and retired to the best and biggest cabin on the ship. After that he hardly ventured out, except at mealtimes, when he hastily swallowed the food on his plate, replied politely to the questions of his fellow passengers, and vanished into his cabin again.

The only one Avraham was prepared to talk to was Theodosios himself, the floor of whose monastery, carved out of a gigantic catapult stone that had fallen out of the sky and landed on the narrow ledge of a windswept mountain, he had once covered with immense Persian carpets. In the wake of this work Avraham had received commissions from neighboring monasteries, hollowed out of skyscraping stones covered with stardust and teetering between heaven and earth on the edge of barren cliffs. Loading the great, heavy carpets on the iron hooks let down from the monastery walls was a skilled and difficult operation, about which Avraham was happy to reminisce with Theodosios, recalling the creaking of the chains, the frightened shouts of the porters, the calm replies of the monks, and the laying of the carpets on the monastery floors.

On the last day of the voyage the sea was smooth as a mirror, cradling the passengers with a gentle rocking motion. Then Avraham told Theodosios the purpose of his journey. He was going to see his family in Jerusalem. His wife, who was the most beautiful woman in the world, had golden hair that covered her body from head to foot. His daughter, who was a baby when she sailed for Palestine, and had already mastered several languages, was about to be married. About his beautiful mute son too he told Theodosios, and how they had consulted all the doctors and magicians without finding a cure. He was bringing many gifts for his family, he whispered into the monk's ear, lest the rumor reach greedy ears. There were carpets rolled up in his trunks, to cover the cold stone floors and warm their feet on the winter nights. Bolts of silk from China, red and gold, to sew them dresses; thick, handwoven cotton from Egypt to cover their beds. And carved crystal goblets to dazzle their eyes with their beauty and tickle their ears with their icy tinkle; and heavy silver spoons, wrapped in wool to keep them from turning black, to eat the feast of the seven blessings after the wedding. And many gold coins were hidden in the trunks, too, all the money he had received for the shop that he had sold after the death of his parents. With their help he would open a carpet shop in Jerusalem and support his family in style.

When he got off the ship and was carried ashore on the shoulders of the Arabs, whose feet were as swollen as sponges, he watched like a hawk to make sure that his trunks had been unloaded with him, and he was not satisfied until he was standing on the shore with all his belongings stacked around him. He looked around for a carriage to take him to the railway station, and then he saw her.

Who she was, what she looked like, and what she was wearing the monk Theodosios was unable to say, but he remembered her hair very well. All his life, until he died at a ripe old age in the Great Greek Monastery in Jerusalem, whenever he remembered that hair it glinted and glittered before his eyes, dazzling them even when they were blind with age. And if he was asked, he was always happy to describe it, as if the gleaming memory illuminated the darkness of his old age and filled his blind eyes with radiance.

The moment Avraham saw her the gold struck his eyes and dazzled him and he cried: "Sara!" She turned around, looked at him, and he murmured her name as if mesmerized and followed the deceitful radiance, the apparition that confounded him and brought catastophe down on his head. And she walked away with her head held high, with her hair trailing after her like the train of Lilith's wedding gown, and leaving the delicate traces of a tangled web in the sand. Avraham stumbled after her, his damp eyes fixed on the shining aureole dancing before him as he followed the prints in the sand swept by that golden broom. He did not bother to look behind him and check the porters running after him, bowed beneath the load of his luggage. Theodosios the monk brought up the rear of the procession. Lurching like a man struck by lightning he too followed the wheel of radiance, the hem of his long black habit blurring the delicate traces of the sweep of golden hair and covering the footprints of the barefoot porters, sunk deep in the sand due to the heaviness of their load.

Without looking back she led Avraham to a squalid little hotel. Her hair swept the filthy, dust-covered wooden steps that led to a narrow, windowless chamber. There she shook out her hair and with a waterfall of light banished the darkness from the room, barred and sealed like a tomb with Avraham's three iron trunks stacked up against the door. In the sealed room he shut himself up with her, and their bodies united on the damp, moldy mattress stained with the secretions of its previous occupants and covered with graffiti of lust so tortuous that nobody has ever succeeded in deciphering them.

What happened to him there he told the monk Theodosios the following morning. After searching for her throughout the length and breadth of Jaffa he met the monk, and asked him for a little money, which he promised to return. The moment they arrived in the room, he recounted, she took off her clothes and wrapped herself in her hair, which covered her body and fell all the way to her feet. And its color was dazzling gold and its touch was like the finest silk. Trembling he stretched his hands out before him and touched it with the tips of his fingers, felt it and weighed it in his hands as the tears streaming from his eyes wet and darkened the silken strands he clutched despairingly, like a drowning man.

When his stiff fingers began to knead her scalp she pushed them away, permitting him to touch only the hair covering her head. Then they lay down on the bed, her hair covering both of them, tangling and coiling between their sweating bodies, and her black pubic hair glittered at him invitingly, like a dark temptation. Before he penetrated the darkness of her body he came in a strong jet, wetting the blanket of hair enveloping his body, which shuddered in rhythmic waves of pleasure. At that moment he closed his eyes, saw her face opposite his, and shouted her name in a terrible voice. Afterward he fell asleep, his nose buried in her hair, and its smell, mingled with the smell of the dust from the street, assailed his nostrils and overwhelmed him with longing.

When he woke up his hands were tangled and trapped in her long hair, as if they had been fastened in golden fetters. All day long he lay bound on the bed, calling to her and begging her to release him, shouting and crying until his throat was hoarse. When people came to rescue him, breaking into the dark room through the door barricaded by the iron trunks, they found him curled up like a naked fetus on the bed, with her golden hair scattered all over the room, as if it had taken fright at his cries, deserted her head, and fled in all directions. Sheaves of hair lay on the pillow stained by the rouge of her lips and kohl of her eyes. They found locks of it tangled in his clothes, padding his shoes, coiled around his pubic hair, and piled up on the floor. Naked he crawled round the room on his hands and knees, collecting the golden strands and tying them up in a bunch. He even wriggled under the bed, where he found long hairs clinging to each other as if locked in a desperate embrace, glittering at him amid the dim shadows cast by the bed on the floor, which was covered by a gray fuzz of dirt. Then he got dressed and set out to look for her.

First he opened the doors leading off the corridor, where he was greeted by the sight of hairy backsides crouching between outspread legs. Then he went downstairs and asked about the woman with the long golden hair. The gaudily dressed women with the crudely painted faces replied that they had seen no one matching his description, and if they had, they would surely have remembered. Only one woman, whose face was plastered with a thick layer of white paint, cracked and fissured like parched soil thirsty for water, said that such a woman had once been there. When he asked where she was now, the white-faced woman told him that she had arrived many years before, with a lot of luggage and two babies, and that she had gone out and come back to the hotel without her golden hair, which had vanished without a trace.

When he wanted to leave he was told that he had to pay. He put his hand in his pocket and found that his purse had gone. In a panic he rushed upstairs and opened his trunks, only to find them empty.

Theodosios helped him to look for her. In all the town they left no stone unturned. They ventured into opium dens where they encountered the stares of men with red, sunken eyes that never saw the light of day, into gambling dens, rooms in cheap hotels, squalid slums, and prostitutes' hovels; they scoured the harbor and the ships, and even investigated the cellars of the monasteries. Everywhere they went Avraham asked about the woman with the long golden hair, produced the crop of gold he had collected in the hotel room, and dazzled the eyes of his interlocutors. But she was nowhere to be found. She had vanished as completely as if she had been swallowed by a whale.

If Theodosios had not been with him to confirm his story, people would have thought that he had lost his wits, and dragged him off to the place where all the lunatics of the town were congregated, swarming and wailing behind lock and bar in the cellar of the monastery next to the seashore. For three days he walked the streets of Jaffa and searched for her, buttonholing passersby, cross-examining gangs of urchins, and begging everyone he met for information about her, but to no avail. It was as if everyone had entered a conspiracy of silence against him. No one had seen her, no one had heard of her. Even the porters who had carried his trunks when he followed her to the hotel stared at him dumbly.

After three days he too disappeared. What happened to him and where he went, nobody knows. Some say that he went to the new town of Tel Aviv and worked there with bricks and mortar and built new, white houses, flooded with light and sun. Some say that they saw him getting on a ship with his empty trunks, out of his mind, and some swore that the Turks arrested him and since he had no papers on him, they sent him to the wars. The money he borrowed from Theodosios was never returned.

✵ ✵ ✵

The absence of the father did not mar the joy of his daughter's wedding. The food and drink, the witticisms of the jesters, and the singing of the women delighted the guests. Rahamim the photographer immortalized the excited couple under the wedding canopy. And after the guests had dispersed, he took them to his studio, where he photographed Pnina-Mazal, in her splendid wedding gown from America, and her brand-new husband David against the background of waterfalls and mountain cliffs painted on the back wall of his shop.

The day after the wedding David went off to his yeshiva as he did every day, and Pnina-Mazal came into the kitchen with a beaming face, dragging a chair behind her. She tied a white napkin round her neck, handed Sara a pair of heavy sewing scissors, and sat down on the chair.

"Cut it off," she commanded.

"Why?" asked Sara.

"I'm a married woman now, and in any case I'll have to cover my hair with a kerchief. I don't need it. David asked me to cut it."

In order to forestall an argument with her daughter, Sara plaited her hair into a braid, and lopped it off with the scissors. Pnina-Mazal rumpled her remaining hair happily with her hand, and hastened to cover it with a green kerchief embroidered with red and purple flowers. Sara looked at her face and it seemed to her that her daughter had grown up overnight. She wrapped the braid in a piece of cloth torn from a sheet and stored it behind the pantry for safekeeping. The radiant expression never left Pnina-Mazal's face, and every day she would wander dreamily about the house, reliving the experiences of the night before, her knees turning to water at the thought of the night to come.

Every night the sound of their voices kept Sara awake. Their giggles and stifled moans made the ground slip from under her feet and rocked her on the stormy ocean waves. The storm only subsided when she rubbed the inflamed spots on her body and calmed them. The louder and more frequent the sounds from the room next door, the louder and more frequent were the stifled moans bursting from her throat. And when silence fell in the adjacent room, her own body would grow quiet, and she would snuggle up in the dense, sweet honey spreading from the tips of her toes to the top of her scalp, still prickling with pleasure, and surrender herself to sleep.

*   *   *

Despite the rumors that Avraham had landed in Jaffa and despite the rumors of his disappearance, the monthly stipend continued to arrive at the Austrian Post Office, and the sum was even increased, so that the young couple too were amply provided for. Even though she had no need to work, Pnina-Mazal presented herself to Lizzie Farkash, the headmistress of the school for girls, upon whom the years that had passed seemed to have left no mark. Miss Farkash still clung to her airs and graces, her ruffled dresses and the cups of tea she still sipped every day at precisely ten o'clock in the morning and five o'clock in the afternoon, and her Sudanese coach driver still drove her home every day from school. But Pnina-Mazal noticed her slackened lips, the deep lines etched on her face, and the threadbare state of her dresses. The headmistress was glad to welcome the girl who had come back to her as a married woman, and offered her the English classes to teach.

Grateful for the work she had received, Pnina-Mazal went home radiant with happiness. At supper, while David silently twisted his beard around his fingers, his eyes veiled as he relived the pleasures of the previous night, Pnina-Mazal happily announced the news of her new job.

"Why do you have to go out to work?" he asked her gently. "The money your father sends us is more than enough. Your mother needs you to help her take care of Yitzhak and Ben-Ami, and you want to fly the nest?"

Sara looked at her daughter's disappointed face and decided not to interfere in the conversation.

In spite of her husband's objections Pnina-Mazal took up her post as an English teacher in Baroness Sarita Cassuto School for Girls.

"Go," Sara encouraged her. "I can manage with the two boys on my own. Go, and don't let David influence you."

Her eyes sparkling with happiness Pnina-Mazal would leave the house every morning. And when she came back in the afternoon, she would sit in the kitchen with Sara, sorting rice, removing peas from their pods, and telling her mother about her day at the school. In the evening, when David came home from his studies, she would greet him with hot coffee and fresh cookies. When he had revived, she would ask him to read her the new tractate he had studied that day. When he encountered a problem or a difficult passage, she would discreetly offer her own interpretation. He would always dismiss her words with a faint smile curling his lips in a forgiving expression, but he would engrave them in his memory, imagining the surprised expressions of his peers when he slipped these new interpretations into his words the next day. When the rest of the house was asleep, the husband and wife would sit at the kitchen table and in the light of the oil lamp casting flickering shadows on their faces, they would look deeply into each other's eyes.

And when they retired to their room, David would seat his wife on the edge of the bed, press his face against her flat belly, and cup her burgeoning breasts in his hands, until her heavy breaths united with his. The next morning Sara would look long at her daughter's face and discover on it the traces of the night before.

When a year passed and Pnina-Mazal's womb still refused to open and absorb new life, Sara took her to the doctors. And when they could find no cure she took her to the rabbis. After that they made the rounds of the magical healers and kabbalists. After every such visit the pillow at David's head would bulge with the new additions to the stock of parchment scrolls bearing spells and invocations, bits of blue glass to banish the evil eye, and amulets inscribed with the names of the angels of fertility hidden beneath it. When the potions and spells did not work, Sara would lie on her bed at night, making promises and taking vows. And when yet another year passed and Pnina-Mazal's belly still refused to swell, the suspicion crept into her heart that her daughter was being punished for Sara's own sins.

*   *   *

The rumor about the end of the world was brought to Sara by her neighbor Esther. More than anything Esther loved spreading hair-raising stories that sent shivers down the spines of her terrified audience. Nothing happened that day to hint at the doom awaiting Esther, Sara, the neighborhood, Jerusalem, the country, and the world at large.

"Next week, on Wednesday," said Esther to Sara in the garden, under the mulberry trees with their intertwining branches, all her double chins quivering with the importance of her doom-laden news. "A star is going to fall on us, the star with a tail—*la istaria con cola*. It will come from the east, and bring trouble to the whole world: wars, plagues, and unnatural deaths. A terrible, fiery star—if it falls on a tree, the tree will burn, if it falls on your house, its effect will be worse than lightning. And if we're lucky and it falls into a pool of water, it will be extinguished and turn into a smouldering ember."

"How do you know?" asked Sara, accustomed to her neighbor's tales of gloom and doom and the way in which she invented calamities and catastrophes on a daily basis.

"Benyamin the watchmaker told me he had read it in the newspaper, and if it's in the newspaper it must be true," she said decisively. "And in the newspaper it's called 'Halley' and people all over the world are throwing themselves off high buildings for fear of burning in its fire."

"And what must we do?" asked Sara, a note of apprehension creeping into her voice.

"Shut ourselves up in our houses and pray to God Almighty to save us. And sinners are the first in line to burn in its fire," she replied, drawing her loose dress tightly around her body, as if in preparation for what was to come.

With the rumor of the fire giving her no peace, Sara drew great quantities of water from the public well and surrounded the house with jugs, jars, basins, and buckets of water. She prepared the interior of the house for disaster, too, filling every vessel she could lay hands on with water. Then she went to the market and laid in supplies of rice, lentils, beans, flour, and oil and several loaves of bread in preparation for the seige. When Esther came to visit her she praised her foresight, and mobilized the other women of the neighborhood to join forces and prepare for the worst.

All that week the gurgling of the pump at the mouth of the well was heard without a pause. When one woman tired another took her place and filled jars and bottles, jugs and kettles with water. The women stood side by side in a chain, passing an empty pail from hand to hand until it reached the woman stationed at the pump, who passed it back down the line until it reached its destination in one of the houses of the neighborhood, taking up its place in the ranks of brimming vessels already standing there.

And all that week the husbands complained that there was no hot food in the house and the children were abandoned to their own devices. At night the women bandaged the blisters sprouting on their hands from the pumping and the hauling and waited for the end of the world. On those nights the moans and sighs rising from the innermost chambers of the houses were particularly loud. The men and women clung to each other in their beds, and sank their dread in each other's bodies. And afterward, when their bodies were calm and satiated, they would raid the pantries and retire to the kitchens, where they ground and kneaded, boiled and fried and roasted, and held midnight feasts, like their Muslim neighbors devouring their one and only meal in the last watch of the night during the month of fasting imposed upon them by their prophet.

During those days the women of the neighborhood looked sleek and satisfied, their cheeks rosy with the fat of the land and the sweet expectations of disaster. The expectations came to an end nine months later, when they gave birth to their children under the sign of the star. These children, so the rumors said, were born with a red mark in the shape of a comet on their backsides. The birthmark faded over the course of the years, changing color from dark red to pale pink, until it disappeared, together with the memory of the comet that passed through the sky and terrified the inhabitants of the town.

∗　∗　∗

When dawn broke on the morning of the fourth day, the day on which God created the lights in the firmament of the heavens, it was colder than usual, and the icy air cut to the bones of the people huddled in basements and cellars. Sara covered her children and her son-in-law, arranged the vessels of water around them, and went outside. The street was silent, and the people waiting patiently for their end looked at her through the cracks in their shutters, shaking their heads and clucking their tongues at the folly of this woman, who had abandoned her children and was running wild in the streets, mad with grief about the imminent destruction of the world.

But Sara was drawn outside by the sound of singing she heard coming from the direction of Jaffa Road. Wrapping herself tightly in her coat she followed the sound of the voices and gazed at the people swaying like drunks in the streets. Yeshiva students were embracing virgins, and virgins were embracing yeshiva students, touching each other's flesh and clinging to each other as if they were drowning. Sara joined in the procession of people wandering like sleepwalkers under the sky studded with stars that shone with an unfamiliar brilliance, and her eyes flashed yellow sparks at the threatening heavens. Suddenly silence fell and the people stopped dead in their tracks. One shining star detached itself from its fellows hanging in the cold sky; its head turned bright red and its light flickered. Then it began to fall toward the treetops, shooting fiery sparks in all directions as its tail cleaved the starry sky from west to east and split it apart. At that moment the crowd, like a single body with its eyes raised to the sky, uttered a cry of terror and awe. Then too she felt the hands of the yeshiva student behind her clutching her body and his nose pressing into her hair with the terror of the sight. The warmth spreading through her body thawed her frozen flesh, her legs gave way beneath her, and she collapsed with him onto the ground, showered with the red sparks falling from the sky.

Chapter Twelve

In the morning everyone woke to a clear sky and a new day. Sara, her hair gathered on her nape, boiled the water she had stored up for the catastrophe and washed her sweaty, dusty body. When she was clean, she collected all the water from the vessels scattered round the house in the laundry cauldron and put it on to boil. Even though it was not her laundry day she washed her clothes, and when she saw that there was still plenty of hot water left, she threw in the children's clean clothes, which she pulled out of the wardrobe, followed by the spotless sheets that she tore off the beds. That evening, when she got into bed, her body rosy and shining from the scrubbing she had given it, she examined her red hands in the light of the oil lamp. They were wrinkled and swollen, as if the water had seeped right into them, covered with transparent blisters as full and quivering as little pools of purifying waters, and painful to the touch.

Before she could lay her head on the pillow, Esther burst into the house and announced that although the comet had spared Jerusalem, it had burned the lands of Ethiopia and Persia to the ground with its tail. Jerusalem had been spared this time, but a great evil would soon fall on the town and devour its inhabitants.

"Wait and see, the curse will weed out the wicked and leave only the righteous alive," she promised, waving her finger at Sara threateningly.

And some say that the great and terrible war that set one nation against the other broke out as a result of the comet. Four years after the tail of the comet disappeared from the sky and the inhabitants of the town stopped talking about it, the news of the Great War arrived.

Troubles and disasters fell thick and fast on Sara's head. First came the rumor of war, and it emptied the shops of flour, oil, sugar, beans, and lentils. People bought everything up and hoarded it in their homes until the houses themselves looked like grocery shops. When Sara saw the stores of food laid in by her neighbors for the hard times ahead, she realized that the war raging in distant lands would last a long time, and she roamed the streets of the town with David in search of a shop that would sell her food. When they finally found a shop that had a little stock left, the owners took a long look at Sara's fine clothes and doubled and tripled their prices. Sara took out her dwindling bundle of money, undid the string, and bought food for her family. Then they made their way slowly home, David bowed beneath the weight of the sacks of flour and sugar on his back, clutching tins of olive oil under his arms.

A few months later the rumor swept through the street that all the foreign post offices were closing down. Sara, who received her monthly allowance through the Austrian postal service, hurried to the Austrian Post Office. The clerk with his butterfly bow tie, together with two other clerks she had never noticed before, were busy tying up bundles of dusty papers and loading them onto donkeys. That same month the post office closed down and the money stopped arriving.

And throughout the town rumors were rife of a cruel war that would rage for years, while the stocks in the pantry dwindled. They were forced to lock Yitzhak up in his room so that he would not stuff himself with their diminishing supplies, and Sara allocated every member of the household a daily ration of one pita, a handful of rice, and a bowl of lentils. One day Yitzhak broke down the door to his room, and while she was busy hanging out the washing in the yard he stole into the pantry, tore a hole in a sack of sugar, set his mouth to the hole, and emptied the sweet stuff into his belly. The next day he did the same with a sack of lentils. They found him crouching by the sack, grinding with his strong teeth the hard green lentils that were supposed to provide a month's supply for the entire family.

The pantry emptied rapidly and Yitzhak grew thinner and thinner, as all the reserves of fat accumulated by his body dwindled away. And the skinny Pnina-Mazal, too weak to continue teaching the English class which in any case had been deserted by almost all its pupils, spent most of the day lying in bed and staring at the ceiling. Ben-Ami suffered more than anyone. He was used to dainty food and refused to eat the hard pita bread Sara baked from millet in the clay oven she fired with twigs of wood, since coal too was unobtainable. Sara would soften the bread with the tea she brewed from herbs, and try to coax him to eat it, and Ben-Ami, who had lost his gentle, placid nature, cried enough to make up for all the years when he never cried, and his belly grew bloated with hunger, his navel sticking out in the middle.

For fear of the Turks patrolling the streets and picking up the young men for forced labor in the army, Sara decided that David would spend the days hiding in the attic. And only at night, after she had locked the iron door of the house, did she allow him to come down and unite with his wife in their room. And the town of Jerusalem starved and its population dwindled. Some died of hunger, others of epidemics, many fled the dreaded conscription into the Turkish army, and others hid in attics and in the hills surrounding the town. The only people remaining in the neighborhood were the old, the women, and the children.

And the mornings brought surprises. One morning Sara woke to the sound of an axe hitting wood. A number of ragged Turkish soldiers with unkempt beards were hard at work trying to chop down the mulberry tree in her garden. The hard tree trunk submitted meekly to the blows, and the wound gaping in its side grew bigger. When it seemed to them to be hanging on by a thread, they began hurling their emaciated bodies against it, trying to fell it to the ground. But the tree clung stubbornly to life and refused to be parted from its trunk. They attacked it again with the axe, but only succeeded in blunting the blade. The defeated soldiers glared angrily at the tree, spat on the ground, and turned their attention to the vegetable beds. Sara stared at them numbly as they trampled her cherished garden, uprooting the still-green cauliflowers and devouring them voraciously together with bunches of parsley and mint.

After wiping their mouths with their filthy khaki sleeves, they went into the yard next door. Respectfully they examined the broad trunk of Esther's mulberry trunk, whose uppermost branches were tangled with those of Sara's tree, and evidently decided to leave it alone. Having failed in their efforts to lay the first mulberry tree low, they saw little chance they would succeed in overcoming its bigger brother. As soon as Esther heard them in her garden she came running out, yelling at the top of her voice and shooing them out of her vegetable beds. The shadow of a smile crossed their haggard faces as the fat woman began to chase them round her garden, brandishing a rolling pin in her hand.

Still busy chewing Esther's vegetables, two of the soldiers set about trying to catch the pair of chickens she kept in her yard. After gaining a grip on the legs of the chickens, whose screeching outdid the by now hoarse cries of their mistress, the soldiers swung their victims round their heads and then brought them down hard on the screaming Esther's head. The desperate shrieks of the chickens grew louder, and Esther's hair filled with brown and orange feathers as they flapped their wings hysterically. The terrified Esther strained her throat to renew her screams, but her voice grew weaker, and the soldiers slapped her fat buttocks, pinched her sagging breasts, and promised to return.

The next day they came back to the neighborhood, where all the doors were locked and all the windows shuttered. They kicked the door of Sara's house with their nailed boots and ordered her to open it. Sara hurried to lock the children in her room and made sure that Yitzhak was hidden in the attic. She put on her most ragged dress, smeared her face with coal dust, and poured the little oil left in the pantry over her hair. The soldiers recoiled at the sight of the dirty woman with the rat-tailed hair who opened the door to them. They pushed her aside and roared *"Akmak"* ("bread" in Turkish), charged into the kitchen, and began devouring everything in sight. When they had finished their work and left the house, the kitchen floor was covered with a thin layer of sugar ground to dust by their nailed boots. Only one tin of beans, which she had hidden under the stove, had escaped them.

⁂ ⁂ ⁂

That week Sara went to Yisseschar, the haberdasher, with a tin box in her hands. There she emptied the contents of the tin into the pillow cover he held out to her. Dozens of amulets, silver jewels, and parchment spells came spilling out. She left the shop without even bothering to count the bishliks he had thrust into her hands. She succeeded in purchasing a little rice and lentils and a small jar of milk and went home.

A few days later the food she had bought ran out, and the smell of cooking was absent from her house for many a day.

One morning an elegantly dressed man with smooth black hair combed back and anointed with oil knocked at her door. As he stood on the doorstep it seemed to Sara that it must have been his thin, hooked nose that had led him to her. With flaring, transparent nostrils he breathed in the odorless air of the kitchen, and he looked with satisfaction at the empty stove and bare kitchen. He sighed greedily, looked into Sara's eyes, and his eyes glittered with lust.

"Your reputation for being the most beautiful of the daughters of Jerusalem is a just one," he commenced.

"And who are you, sir?" she asked, full of foreboding.

"Samuel." He introduced himself with a flourish and peered over her shoulder into the dark house as if seeking something there.

"What do you want?" she asked coldly.

"Your son-in-law—David is his name if I am not mistaken—is shirking military service. If you wish, I can save his skin."

"State your price," she said shortly.

He looked into her eyes, lowered his eyes to her lips, let them slide down to her bursting breasts and massaged them with his look, fawned on her stomach, slithered down to her private parts, and concluded with her feet. Then he gazed deep into her eyes again and licked his fleshy lips crowned with a long, thin mustache, and his sinewy out-thrust neck contracted in a swallowing movement.

"Woman, you know the price."

Blushing furiously she locked the door behind him and sat down, gasping for breath. Pnina-Mazal came hurrying toward her.

"What did he want?"

"To sell me food at black-market prices," she lied.

Esther, who had witnessed the scene from her window, ran to Sara's house with her hair standing on end. "The destroyer of homes has visited you," she panted. "Be careful. He pries into people's homes and informs the authorities about men evading military service. If you didn't give him what he wanted he'll come back again."

The next day he returned with a wicker basket full of fresh pitas, bags of lentils, and vegetables.

"Your son-in-law will be saved and every day fresh supplies of food will be delivered to your house. I heard that your son is dying of starvation," he said, staring rudely at her private parts and feeling her breasts with his eyes under the flimsy material of her dress.

"I'll thank you never to come here again," she replied, pushing the basket he tried to give her away and closing the door in his face.

The next day she found the iron door wide open, with Pnina-Mazal standing in the doorway, Ben-Ami clasped in her arms, and hot tears streaming down her emaciated cheeks.

"They were here," she said between her sobs. "One of the neighbors must have betrayed David to them. The military police came. They found him, tied up his hands as if he were a dangerous criminal, and took him with them to the Kishleh jail."

Without wasting any time Sara hurried to the police station, a gold napoleon hidden under her dress.

The eyes of the station commander widened when he saw the beautiful woman standing before him. In a magnanimous gesture he refused to touch the gold coin glittering on her palm.

"Yes, you can see your son-in-law and even bring him food, but he will be sent from here to the front with the rest of the men," he said, and led Sara to the jailhouse.

David was lying on a filthy, sticky mattress, his sparse beard erect and stiff with dirt.

"How is Pnina-Mazal?" was the first question he asked.

The next day Sara arrived with Pnina-Mazal and the little food she had managed to spare from her own mouth.

David pressed against the iron bars, looked into his wife's eyes, slid his eyes over her stomach, smiled at her reassuringly, and whispered something in her ear. A blush darkened Pnina-Mazal's pale face and spread to the roots of her hair.

"What did he say to you?" asked Sara when they left.

"He told me that I was pregnant and that I would have a daughter," she said, the blush returning to her face.

Sara looked at her intently. "He's right," she said. "You are with child."

Pnina-Mazal looked at her in disbelief. "How do you know?" she asked, as if the two of them had entered into a conspiracy against her. "For six years nothing has happened. And precisely now, in wartime, and when they're taking him to the army! And besides," she added, "I'm not late and you're both wrong."

Sara did not reply, but in her heart she began to recite girls' names that would suit her first granddaughter.

A week later, on a Friday afternoon, one of the neighborhood children arrived panting at her house and told her that he had seen David being led with the other prisoners to the railway station. Sara called Pnina-Mazal, who was lying in bed and staring at the ceiling, and they stopped a wagon and rushed to the railway station. There they found him standing in a straight row with dozens of other men, some of them sick and old, while a Turkish band played them off with merry tunes as if they were on their way to get married. In the deep, jarring silence that fell when the band stopped playing rose a cry of "David!" He turned round, met Pnina-Mazal's eyes, smiled at her as if he were setting out on a holiday, and stepped onto the train.

The lights of the Sabbath candles were already flickering in the windows as they made their way home.

Their food ran out and the situation of their neighbors was no better. With nothing left in the house to eat, Sara and Pnina-Mazal went to the German army camp. There they joined the emaciated, wild-haired women watching with yearning eyes as the soldiers in their clean, pressed uniforms fed their horses oranges and sweet carrots. With the help of Pnina-Mazal as a translator, Sara offered to wash the soldiers' clothes in exchange for bread and legumes. She was not the only one. The soldiers looked at the starving women, whose ribs were showing through their threadbare cotton dresses, placed some dirt-stiff worn uniforms in their outstreched hands, and snatched them away again to the sound of loud, coarse laughter.

The uniform of one young soldier fell into Sara's lap. He did not snatch it back, and Pnina-Mazal told him in his own language that it would be returned to him, clean and pressed, the next morning. But as they were about to leave with their booty in their hands, the eyes of the camp commandant fell on Sara's lowered face. He beckoned her to approach him and Pnina-Mazal accompanied her mother with her arms around her.

Sara's eyes were transfixed by the glittering sword adorning his thick waist like a precious jewel. The officer appraised her with his pale eyes like a cattle dealer trying to guess the weight of a cow. With downcast eyes she stood before him. He took hold of her chin and raised her head roughly until her eyes were level with the splendid row of medals

and ribbons decorating his broad chest. Then he lifted her head higher
and forced her to look into his eyes. When eye contact had been
achieved he barked something at her.

"What did he say?" asked Sara.

"Come, let's go," Pnina-Mazal replied, tugging at her arm and trying to pull her away.

"I need the money, I'm prepared to do any work, just tell me what
he wants," her mother demanded.

"Let's go, it would be better to starve to death," said Pnina-Mazal.

"I'll go, but only after tell me what he said."

"He said that you're a beautiful woman and that he wants you to
come to the camp tonight and he'll give you a loaf of bread and a bag
of sugar in exchange."

Sara turned pale, looked at the officer with flashing eyes, and walked
away, her thin body supported by Pnina-Mazal.

When the last lentil in the house was gone, Yitzhak lay in his bed
too weak to say "food," and Ben-Ami was too exhausted to cry, Sara
strode resolutely to the camp. In the evening she returned, her body
crushed and broken and in her folded arms a loaf of coarse black bread,
a bag of sugar, and a few potatoes.

*   *   *

The last summer of the war was the most terrible of all. The blazing
heat lay over Jerusalem like a thick blanket and a fine white dust descended from the sky and covered the town, the hills around it, the
houses high and low, the surviving trees, the fences, the streets, the
beards of the men, and the faces of the babies; it penetrated the necks
of the women's dresses, powdering their breasts with a deathly white
dust, and made people's teeth gritty when they opened their mouths to
speak. And when they tried to strengthen their spirits with words of the
Torah, the dust penetrated their throats and made their speech hoarse
and halting. When they tried to quench their thirst with precious water
from the wells and pumps, the stinking bilge slid down their throats and
lined their stomachs with a layer of sticky mire. And whenever they
breathed the blazing air into their lungs, the dust tickled the insides of
their flaring nostrils and their thin bodies were convulsed by violent
sneezes.

In those days Sara and Pnina-Mazal were busy from morning to night sweeping the layers of dust settling over the house and searching for food. There was no coal to be had for cooking in all the town. First they burned the wooden doors of the cupboards in the alcoves of the rooms, then they burned the kitchen shelves, and when there wasn't a stick of furniture left in the house they roamed the fields gathering twigs and straw. And when they came home they picked the leaves from the mulberry tree, the wild mallow and the sorrel sprouting in the vegetable beds, and made them into thick soup and rissoles.

The food Sara brought home from the German army camp did not improve the condition of her little boy. Ben-Ami lay supine on his bed and mumbled the word "food," like his brother Yitzhak. The smiles that had once wreathed his face disappeared, and it now resembled a twisted mask, like the face of a shriveled old woman for whom the Angel of Death lay waiting in a dark corner. Sara and Pnina-Mazal stood over him every evening, pulling faces and making funny noises, until he consented to open his dry mouth and swallow a few crumbs of millet bread soaked in soup.

Double-chinned Yitzhak was to be found gnawing the bark of the surviving trees, licking the grass of the fields, sticking straws into ant holes, chasing the ants out of their dens, picking them up one by one, popping them into his mouth, and smacking his lips with relish. When he was finished with the ants, so the neighbors said, he would turn his attention to the sage bushes and finish his repast with a bunch of bitter leaves. If he was lucky and a grasshopper, a locust, or a beetle fell into his hands, the noise of the insect's armor snapping as he pulverized it between his teeth could be heard from afar. Sometimes he went to the nearby Arab village, and with cries of *"Majnoon, majnoon"* (madman) pursuing him, he would stand in the doorways of the mud huts, point to his mouth, and demand: "Food."

Sometimes he would encounter the few flocks that had remained to the villagers on his way. The moment his fair head appeared on the horizon, the little shepherds would flee, kicking up a great commotion and placing their entire flock at his disposal. Then he would scan the animals for a black nanny-goat with a baby kid by its side. And if he found one, he would run up to it, and while it bleated and stamped with its slender hooves he would lift it in the air and raise it above his head, as if it weighed nothing at all. Then he would throw back his head, clamp his mouth around its teat, and suck for all he was worth.

When its udder was dry, he would drop it to the ground from his great height, where it would bleat with the pain of the blow, and limp back to its abandoned kid. The shepherds knew that the kid butting its head in vain at its mother's empty teats and trying to extract a drop of milk from them would go hungry that day. And they said that after Yitzhak left the flock with his belly full, there would be deep, bloody holes on the necks of the exhausted goats, as if they had been pierced by a pair of blood-sucking fangs. In the evening he would go home with his stomach full of milk in which floated bits of grass, bark, ants, and grass-hoppers.

The more the flesh of his brother dwindled, the redder Yitzhak's cheeks grew, and his fair skin was stretched as firm and taut over his bones as that of an athlete who spends his days cultivating his body. Davida too provided Yitzhak with food. On her weekly visits she would bring him a nibbled pita made of millet, or a handful of raisins that had shriveled of their own accord on the tendrils of the vines. Sometimes she brought a few figs that she had succeeded in picking laboriously from the top of the big fig tree on the outskirts of the Arab village. He would eat everything she brought, and Sara didn't have the heart to ask her to share her bounty with little Ben-Ami, too, who lay languishing in his bed.

When Sara looked at her children in the evenings, it seemed to her that of them all the one least affected by the famine was the pregnant Pnina-Mazal. Her budding breasts had rounded, her belly had swelled, and there was a healthy rosiness in her cheeks. Pnina-Mazal delighted in her pregnancy and counted the months that passed in sweet expec-tation of the birth of her baby and the return of her husband from the war.

And death struck all the houses of the neighborhood. First to die were the toothless old people and infants, who could not chew the coarse food, and after them death sank its sharp fangs into the necks of the children and the adults, and Sara's house was not spared either.

"He's dead," Pnina-Mazal screamed at Sara when she came back exhausted from the German army camp. "I tried to feed him and he spat it out, made a rattling noise, and gave up the ghost."

Swaying on her feet and supported by her neighbors Sara entered the room that had been visited by death. Ben-Ami lay on his bed. His arms and legs stuck out from his body shriveled as dried figs on a string;

his mouth was wide open, as if he were trying to drink in one more gulp of air; and his eyes sunk in their dark sockets were open. Sara recoiled.

Her son's face looked like the death mask of his grandmother Mazal. She sank sobbing to the floor, and the sound of her terrible screams went on ringing in the ears of her neighbors all night long.

"He's better off dead than alive," spiteful tongues gossiped. "What kind of a life could he have with a father who isn't there, a whore for a mother, and a crazy brother."

He was buried on the Mount of Olives, next to the fresh graves of the many other residents of the town whose strength had failed them, and she visited his grave every day, decorating the loose soil with the wild chrysanthemums and grasses she picked on the way. She stopped going to the German camp, and roamed the streets knocking on doors and asking for work in exchange for a slice of bread and a handful of lentils. With her tall stature and beautiful face she looked like a princess fallen on hard times, and the residents of the wealthy neighborhoods didn't have the heart to employ her on menial domestic chores and sent her away with a few scraps of food.

And disaster continued to plague her. On the day she saw Pnina-Mazal waiting for her on the doorstep with her belly about to burst, she knew that David too was dead. They received no official notification, but a solider who returned from the front with a leg amputated told Pnina-Mazal that her husband had not even had time to fight. As soon as they arrived in Constantinople he contracted smallpox. His whole body was covered with pustules, and he lay screaming in terror and scratching his body until it bled. They dumped him in a military hospital, and there, on a filthy, blood-soaked mattress, among the soldiers with amputated legs and arms and bandaged heads, he departed this world. They buried him in haste and at night, in a large mass grave.

*   *   *

During the seven days of mourning Pnina-Mazal beat her belly as if to hasten the birth of her son or to kill him with her fists, and the sound of her weeping kept the neighbors from their in any case restless sleep. At the end of the shiva Sara went out into the garden, and as she bent down over the barren vegetable beds tears poured from her eyes and heartbreaking moans burst from her lips.

A faint moaning echo suddenly rose from somewhere near the house. Sara pricked up her ears and moaned again. And again there was a deep moan, as if some clown were hiding in her garden and mimicking her mockingly. Sara kept quiet and the moans increased. She ran round the house, and under the mulberry tree she saw her, a fat Arab peasant woman squatting on a filthy sack, as if she needed to void her bowels, her dress hitched up round her waist and her heavy stomach rising and falling with every groan she uttered. As soon as her eyes fell on Sara a sharp scream burst from her throat, as if she had seen a devil standing in front of her and threatening to take her life. Together with the scream, which seemed to go on forever, a strong stream of water broke out of her body, after which a baby's head emerged between her legs. Sara ran into the house, poured hot water from the kettle into a basin, grabbed a kitchen knife, took a clean sheet from the cupboard, and hurried outside. At that very moment she heard similar groans coming from inside the house. She turned on her heel and ran in alarm to Pnina-Mazal's room.

Wide-eyed, Pnina-Mazal stared at her mother standing disheveled in the doorway with the kitchen knife in her hand, like some Lilith threatening to cut open her stomach and steal her fetus. She screamed as if possessed and looked wildly at her mother. Paralyzed by her daughter's demented stare Sara stood there with the knife in her hand and saw the dam open and the warm waters come bubbling out, gathering in a pool around Pnina-Mazal and soaking her clothes. The contractions began immediately, convulsing her body and squeezing agonized groans from her throat.

The baby slid out, thin and fragile, her head covered with stiff, bristling red hair. The moment she emerged into the world she opened her mouth in a loud, trumpeting cry, as if to announce: Here I am. Alarmed by the violent cries of the newborn baby, Sara roused herself from her paralysis and with the kitchen knife that was in her hand cut the cord of life connecting mother to daughter. Then she inserted her finger into the baby's mouth to clear it of phlegm, and in exchange received a bite that left two bloody dents in her finger. Too excited to pay any attention she wrapped the baby in the sheet and hurried outside to see to the second delivery.

But only a pool of water with blood on its edges remained. The mother had vanished, with her naked baby clamped to her nipple, and the afterbirth bundled into a sack and placed in the wicker basket on her head, together with the medicinal herbs she was taking to the market.

Sara went back into the house, picked up her granddaughter, cooed at her clenched fists, and dipped her in the basin of warm water she had prepared for the vanished Arab baby. As she was washing off the oily layer that made the little body as slippery as soap, the baby seized her hand in her mouth, and left two more slits in it. In her astonishment Sara let her drop, and she sank into the water and popped up again like a cork, her gaping mouth emitting a stream of soapy water between the two pointed teeth sticking out of her gums.

Pnina-Mazal smiled for the first time when Sara placed her freshly bathed daughter in her arms. The infant rooted for the nipple with her nose, and began sucking delicately from her mother's bursting breasts, as if afraid of hurting her with the teeth she had grown in the darkness of the womb.

"This child will bring the Messiah," Pnina-Mazal said to Sara, looking at the baby as if she refused to believe the evidence of her eyes. "Redemption is at hand," she exulted as she looked at the crumpled little face. "We'll call her Geula." (*Geula* means "redemption" in Hebrew.)

"They do say that a girl born with teeth will marry the Messiah," Sara confirmed, touching the sharp teeth in the little mouth cautiously, as if afraid of receiving another bite.

Chapter Thirteen

Tidings of imminent redemption came on baby Geula's very first day. Rumors of the defeat of the Turks and Germans next to Beersheba began to arrive in the town, and in the wake of the rumors the horseless carriages of the Germans were to be seen driving away with a dreadful noise, leaving clouds of dust behind them. And in the wake of the German carriages the Turkish cavalry galloped down the streets, leaving Jerusalem in a turmoil, with everyone waiting for the English Messiah to come and redeem the town from its terrible suffering. With the sound of cannon fire rattling the windows and black iron birds circling the sky like vultures seeking their prey, Pnina-Mazal was jubilant. "The English are coming!" she cried.

Sara, who was always suspicious of her love of the English, paid no attention to her exultant cries and instead listened to the dire predictions of the neighbors, who said that Jerusalem would be smashed to smithereens, the mills destroyed, the wells poisoned, and the people of Zion cast into the darkest dungeons of the prison houses.

On the Saturday night preceding the redemption the earth trembled. The Turkish cannons thundered without a pause, and with every shell that exploded Pnina-Mazal, clasping Geula to her bosom, became more radiant, murmuring to herself: "Redemption is at hand, redemption is at hand." And as if the noise of the cannons weren't enough, the worst storm in living memory chose that day to burst upon the town. The noise of the thunder rivaled the noise of the cannon fire, and fierce flashes of lightning lit up the sky, until it split open and flooded the parched and dusty town. And the louder the noise outside grew, the more the sky shuddered and the earth shook, the more Pnina-Mazal's heart filled with joy. She pressed her nose to the window shuddering with the blast of the explosions and rattling with the deafening noise of the thunder, and tears of happiness ran down her cheeks and wet the inside of the windowpane as well. Only after midnight did the stillness of death descend on the town, as if the thunder and the cannons had declared a truce.

Then the sound of the retreating army was heard in a soft shuffle of hasty feet, shod in rags or whatever substitutes for shoes the men could lay their hands on. By morning the sound of the soldiers' footsteps was stilled, and the rumor spread through the town that the Turkish army had surrendered to the British army on the hill of the village of Lifta. Then the emaciated figures of the population of Jerusalem began to emerge slowly from their houses. First they stumbled out like rats peeping from their holes and blinking their blind eyes in the light of the sun. Then they gathered courage and walked with their heads high down the streets scattered with rags and human remains, growing braver as they made their way to the Turkish government offices in the Kishleh. Like a swarm of locusts they descended on the building. They invaded the rooms, broke down the doors, flung the papers off the wooden desks, tore up the floor tiles, dug into the plaster of the walls, exposed copper pipes and ripped them from their places. When nothing was left and the building was naked and bare, they climbed on the roof and tore up the red roof tiles. After that they clustered in the streets, delighting in their freedom to stand together in a crowd, shoulder to shoulder with their fellows. They were no longer beholden to the Turkish laws, which forbade gatherings of more than three people in the streets of their town. All who defied this law did so at their peril, for the Turkish police would beat them with batons, search their pockets, rob them of their last pennies, and send them with aching backs and empty pockets to jail.

Leaving Yitzhak in the faithful care of Davida, Sara and Pnina-Mazal with the tiny baby pressed to her bosom joined the crowd at the Jaffa

Gate to see the entry of the God-sent English Messiah into the heart of Jerusalem.

"The General was full of light," Pnina-Mazal said later. "The sun brightened his hair and the flashing of the bronze buttons on his uniform hurt my eyes. On foot the General entered the gates of the Old City, and there, on the steps of the citadel, he read us our rights in eight languages, and the words he spoke in one language fit the words of the language before it like a glove."

And a guard of honor stood around General Allenby. There were dark-skinned soldiers whose white teeth flashed in their black faces, and others wearing short plaid skirts. Soldiers belonging to other regiments wore broad-brimmed hats on their heads, and they all spoke English in different accents, and Pnina-Mazal, straining her ears to hear their whispers, understood them all.

Happy and content, Sara hugged her daughter and her granddaughter and gazed at the scene in front of her. Suddenly she felt giddy as the world before her eyes was bathed in blue. Overcome by weakness, she leaned on her daughter as a strong hand reached out and gripped her elbow. She found herself gazing into Edward's eyes as he stood before her armed with his tripod and black camera.

"I've come back," he said, and then recoiled as he saw Pnina-Mazal and the red-haired baby in her arms. And he immediately resumed his place by the side of the General, leaving Sara with the painful longings that racked her body.

And when they walked home, they saw lights flickering in all the windows. The first candle of Hanukkah had been lit in all the houses of Jerusalem, the first candle of redemption, and Sara began to believe in her daughter's prophecies. For with her own eyes she had seen her redemption today, and looked it in the eye.

✳ ✳ ✳

When the two women came home exhausted from the citadel, they found Yitzhak and Davida sitting on the big brass bed, holding hands, Davida's green eyes looking deeply into Yitzhak's blank ones. On his face was an expression of satisfaction, as if he had just polished off a rich repast of chickens dripping fat and mounds of sweet rice. Sara stood in the doorway breathing hard.

"I'm getting married," announced Davida in the silence that had fallen in the room, as if she were addressing a hall full of people, and she avoided Sara's eyes.

"Congratulations," Sara said, and a feeling of relief spread through her. "Who's the bridegroom? Do I know him?"

Davida giggled. "Yitzhak," she said without batting an eye, and she planted a kiss on his lips as he tightened his grip on her hand.

Sara sat down heavily on the bed next to them and looked at her son. His eyes had a strange, different look, and his face was shining. She had never seen him like this before. For a moment it seemed to her that his expressionless face showed signs of animation, and that he was about to engage her in conversation.

"But he isn't capable of getting married," Sara said, with the taste of the dust that had disappeared from the streets of the town on her tongue, as if it had returned to take refuge in her mouth.

"I've chosen him to be my husband," Davida declared firmly. "And I've given the matter a lot of thought," she added, as if to justify her choice.

"But he isn't capable of supporting you," Sara tried again.

"I've found a solution to that too. Tomorrow I'm going to start looking after the children in the kindergarten, and my salary will be enough to support us both," Davida said confidently. "And apart from that, I'm sure you'll be happy to have him continue living here, and me with him."

"And the children you'll have, what will happen to them?" Sara wrung her hands.

"We'll worry about that when they arrive," Davida replied absentmindedly and pressed Yitzhak's body to hers in a tight hug. Her arms were too short to encompass his great girth.

Sara looked at them and thought she saw her son closing his eyes and basking in the unfamiliar pleasure spreading through his limbs.

"And how will he consecrate the marriage?" she asked.

"With a ring," Davida replied, and burst out laughing.

"And what will you talk to him about?"

"Since when does a wife have to talk to her husband?" she replied with a question.

Sara, feeling utterly exhausted, called Pnina-Mazal and asked her to talk to her brother.

"He wants Davida," she reported to her mother later. "And we should be delighted that he's found himself a wife."

"And from now on I have another mouth to feed," Sara said resentfully. But she decided not to interfere in her son's decision.

❋   ❋   ❋

Davida's parents were no longer alive, and so Sara found herself making her way through the alleys of the Old City to Mrs. Nahmias's mikvah. Davida took off her clothes with open enjoyment and without any hesitation and with light, dancing steps hopped into the pool. At the command of the rabbi's wife she sank several times into the black water, her hair sinking with her, and emerged clean, pure, and ready for her wedding night.

Under the hastily erected canopy she was awaited by Yitzhak, worn out by the daylong fast imposed on him and muttering the word "food." His fair hair was combed and parted down the middle of his head, and his new suit lent him the look of a European aristocrat on a slumming expedition. Davida stood festive beside him, a bunch of white lilies in her hands. Her thin body was squeezed into Pnina-Mazal's wedding gown, despite Sara's disapproval and protests.

"She wore this dress to marry David, and he's dead. It will bring you bad luck. I'll sew you a new one," she said, trying to dissuade Davida from wearing the dress.

"I'll get married in this one and this one only," pronounced Davida.

To the sound of sniggers from the few guests gathered round, Davida put the ring on her own finger, repeated the rabbi's words, and consecrated herself to Yitzhak in a clear, firm voice. Then she took the glass of wine, sipped it, and handed it to Yitzhak. Yitzhak held the glass in both hands, gulped down all the wine with a deafening noise, threw it to the ground, and demanded food. Gently Davida lifted his foot, placed it on the glass, and pressed it down hard until the glass cracked.

"Mazal tov," the congregation called weakly.

When the ceremony was over Davida linked arms with her elegant husband, circulated among the guests, and fed him tidbits from the table like a bird feeding its famished young.

All that night Sara never slept a wink. Even though she tried to shut her ears, she could not help hearing the heavy grunts of her son and the squeals of delight with which Davida responded to him. The next day they stayed in bed, and Sara brought them breakfast on a tray. Davida noticed Yitzhak's hand stealing toward the fresh pitas and slapped it lightly. Daintily she split the top pita, broke off a little piece, and popped it into his open mouth, after which she planted a kiss on his lips.

After spending a week in bed, Davida began making her way weakly to work at her new job, leaving Yitzhak cosily ensconced in bed, waiting for her return. When she came home she would nibble at the food prepared by Sara, take off her clothes, and join her husband in bed. And again Yitzhak's grunts would invade the house, accompanied by squeals of delight and deep, throaty moans from his wife. Davida's thin body grew thinner, and black circles darkened the hollows under her eyes, as if someone had maliciously painted them with kohl.

The day she discovered that she was with child, she stopped sharing her husband's bed, and he would wait for her in vain, lying on his back between the quilts and the pillows. After she moved her bedding into Pnina-Mazal and baby Geula's room, he would stand at the closed door, his tongue lolling from his dribbling mouth, with the look of a beaten dog in his eyes. During this period her small breasts grew round and heavy and the sharp angles of her body were padded with flesh.

And it was as if all the troubles in the world had descended on Davida. Sara would find her dissolved in tears, and when she made her bed in the morning the pillow was soaked. It seemed as if the baby in her womb had breached a dam of tears within her and filled her with an incomprehensible sorrow.

When Sara tried to talk to her and find out what the matter was, she would shrug her shoulders and snap, "Nothing," and put an end to the conversation. Tactfully Sara and Pnina-Mazal tried to urge her to return to her husband's bed, but she stubbornly refused, and avoided any contact with the father of her unborn child.

*   *   *

About six months after Geula's birth, an event occurred that changed Pnina-Mazal's life. The polished English officer stood in the doorway as if struck dumb, staring at Sara. Her eyes opened wide in astonishment, blurring the network of fine wrinkles surrounding them. It wasn't every day that a tall English officer in an elegant uniform knocked at her door. He cleared his throat, straightened his uniform, adjusted the angle of the hat on his head, opened his mouth, and failed to find the right words. Sara invited him to come inside. The officer took off his hat, bowed his head politely, and followed her into the house.

As if she had been entertaining English officers all her life, she seated him on the sofa in the front room and went to look for Pnina-Mazal, who was hanging out Geula's diapers in the yard.

Pnina-Mazal handed her baby to her mother, tidied her clothes, tightened the kerchief over her hair, which had begun to grow, and went into the house. The Englishman, sitting straight and stiff as a ramrod on the sofa, rose hurriedly to his feet when the two women entered the room. Pnina-Mazal greeted him in his language. It seemed to Sara that a look of relief spread over his face, and after drinking a glass of cold water he entered into a long conversation with Pnina-Mazal. Pnina-Mazal had always loved talking English, and the longer he spoke to her the more her face glowed. Every now and then she gave voice to a contented chuckle, and immediately resumed her serious expression. It seemed to Sara that she agreed with everything he said. When the officer parted from them with a slight bow and a click of his heels, Sara stared at her daughter's exultant face.

"What did he want with you?" she asked even before he had turned his back and walked out of the door.

"Edward sent him."

At the sound of the name Sara turned pale.

"He came to offer me work," Pnina-Mazal quickly explained.

"Where?" whispered Sara.

"Edward recommended me," she repeated slowly, as if the mention of his name had rendered her mother incapable of taking anything in. "They need a translator fluent in English and the local languages."

"And what did you tell him?"

"I told him yes. We need the money, and he said he would pay me generously."

"And what about Geula?"

"We'll give her to the Arab woman from the village to nurse, the one who gave birth the same day I did. Her breasts are bursting with milk. Esther told me she came back to the neighborhood looking for Jewish babies whose mothers' milk had run dry, so that she could nurse them and earn a few pennies."

"I have no intention of letting my granddaughter roll around in a filthy peasant's hut together with the sheep and the goats," Sara heard herself announcing. "And think of all the fleas and the lice the place must be swarming with," she added.

"We can ask her to bring her baby here, and in the evening, when I come back, she can go home."

Sara made no reply and busied herself with the dough she was rolling out for pitas.

With Geula clasped in her arms Pnina-Mazal kept at her mother all day, until Sara unwillingly gave in, and together they set out for the nearby village to pay their respects to the Arab woman. The village children, barefoot and filthy-faced, accompanied by swarms of glittering green flies, ran happily in front of them to show them where Fatma lived. The dirt path that led to the house was trodden firm by innumerable footsteps and adorned by the small, pointed hoofprints of the goats and by their round black turds. The two women bent down to go through the door and blinked their eyes. Their pupils dilated to adjust themselves to the chilly darkness of the interior after the dazzling sunlight outside.

From the dark recesses of the hut a short, fat woman with a pleasant expression hurried toward them. When she saw who her visitors were she wiped her hands on the gray apron tied round her waist, hastened up to Sara, took hold of her hand, and kissed it. Sara's eyes, having accustomed themselves to the cold darkness of the hut, scanned the room mercilessly. In one corner stood a pile of colored mattresses, set one upon the other with military precision, with a number of noisy, black-faced infants jumping merrily on top of it. They climbed up the mattresses as if they were a soft ladder leading them to their heart's desire, jumped with suicidal leaps to the floor, and clambered up again. Fatma silenced them with an *"Uskut,"* which did not appear to make much of an impression on them. They froze for a moment on top of the heap, giggled, and continued their game.

Sara went on scanning the room with prying eyes. There was not a goat or a sheep to be seen, nor even a broody hen. The floor, which was paved with big stones, had just been washed, and it shone at her with a cool, welcoming wetness. Next to the window stood a baby's cradle made of iron, which rocked on curved legs. Plump hands poked out of it and waved cheerfully in the air, accompanied by the soft gurgle of a well-fed baby singing a private lullaby to himself before he went to sleep. Fatma hurried to the big clay water jar standing sweating next to the door and offered them chipped tin mugs, cool to the touch, full of cold water. While Pnina-Mazal sipped her water and Fatma hurried to the smoking clay oven outside and pulled out thin pitas, Sara examined the thick walls enclosing her, which were painted a fresh turquoise, and sensed the minty taste of the color on her tongue.

Fatma quickly came back and laid before them on the bench olives, a big, steaming pita that had been folded in four, and a slab of salty goat cheese, apologizing as she did so for the modesty of the refreshments.

Without beating about the bush Pnina-Mazal turned to her and explained in Arabic the purpose of their visit.

Fatma's eyes widened in delight and she kissed the hand of her benefactor.

"Ever since the death of my husband I have been struggling to support my five children. There is only a year between them, and they are all boys," she said proudly. Without being asked she hurried to the cradle in the corner of the room and picked up the sleeping baby. Cradling him in her arms in front of the two women, she unwrapped his swaddling clothes and proudly displayed his plump body. Muhammad's legs kicked in glee at the unexpected nakedness that had fallen to his lot, and Sara felt a pang as she compared his fat, juicy legs to the skinny, transparent limbs of her granddaughter.

With her sharp instincts Fatma placed the heavy, kicking baby in Sara's lap and pulled her black dress with its embroidered bodice over her head. The women's eyes widened in wonder. Above her white cotton bloomers hung two enormous cone-shaped breasts equipped with stiff black nipples, which stuck out in the cool air of the room like two spears threatening to pierce the eyes of the beholder. Smilingly she held out her breasts, like a peasant woman in the market displaying two bursting watermelons to the shoppers. Then she asked Pnina-Mazal to feel her breast. Obediently Pnina-Mazal tried to take hold of the breast looming up in front of her, and found that one hand was not enough to encompass its girth. She enlisted her second hand too, and enviously felt the weight of the Arab woman's breast.

"I only finished feeding Muhammad a few minutes ago," Fatma said, and she retreated slowly to the end of the room with her breasts swaying in front of her, facing them all the time as if afraid they might run away if she turned her broad back to them.

When she reached the wall she leaned against it with her back and lightly pressed the base of her breast. A strong jet of steaming milk burst from the prickly nipple and fell at the feet of her guests in a white puddle, which gave off a sweet, dense smell. The milk went on streaming from her breast even when she let go of it.

"I have to do this every day," she apologized, but there was a note of pride in her voice. "Otherwise Muhammad would choke on the stream of milk and it would make him cough and burst out of his nose too," she added with a smile, taking the whimpering baby back to his cradle. "Don't worry," she added, "Allah has blessed me with enough milk to satisfy a whole village full of babies."

She wriggled back into her black dress, squeezing her enormous bosom into the embroidered bodice, where a wet stain appeared and spread to her waist, ran down to the hem of her dress, and collected in a puddle at her feet. Leaving a trail of little white puddles behind her she went up to the washing line next to the cradle and took down a cloth, which she pushed down the neck of her dress to her dripping breasts.

An expression of gratification spread over her face. "The thought of a new baby to suckle is making my breasts drip," she explained apologetically, and added: "When will you bring him to me?"

"It's a little girl," said Pnina-Mazal, who had not yet recovered from the sight of the wet-nurse's breasts.

"As long as they don't fall in love with each other," chuckled the wet-nurse, and immediately took fright at her boldness. "They will be brother and sister in my milk, and she will be like my daughter in every respect," she solemnly declared.

"I will be starting work next week, and then you will have to come to our house every morning," said Pnina-Mazal.

Fatma's face fell, and the stream of milk stopped. "And who will take care of Muhammad?" she asked weakly.

"Bring him with you," Pnina-Mazal offered generously.

"And who will look after the other four boys and feed them?" Fatma demanded bleakly.

Here Sara intervened. "Geula can stay in Fatma's house. I can't see any reason why not, and you can bring her here in the automobile that will take you to the office, and fetch her again at the end of the day."

Pnina-Mazal looked at her mother incredulously.

"And what about the dirt, the goats, the fleas, and the lice you talked about before we came?" she asked her in a whisper, in Hebrew.

"I've examined the house and there's nothing to worry about. She's a good woman, her baby is well fed and well taken care of, and the house is clean."

Pnina-Mazal looked at her with a hurt expression, as if her mother were abandoning her only granddaughter.

"I'll have to think about it," she said faintly.

"If you have any other solution I'd be glad to hear it. As long as you're determined to go out to work, you have to find the best solution for Geula. In my opinion, you should stay home with her until she grows up, and in the meantime we'll find some other way to make ends meet."

Pnina-Mazal looked at her suspiciously, afraid that she would try to prevent her from going out to work, and told Fatma that she would let her know her answer soon.

The next morning she presented herself at Fatma's door and announced that next Monday she would bring Geula to her.

⁎　⁎　⁎

On Monday morning the long black car stopped at the end of the street and blew its horn twice. Pnina-Mazal emerged from the house in a new suit, carrying Geula in one hand and a bundle of diapers in the other. The driver opened his eyes in astonishment, and before he could open his mouth she ordered him to drive to the Arab village.

The car bouncing over the stones on the dirt road sent up a thick cloud of dust, covering the train of urchins running behind it in a layer of white. Some of them, whose faces Pnina-Mazal could see clearly through the window, succeeded in hanging on to the rear mudguard before they fell back again and resumed their pursuit, their thick-soled feet kicking up little puffs of dust in their wake. Accompanied by an entourage of small children, Pnina-Mazal got out of the car and walked up to Fatma's door, her tight skirt shortening her steps.

The floor had just been washed, and a smell of soap lingered in the room. Next to Muhammad's cradle, whose occupant was waving his plump, dimpled fists in the air, stood a new iron cradle. Pnina-Mazal examined the puffy mattress and saw that the material was new and shining. Gently Fatma took her baby from her hands, and immediately noticed the pitifully thin, stiltlike legs.

"She has two teeth already," Pnina-Mazal warned the wet-nurse. "She was born with them."

Fatma laughed incredulously, clucked pityingly, undid the buttons of her blouse, and offered her nipple to the baby's lips. A warm smell of milk rose from her breast and Geula inclined her red head toward it.

Without the kind of games she played with her mother, the baby took the stiff nipple between her lips and sucked noisily, waving her hands contentedly to and fro. On her face was an expression of pure pleasure, which Pnina-Mazal had never seen there before. She felt a stab of envy, but it disappeared when the baby began to choke on the abundant stream filling her mouth, making gurgling sounds in her throat and spraying the milk in all directions.

"Never mind," Fatma quickly reassured Pnina-Mazal, who tried to tear the baby from her arms. "She has to get used to the stream. My Muhammad had problems at the beginning too. Before the day is out she'll learn to use her mouth and lips to regulate the flow," she said and pressed the baby against the cleavage between her breasts, where she groped blindly for the new fount of plenty that had come her way, and stuck her mouth to the nipple like a leech. Pnina-Mazal waited patiently until Geula's stomach grew round and the nipple slipped from her mouth. Fatma touched the baby's sharp teeth wonderingly, allowed her mother to cuddle her on her shoulder to burp her, and then set her gently down in her cradle.

Before she left the house for the waiting car, it seemed to Pnina-Mazal that she saw Muhammad, who had woken up the meantime, fix his eyes darkly on Geula's white face. She quickly banished the disturbing thoughts from her mind and sat down next to the driver.

Before he had time to start the car, Fatma appeared in the doorway and waved her arms. She hurried heavily to Pnina-Mazal and pressed a bunch of dried sage into her hand.

"Put this in your tea," she whispered in her ear, as if afraid her words would reach the stranger's ears. "It will dry up your milk. Why should you suffer?" she added.

Pnina-Mazal hesitated, but when she thought of her breasts leaking inopportunely and shamefully at the office, she thanked her and took the herbs.

In the evening, at the end of her first day in the office, she returned to the village. The driver, after dropping the other passengers off and remaining alone with her, turned on the headlamps of his car. The lamps illuminated the rutted road before them in a beam of light that brought the urchins running out of their houses to escort them. When they arrived at the house she found Fatma sitting in the light of the oil lamp, naked to the waist, cradling two infants in her arms, one whose head was crowned with a soft, shining black forelock, and the other whose spiky red hair stuck out in all directions. They had their mouths clamped to their respective nipples and were sucking greedily. Their hands, which were waving with spasms of pleasure at their sides, kept touching each other's bodies, and it seemed to Pnina-Mazal that they were dancing together. Gently Fatma removed the open mouths dripping with milk from her breasts and smiled at Pnina-Mazal. Only then did Pnina-Mazal realize that although Fatma was years younger than she, she was almost completely toothless.

"Each of them chose a breast," she said. "The baby girl chose the breast that covers the heart. I tried to give her Muhammad's breast and she spat it out," she added with an ingratiating smile, handing Pnina-Mazal a pile of freshly laundered diapers.

Pnina-Mazal took Geula in her arms, and she could have sworn that the day spent fastened to Fatma's nipple had already put flesh on her bones.

⁎   ⁎   ⁎

At home Sara was waiting for her with a hot meal on the table.

"How was it at the office?" she asked curiously.

"And you don't ask about Geula?" demanded Pnina-Mazal, insulted.

"I know that everything's all right," she said, without telling her that she had spent hours at Fatma's house inspecting everything she did.

"After I give birth and go back to work, perhaps a similar arrangement can be made for me," said Davida in a pampered tone, stroking her slightly rounded belly. "I'll have to go back to work, because who will take care of me?" she added with the note of complaint that had invaded her voice ever since she found out that she was pregnant.

Sara preferred to ignore the rhetorical question, and Pnina-Mazal gritted her teeth and looked hard at Yitzhak.

"Yitzhak would be happy if you returned to his bed," she said shortly, after she had finished talking to Yitzhak with her eyes.

"And what will happen to the fetus?" Davida's eyes widened in self-pity. "He wants me all night, every night."

"Plenty of intercourse enriches an embryo's blood," Pnina-Mazal said, remembering with longing the sleepless nights she had spent with her husband. "And you can thank God that you've got a husband," she added in a venomous whisper.

Davida, whose eyes would fill with tears on the slightest provocation ever since her pregnancy began, pushed her plate away and rushed to her room, from which the sounds of her sobbing reverberated throughout the house.

After the sobs had subsided and Sara had taken Yitzhak to his room and soothed him with kind words, she was ready to hear about Pnina-Mazal's experiences on her first day at work.

"The building of the Governor's offices is like the Tower of Babel, and it's my job to introduce order into all the languages before they start fighting and killing each other," Pnina-Mazal said. "After I translated documents the Governor calls 'Proclamation' into Hebrew, Arabic, French, and Russian, he asked me to come and translate for him at a meeting he had called."

"What did you translate for him?" Sara asked curiously.

Pnina-Mazal blushed faintly and continued: "At the meeting there were Jews, Christians, Muslims, Armenians, and—"

"But what did you translate today in the Proclamation?" Sara asked again.

Pnina-Mazal took a deep breath, avoided meeting her mother's eyes, and said, "It was an official announcement about brothels."

"And what did it say?"

"I don't remember. You can read it tomorrow. It will be pasted up all over town."

"How many languages did you say you translated the announcement into?" Sara inquired.

"Four," she replied obediently.

"And how is it that after translating it into four languages you don't remember what was written there?" Sara persisted.

" 'Heavy fines will be imposed on anyone soliciting men, especially members of the armed forces, by word or gesture, and the activities of prostitutes will be confined to specified locations,' " she recited.

"What locations?" Sara asked.

"Nahalat Shiva and the Shlomo Milner quarter next to Meah Shearim. Any prostitute caught plying her trade outside those places will be put in jail for a month and fined ten Egyptian pounds."

Sara giggled, trying to imagine a row of prostitutes standing in the doorways of the houses in Nahalat Shiva, all powdered and painted and dolled up to the nines, with the respectable residents of the quarter stealing past them like thieves in the night. She laughed aloud as she imagined how the residents of Nahalat Shiva, who considered themselves so superior, would be forced to watch the abominations taking place right under their noses.

Sara detached herself from the scenes floating in front of her eyes and asked her daughter to tell her about the meeting called by the Governor.

"The Mayor was there, the mufti, rabbis, church dignitaries from the Franciscans, the Armenians and the Italians, and also representatives of the Arabs and the Americans—"

"Who was the American?" Sara interrupted her.

"We don't know him," Pnina-Mazal hastily reassured her mother. "He's new in town. Since there was such a confusing medley of tongues, and I and one other translator had to cope with all of them, it was decided to conduct the meeting in French, and I translated everything for the English speakers, including the conversations being conducted around the table in Arabic, Armenian, Hebrew, and French."

"And what did they discuss?" Sara asked, as curiously as if the decisions made there would have a decisive influence on her own personal life.

"They set up an association on behalf of Jerusalem to deal with the affairs of the city," Pnina-Mazal said with undisguised pride at her important role in the life of the town.

＊   ＊   ＊

Loud screams coming from the room Pnina-Mazal shared with Davida interrupted their conversation. They rushed to the room in alarm, and there, in the gloom, they saw Yitzhak crouching over the screaming

Davida, his backside rising and falling above her body in a rhythm unique to him. The shrieks of the terrified Davida, who did not notice the women rushing to her rescue, gave way to squeals of delight, and she crossed her legs on her husband's back, adjusting the movements of her pelvis to the rhythm he dictated. Her moans rose to a crescendo in time to Yitzhak's grunts, and when it was all over, and his penetrating thrusts were stilled, she stroked his sweating face and wiped his drooling mouth.

The two women, who had been standing rooted to the spot, tiptoed out of the room. That night Pnina-Mazal slept with Geula in Yitzhak and Davida's bed, while they pleasured each other on hers.

The next morning Davida greeted them with sparkling eyes and announced that she would never neglect her husband again, and she stole a fond look at his face as he sat staring at some invisible point on the wall, while an expression reserved for very special moments of grace spread over her face.

Chapter Fourteen

Pnina-Mazal spent more and more time at work, and sometimes, when she was obliged to remain at the office until the small hours of the morning, she did not bother to collect Geula from Fatma's house but left her there all night long. On Saturdays and Sundays, when she was off duty, she tried to quiet her conscience by playing with the child and taking her for walks in the fields, teaching her about the plants, the butterflies, and the little animals they met on their way. Geula, who had already learned to walk, and whose body had rounded and grown broad and strong, insisted on speaking to her mother in Arabic, while Pnina-Mazal made determined efforts to return her to Hebrew.

The day she came back from work and found Geula and Muhammad wrapped in each other's arms, murmuring to each other in a language known only to them, she gave Fatma notice that the child had to be weaned. The Arab woman's eyes filled with tears and the milk burst from her left breast in a strong jet that hit Pnina-Mazal and wet her dress. Filled with revulsion she ran to the water jar and tried to remove the milk stain. The stain spread wetly over the front of her dress and a nauseatingly sweet smell of milk filled her nostrils.

"There's no choice in the matter," she said to the weeping Fatma.

"She has to be weaned. She's already walking and talking, and you can't go on breast-feeding her forever."

"But I'm still breast-feeding Muhammad," she tried to persuade her. "And I shall go on doing so for two more years at least. Don't take her away from me," she begged, "she's happy here, and from the day she arrived she hasn't had a day's sickness and she's grown big and fat."

Pnina-Mazal hardened her heart even though she secretly agreed with Fatma, and she notified her again, before she could regret it, that from Monday Geula would not be coming to her anymore. She averted her eyes from the wailing Fatma, who beat her left breast as if she had just lost her daughter, and left the house.

On Monday she left Geula with her mother and hurried to work. Before the hour was out, Reuven, the neighbor Esther's son, burst into the room where Pnina-Mazal was translating the words of the head of the Jewish council, who was protesting the closure of his neighborhood school.

"Your mother wants you to come home right away," he said, panting for breath.

Pnina-Mazal hurried home and found Sara at her wits' end with Geula screaming and arching her body in her arms, her red hair bristling.

"She won't eat a thing. She spat out everything I gave her and screamed for Fatma."

Pnina-Mazal quickly took the red-faced child in her arms, where she writhed about and tried to free herself.

"Fatma, I want Fatma," she shrieked in Arabic, vomiting onto Pnina-Mazal's elegant dress the remains of the lunch that had been pushed into her mouth by force.

"We'll go tomorrow," promised Pnina-Mazal, sure that the child's memory would not last that long.

Geula calmed down immediately and allowed her mother to wash her face and change her clothes.

The next day the little girl woke up unusually early, singing to herself an Arabic song Fatma liked to sing while she was breast-feeding her. For the first time in her short life she allowed her mother to comb her rebellious hair, and as soon as she heard the car she ran out of the house.

With cold calculation Pnina-Mazal distracted her and sent her back inside to fetch a change of clothing. The moment the child tottered into the house, waddling like a fat goose on her little legs, Pnina-Mazal slipped into the seat next to the driver and ordered him to drive full speed out of the neighborhood. When she looked back she saw the deceived Geula standing in the doorway, her mouth wide open, screaming at the top of her lungs. All that day Pnina-Mazal could not concentrate on her translation work, seeing before her eyes her daughter's flushed face, her mouth gaping and screaming in the astonishment of her betrayal.

When she came home in the evening she found Geula, clean and calm, playing with her grandmother.

"How did the day pass?" she asked, holding her breath.

"All right," Sara answered shortly.

"What did you do?"

"Nothing special," her mother said, and busied herself at the kitchen sink.

Only when she put her daughter to bed did the placated Geula tell her how her grandmother had taken her to Fatma's house, where she played with Muhammad and drank milk.

Pnina-Mazal returned to the kitchen with her eyes flashing. "Don't ever do anything like that behind my back again," she snapped at her mother.

"I couldn't bear to see the child suffering," Sara replied calmly. "You would have done the same thing yourself. It's too late now to detach her from her wet-nurse. She's become the daughter Fatma never had. You should have thought about it before you went out to work and before you abandoned her to the mercies of strangers," she concluded rebukingly and retired to her room.

Pnina-Mazal ran after her. "And tomorrow? If she asks for her tomorrow will you give in to her again?"

"You would have done the same thing yourself if you had to stay with her the whole day and listen to her heartbreaking screams," Sara repeated firmly.

The next day Pnina-Mazal took Geula to Fatma. Muhammad, who was playing in the yard, clapped his hands when he saw her, and she tottered toward him on her chubby legs and fell heavily into his outstretched arms. Pnina-Mazal pretended not to see what was happening in front of her eyes.

Fatma, who came out into the yard at the sound of the voices, ran up to the little girl and knelt tenderly in front of her, and Geula immediately inserted her little hand into the neck of Fatma's blouse and tried to pull out her left breast.

"She will decide when she's ready to be weaned," Fatma whispered gently to Pnina-Mazal.

Without a word Pnina-Mazal turned away and walked down the path to the waiting car.

∗　∗　∗

It seemed to Sara that Davida would never give birth. Nine months passed and her belly went on swelling like rising dough. The tenth month passed, and every day Davida stroked her stomach, complained of the weight, and refused to give birth. Sara tried to coax her to go to the doctor, but she refused on the grounds that she was perfectly happy as she was.

"The birth frightens me," she said to Sara. "I've been told that the baby will tear me apart, spill my blood and hurt me all over. Let him stay where he is," she added, stroking her kicking belly, soothing the baby inside with endearments, and putting him to sleep with lullabies. And if his little hand clenched into a fist and beat against the walls of her belly as if to make them open, she would push it back and scold the mischievous scamp.

At night she slept on her back, with her belly, twitching and dancing in all directions, looming up in front of her. Yitzhak would try to mount the hill, which shuddered as light tremors passed through it, but was unable to push himself into her body. He would fall defeated onto his back and look anxiously at the white belly stretched as tight as a drum.

Anxious for the fate of the fetus, Sara found herself consulting Fatma as the two toddlers hung from her breasts like weights, greedily imbibing their milk. Glad to be of help, Fatma detached the children from her breasts and sent them into the yard with a light slap on their backsides. Then she hurried to a niche hidden behind the pile of mattresses, and took out a brightly colored tin box, which she opened with a flourish. A strong smell, which tickled Sara's nose and made her sneeze, spread through the room. In a confidential whisper, as if the room were full of invisible spies, Fatma breathed her instructions into Sara's ear.

In the evening Sara gave Davida a drink to "strengthen her bones and teeth," and waited until she had drunk it to the dregs, wailing and holding her nose. The next morning her body gave off a strange smell, and even Yitzhak avoided her. All day she complained of pains at the bottom of her abdomen.

"You'll give birth soon," the beaming Sara announced.

"I won't let him out," screamed Davida in a panic. "I won't let the baby tear my belly open," she added decisively and hugged her stomach.

The birth took place a few days later. That morning Davida stayed in bed with Yitzhak's arms around her and refused to go to work. "You'd better send someone to tell Regina, the kindergarten teacher, that I won't be coming today," she said to Sara in a pampered tone.

Sara brought them breakfast in bed and discovered that the mattress was soaking wet.

"Your waters have broken," she announced. "The birth has begun."

"And I thought Yitzhak did it," Davida said, and burst out laughing. Sara was astonished by her jovial reaction, but put it down perhaps to the drink she had forced down her throat to change her mood. Supported by Sara, Davida went into the kitchen leaving a little trail of water behind her, and stood there in the puddle collecting round her feet.

"I'll send for Pnina-Mazal to come at once with her automobile to take you to the hospital. It will be safer for you to give birth there, and we'll be better off without Yitzhak getting under our feet too," Sara said in a tone that brooked no argument.

Giggling as if all her fears had vanished, Davida got into the car sent by Pnina-Mazal, gave the driver a provocative look, and stuck her head out of the window so that the whole neighborhood would see her driving past.

At the hospital she was given a white gown and led groaning with pain to a large hall, where her eyes were met by rows of mountainous bellies. Loud groans rose in the air and doctors armed with wooden ear trumpets passed from woman to woman, pressing the trumpet to the mountain in front of them and listening to the muffled sounds of the fetus.

Sara was told to go home and come back in the evening. At home she was greeted by a questioning look from Yitzhak, who was sitting alone in the kitchen and staring into space.

"Davida is going to bring you a son," she heard herself saying to him. His expression did not change. Sara felt as if his eyes were boring through her body and sticking in the wall behind her.

In the evening she returned with Pnina-Mazal to the hospital, where Davida was waiting for them with a red-faced baby in her arms. It was as wrinkled as a venerable old man.

"Why didn't you tell me it hurt so much?" she hissed at them with a hard, unfamiliar look in her eyes.

Sara ignored her question and looked at the baby's face. He was a healthy pink-skinned baby with downy fair hair covering his head and falling onto his forehead and neck. "Mazal tov, mazal tov," she said emotionally, picking up her new grandson and rocking him in her arms. "Let's call him Avraham, after his grandfather who disappeared. What do you think?" she asked Davida without waiting for an answer.

Davida and Avraham came home two days later.

*   *   *

Yitzhak stared at the tiny baby they held out to him and went on chewing the slice of bread Sara had given him. In the evening, when the tumult of the day had died down, Davida went up to her husband with the baby in her arms and he looked at his wife and son with expressionless eyes. Davida shook the baby in front of him but not a muscle moved in his frozen face. She tried to put the baby on his lap but his hands resting motionless on his knees refused to open and accept the new life thrust into them. In desperation Davida held the baby to his nose. His nostrils refused to open and take in the new smell that had invaded the house. At that moment the baby whimpered. Yithzak didn't bat an eye, as if the voice had failed to reach his ears. When the whimpering turned to loud wails Davida sat down by her husband's side, unbuttoned her blouse, took out her breast, which had swollen to the size of a grapefruit, and pushed the nipple into the baby's tiny mouth. He seized hold of it immediately and began to suck with loud, gratified noises, his hands waving in the air.

Nobody knows for certain what happened there in the kitchen. Later Davida said that Yitzhak, whose eyes had been fixed on an invisible point on the wall all this time, stood up, uttered a terrible, desperate cry, and tried to tear the infant from her arms. "He kept shouting 'Food, food,' and hitting his chest like a madman. I was afraid he was going to kill the child and I ran away."

Pnina-Mazal, who came running at the sound of the shouts, could not understand her brother, who was howling loudly and repeating the word "food" like a scratched record. Later on, when she sat with Sara in the kitchen and mulled over the events of the day with her, she said that she thought Yitzhak was afraid that the baby was going to eat Davida and wanted to rescue her from him.

"But he saw you breast-feeding Geula and he didn't react," said Sara.

"True, but Davida belongs to him and he doesn't want to share her with anyone else," argued Pnina-Mazal.

All that night Yitzhak banged his head against the wall, hot tears streaming from his eyes and his teeth chattering feverishly. The next day three burly men arrived at the house and restrained Yitzhak in a white shirt with long sleeves that they wrapped around his body. Trapped and kicking, Yitzhak was led to the lunatic asylum that was housed in a new building outside the town, surrounded by newly planted pine forests. Later that morning, when Davida pushed her nipple into Avraham's mouth, he seized it firmly between his pink gums and began sucking voraciously. But he quickly spat it out again with an insulted grimace and burst into tears.

Davida joined in, and the sound of their combined weeping brought Sara hurrying to the room.

"Your milk has dried up," she said after lightly shaking Davida's breast and squeezing the nipple with her fingers.

"So will we take him to Fatma?" asked Davida, a spark of hope gleaming in her eyes.

"Certainly, if she agrees."

Fatma, delighted at the prospect of a new baby to nurse, once again displayed her impressive breasts and squirted her milk across the room, this time for Davida's benefit, and immediately accepted the job. Every morning Pnina-Mazal would get into the car carrying the baby in her arms, and Geula, sitting next to her mother, would suck her thumb and glare at him with all the fury of a deposed queen.

That same week Sara traveled to the hospital to visit Yitzhak. She found him lying in a big room full of white iron beds containing faceless, anonymous people, sighing and mumbling and throwing their heads from side to side.

She went up to his bed and a little spark of recognition flashed in his eyes before they resumed their customary blankness. He tried to sit up in bed, but with every attempt he was flung back on the mattress with a force that shook the iron bedstead.

This must be some new illness, Sara thought as she examined his immobile body, only to discover that his arms and legs were fastened with thick leather straps to the edges of the bed. She burst indignantly into the doctors' room, where she encountered a hard stare from the nurse.

"Free my son from those restraints immediately. He isn't an animal. He isn't dangerous. How can you treat him so heartlessly?" she shouted at her.

"When he was brought here he went berserk and tried to break things and to harm himself and others," the nurse said without moving a muscle and with no change in her stiff expression. "If we free him he'll hurt himself. When he calms down he'll be transferred to another room where he'll be free to move about," she promised.

With her back bowed Sara went back home, and all that evening she avoided looking into the eyes of her daughter-in-law, who was busy with the baby and showed no interest in her husband's fate.

*   *   *

While she was brushing her hair in front of the mirror before she went to bed, Sara looked intently at her reflection. The tired eyes looking back at her were sunk in their sockets and framed in a network of finely etched wrinkles. Her cheeks fell slackly and she tried to pull them up with her fingers, but they immediately fell back again, as if intent on uniting with the withered flesh of her thin neck.

She examined the hairs pulled from her scalp by the comb, laying them one by one on the table in front of her, and drew up the oil lamp to scrutinize the specimens she had collected. A little pile of long coiling hairs rose before her. She picked one hair from the pile, held it at both ends, and examined it in the lamplight. One end of the hair had preserved its original color, but the closer it came to the root the more it faded, until it finally turned snowy white. She gathered all the hair into a ball, threw it into the wastepaper basket, and took off her blouse.

She pulled down the straps of her woolen undershirt and examined the reflection of her breasts in the mirror. They were still full after feeding three babies, and the nipples stared into their own eyes in the mirror. With a tug of her white petticoat she exposed her belly, which had rounded with the years, and stroked it with her hands, where veins had begun to twine like a vine sending its tendrils in all directions. The mirror was too short for her to examine her thighs and calves, and she promised herself that she would do so early in the morning, when her daughter and daughter-in-law were sound asleep, and she would be able to climb onto the bed and inspect the lower half of her body.

That night when she was about to blow out the oil lamp the achingly familiar knock was heard at the door. Holding the lamp in her hand she hurried to the door, where Edward was waiting on the threshold with an ingratiating look in his eyes. In the light of the lamp she examined his hair, which had thinned and turned white, and the deep lines etched by the years on his face.

"Get dressed and come with me," he said, and she hurried to her room and quickly pulled on her best dress.

The house that had been locked up all these years greeted her with familiar smells. Edward carried her to the bedroom, rocking her in his arms as if she were a baby.

"You're the most beautiful woman in the world," he said to her, his eyes melting with tenderness.

Sara giggled uneasily. "I'm already a grandmother," she warned him.

"The most beautiful grandmother in the world," he retorted, and laid her gently on the bed, which sank beneath her with a familiar softness and enveloped her in a gentle, cradling motion.

When they were satiated she lay in his arms and told him about Ben-Ami, about David, about Yitzhak and Davida, about Geula, and about Fatma. The more she spoke the more the tears rolled down her cheeks, and she sucked them in and felt their saltiness on her tongue.

"And to think that during all that time I was in America living off the fat of the land, enjoying myself at plays and moving picture shows," he said. "I wrote you dozens of letters and sent you telegrams, and at my post office they told me there was no chance that you would get them."

When he calmed down he told her about Elizabeth, who had not been cured, and who had written books about her childhood in Palestine, which had brought her fame and earned her a lot of money. He told her too about the difficulties of his divorce from Rachel, who refused to let him go even though he told her of his other love, and about his wanderings in the desert with General Allenby's army.

When day broke in the windows and he tired of speaking, he piled big biscuit tins on the bed and put them in her hands. Inside them she found his past: Rachel, Elizabeth, and portraits of other people, some of whom she knew. There were pictures of General Allenby and his camp; the Turks abandoning the beaten city; the General's entry into Jerusalem and the ceremony on the citadel steps; pictures of skyscrapers and of beautiful women with cropped fair hair, wearing short dresses, which exposed their long legs, and long strings of pearls; strange animals whose likes she had never seen before; and the streets of a foreign city full of motorcars. The last bundle of photographs he dropped into her lap was wrapped in a piece of cloth. She unwrapped it carefully and a cry burst from her lips. Edward came up and put his arms around her.

In some of the pictures she saw herself on the ship with her long hair, carrying little Pnina-Mazal and holding Yitzhak by the hand, sur-rounded by people who were devouring her beauty with their eyes. In another picture she appeared as a young woman stretched out on a deck chair on the ship and soaking up the sun. Her hair shone round her like a radiant halo, leaving an aureole of colorless light around her head. In another picture she saw herself leaning against the ship's railing and looking at the approaching coastline of Jaffa.

When she reached a sheaf of pictures tied together with a thick string, Edward snatched them from her hands. Sara slapped his hand lightly and tried to take them back. Edward resisted her and slipped the packet under the pillow, upon which he laid his head. Sara refused to give up and tickled his ribs until he burst out laughing and raised his head. She quickly slid her hand under the pillow, groped for the packet, and pulled it out. With her back to the still-laughing Edward she untied the string and gazed incredulously at the pictures.

She saw herself as naked as the day she was born, smiling through the hair covering her face. In another picture she was lying on her stomach with her firm buttocks sticking up, like the bare behind of a baby photographed in honor of its first birthday, on a white studio bearskin that had borne innumerable bare-assed babies before it. In an-other picture she was crouching on all fours, with her breasts resting on the bedcover.

"And you told me that all the pictures were burned," she flared up angrily. "How could you?"

"I had to photograph you again and again. For me you'll stay like you were then and that's how I'll always remember you," he answered quietly.

Sara compared her tired body and lined face as she had seen them reflected in the mirror in her bedroom at home to the pictures she was holding in her hand. She dropped the pictures onto the floor and held out her arms to Edward, who entered her body gently, murmuring her name.

In the morning, when she went home with her body saturated with love, she was greeted by Pnina-Mazal's accusing looks and Davida's aggrieved ones.

"And you, where were you?" her daughter-in-law demanded. "Avraham cried all night. Tomorrow's the brith and you disappear like a ghost in the night."

Sara bit her lip and did not react to the accusing looks and words. She hurried to the stove, put on the kettle, and made them tea.

"Perhaps the time has come for you to learn to make yourselves a cup of tea," she said as if to herself, without looking at them. "I won't be with you for the rest of your lives, and you had better begin to prepare yourselves."

Pnina-Mazal felt a guilty pang and made haste to embrace her mother. "I didn't mean it, I was just worried about you," she tried to appease her.

"I'm responsible for myself," Sara replied loudly, so that Davida too would hear from the next room, where she was busy with the baby. "And don't ask me where I was," she added in a whisper, although her shining eyes told her daughter everything.

"How are Rachel and Elizabeth?" asked Pnina-Mazal innocently.

"Elizabeth has written a book about her childhood in Jerusalem," she said proudly, as if it were her own flesh and blood she was talking about. "And the book sold very well and brought her great honor and plenty of money."

"And Rachel, what about her?"

"They're divorced, and she's decided never to return to the Land of Israel," Sara replied, and left it at that.

"Ask him for their address," Pnina-Mazal requested. "I'd like to tell them our news. And besides, why don't you try to find Father and ask him for a divorce? He abandoned you years ago and it's time you freed yourself from him." Without waiting for a reply she left for the wet-nurse, with Avraham in her arms and Geula tottering behind her, her red hair bristling.

✻ ✻ ✻

The day after Avraham's brith Sara woke up in the morning to the baby's hungry crying, went out into the garden, and in the fury usually reserved for pulling out weeds she tore up the parsley beds, stamped the mint with her heels, and uprooted the turnips and the cabbages. She worked like a lunatic, and the corpses of her cherished plants piled up around her, their exposed roots shivering miserably in the morning wind.

Pnina-Mazal ran out after her, hugged her with her thin arms, and asked her in dismay: "Have you taken leave of your senses? What are you doing?"

"This garden does me no good," replied Sara with her back bowed, furiously pulling up tomato bushes full of tiny green tomatoes.

"But why are you pulling them up by the roots? Isn't it a pity?" Pnina-Mazal tried to restrain her from wreaking further destruction.

"I'm going to plant red roses instead."

"And what will we do with them? Eat them?"

"I'll make rose water from them," she replied, her nostrils quivering in anticipation of the as yet nonexistent smell, which sent a frisson of pleasure from the tips of her toes to the roots of her hair.

"And what will we do with rose water?"

"We'll sell it in the market."

"And how will you make it?"

"Fatma promised to teach me, and I'm going there with you today."

"But what do you need it for? I bring home enough money for all our needs."

"And if you marry somebody else, what will become of me?"

"I'll never marry anyone else," she promised. "I'll always be with you."

"But I want you to have a family."

Pnina-Mazal was silent, and lowered her eyes to the tips of her shoes.

* * *

On the stone floor, smooth with years of polishing, Fatma waited with
a festive expression, surrounded by glass jars, pipes, bottles, kettles, funnels, and big copper pots. The house smelled strongly of roses, as if all
the painted whores of the town had spent the night having a party there.

"First we'll feed the children," she said, and took out her watermelon breasts. Muhammad and Geula ran up to her, took possession of
a nipple each, put their arms around each other, and set to work. When
their bellies were full they went outside holding hands as if they had
been born from one womb, tottering like drunks on their fat legs. Then
Fatma took Avraham on her lap and he turned his eyes and nose to the
black nipple, took it in his mouth, and the room filled with the sounds
of his sucking. When he had finished and given vent to a loud belch,
like a Bedouin sheik after a particularly rich meal, Fatma put him down
in Muhammad's cradle.

"And now to the roses," she said, and moving quickly, as if she
feared that with their exposure to the air of the room their fragrance
would evaporate and disappear, she removed the sheet covering a little
pile of roses.

That evening, when she went home, Sara brought a fresh scent of
roses in her wake. And when everyone had gone to bed, she went to
Edward's house, with the scent preceding her as if to announce her
arrival. There, on the bed, he sniffed her fingers one by one, smelled
her armpits, let his nostrils stray over her breasts, thrust the tip of his
nose into her navel, tasted her pudenda, roamed down her legs, parted
her toes, sucked them one by one, breathed in the heavy, unfamiliar
scent, and searched for its source like an explorer searching for the
source of a river with many tributaries. And when he entered her he
sailed between the perfumed gardens of her body, and the strong scent
stiffened his member. And when she left his bed at dawn she left behind
her on the sweaty sheets a heavy scent of flowers. In the morning, when
he shaved his beard with a razor, the smell of roses wafted from his
hands as they slid the razor over the stubble on his cheeks. For hours
he labored with soap, with scouring powder, and with hot water to rid
his skin of the smell, but to no avail. The scent clung to him, seeped
into all the cells of his body, and refused to go away. When he went

about his business in the town that day people sniffed suspiciously and turned their heads as he walked past them.

✳ ✳ ✳

On her way home Sara bought red rose seedlings. She collected chicken droppings from Esther's henhouse and strewed them over the soil, planted the seedlings in the gaping holes left by the uprooted vegetables, and watered them with water she drew from the pump. When she was finished she went to the market and bought transparent glass bottles, a large kettle, a broad-brimmed basin, flexible copper pipes, and wide-mouthed funnels, exactly as she had seen at Fatma's house.

When the rose bushes sprouted velvety red flowers, she recruited her daughter and daughter-in-law to pick them. Pnina-Mazal pricked her fingers on the thorns, gritted her teeth, and plucked the heads of the flowers. Davida had lost weight after giving birth; her arms were as thin as pale sticks, with sharp, protruding elbows, and her knuckles were hard and knobbly. She picked the flowers with sharp, quick movements, as if in a rage at the whole world, pricking her transparent fingers again and again, and with a pricked finger thrust into her mouth complained tearfully that she was sacrificing her blood on the altar of Sara's roses.

When the bushes were bare and there was no red left on them, they took the fragrant basket into the house and pulled the red petals off the heads of the flowers. When they had finished their work Sara asked them to leave her alone, put the great copper kettle she had bought in the market on the stove to boil, and stood over it with her face flushed, like a witch brewing magic potions. She completed her work in the morning, and when the girls woke from their light sleep accompanied by the crying of hungry babies, she was waiting for them in the kitchen, her face shining with sweat, an array of bottles sealed with wax and filled with scented water in front of her.

"On that machine of yours in the office, the one that writes, write on little slips of paper in Hebrew, Arabic, and English the words 'Sara's Rose Water,' and if you have the time, draw a picture of a rose in red ink on them," she asked Pnina-Mazal.

"You write and I'll draw," piped up Davida, who since giving birth had sat idle at home. "I drew red roses for the children in the kinder-garten all the time; I can draw them with my eyes closed."

"I don't think they'll approve of you coming with me to work," Pnina-Mazal said, trying to put her off.

"Go, go," said Sara to Davida, ignoring the note of hesitation in her daughter's voice, "and this evening, when you come home with the labels, we'll stick them onto the bottles."

Unwillingly Pnina-Mazal took Davida with her to the office, where she ordered her to sit in a corner, not to talk to anyone, and to draw roses on the pieces of paper she cut out for her, after typing the required words in duplicate and triplicate with the aid of carbon paper.

After devouring the room and the typewriter with her eyes, and accustoming her ears to the bustle and commotion, Davida settled down to her task, which she performed with small, sharp movements.

A sudden shadow fell on the red rose she was drawing. She raised her eyes, and saw a fair-haired, blue-eyed man, wearing a spick-and-span khaki uniform with decorations and medals on his chest, smiling at her from under the visor of his cap.

"Roses?"

"Yes," she answered faintly, afraid to look at him lest he notice her palpitating heart and her cheeks that were redder than the drawings of the roses. Her hands trembled as she went on drawing and the petals came out ragged and miserable, as if they had been afflicted with a mysterious disease or premature old age.

The tall man went on asking her questions she could not understand. Blushing hotly, she silently cursed the English teachers who had failed to teach her anything. "He says you're very beautiful and you remind him of his mother." Nissim, the translator who worked with Pnina-Mazal, came to her aid.

"Thank you," Davida finally succeeded in getting out of her mouth, and she sent the man a green, liquid, sidelong look.

∗ ∗ ∗

At home Sara was waiting for them impatiently with a paste she had cooked up from flour and water standing in a bowl on the floor.

"And now let's begin to paste," she commanded.

Obediently they smeared the paste on the paper and stuck the labels on the bottles, until the bottles ran out and the pile of labels illustrated with red roses diminished.

That night, as Sara communed with her bottles in the kitchen, breathing on the glass and rubbing them with a clean cloth until they shone, straightening the labels and polishing the wax stoppers, Davida sprayed herself with rose water and stole out of the house.

George was waiting for her on the outskirts of the neighborhood, clasping his hands in excitement. He took her to the officers' club, and there, gliding in his arms and steeped in the smell of roses, she found that her feet danced of their own accord to the strains of the records fed without a pause to the giant-eared gramophone.

Flushed and excited she returned home, where Pnina-Mazal was waiting for her, her eyes flashing in the darkness of the room. "The government doesn't approve of its soldiers fraternizing with Jewesses," she shot at her.

"He calls me Rose," Davida replied with misty eyes, then curled up under the blanket, imagined his big body breathing next to her, purred to herself like a satisfied cat, and fell asleep immediately.

The next day Pnina-Mazal refused to take her with her to work. The note fixing the rendezvous with George she received secretly from Nissim.

That week, when Davida was alone with Sara and her bottles in the kitchen, she told her that she wanted to go to the rabbi and institute divorce proceedings.

"Help me to take the bottles to the market, and after that I'll go with you," Sara replied calmly, as if she had always known that it would happen, and prepared herself in her heart.

Armed with wicker baskets full of crowded bottles knocking into each other and making tinkling noises, they made for the perfume market. The merchants turned to look at the women walking past them and leaving a long train of flowery scent behind them. Long after they had gone the men went on standing there lifting their noses like desert jackals and sniffing the fresh fragrance still lingering in the air.

Sara felt the tension rising inside her as she bargained with the shopkeepers, lugging her bottles from one to the other until she found one who was prepared to pay her a few more pennies because of the label with the drawing of the rose adorning the bottle. On the way home, their baskets empty, they went to the rabbis, who after a short consultation promised Davida that by the end of the week she would be free to marry again.

❖   ❖   ❖

With the parchment scroll of her bill of divorcement in her hand and her baby in her arms, Davida confronted Sara and Pnina-Mazal the next day and announced that she was going to marry George and sail with him to England.

"George has been released from the army to marry me. He's going back to England and taking me with him. In his country, he told me, they'll call me Rose."

"But he isn't Jewish," Pnina-Mazal said, trying to dampen her enthusiasm.

Davida looked at them with hard eyes. "He isn't the only gentile man you know," she said coldly.

"You don't know English, how will you talk to him?" ventured Sara.

"Who said you have to talk to your husband?" she replied.

"And the baby, what about the baby?"

"If you like, I'll leave him with you," she said magnanimously.

That same week she packed her bags, said good-bye to the neighbors, parted from Pnina-Mazal and Sara, kissed the baby on his cheek, and left the house. Months later she sent them pictures of herself arm in arm with George in the snow, her thin body draped in a black fur coat. In other pictures they saw that she had cut off her long hair, stuck strange feathers in what was left, and shortened her skirts. She inquired after their health, asked about the baby, and made no mention of Yitzhak.

Chapter Fifteen

One week after selling the bottles of rose water in the market Sara went apprehensively to the perfume shop to ask what had happened to them. The smell of roses that preceded her, like a herald announcing his mistress's arrival, brought Mustafa the perfume seller running to meet her. He took both her hands in his scented ones.

"Madam Sara," he whispered. "They're all sold. People who bought one bottle came back for more. It must be your beauty that penetrated the water and gave it special properties. Bring me more. They'll buy it all. People told me that they didn't only use it for cakes and sweets," he continued enthusiastically. "If they bathed their faces in it, it made their skin fairer, and if they bathed their eyes, they grew clearer and were cured of inflammations."

Sara went home that day with new roses to plant in her own garden and the gardens of her neighbors Esther and Bracha. And the rose bushes grew prodigiously. If she picked a flower, the next day a new bud sprouted in its place, and if she cut off a branch, within a week there would be a new one, covered with buds. All the bushes were full of blooms, but also of thorns, sharp as spurs, as if they wanted to draw blood in exchange for every plucked bloom whose essence was squeezed into the rose water. Try as she might to avoid the thorns and pick the flowers without being scratched, they would spring out at her, tear her delicate skin, penetrate her flesh, and draw her blood. Some of them, particularly obdurate, buried themselves like hooks deep in her body and resisted all her attempts to pull them out. They remained inside her; new skin grew over them and they became flesh of her flesh.

Every day, late in the morning, when the dew had dried on the flowers, the neighbors would gather in the rose gardens, where the air was steamy with heavy scents, to chat, tell stories, and gossip. They picked the most fragrant of the red blooms, scratched their hands, and licked the blood that dripped onto the silken tissue of the petals and collected in little pools. The next morning they were rewarded for their pains by bottles of fragrant rose water, which they used to lighten their complexions and to cure the pustular sores on their hands and the suppurating eyes of their children.

The news of Sara's miraculous rose water spread far and wide, and people besieged her with requests for a bottle of the magic panacea that could alleviate the pain of labor, cure sore throats, bring straying husbands home, calm naughty children, and heal the afflictions of body and soul. And even the famous eye doctor, Dr. Ticho, came to her and bought a bottle. Afterward they said in the town that the doctor returned the next day and bought up her entire stock. And when a patient came to him with his eyelashes stuck together by yellow pus, the doctor would take a toothpick covered in cotton wool, dip it in the fragrant water, and open the blind eyes. Dr. Shapiro, from the new hospital, heard that gargling with Sara's rose water cured sore throats and cleared up nasty inflammations on the spot, and he too came to buy her bottles.

She told nobody how she made the rose water, as if revealing the secret of its preparation would rob it of its magic properties. Fatma the wet-nurse agreed to reveal the secret to the neighbor women after they pressed coins into her hands and swore not to tell Sara. But the rose water they prepared according to her instructions, while fragrant and refreshing, lacked the miraculous properties possessed by Sara's. When they bathed their faces in it their skin remained dark and cracked; eyes blinded by trachoma did not see; wombs did not open to receive sperm; and broken hearts did not mend.

Sara picked the roses in the late hours of the morning, when the dew had dried and disappeared from their petals. She collected the heads of the flowers in a white cloth bag and took them into the house. There she dipped them in water, washed them well, and between her thumb and forefinger she rid them of all the pestilential creatures, the winged and the wingless, the soft and the hard shelled, the earwigs and the centipedes, that had made their homes among the scented petals.

After cleaning the petals she filled the big kettle with water and put it on the stove to boil. Into the water she crammed the red petals and pressed them down. Then she attached a long, flexible copper pipe to the spout of the kettle, sealing the mouth of the spout tightly with a cloth so that the fragrant steam would not escape. The other end of the pipe she inserted in a clean glass jar that she stood on the kitchen floor. She plunged the copper pipe that was on its way to the glass jar into a deep tub of cold water. And when the petal-filled water in the kettle boiled, the vapors passed into the pipe through the spout of the kettle, and in the place where it was plunged into the cold water, they turned into drops of dew saturated with the scent of roses. And drop by drop the fragrant drops fell into the jar. After the jar was full to the brim, she pushed a funnel into the mouth of one little bottle after the other and poured the water steeped with the essence of roses into them. Then she sealed the bottles with fresh wax and pasted on the labels bearing the picture of a rose.

❊   ❊   ❊

In those days the smell of roses pervaded all the houses of the neighborhood. Every night the women, their hands scratched, their hair wild, and their faces flushed, brewed the fragrant potion. And the smell of dying roses accompanied them wherever they went, and everyone who met them on their way could tell by their smell that they were Sara's neighbors. But only Sara's rose water possessed magic properties, and when she walked through the streets of the market with her bottles rattling in her big wicker basket, she was accompanied by the heady scent of freshly plucked roses.

And when the demands for Sara's magic rose water multiplied, so did the money in her pockets, until she purchased a broad field next to the neighborhood wall, and planted it with straight rows of red-flowered bushes. Then too she went to Fatma's village and recruited the children to pick the roses. And she built a wooden shed next to the field and set up a distillery in it, where she and Fatma were busy all day long, distilling the blessed water from the rose petals and filling the bottles with it. And

Fatma brought her children with her, and Geula, Muhammad, and Avraham played at her feet, and when they were hungry they undid the bodice of her dress, exposed her breasts, and drank their fill of rose-scented milk.

Edward too offered his services to the fragrant enterprise and generously donated his old carriage, which had been replaced by a motorcar, to transport the bottles. The aged horse, whose ribs stuck out of his walking corpse and threatened to tear his parchment-thin skin, would trudge through the streets of the town, his hooves ringing, pulling the bottled miracle water behind him, and after every few steps he would turn his head and with avid, flaring nostrils sniff his fragrant freight.

Soon the breath escaping from his yellow-toothed mouth began to smell like roses, and the sweat pouring from his body too gave off a heavy scent of roses. His brother horses would come and sniff his black coat, and with soft neighing noises they would rub their bodies against him in order to soak up his smell. And thus the streets of Jerusalem were walked by delicately scented horses. And when they arched their tails and dropped damp, steamy turds behind them, even these turds would give off sweet smells.

And when the famous travel writer Irwin Thomas came to the Holy Land on his way from India, Yemen, Ethiopia, Egypt, and the Sudan in order to write about the Christian holy places, and arrived in Jerusalem, he stood amazed before the horse manure that spread its fragrance throughout the town. And the story of the sweet breath and fragrant turds of the horses of Jerusalem was printed in *The Times* of London, where his articles were published. "And the holy air of the city turns even piles of stinking horse manure into an essence of perfume which the most refined London lady would gladly dab behind her ears and in the creases of her elbows before setting out for the Opera, smelling of the sweetest scents which have ever reached your noses," he wrote in an article entitled "The Sweet-Smelling Holy Manure of the Horses of Jerusalem." Angry letters were written to the editor. Many readers demanded that Irwin Thomas be fired, claiming that the holy air of Jerusalem had deprived him of his wits, so that he had begun to write of bodily excretions and horse manure instead of the holy places, and saying that it was blasphemous to mention holiness and horse manure in the same breath.

In the end the poor man went out of his mind, and was found

walking naked in the streets of Jerusalem, digging a blackened silver teaspoon into the piles of dung, lifting it to his nose, breathing in the smell with quivering nostrils, and then tasting the contents of the spoon while smacking his lips in enjoyment. After this he would roll around in the dung, smear it on his hair, and roam the streets with his naked body smelling of roses, setting women and girls of tender years to flight and proclaiming the gospel of the holy smell to the harsh stones of the city.

Finally men in white coats caught him, restrained him in a long straitjacket that covered his nakedness, and led him to the lunatic asylum on the outskirts of the city, where the young pine trees had already grown soft crests. There they put him in the ward for the incurable, where his strapped bed stood next to Yitzhak's. And he would talk feverishly of the holy air that turned manure into fragrant gold, and say that the moment he was released he would collect the turds and send them to London, where he would be paid for them in gold. Yitzhak would stare right through him and widen his nostrils to breathe in his smell.

In the wake of Thomas's article the noted equine nutritionist Dr. Henry Cook arrived in Jaffa and took the train to Jerusalem. It was said that he was seen wandering the streets of the town, collecting the turds in glass jars and sealing them with thick cork lids. And when he reached his room in the Allenby Hotel he opened his trunk and took out the instrument that magnifies a fly into an elephant, crumbled the manure between his fingers, and inspected the results closely through the thick lenses. Then he hired a horse and carriage and examined every aspect of the animal's life. He took a particular interest in the sack of fodder tied around the horse's neck, felt its contents with his snuff-stained fingers, removed a few stalks of straw and sniffed them, stuck them in his mouth, and chewed them with his strong teeth.

When he returned home he took with him in his suitcase specimens of manure and fodder in well-sealed jars. And when he opened the suitcase for inspection at Dover, the customs shed was filled with a heavy fragrance, and he was given a fine for smuggling unknown oriental perfumes in solid form and commercial quantities into the country. And when he argued that all he had with him was horse manure they looked at him as if he had gone mad, and confiscated the sweet-smelling stuff. And at a congress in Kent on the subject of "the nutrition of English

race-horses and its influence on their performance on the track," he
stood on the platform and took from his pocket the one test tube he
had managed to save from the customs officers, displayed the dried-up
manure it contained to the delegates, and spoke at length on the diet
of the horses in the Holy City that turned their excrement into perfume.

✳   ✳   ✳

And the smell of the roses wafting from Sara's distillery evaporated in
the air, perfumed the surroundings, and rose up to the clouds. And when
the first rains fell on the town covered with the gray summer dust, the
water bathed the dirty streets in a sweet smell. And barefoot children
whose eyes were clogged with yellow matter raised their faces to the
showers falling from the clouds, like members of some ancient tribe
dancing for joy outside their caves at the advent of the first rain, wid-
ening their nostrils like savages to sniff the smell and washing their faces
encrusted with dried sweat and summer dust. And purblind eyes were
opened, filthy faces were cleansed, and sores left by lice and bug bites
were covered by pure new skin.

And when the demand for the rose water increased, and customers
began arriving from Motza, Bethlehem, and Hebron, Sara bought another field with the money she had earned, recruited more children,
and expanded the distillery. Fatma brought her neighbors from the village, and together, enveloped in the heavy scents, they distilled the
healing waters. At night Sara would count the money she had earned
that day, and the next morning she would send Pnina-Mazal to deposit
the stacks of coins in the Anglo-Palestine Bank. And the more the
money accumulated the more the beggars and tramps multiplied outside
the house and the distillery, refusing to leave until she handed out bread
and cheese and distributed a few coins among them.

One morning the door to the house was barred by a man dressed
in rags, his beard matted and stiff with dirt. He refused the coins she
offered him and declined the bread and cheese she had prepared the
night before for distribution to the poor who came knocking at her
door. His prematurely aged hands, covered with pale brown spots,
gripped a bottle of water.

"Saint," he addressed her reverently, "bless the water, my wife is
very sick."

"If you wish I'll give you a bottle of rose water for her," Sara said.

"I'm not a beggar. I don't want your charity. Just hold this bottle in your hands and your healing powers will enter the water and my wife will be cured," he replied.

"I'll give you money for a doctor. That water won't help her," Sara said, obediently holding the bottle of water he put into her hands. One week later he knocked at her door and thanked her for his wife's recovery. In the following days more people arrived with bottles of water in their hands, and they asked Sara to hold the bottles and to bless their households. And the line lengthened from day to day. They stood there patiently in the burning sun, teenage virgins who wanted a husband, barren women whose wombs had not yet opened, children afflicted with boils, the lame and the paralyzed and the insane, children with bloated stomachs, and even a lame horse brought by the neighborhood coachman together with a bucket full of water for her to bless. And Sara would go out to them and bless their bottles with her scratched hands. And when the sick were cured others took their places, and her hands were full, and Fatma remained alone in the distillery.

And there came a day when the rose water merchants stopped coming to her house. When she asked them why, they explained that there was no longer a demand for her rose water. "In any case you bless the plain water, and it too has healing powers, so why should they buy the rose water for money if they can get the same thing for nothing?"

And when the demand ceased, Sara was obliged to curtail the rose picking; she sent the children home and scaled down her business. The people who besieged her door with their bottles occasionally bought her fragrant rose water too, but most of these unfortunates lacked even the money to buy a crust of bread, and Sara soon found herself feeding as well as blessing them. In the end she sold her fields to a wealthy contractor, who built large new houses with flat roofs on them. Sara went home and continued to bless the dozens and hundreds of bottles of water held out to her every day.

＊　＊　＊

When she succeeded in getting away from the wretched supplicants standing patiently at her door, she harnessed Edward's old horse to the fragrant carriage, packed a few bottles of rose water, and set out for the hospital to visit her son. Before she entered the room, Irwin Thomas would avidly breathe in the scents that announced her arrival, smacking his lips with relish as if the smell had penetrated the taste buds on his tongue too, and excitedly shake Yitzhak as he lay flat on his back in his white bed and stared at the ceiling. And when she sat down on the white-painted wooden chair, Irwin Thomas would sit at her feet, bury his head in her lap, and breathe in her smell while shudders of delight ran up and down his body. Yitzhak would look right through her and greedily drink the rose water she brought him. Sometimes he would polish off all three bottles without any perceptible effect. But when she said good-bye she felt as if he looked at her and understood everything she said.

And when time passed and Yitzhak's hair began to turn white and his body grew slack and obese, and rolls of quivering fat appeared beneath his chin, she asked permission to take him home, and her request was granted. For days on end Yitzhak would sit in the garden, warming his bones in the sun and browning his skin, which had grown white during his years in the hospital. He would sit without moving for hours on end, and the neighborhood urchins would steal up to him, utter shrill, sudden cries, and throw dead lizards and snakes into his lap. When he didn't move they grew bolder, came right up to him, and danced round him like savages. And Yitzhak, as if he had turned into a pillar of salt, would stare in front of him, blind to the commotion surrounding him.

In the neighborhood people said that one day the wickedest of the little boys collected dry branches and lit a fire at his feet. The smoke coming in at the kitchen window brought Sara running into the yard to rescue her son, who sat quite still, as if he did not feel the flames licking at his shoes. From that day on she left him sitting on a chair inside the house, in front of a window overlooking the yard. The children would walk past the window, make faces, and throw little stones at him, and he would stare at them without moving a muscle of his big, flaccid body. And when strangers came to the neighborhood they would see him sitting in the window and ask him for directions, and when he failed to reply they would shrug their shoulders and continue on their way.

*   *   *

Geula's behavior kept Sara awake at night. She had grown into a strong, skinny child, with sharp white teeth, freckles all over her face, and rebellious red hair that stuck out stiffly in all directions. She would wander round the house naked as the day she was born, refusing to put on her clothes even on cold winter days. And when her mother tried to dress her in a frock and long stockings, as was right and proper for a girl of her age, she would bite her mother's hands, stamp her feet, and refuse to put them on. The only clothes she agreed to wear were the wide, shabby, patched trousers and the plain striped shirt that she had received from Fatma.

When her mother combed her long, tangled hair she would protest vociferously, filling her lungs with air and letting out bloodcurdling shrieks that startled even Yitzhak's motionless body from its place. Nor would she allow her mother to wash her hair, and Sara would steal up and pour water over her head while she was splashing naked with Muhammad in the copper basin used for washing the rose petals. On a number of occasions Sara caught her attacking her long hair with the heavy scissors once used for cutting the roses. Thick locks would fall to the floor, leaving the little girl's scalp full of round pits and bald patches, around which her long red hair grew wild.

When Geula went out to roam the neighborhood streets mothers would make haste to call their daughters in and shut the door. She would pull the little girls' hair, smack their bottoms, tear their dresses, throw the beetles and lizards she collected in the fields at them, and incite the boys to pelt them with stones.

She was very fond of the mulberry tree, especially in the summer, when its lumpy berries attracted the birds of Jerusalem, which settled on its branches in droves and pecked greedily at the soft fruit. With their bellies full they would fly off again and shed their droppings unerringly on the spotless laundry hanging on the washing lines, leaving purple stains that the most strenuous efforts of the housewives failed to remove. And in the summer nights the bats swooped down with squeaky little cries and hung upside down from its branches, filling their hairy bellies with its sweet fruit.

The mulberry tree was Geula's hiding place. Here she would sit, ignoring Sara's calls for her to come inside, and it was only after all the treetops roundabout had been scanned that her red hair was finally discovered flaming on the uppermost branch of the great mulberry tree, where even the cats could not climb, and if they did they were unable to come down again, and remained where they were, wailing and mewing for help. Geula on the other hand would look down scornfully at the search party gathered at the foot of the tree, smile her sharp-toothed smile, and only when she felt hungry climb down as lightly as a dancer.

After she climbed to the top of the tree, concealed by the green foliage, she would pick the plumpest mulberries, fill her mouth with juice, and spit the purple pulp mixed with her saliva onto the heads of the passersby. When she succeeded in hitting the back or chest of a yeshiva scholar she would rejoice to see the ugly purple stains spreading over his spotless white shirt. In those days her backside was red with Sara's slaps, and Sara's hands were sore from hitting her granddaughter's hard backside. During these beatings Geula would close her eyes and grit her sharp teeth, and she never made a sound.

All their efforts to separate her from Muhammad failed, and he remained her bosom friend even after they were both weaned from his mother's breasts. There was already talk of sending her to school, but at the very mention of the idea she would cling to Muhammad with the desperation of a drowning man, scream at her mother, and refuse to let go of him. And so the two of them were left to their own devices, scampering about the house, chattering to each other in their own private language, which only Pnina-Mazal could understand, and using Yitzhak's broad lap as a playground. They would climb up his thick legs as he sat motionless in his chair or bounce up and down on his feet as if he were a seesaw. And when they grew tired they would climb into his lap and nestle there like birds in a nest. And when they had rested they would clamber up his chest, climb onto his shoulders, and perch by turn on his big, fair head, straddling it with their legs. Then they would rise carefully to their feet and jump from his head to the floor, shrieking with fear and delight.

Fatma's dwindling breasts they left to Avraham, Yitzhak's fair-headed son, who stuck to them like a leech for hours at a time. And when the fancy took them, they would include the tiny toddler, whose nose was always running, in their games. Then they would stand him before his father and command him in their unintelligible language to climb into his lap. Avraham would stand opposite the motionless lump of his father, one finger in his mouth and the other deep in his nose, and survey him with his mother Davida's green gaze, like an art critic contemplating a painting in a museum. At such moments Sara could have sworn that she saw tears welling up in the eyes of her son.

❈   ❈   ❈

Although she had her hands full with her healing work, Sara occasionally found time to try to restrain her wild granddaughter and to talk to her in Hebrew. Geula would agree to stay with her in the kitchen only when she bribed her with cookies soaked in rose water. Then she would swing her legs over the edge of the chair, open her mouth like a baby bird, and thank her grandmother with a polite *"Shukran"* in Arabic.

"Say *'Todah,'* Geula," Sara said, trying to teach her Hebrew.

"Shukran," the little girl repeated obstinately.

In the evening, when Pnina-Mazal came home tired from the British staff headquarters, Sara would try to talk to her about her daughter.

"The main thing is that I understand her," she would say whenever her mother brought up the subject of the secret language Geula spoke to Muhammad and the Arabic she insisted on speaking to her. "And the fact that she insists on speaking Arabic to you doesn't matter. She'll learn Hebrew when she goes to school."

"But school has already started. And she refuses to be parted from Muhammad," Sara tried to argue.

"I'll take care of it," said Pnina-Mazal wearily.

That same week Geula was led to the first-grade class in the Lady Meyuhas School for Girls, screaming and kicking, trussed up in the "best dress" that she had never worn before.

That afternoon Sara was summoned from home and asked to present herself at the school. In the headmistress's room her granddaughter was waiting for her, her new dress covered with blue ink spots. Her long hair, which had been braided and tied with red ribbons when she left home, was loose and wild. She sat squirming on the chair and baring her pointed teeth in a vicious expression.

"I don't think the child fits into the framework of our school," said the headmistress, examining Sara's elegant gown. "She refused to speak Hebrew and answered the teacher in a strange language. She only agreed to speak in Arabic, to the girls from Haleb and Egypt. And that's not all. The teacher handed out ink-pots and pens, and she dipped her fingers in the ink and drew blue roses on the blouse of the little girl in front of her. Then she grabbed hold of the lid of the desk and kept opening and shutting it. And when she was finished playing with the desk she began climbing on and off the chair. And when the teacher lost patience and tried to drag her to the corner she bared her teeth and threatened to bite the finger she was admonishing her with. I advise you to take her home and keep her there until she's ready for school."

With her face flushed, Sara seized her granddaughter's arm, making white marks on the skin, and left the school. That evening she decided with Pnina-Mazal to hire a private tutor to teach Geula Hebrew.

Pnina-Mazal found a new immigrant from Russia, Gershon, who spoke a polished Hebrew and was ready and willing to teach the child. Although he really wanted to do manual labor, work on the roads and build the country, he had been rejected for these jobs on account of his weak, fragile body.

Wearing an embroidered cotton shirt with a high collar, tied round his slender waist with a tassled cord, his sparse hair neatly parted in the middle, Gershon surveyed, through the lenses of his round glasses, the little girl who burst into the room. Geula clung to the skirts of her mother's dress, looked contemptuously at the teacher they had brought her, and announced in her private language that she would only agree to be taught by him if they brought Muhammad too.

"You have to learn Hebrew," Pnina-Mazal said, "and Muhammad will learn Arabic."

"I won't learn without him," the child insisted.

Pnina-Mazal gave her a hard look and walked out of the room, slamming the door behind her.

In the afternoon, when Sara was busy with the supplicants, the bottles, and the holy water, Gershon emerged from the room disheveled and deathly pale, painfully holding his left hand, which was embellished by two bleeding crescents of sharp-toothed bite marks.

"She refused to talk to me," he said later to Pnina-Mazal. "And when she did talk she did so in a guttural language I've never heard before. And then she spilled the ink on the table, painted with her fingers, made a mess everywhere, climbed up my legs, and used my body as a swing and my head as a springboard. In the end she gave me this bite in the bargain," he said, and waved his hand before her eyes. "If things continue like this I don't think I'll be able to go on."

Sara hurried to give him a well-sweetened cup of coffee and sprinkled blessed water on his bleeding hand.

The next morning she sent Pnina-Mazal to Fatma's village. She returned holding Muhammad by the hand. As soon as Geula saw him she ran up, spoke to him excitedly in their language, took his hand, and sat him down beside her. And thus they sat obediently, hand in hand, throughout the lesson. At midday Gershon came out of the room with his face wreathed in smiles.

"There's still hope," he said to Sara. "Both children learned a few basic words in Hebrew today and agreed not to talk their strange language."

When the lesson was over the children ran up to Yitzhak's chair as usual, curled up in his warm lap, and went to sleep.

Chapter Sixteen

 In those days the first murder took place in the neighbor Esther's yard. She came running to Sara's house in alarm, clutching a pile of bloody feathers in her hand.

"All night long I didn't sleep a wink," she said in agitation. "All night the chickens cried for help and my husband wouldn't let me go out and see what was happening for fear I might step on a snake or bump into a jackal. And see what they did to me. They killed my Shoshana. They robbed me of my best layer, and left me with the feathers."

Sara crossed the yard with her and entered the chicken run. Signs of a bloody battle were evident everywhere. Broken eggs were squashed on the ground, their sticky contents providing a feast for the glittering green flies, who finished off their meal with the blood smeared on the feathers flying all around.

"We'll wait for tonight," she said to the terrified Esther. "If nothing happens tonight, it won't happen again."

"But who did it?" cried Esther, who had loved the plump Shoshana best of all her brood. Shoshana had come to her as a little yellow ball of fluff and down. Since the first sight she saw in her life, which had now come so abruptly to an end, was Esther's doughy face, she would eat from her hand and follow her like a shadow wherever she went.

Even when Esther stood in the kitchen cleaning the carcass of a chicken that had been taken from the henhouse and slaughtered in the yard, its head chopped off its bleeding neck before her very eyes, Shoshana's blind faith in her mistress did not falter. She would cuddle up to her benefactor's feet with her warm, feathery body even when the steamy air of the kitchen was full of swirling down, and the smell of singed feathers spread throughout the house. When the aroma of roasting chicken filled the kitchen and soup glistening with fat and full of necks and clawed feet bubbled on the stove, she would gaze at her mistress with her yellow eyes full of love and trust.

In the neighborhood people said mockingly that when it snowed in Jerusalem Esther would steal into the henhouse and despite her husband's vociferous protests and her children's scornful sniggers, smuggle Shoshana into the house wrapped up in her woolen shawl. Then she would thaw her icy feathers under the down quilt on her bed, and warm her frozen body with her own plump flesh.

That night Esther did not sleep a wink, mourning her beloved chicken and listening to the sounds of the night. The screeches from the henhouse were not repeated. But the next morning, when she went to feed the chickens, she was greeted by the same atrocious scene as before. Another broody hen had disappeared, leaving a heap of bloody feathers behind her. Again Esther burst into Sara's house, alarming the women waiting on her doorstep with her ghastly expression and bloody hands.

She spent yet another sleepless night standing at the window overlooking the henhouse. There was no suspicious movement in the yard, and the henhouse was as still and dark as usual. Once, she was startled by the sound of a little screech breaking the silence, but when she hurried out she discovered that it was only a dream that had disturbed the rest of one of her broody hens, which fell asleep again immediately, tucking its head into the warm down of its body. The next morning she woke up in her chair, her head giddy from lack of sleep, her mouth dry, and her limbs stiff. She ran to the henhouse and again she found a sticky pool of broken eggs and a vanished chicken.

In despair she went the same day to the tinkers' market and came home with a large wooden board to which a strong coiled spring was attached by a thick square wire. "It's a trap," she explained to Sara. "I'm going to bait it with a piece of meat and put it in the henhouse tonight, and we'll see what's caught in it."

That night Esther slept the sleep of the just, and the next day she found the usual upheaval in the henhouse. The trap stood on the floor where she had left it, but the bait had vanished into thin air. The same thing happened on the following nights. When only one scrawny hen and one red-combed rooster were left in the henhouse, she decided to bring them into the house at night, but she left the trap in the henhouse nevertheless. Before the first rays of the sun appeared in the sky, the rooster under her bed began to ruffle his feathers. He stretched his body, lengthened his neck, and a triumphant crow burst out of his scrawny, naked crop. Afraid of the reaction of her family, who had been woken by the noise echoing throughout the dark house, Esther began to run after the rooster, which hopped onto the beds, pecked at their occupants' hair, and crowed loudly into their ears. The chase ended in the kitchen, where she found the rooster perched on the wooden table, pecking at the remains of their last meal.

With much effort she managed to catch both birds, then put on her slippers and shuffled outside, determined to return them to their rightful home. As she shuffled across the yard, with the fowls flapping their wings under her arms, she saw a sight that tore a scream from her lips. Two pairs of glittering eyes greeted her in the forefront of the henhouse, one at the height of the ground and the other floating above it. Rooted to the spot, with the chickens struggling soundlessly in her hands, she stood still and stared at the demonic eyes gleaming at her. She heard a little girl's voice and another voice gurgling in reply. When the two pairs of eyes encountered her corpulent stock-still figure, they opened wide and flashed green sparks at her. Immediately after that the sound of pattering feet was heard. One pair of eyes came quickly up to her and slipped between her feet planted at the entrance to the henhouse. From close quarters she could make out the pointed nose, the short legs, the small, elongated body, and the bushy tail dragging on the ground and leaving a long train like a feather duster behind it.

Esther let go of the chickens and they dropped to the ground with clucks of relief and started running round the yard in search of worms for breakfast. She advanced in the direction of the remaining pair of eyes gleaming at her from the darkness of the henhouse. Her hands groping in gloom in front of her encountered wiry, bristling hair. She immediately recognized it as Geula's, from all the times when she had grabbed her by the hair and led her to her grandmother's house.

"What have you done?" she screamed at her. "Why did you let him kill my hens?"

Her body trembling, the little girl mumbled, "I didn't want the fox to die. All I did was free him from the trap."

Esther, always merciful, led Geula home, asking her only: "If you see him tomorrow, tell him not to come. And if my chickens are spared, I won't tell your grandmother."

That night the chickens slept as usual in the henhouse. The next morning Esther heard the rooster's voice announcing the dawn of a new day. She hurried out to the henhouse and found both her surviving chickens without a single feather missing from their tails. Whether Geula had watched over them all night or chased the fox away Esther did not know. From that day on she called her Vixen. When Sara asked Esther to explain the nickname, she said that the color of Geula's hair reminded her of a fox's fur, her pointed teeth of a fox's teeth, and her cunning of the cunning of the animal that she had never succeeded in seeing face to face. From then on, whenever Esther cooked a chicken, she would place its head, its innards, and its clawed, chopped-off toes on an old tin plate at the entrance to the henhouse. The next day the plate would be empty. To anyone who asked about this strange custom of hers, she replied that this was the only way she could ensure that her family would always have chickens to eat.

*   *   *

As usual, it was Esther who brought the bad news. "The Arabs are getting ready to kill us all," she panted, hanging on tightly to the buttons of her blouse as if to keep her heart from jumping out of her skin in its terror. "They're going to gather after the Friday prayers and invade our houses, rape the women, and smash the children's skulls," she said, and her eyes darted from side to side as if counting the heads of her vast brood of children and grandchildren, to make sure that none of them were missing. Pnina-Mazal, who had come home early from work, confirmed the rumor.

"It's true, they're talking about it at the staff headquarters too, and trying to make preparations in time. The Arab nationalists are raising their heads," she admitted. "Don't leave the house this Friday, and don't let Geula and Avraham roam the streets. Lock yourselves in and close the shutters."

While Sara and Pnina-Mazal were sitting in the kitchen and discussing the evils about to befall them, Fatma burst through the door, her hair wild as a keener's at a funeral and her immense bosom heaving with every breath. "I heard they're coming here too. Come and stay with me. There they won't dare touch you," she urged, distractedly stroking Geula's untidy hair. Sara looked at the line of supplicants waiting outside the kitchen door and shook her head.

"I'm staying here with the children. Nothing will happen to us. Stop worrying," she said to Fatma, and handed a bottle of water to the old man standing at the head of the line, placing his shaking hands in hers. "Take a sip of the water twice a day, and you'll feel better," she said gently.

On Friday Pnina-Mazal went to work, leaving Yitzhak planted in his padded chair and Avraham playing with a pile of empty bottles in the kitchen. Since there was no line waiting at the door as usual, Sara busied herself with baking bread for the Sabbath and waited for Gershon to arrive for Geula's morning lessons. But the teacher did not come. With her hands sticky with dough Sara opened the door of the children's room. Trousers, shirts, and panties were strewn around the room as if a violent hurricane had passed through and scattered the contents of the drawers in all directions. There was no sign of Geula. Alarmed, she went out into the yard, but the little girl was nowhere to be seen.

Holding her sticky, floury hands out in front of her, she knocked impatiently at Esther's door, leaving doughy traces behind her. A frightened pair of eyes peeped out of the window, the door opened a crack, and Esther's sturdy arms pulled her inside.

"What are you doing outside? Have you taken leave of your senses? You nearly made me die of fright."

"Geula, where's Geula, is she with you? She's not at home," said Sara weakly.

"Have you checked the top of the mulberry tree?" said Esther mockingly.

"You know very well that she doesn't climb up there anymore," Sara replied. "Are you sure you haven't seen her this morning?"

"And who told you that she went out this morning?" Esther retorted. "Sometimes when I wake up in the middle of the night to inspect the chickens I catch a glimpse of Geula in the yard, whispering with strange men in the dark. Once I even saw her leaving the boundaries of the neighborhood, and that wasn't in the morning or the afternoon either," she said, with a note of rebuke in her voice.

"Why didn't you tell me before?" asked Sara tearfully.

"You're busy with your bottles, and I was sure you knew about it; after all, you let her run wild and put no limits on her freedom. She doesn't want to go to school—you bring her a private tutor at home; she doesn't want to wear dresses—you let her wear Fatma's children's cast-off trousers; she doesn't want to be by herself—you bring her the Arab boy for company. If she wants to, she stays on the top of the tree; if she wants to, she comes down. Why should I tell you anything if you let her do whatever she likes? She's been a bad example to my daughters and granddaughters from the day she was born. 'Why is Geula allowed to play outside all day?' and 'Why doesn't Geula have to help with the housework?' That's all I hear all day long. And now you don't know where she is? Don't you worry about her. From what I've seen up to now she knows how to look after herself," she snapped, gathering her brood about her and counting their heads with her hands.

* * *

Sara left feeling chastised. The dough on her hands had hardened, sticking her fingers together, and she had to knock on Bracha's door with her elbow. A little hatch opened up on the door and she squeezed through it into the dark house. Geula was not among the children clustering fearfully round Bracha either, and after taking a sip of the sugar water she offered her, Sara left her house feeling weak with anxiety. When she failed to find Geula in any of the neighbors' houses, she began running round the streets of the deserted town calling her name, while people peered at her through the slats of their closed shutters and shouted at her to take shelter because the pogromists were coming. Her eyes blind with fear, Sara hired an Arab coachman, who only after seeing the money in her hand agreed to take her where she wanted to go.

Sara arrived at the British staff headquarters and burst into Pnina-Mazal's office panting for breath. Without hesitation Pnina-Mazal ordered the car and the driver to take them to Fatma's village.

"She's here with us in the village," Fatma said calmly, as if she had been waiting for them all morning, and her eyes gleamed at them from the darkness of the room.

"Where?" both women asked at once.

"The teacher Gershon is with her, too, and so is Muhammad"— she added the name of her son even though it was self-evident that he would follow wherever Geula went.

"And what has Gershon got to do with it?" asked Pnina-Mazal.

"He came with her last night. They knocked at my door. Muhammad went out and they went off together, and I haven't seen them since. People say that they've shut themselves up with some other Jews in a house at the edge of the village, and they're printing a newspaper and talking all day."

One of Fatma's children volunteered to lead them to the house. He pointed from a distance at a stone house surrounded by a thorny hedge, with all its windows shuttered by heavy iron blinds. Then he turned on his heel and ran for his life, as if the house were full of evil genies. Muffled voices and the creaking of a rusty machine reached their ears.

With trembling hands Sara banged on the door and ordered them to let her in. The muffled voices fell silent abruptly, and someone opened the slat of a blind to see the cause of this unexpected interruption. When the door failed to open she went on banging on it, using her knees as well. Exhausted, the women collapsed outside the locked door, and in the meantime the village rabble crowded round them.

"They won't harm us," said Sara to Pnina-Mazal, who stole an apprehensive look at their audience. "They regard Geula as one of them and we're her family."

Youths armed with sticks and iron bars arrived and rammed the doors of the house. When their efforts were unsuccessful they gathered the remnants of their pride and set out for town to "kill the Jews." After they disappeared, a few youths in light khaki uniforms burst round the bend in the lane and, in Hebrew, ordered the people hiding in the house to open the door. At this command the door opened, and people began streaming out, their faces stiff with fear. Among those bringing up the rear were Gershon, Geula, and Muhammad, holding hands and looking exhausted. Muhammad nodded politely at Sara and Pnina-Mazal, as if he had just met them in pleasant social circumstances, and then he stroked Geula's cheek, smoothed her unruly hair, and holding his head high marched toward his house.

For the first time in her life Geula burst into tears and asked to be taken home. On the truck belonging to the khaki-uniformed youths she folded her long limbs and cuddled up in Sara's lap like a baby, burying her head in her bosom at the sounds of the shattering glass, shots, and screams of the victims. Pnina-Mazal, avoiding her daughter's eyes, listened to the frightened conversations in Russian between the people who had been besieged in the house.

"Mother," she breathed in horror into Sara's ear, "Geula was with the Palestiner Kommunistisher Partei, the Communists." She said the last word aloud and turned to Gershon. "You're not working for us anymore. Geula will go to school. Five years with you were more than enough."

Gershon let his head fall onto his chest as if she had delivered a blow to his trembling stalklike neck.

He was never seen in the neighborhood again. Later his friends told Geula that since he had failed to get rid of the British army, put an end to the Mandate, abolish the Balfour Declaration, and expel the Jewish invaders, and failed too in his efforts to bring about an agrarian revolution among the Arab peasants, he had left the country. He also knew, so they told her, that Pnina-Mazal had given his description to the British police. He had left early in the morning, by train, dressed as an Arab fellah. Afterward he had reached the Suez Canal, where he had boarded a ship on his way to Moscow. Years later, when Geula tried to pick up his traces, she was told that he had been caught up in Father Stalin's purges and sent to a labor camp in Siberia.

* * *

Before I was born my mother lived in Meah Shearim. To be exact, she hid there. It seems that there were a lot of people looking for her. The Hagana were looking for her because of her ceaseless efforts to incite the Arab population against the Jews. She was in the habit of introducing the sentence "Annul the Balfour Declaration and expel the Jewish invaders" into her speeches and repeating it tirelessly at every opportunity that came her way, and the words acted on her audience like a red rag waved in front of a raging bull.

The British declared her to be a Soviet agent, put out a poster with the picture of a young girl with bristling hair and a smile that exposed pointed teeth, and promised a reward for information regarding her whereabouts. As a result, even her comrades in the Party felt that she was endangering them with her extreme views, and tried to keep her at arm's length, on the pretext that "the Comintern was dissatisfied with her activities."

Meah Shearim was an ideal refuge for her. No one would have dreamed of looking for her in this ultra-Orthodox neighborhood, where the women covered their shaved heads in dark kerchiefs, and the men slipped like black shadows through the narrow alleys. She arrived in the neighborhood wearing dark glasses as a barrier between her and the world, her dyed hair cropped like a man's and resembling the bristles of a black boot-brush, and her slender body clad in a loose, shabby man's suit. There she settled down with a large heavy suitcase full of books in a dark, narrow room that shared a wall with the Hassidei Tzaddikim yeshiva and its pure and pious young scholars.

At first the landlord refused to rent her the room, even though he needed the money and she was prepared to pay handsomely for the moldy room. He decided that he could not possibly allow this woman, so brazenly and blasphemously dressed in men's clothing, to live in the room, in case, God forbid, she should lead astray the young men who spent their days and nights studying the Holy Books and purifying their souls.

The next day a bearded young man in the black garb of the Orthodox knocked at his door, pulled out a thick wad of notes, and asked about a room for rent. The landlord was only too happy to rent him the room. A couple of hours later she appeared with her suitcase, and the signed contract in her hand. Who that bearded man was nobody knows, for the moment he received the bronze key in his hand he disappeared, never to be seen again. After the event the landlord complained tearfully to everyone he met how he had been tricked by a smooth-talking pimp in disguise into renting the room to his undesirable tenant. The imposter he described as a Sephardic Jew who spoke with an Oriental accent.

The landlord's wife, who had been present throughout the negotiations and more than once had poked him warningly in the ribs with her sharp elbows, informed her neighbors with mournful sighs that even though her husband claimed that the imposter was a Jew, she was sure that he was an Arab. Her intuition had never deceived her, and she was ready to swear that he was an Arab disguised as a yeshiva student. She, who was immediately aware of the fraud, had tried to warn her husband. But he, with the smell of Mammon rising in his nostrils and the bribe money pushed into his pockets, had silenced her with "Be quiet, woman" whenever she tried to say something and had brushed away her elbows digging into his ribs.

"And this is the result. Instead of a pure, pious yeshiva scholar studying in the room and steeping the place and its owners in an atmosphere of holiness and the blessings of the righteous, we had this slut in man's clothing. She paid, naturally she paid the money, but she brought no blessing. On the contrary, all she brought was trouble—imagine, an illustrious yeshiva, and right next door to it that whore in dark glasses that she wore even when it was raining, even when it was dark outside. As if the Lord's light wasn't good enough for her, as if she had to filter it before it reached her eyes."

She had hardly moved in before the rumors spread. Those were palmy days for the tenant who occupied the rooms above her, Fruma Itzikovitz. Everyone began to greet her warmly in the street, and to offer her the freshest produce in the market, and all they wanted was for her to spy on her black-haired neighbor, who emerged from her room like a blind mole from its hole. At first Fruma didn't know what to tell her avid questioners. She neither saw nor heard her. If she left the house at all, it was always late in the evening when all the inhabitants of the neighborhood were shut up in their homes. But later on she found plenty to tell them, so much that she didn't always know where to begin and where to leave off.

She told them that young men and women had begun to go in and out of her neighbor's room as if it were a railway station, both sexes crowded together in that narrow little room, scandalizing heaven with their immorality. What they did there, she didn't know. The woman told Fruma that she was a student, and her friends came to study with her. And when she asked her why she had picked a room in their neighborhood of all places, she said that it was the cheapest room she could find. Later, in the strictest confidence, Fruma told the women bathing with her in the mikvah that an Arab youth dropped in on her all the time, as familiar as if he were her husband. He always came with his hands full. Sometimes he brought a basket of vegetables. In the summer he came bearing a great watermelon, sometimes he brought eggs, once she saw a slaughtered chicken poking out of his basket, and he even brought bunches of wildflowers. When he came to visit her and she wasn't at home he would take the key from under the flowerpot next to the door and go inside and make himself at home as if he owned the place. In a whisper that went from mouth to ear she recounted how one night when baby Itzik kept her awake because he was teething, she was standing at the window and she saw the Arab slipping out of her neighbor's door early in the morning, after apparently spending the night with her.

Fruma was also the only person in the neighborhood who had actually been inside her room. This happened after the diapers she hung out to dry were blown off the line by the wind and fell into the courtyard. Geula picked them up and took them inside, and thus Fruma found herself knocking at her door, afraid that it might be opened by the Arab, or that Geula might have other company and she would find herself at close quarters with a strange man, God forbid. But it turned out that Geula was more frightened of Fruma than Fruma was of her. Only after cross-examining her did she agree to open the door, and then only a crack. At those moments she looked like a hunted animal. She asked her politely not to let her washing fall into her courtyard again, as she did not want to be disturbed. The brief visit and quick survey of the room satisfied Fruma's curiosity. There were no young men there, to her relief, nor girls either. It was a small room with piles of books in every unoccupied corner. Just like a yeshiva student.

❋   ❋   ❋

For a few months Geula lived in the room, and then she disappeared. Some say that her disappearance was connected to the great scandal that inflamed people's passions and caused a commotion in the entire neighborhood. The scandal led to a schism in the community, to quarrels between brothers, and in the end to a shameful article in the Zionist press and a campaign of vilification against the head of the Hassidei Tzaddikim yeshiva, which adjoined Geula's room. To this day, so many years after it happened, the affair has not been forgotten, and the story comes up again every Purim eve, diluting the joy of the holiday with the dire threat of splitting the community into two camps: those who believed in what had happened and the sceptics who claimed that nothing of the kind had ever taken place.

The news of the abomination that ostensibly had taken place within the walls of the yeshiva fell on the neighborhood like thunder from a clear sky. The yeshiva housed a collection of fine young scholars who came from all over the world to study there, and who, so it was said, took no interest in the vanities of this world. They rose before dawn to do the work of the Creator, washed their naked bodies in icy water, and went out into the fields in summer and winter to welcome the Holy Spirit.

The event that brought hatred and strife to the community took place on the day after the festival of Purim. One of the most brilliant scholars at the yeshiva asked for a private interview with the rabbi. Speaking haltingly, his eyes downcast, he told the rabbi about a disgraceful act committed by himself and his friends. The story spread through the neighborhood like wildfire. If the young scholar had not escaped from the yeshiva in time, he would no doubt have been lynched, beaten till he bled, and tarred and feathered to boot.

After his confession the young man packed his possessions, hired a cart and mule, loaded it with one chair, a down quilt, a little bookcase, and a set of all the volumes of the Talmud published in Warsaw. Then he climbed onto the cart and left the neighborhood. People say that as soon as he reached the first secular neighborhood he took off his Hassidic coat and hat, went into a barbershop, and asked the barber to shave off his earlocks and beard. In the end, the rumors went, he returned in disgrace to America, abandoned his studies, opened a liquor shop in a black neighborhood, fell in love with a black woman, married her in a blasphemous ceremony, and spent the rest of his life living with her and bringing up their coffee-colored children.

And this is the story he told the rabbi, a story that leaked to the newspapers and in whose wake Geula locked the door of her room behind her and disappeared from the neighborhood forever. It happened on the eve of Purim. The yeshiva students, merry with wine, kicked up a racket, danced on the tables, waved bottles of wine over their heads, and raved and ranted at the tops of their voices. When they emerged into the courtyard a figure approached them. Whether it was the figure of a man or a woman, the student could not say. This figure, whose face was smooth and whose body was draped in a man's coat, demanded that they be quiet, because their noise was making it impossible for it to concentrate on its studies.

"But it's Purim," the yeshiva students chorused in reply.

And the figure stood its ground and insisted that they stop their revels. Playfully they formed a circle round the figure and began teasing it, first with words and then with taps on its bare head, and they began throwing it round the circle from hand to hand, tickling it between the ribs, pinching its lean flesh and laughingly pulling off its big coat. The figure tried to fight back, begged for mercy, and tried to run away, but they would not stop. The more the figure pleaded, the more arrogantly they behaved.

In the end the wretched figure was lying flat on its face on the ground, its trousers pulled down and its ankles trapped inside them, its bare buttocks rising cheekily and temptingly in the air, while the pious youths crouched over it, came at it from behind, and performed unspeakable acts on it. And when the figure cried for help they shoved the neck of a wine bottle into its open mouth. And when it went on screaming, they sat on its back, held down its waving arms and kicking legs, and poured gallons of wine down its throat. The wine burst out of its mouth and nose like a fountain and wet its clothes. They kept on pouring wine down its throat until the figure lost consciousness and lay still, its face buried in the dirt, and they had their will of it. At dawn they departed, leaving behind them the body spread-eagled in the dirt. And when they sobered up a few hours later and hurried to the scene, the body was gone and they tried to wipe the memory of what they had done from their hearts. But for the student whose conscience drove him to confess to the rabbi, nobody would ever have known.

The day after the incident my mother crammed all her books into her suitcase, locked the room behind her, and stole out of the neighborhood never to return. Fruma, at her observation post, saw her stumbling out of the room, deathly pale and leaning on the Arab's arm. After that the Arab showed up at the landlord's door, put a month's rent on the table, returned the key, and disappeared. Fruma, with the fount of her stories dried up, deprived of her occupation as a sleuth, turned her attention to interpretation, and told whomever was interested that her heathen neighbor had left because she believed the slanderous rumors about the fine, upstanding yeshiva scholars. Presumably, she said, the girl had run away because she was afraid the same thing might happen to her.

⁕   ⁕   ⁕

The year my mother left Meah Shearim the War of Independence broke out. Most of the houses in the ultra–Orthodox neighborhood were damaged by shots fired from the adjacent Arab neighborhood. Men, women, and children fell like flies, and only the yeshiva, its students, and the houses next to it escaped unharmed, which was seen as a sign from heaven by those who had refused to believe the rumors and denied that the incident had ever taken place.

After the war was over the yeshiva was closed down. Today the premises are occupied by a welding shop famed for the quality of its window bars, and the soft murmur of Talmudic debate has been replaced by the noise of metal saws, blowtorches, and soldering irons. They say that attendance at the yeshiva had fallen off sharply before it closed down, and the few students that remained dispersed and went to study elsewhere. To anyone who asks, Fruma says with a sigh that pure souls like the boys who studied at the old yeshiva are impossible to find today.

Chapter Seventeen

The letter with the purple stamp picturing a man's crowned head was waiting for Pnina-Mazal on her office desk, hiding between the heavy wooden boxes. Notice of the liquidation of the office and orders to pack up the documents had reached them a month before, but she had done hardly anything about it. The date came closer, and she still had not succeeded in overcoming the weakness that took hold of her at the thought of burying her life in the pale wooden boxes smelling pungently of the best black Ceylon tea.

She recognized the handwriting on the envelope, and carefully, in order not to damage the stamp, she opened the letter with the ivory paper knife she had received as a prize for outstanding work.

At home, she told Sara about her day and casually mentioned the letter and the news that Davida was coming to take Avraham and save him from the war about to break out.

"Now she remembers," Sara responded sarcastically. "Never mind, let her come. Let's see her running round the country and looking for her overgrown son in all the kibbutz training camps."

On Saturday Avraham came to visit them. He was tall, long-limbed, tanned, with his fair hair combed back to reveal a high, lined forehead. He gave his father, planted in his chair, a friendly pat on the shoulder and tousled the few hairs left on his head. Then he stood opposite him, tried to catch his eye, and shouted at the top of his voice, as if his father were deaf: "Next month I'm getting married."

Sara and Pnina-Mazal came running startled from the kitchen, wiping their hands on checked towels.

"What were you yelling at Yitzhak like that for?" asked Sara.

"I was just informing my father that I'm getting married," he said lightly, as if he were talking about the breakfast he had eaten on the kibbutz before coming to Jerusalem.

The two women rose on tiptoe to kiss his cheeks, which smelled of the sun. His green eyes laughed at them.

"Mazal tov, and who's the bride?"

"A girl I met on the kibbutz, a refugee from the camps in Europe. Next time I'll bring her to meet you. And what do you think?" He turned to address his father. "Will you give me your blessing? Because if you don't I'll be forced to spend the rest of my life on an armchair next to yours," he added and slapped Yitzhak's shoulder with a force that jolted his slack body and made his head drop to his chest.

"If you see her you'll wake up," Avraham said with a wink. "She's beautiful. She reminds me of you," he said teasingly to Sara, who ran after him and tried to hit him with the wet kitchen towel in her hand.

"What are we going to do about your mother?" she asked him later that night, after telling him about the letter.

"We'll invite her to the wedding."

"She's coming here to take you back with her, to save you from harm in the war that's going to break out when the British leave the country."

Avraham looked at her in amazement, as if he couldn't believe his ears, and then burst into loud laughter and slapped his thighs as if he had just heard a good joke. "Are you serious?" he bellowed with laughter.

"Here's the letter," she said and handed him the letter, which was written in poor Hebrew.

The expression of amusement on his face gave way to one of astonishment. "I've got a crazy family. A father who's put down roots in an armchair and a mother I haven't heard from in thirty years and who suddenly wants to shelter me under her wing."

❖　❖　❖

A month before the final liquidation of the office Davida walked into Sara's kitchen as if she had just popped out to visit a neighbor and was returning after a couple of hours' absence. Her sparse hair was dyed blond, her lips were red, and two round pink spots of rouge adorned her sagging cheeks and gave her the look of a china doll. Her skinny body was clad in a suit of fine gray wool and on her head she wore a little felt hat. Her pale green eyes examined Sara in the dim light of the kitchen lamp and her transparent nostrils sniffed the scent of roses that pervaded the house.

"Where's Abie?" she asked as if they hadn't been separated for almost three decades.

"Avraham lives on a kibbutz, and next month he's getting married, God willing," Sara calmly replied, continuing to knead her cookie dough.

"He's coming back with me to England," Davida announced firmly. "The British are leaving, and you're all going to be slaughtered like sheep. That's what it says in the papers. He's my son and he'll do whatever I tell him."

"Try," said Sara pleasantly, and served her coffee and bagels strewn with sesame seeds, which she had just removed from the oven.

And so Davida—now called Rose—sat with her in the kitchen and told her about her husband, her life in England, and her daughter Helen, to whom she had given birth after a lot of difficulties.

"Don't you want to see Yitzhak?" Sara asked the unavoidable question.

"Of course, how is he?" she inquired perfunctorily.

Sara led her to his room, and there he sat, his face to the window and his back to them. Davida-Rose entered the room hesitantly. At the sound of her footsteps Yitzhak suddenly turned his head and looked for a long time at his former wife standing in front of him.

"Oh dear, he's losing his hair," she exclaimed shrilly, gave him a little pat on the back, and left him rooted in his chair. Sara, who followed her out of the room, noticed that the corners of her son's eyes were moist.

That was the last time Rose paid any attention to her ex-husband. From that moment on she treated him like a piece of furniture, even though his eyes filled with life whenever they fell on her and followed her round the house.

The following Saturday Avraham arrived accompanied by a short young woman whose dark eyes darted round the house with a hunted expression, like a trapped animal looking for a way to escape. When she calmed down she smiled at Sara and accepted her invitation to dunk freshly baked cookies in a hot cup of tea. Then Avraham took her on a tour of the house and introduced her to his father.

"Yitzhak, my father," he said to her. "Flora, my wife-to-be," he said to his father. Flora's hand reached out automatically to shake Yitzhak's and remained suspended in the air. Avraham gently lowered her hand, whispered something in her ear, and together they left the room.

A few minutes later Rose's shrill voice was heard at the door.

"Where's my Abie? My child, Mummy's here!" she announced at the top of her voice when they opened the door. Rose wasted no time on Yitzhak, who tried to catch her eye as she passed his chair. She burst into the kitchen and recoiled at the sight of the strange man who was sitting there and filling the little room with his big body.

Sara nodded her head.

"Abie?" Her eyes opened wide in astonishment.

"Mother!" he declared with a little smile and a nod of his head, gathered her in his muscular arms, and pressed her to him. "It's me, Mother. I'm so glad you could come for my wedding," he added, and introduced her to Flora.

Flora looked at her like a frightened rabbit.

"Flora, meet my mother, whom I haven't seen for thirty years."

Flora hesitantly held out her hand, and Rose's eyes were transfixed by the number tattooed on her arm. She took a firm grip on Flora's hand, put her finger in her mouth and wet it with spit, and by vigorous rubbing tried to erase the number from her skin. Flora attempted to pull her hand away, but Rose tightened her grip, leaving white marks on the girl's tanned wrist, wet her finger again, and made strenuous efforts to remove the blemish from her future daughter-in-law's arm.

"Mother, it doesn't come off, that's how she came to me and that's how she'll go to her grave," said Avraham with a smile.

"And what kind of a person brands herself with a number like cattle sold in the marketplace?"

"I'll explain it to you later," he promised, and immediately changed the subject to the preparations for the wedding, to the kibbutz, and to the big cabin they would be given to live in after they were married.

∗ ∗ ∗

Without being asked Sara spent the whole week baking crisp sesame cookies and packing them in tins. On the eve of the wedding she took out the red velvet dress she had made herself in honor of Yitzhak's bar mitzvah and hung it out to air on a branch of the mulberry tree in the yard. Then she filled the big tub, once used for washing the rose petals, with boiling water, and hung the dress over it to smooth out all the creases. That evening she tried it on and smiled to herself with satisfaction after inspecting her reflection in the mirror. The next day, after getting dressed, she combed her long white hair, gathered it up in a bun, and pinched her cheeks to make them pink.

Armed with maps and directions Edward drove Sara, Pnina-Mazal, and Rose straight to the dining room of the kibbutz, where the wedding ceremony was to be conducted. Rose, wearing a tight white silk dress with black polka dots and a matching black hat with a tulle veil that covered her face, was greeted by gales of laughter. A couple of wits even asked her to donate her hat to their poor kibbutz after the wedding so they could wear it to extract the honey from the beehives, "where it would no doubt scare the bees away," they added with a wink. And Rose, angry and offended, turned her slender back on them.

After the ceremony Rose did not take her eyes off her son and daughter-in-law, her looks following them wherever they went and turning giddily with them as they danced the hora in the middle of the circle that had formed around them. Afterward she took her daughter-in-law aside and conferred with her at length.

"What did she want?" Sara asked the girl without beating about the bush.

"She said that now I'm married to her son I'm like a daughter to her, and she'll take me back to England with her too."

After that Sara didn't let Rose out of her sight. Late at night, when the accordionist folded his instrument and put it away in its wooden box padded with purple velvet, and the kibbutz women began clearing the dishes off the tables, she informed Rose that it was time to go home.

"I'm staying here, and I won't budge until they tell me that they're coming with me," she announced.

"Avraham's married now, he's not the baby you left behind you, he's a grown man; you can't do as you wish with him," Sara retorted.

Avraham was called to make the peace, and he whispered to his mother so his friends wouldn't hear, "Thank you for coming, and now go back to Jerusalem with Sara, and I'll come and see you next week."

"Next week we'll all be on a ship on our way to London, or else we'll be slaughtered in our beds."

"I'm staying here with my wife," he said like a stubborn child.

"You're coming with me, and if your wife wants to stay here, as far as I'm concerned she can stay."

On her son's wedding night Rose slept over at the kibbutz, and the next day too, and in spite of all Avraham's efforts to persuade her she refused to return to Jerusalem. Later that week Pnina-Mazal sent her an urgent letter by special messenger to inform her that the last of the British had folded their flags and gone back to England. The next day Rose packed her bags and embarked on the last ship sailing from Haifa, never to return.

Six months later they received a letter from her, inquiring about the situation in the country, and asking Sara to keep an eye on her son and not to let him wander around by himself in the kibbutz fields at night. When the war was over and Avraham's son Yiftah was born, she sent her grandson a blue woolen sailor suit, together with an explicit request not to be called Granny.

*   *   *

Geula stood in the darkness at the front door, dark glasses on her eyes and her hair black and cropped like a boy's. Sara paused for a moment before she recognized her granddaughter and fell upon her neck with cries of joy.

"Geula, you've come back, I'm so glad to see you. What happened to your hair?"

"Never mind," she replied impatiently, gave her a light push, and rushed into the house, as if a pack of devils were hot on her heels. "Close the door and lock it," she said in a commanding voice, "and if anyone knocks, don't open. And if people come and ask you about me, say you haven't seen me."

"They've already been here and asked questions, and you have no idea how much trouble you've caused your mother. That was the last thing she needed, working for the British. You should know that she nearly lost her job because of you," Sara said reproachfully.

"Where is Mother?" asked Geula, as if she had just remembered that she existed.

"Translating at a party at the High Commissioner's."

"Don't tell her I was here."

Sara led her granddaughter to the kitchen and inspected her closely.

"You're pregnant," she said dryly. "Who's the father?"

"Let's not talk about the father," said Geula, astonished at her grandmother's powers of perception, which had succeeded in penetrating the walls of her still-flat stomach. "In short, how do I get rid of it? You know. You have the power."

Sara sat down heavily on a chair.

"I have been gifted with the power to give life, not to take it," she said. "It's a girl, and you have to give birth to her. You won't have any more children," she said with cruel frankness.

Geula stared at her in dismay, then she recovered and blurted out, "Nonsense. How can you possibly know, and why should I listen to your nonsense?"

Sara said nothing and put the kettle on to boil.

Suddenly there was a knock at the door.

"Don't open it," said Geula in alarm.

"Don't worry," Sara reassured her. "It's only Edward."

"Tell him to go away."

Sara shuffled to the door, opened it a crack, and whispered to the figure standing outside.

"At least let me say hello to her," Geula heard his voice say.

"She refuses to see anyone. Let's leave her alone today."

Sara closed the door and locked it.

When she returned to the kitchen she saw that all the cookies on the plate had disappeared.

"Come home before the birth," she said. "We'll help you and we can look after the baby if you're busy," she offered generously.

Geula frowned. "If I decide to keep it. You have to understand that it's very inconvenient for me. I had plans to study law, and this is the last thing I need now."

"I told you that we'd help you. There's plenty of room."

Geula pursed her lips scornfully. "Yes, and every day I'll have to fight my way through all the women who thanks to you will bring about a population explosion and deplete the food resources of the world."

Sara was silent.

After providing her granddaughter with a bag full of fragrant cookies she said good-bye to her and repeated her request: "Come back to me for the birth."

Seven months later, when the shells were exploding over the besieged city, Geula returned to her grandmother's house. Pnina-Mazal was the first to see them entering the door, Geula leaning on Muhammad's strong arm, her belly rising in front of her and her face twisted in pain.

"Put the kettle on," Sara said serenely from the kitchen, even before she saw her granddaughter on the doorstep. She spoke quietly and calmly, as if she were asking Pnina-Mazal to to boil water for tea for their guests.

Obediently and without asking superfluous questions, Pnina-Mazal did as she was told and filled the copper tub with boiling water. Geula stole a glance at Muhammad, who stroked her hair, kissed her lightly on the cheek, and went outside. Sara took Geula in her arms and led her to her room. Clean, stiff sheets had been spread over the brass bed, as if Sara knew in advance that her granddaughter's time had come.

"It will be an easy birth. I don't expect any complications," she said to Geula in a reassuring tone.

Chapter Eighteen

About half an hour later I emerged into the light of day on my great-grandmother's big brass bed. From the moment I came alive I used all five senses. The first cry that burst from my mouth was addressed to my mother. She looked into my face with a shocked expression, as if refusing to believe that her body had produced this kicking and screaming red bundle. I looked back at her, blinking slightly in the glaring light invading my eyes, which had grown accustomed to the darkness of the womb.

When Sara dipped me in the lukewarm water in the copper tub, I breathed in the scent of roses, which rose into the air with the vapors of the water, penetrating my nostrils and adhering to my skin.

"It's a girl, it's a girl, it's a girl . . ." were the first words that trembled on my eardrums and made me forget the sound of the beating heart and the gentle murmur of the waters in which I had been swimming for the past nine-and-a-bit months. The nipple that was pushed into my mouth straight after I was born filled it with a warm, dense liquid, which stimulated the taste buds on my tongue, and imprinted one of the gray cells in my brain with the taste "sweet." My hands fluttering around my body became entangled in Sara's hair as she bent over my mother, and as I clenched my fists in what students of babies call the "monkey reflex" I found myself clutching a few long hairs uprooted from my great-grandmother's scalp. These hairs, which were like silk to the touch, remained imprisoned in my fist for a few days after I pulled them out, and they soothed my sleep during my first nights in the air of the world.

⋆   ⋆   ⋆

Edward would arrive every morning in his black Ford convertible, wearing a pith helmet and a white safari suit and boasting a white cane with a gleaming brass knob. At the door he would breathe in the heavy scents, pause a moment, smile to himself, and then knock discreetly on the iron door with the knob of his cane. She would hurry to open it with a welcoming smile, her white hair gathered in a bun on the nape of her neck and her body giving off a strong smell of freshly plucked roses.

In their regular morning ritual he would examine Sara gravely through the lenses of his pince-nez, as if he were seeing her for the first time in his life, kiss her gently on her forehead, and repeat the sentence he said to her every morning, year after year, until the day he died: "You're the most beautiful woman in the world." And she would giggle shyly, like a maid of tender years receiving her first compliment from a young man, and give him the same reply that she repeated word for word all those years: "They have eyes and see not. I'm already an old grandmother." Then she would ceremoniously invite him to come inside, as if he had never visited her house before. After that she would lead him into the kitchen, seat him at the small, scarred wooden table, and serve him strong morning coffee and a sesame cookie still warm from the oven.

Thus they would sit until the line of women lengthened under the mulberry tree and she went out to them with little bottles of water in her hands. While she was busy with the women, he would set up his camera stand and photograph his beloved, who stood out with her white hair, smiling face, and shining eyes among the hard-faced, dull-eyed young women. With his head buried under the black cloth he would hum the verse from the Song of Songs to himself: "As the lily among thorns, so is my love among the daughters."

Every morning he photographed her and every night he developed the photographs in the darkroom in his house. When the pictures dried he tied them in bundles and put them away in square English biscuit tins. Every evening he returned to her house laden with food he bought in the market, sat with her in the kitchen, and helped her to peel potatoes and wash vegetables. After they ate he would lie on his back on the carpet in the sitting room and entertain her with stories of his travels. When she tired he would lead her to bed, lay her down, hold her hand, and put her to sleep with lullabies that he sang to her in English. Then he would kiss her lightly on the forehead, whisper words of love that brought a blush to her beautiful, faded face, and go home enveloped in the scent of roses. And she would remain by herself in her brass bed, with tender ocean waves blissfully rocking her body.

And so it was day after day. He never missed his daily visit. Even in winter, on days when the city of Jerusalem was covered with a blanket of heavy snow that choked the streets and bent the boughs of the cypress trees under its weight, he would put on his galoshes and his warm fur hat and plough through the snow with his stick. With all the furious determination of a knight of old overcoming trials and tribulations to reach his lady love he would beat a path to her door. Then he would thaw his bones at the kitchen stove, and she would rebuke him and say that one day he would kill himself for her sake and that she wasn't worth the sacrifice.

And so it could have continued, but for the stone thrown by an Arab boy next to the Nablus Gate and intended for another. The stone was aimed at a black-garbed yeshiva student on his way to the Western Wall, and cast from the roof of Abu Fasha's café, which was situated at the foot of a hill covered by the rain-eroded tombstones of an ancient cemetery. The murder was witnessed by dozens of men silently sucking their hookahs and contemplating the scene with dreamy expressions on their faces while rolling amber prayer beads between their slack fingers. Later investigation revealed that the stone, which had been uprooted from the paved courtyard of the café, had fallen straight into the open roof of Edward's Ford on its way to Sara's house, and smashed his skull.

✳   ✳   ✳

On the day the stone was thrown Sara locked up her house, sent away the women besieging her door, and armed with bottles of rose water presented herself at the Augusta Victoria Hospital at the Mountain of Olives, where Edward had been taken. As soon as she appeared in the doorway with the fragrant bottles in her hands Edward's bandaged head turned toward her.

His nostrils eagerly breathed in the familiar and beloved smell, and he held his weak arms out to her. With tears streaming down her finely wrinkled cheeks she caressed his bandaged head, stroked his unseeing eyes, kissed his dry lips, which sought hers beneath the bloody bandages, and whispered words of love in his ear.

When the nurse in a nun's wimple left the room Sara raised his head and put the rose water to his lips. Edward swallowed it like a drowning man, and little rivulets streamed down his face and onto his body, seeped into the bandages covering his head, soaked the hospital pajamas, and collected in the heavy mattress, banishing the smell of death and dying of the patients who had preceded him. He turned his unseeing eyes to Sara and whispered, "You're the most beautiful woman in the world."

With tears in her eyes Sara made the usual reply, "They have eyes and see not . . . I'm an old grandmother already." After she had composed herself she looked at Edward. His head beat against the pillow in a desperate attempt to see her, but not a single ray of light penetrated his bandaged eyes to bring him the sight of her beloved face.

When his head stopped thudding, his lips were sucked inward, his ears stopped reacting to her endearments, and his body was still, she called the doctors. They took his pulse and told her that they were sorry. She went on standing silently by his side for a long time, until one of the nuns gave in to her pleas and unrolled the bandages from his face as carefully and gently as if she were treating a feeling, breathing man. Edward's blue eyes were wide open under the bandages. They gazed at her lovingly as if determined not to forgo the sight of her beloved face for a fraction of a second, and his lips, which gave off the scent of wilted roses, were parted in a blissful smile.

In the evening she went to his house and banged on the carved iron gate. The faithful Sudanese servant, whose curls had turned white and whose shoulders were stooped, greeted her with tears streaming down his cheeks. Without her having to say a word he knew the purpose of her visit, and he led her through the rooms of the house, where the cupids on the ceilings looked down with tired, faded faces, the arrows of love unused in the quivers on their backs. With the heavy bronze key clattering on his waist he opened a little side door and pulled a string to switch a red light, which swayed above their heads and spread shadows of blood on the windowless walls. When her eyes grew accustomed to the dim light she saw the tall stacks of biscuit tins he had told her about. With the servant's help she emptied the room and loaded its contents onto the cart she had hired at the Jaffa Gate.

That night, with tears streaming ceaselessly down her cheeks, she opened the tins piled around her and filling her room, and she stroked the faces looking up at her. In her mind's eye she saw Edward standing with his legs planted firmly apart to photograph General Allenby's cavalry, kneeling to photograph little Geula with her arms around Muhammad, looming over her to photograph her head rising above the heads of the women surrounding her.

When the red rays of the sun filtered through the slats of the blinds, she reached the last packet. Her face turned red. For a moment it seemed that she would tear them to pieces, but she calmed down and went up to the old *sandouk* standing in the corner of the room. She lifted the lid and sneezed as a cloud of dust covered her head. Quickly, as if afraid that someone would discover her secret, she pulled out her wedding dress and ripped off a wide band of cloth. Then she wrapped the cloth carefully round the sheaf of pictures in her hand, pushed the bundle wrapped up like a body in a shroud into a little tin box, and buried it deep in the chest. The other pictures she crammed higgledy-piggledy into the biscuit tins, emptied the *sandouk* of its contents, and replaced them, tin upon tin, with the treasure left her by Edward, with love.

Worn out by a sleepless night and by the weeping that had torn her body apart, she hurried to the door in the morning at the sound of a knock from the brass-knobbed cane. A strong smell of withered roses greeted her as she opened the door and she heard Edward's voice saying, "You're the most beautiful woman in the world." This time she did not answer him. She left the door open and went into the kitchen to make coffee for her lover who was no more.

They buried him with due pomp and ceremony in the American colony cemetery, under a rustling glade of pine trees on the summit of Mount Scopus, in a spot overlooking a view of Jerusalem. His eulogists mentioned his contribution to the city and stole hard looks at Sara, who tore the collar of her dress and murmured Kaddish to herself. When the ring of hostility tightened round the fresh grave, she withdrew and went up to the stooping Sudanese servant, and they stood there together and looked at the black, excluding backs of the men of the American colony encircling the grave and performing their alien rites. For a long time she waited with the Sudanese until the last of the mourners left. When she was alone she took a bottle of rose water out of her bag, went up to the grave, murmured words of love, and drenched the parched soil with the scented water.

One week later the war broke out. Edward's house and his grave remained on the Jordanian side of the divided city.

From that time, until the city was liberated, the same scene was repeated month after month, year after year. The members of the convoys to Mount Scopus recounted that at the Mandelbaum Gate checkpoint they would see an old woman whose beauty shone through her black clothes blocking the armored cars with her body. She wanted them to take a bottle of rose water with them up to the mountain and pour it onto one of the graves there. And she explained that it was in the section of the cemetery reserved for the American colony, and the cross engraved on the marble tombstone pointed in the direction of the new city. The members of the convoy never refused her request. After taking the bottle they received her blessing and a bottle of scented water to strengthen their spirits.

They found the grave easily. It was surrounded on all sides by red rose bushes, which gave off fresh, flowery scents. And when they poured the rose water onto the grave, it washed away the dust that had gathered on the tombstone, swept away the pine needles lying on it, and watered the rose bushes planted around it.

After the liberation of Jerusalem she did not go up to the mountain. Nor did she ever return to his house near the Nablus Gate, which in the course of the years had become a luxurious hotel. And when longings pierced her heart she would light her bedside lamp, go up to the *sandouk,* take out one of the biscuit tins, and spend a night of love with her lover who was no more.

*   *   *

The sons and grandsons of Abu Fasha, who inherited his café, did not bother to replace the uprooted paving stone with a new one, as if they wanted to leave the empty space as a memorial to that first stone, thrown before its time, the first in the long line of murderous stones that were to be thrown in the city of Jerusalem in the years to come.

*   *   *

A few decades after Edward's death, in a particularly rainy year, the puddle that had collected in the hole left by the uprooted paving stone in Abu Fasha's café brimmed over. That same evening, when the café was crowded with people, the waterlogged hilltop cemetery collapsed onto the café sheltering beneath it. The dead invaded the living in a landslide of tombstones, yellowing skeletons, human skulls baring their teeth in frozen grins, and mountains of brown mud full of human bones, which choked those sitting in the land of the living with the pipes of steaming hookahs still in their mouths. That same night, when the rescue party was cleaning up the floodlit death scene, the body of Abu Fasha's son was found, his crushed skull stuck in the hole left by the absent paving stone.

✻　✻　✻

One morning the line of women waiting for Sara's blessing was longer than usual. Crazy Dvora ran to and fro, handing out numbers to the perspiring women with round yellow sweat stains spreading under their armpits.

Number one hundred and three accepted her slip from Dvora with a small smile of thanks. She was a middle-aged woman seated in a wheelchair, wearing a white lace dress; a straw hat trimmed with red cherries shaded her face. In contrast to all the other women with their perspiring bodies and exhausted faces, she looked as fresh as if she had just emerged from the bath. Her fair hair, which was streaked with gray, was braided into two plaits that encircled her fair face like a halo. Her tip-tilted nose was delicately strewn with freckles that spread to the middle of her plump cheeks, and her feet were shod in white canvas sandals that had never trodden the ground. Next to her sat a young man in a brightly colored shirt and trousers, with fair hair, pale blue eyes, and heavy sideburns. He was humming a rhythmic tune to himself and tapping his feet.

"Lady, don't you think you're a little too old for a fertility blessing?" asked Dvora in her rude way as she thrust a number slip into the woman's hand. "And as for the wheelchair, Sara doesn't do legs anymore. Only fertility. But if you want to wait, nobody's stopping you. You can always try," she added and turned to the woman next in line.

The springs of the wheelchair squeaked slightly as it rolled into the darkness of the house. Sitting up in bed and smiling, Sara received them in her room.

The woman's eyes, which were straying over the room, suddenly opened wide. Her face paled and she gripped the arms of her chair in a desperate attempt to stand up. Then she dropped back heavily again, took off her round glasses, which had misted over, and wiped them agitatedly on the wide skirt of her dress. The young man followed her look and his eyes came to rest on the picture that had focused her attention. It was hanging on the whitewashed wall, above Sara's bed, between two pictures of men in fezzes.

"That's my father," she said, partly to herself, partly to the young man, who was looking at her anxiously.

"Elizabeth," Sara said, breaking the tense silence in the room, "you've come back. How good it is to see you. How is your mother?"

"My mother died ten years ago," came the halting, somewhat surprised reply.

Silence fell again. Elizabeth sniffed the scented air appreciatively and hesitated before going on. "My father told me about the smells. I've come from the house. I had to wait a long time at the Mandelbaum Gate before they gave me a permit to enter the town, and I have to go back tomorrow. They told me that you have the photographs."

"Yes, your father left them to me," Sara said almost apologetically.

"I'd like to have the photographs of myself and my mother and a few of the town as a memento," said Elizabeth, her voice full of pleading, as if she expected a refusal. "I'm writing a new book about Jerusalem and my family and I'd like to illustrate it with the photographs. If you have no objections, of course," she added.

"Come back this evening, and Pnina-Mazal can help you choose."

As if unable to believe her good fortune, Elizabeth turned to the youth, who was gripping the handles of her wheelchair so tightly that his knuckles turned white, and translated Sara's words to him. A smile appeared on his face, his blue eyes opened wide, and he nodded at her in thanks. At that moment Sara felt the earth slipping beneath her feet as she heard the ocean waves murmuring in her ears, threatening to drag her down to the depths.

"Please allow me to introduce my son Robert," said Elizabeth, noticing Sara's pallor. "He accompanies me everywhere."

"Edward's grandson," Sara whispered, as if to herself.

Robert bent down and whispered something to his mother with a smile. "He wants me to tell you that you're the most beautiful woman he's ever seen," Elizabeth said.

"They have eyes and see not," Sara whispered, turning even paler than before. "I'm already an old grandmother."

At that moment the tension relaxed and Elizabeth turned her wheelchair toward Sara and buried her head in her lap, weeping bitterly. Sara stroked her hair.

"I know he was happy with you," she said. "In all the letters he sent me he told me about his love for you and about all your good deeds."

Sara was moved by her words. She sat leaning forward on her bed, stroking Elizabeth's head, her eyes fixed on Robert as tears rolled down her cheeks and wet the gray head on her lap.

Crazy Dvora burst into the room with an anxious expression on her face. The line outside was growing longer and she couldn't understand what was taking them so long in the room.

Elizabeth, Edward—Dvora," Sara introduced them. And she immediately recovered, cleared her throat, and said, "Sorry, I meant Robert, Edward's grandson."

Dvora and Elizabeth pretended not to have noticed the mistake.

Afterward she asked Dvora to take her guests to Pnina-Mazal, who had bought a spacious new apartment in the suburb of Rehavia and taken Yitzhak to live with her. Sara warned them that Pnina-Mazal's house was full of cats, and anyone who disliked four-footed creatures with whiskers might prefer to meet her outside her home. Elizabeth burst out laughing at the description of the cats and informed Sara that she too had a house full of cats, and that perhaps their common love of the creatures had originated in their childhood, for they had grown up like sisters.

∗　∗　∗

Early that evening Elizabeth, Pnina-Mazal, and Robert burst into Sara's house. Pnina-Mazal pushed the wheelchair and from time to time she hugged Elizabeth's shoulders warmly. So radiant with happiness were the two women that an onlooker might indeed have taken them for a pair of sisters, arbitrarily parted by the cruel hand of fate and meeting again after long years of separation. Robert, deprived of his occupation, stood to one side, Edward's shy smile on his face and his hands delving deep in his pockets as if searching for something to do.

On Sara's scarred wooden table supper was ready: warm homemade pitas, a finely chopped salad in a tahini sauce, eggs fried with fragrant herbs, green olives from the giant jar standing in the corner of the kitchen, and purple mulberry preserves for dessert.

Giggling like schoolgirls Pnina-Mazal and Elizabeth sat and reminisced, and after they ran out of memories they talked about cats, compared numbers and sizes and gave each other advice on rearing and breeding.

After black coffee and sesame cookies Sara led them to her bedroom. "Open the lid of the *sandouk,*" she instructed Pnina-Mazal.

The two women stared in astonishment at the stacks of tins revealed to their eyes.

"You never told me." Pnina-Mazal looked reproachfully at her mother.

Sara ignored the tone of rebuke in her voice and asked them to take out the tins and put them on the bed. When they reached the tin at the bottom of the chest she stopped them and explained that it contained pictures that were not fit to be seen.

With flushed, expectant faces, as gay and lighthearted as a couple of schoolgirls, Pnina-Mazal and Elizabeth opened tin after tin. They spilled the pictures onto Sara's starched bed linen, and fanning them out like hands of cards they inspected and discussed them one by one.

With every picture removed from its tin and laid aside Sara felt as if she had been stabbed by a dagger. When she could bear it no longer she left them to it, and only returned when Robert came into the kitchen some hours later and told her that they had finished. Sara tried to ignore the big pile of photographs lying on Elizabeth's knees as she sat erect in her wheelchair and said good-bye to her with a smile and a hug.

"Naturally I'll send you a copy of my book," promised Elizabeth, raising herself slightly in her wheelchair to kiss the bending Sara's forehead, and she wheeled herself rapidly into the darkness outside as if afraid that Sara would regret it and ask her for the pictures back. Pnina-Mazal and Robert argued over the right to push the wheelchair; Pnina-Mazal won, and pushed her friend through the narrow alleys of the neighborhood.

When they reached the taxi waiting at the end of the road, crazy Dvora caught up with them, panting for breath and holding a flat parcel wrapped up in newspaper in her hand.

"Sara wanted you to have this too," she said and gave Elizabeth the parcel.

Elizabeth put the parcel on her knees. Carefully she unwrapped the newspaper and found herself looking into her father's light blue eyes.

"Sara wants to give me the picture that was hanging on her wall?" she asked incredulously.

"Yes, she asked me to tell you that the picture belongs to you. She only had it for safekeeping," she said, and made her way back up the alley to Sara's house, her wooden clogs clattering loudly on the paving stones.

Elizabeth stared at the picture and tears streamed from her eyes and wet the lenses of her glasses, trickled down her nose, and dripped onto the glass of the frame, where they collected in a salty little puddle.

Pnina-Mazal gently stroked her hair, then opened the door of the taxi and together with Robert helped the weeping Elizabeth to get in and sit down.

Sara and Pnina-Mazal never received a copy of the book. When Pnina-Mazal tried to find out the reason for the delay, she received an official letter from Elizabeth's publisher. The letter, which opened with the words "I am sorry to inform you," explained everything.

Soon after her return to America, the paralysis had spread through Elizabeth's body and she died before she could finish her new book. Pnina-Mazal's letters to Robert went unanswered, and were returned with the stamp: "Address Unknown." The pictures that had been so carefully selected were never found.

✻ ✻ ✻

My grandmother Pnina-Mazal never married again. In a moment of frankness Sara told me that she suspected it was because of her, because Pnina-Mazal didn't want to leave her. Today I'm sure that Pnina-Mazal never remarried because of her cats. She had plenty of suitors, but they were all defeated in the battle for her heart and gave up trying when they saw that her cats were more important to her than they were. The most persistent of them all was Avner from the Main Post Office on Jaffa Road, who was Pnina-Mazal's neighbor. But he too retired from the field after bloody battles with her cats, who drove a wedge between them.

Nobody knows how many of them there were. Thirty, forty, or perhaps fifty. And in every imaginable color: black, white, gray, red, brown, and striped. With red, green, brown, and blue eyes. Only at night they all looked the same: black with red eyes, glittering and dazzling as the headlights of a car. And they were everywhere. On the beds, taking over the down quilts, littering in the cupboards and settling down there with their kittens at their teats. Above all they were drawn to the kitchen, the icebox, and the pantry.

And a strong smell pervaded the air. As if it weren't cats she kept there but skunks spraying the threshold and the doorways with their stink as if to announce: This is where I live, and anyone who doesn't like the smell can go somewhere else. And the noise was unbearable, too, especially in springtime, when the howling of the cats in heat rose into the scented air and drove the neighbors insane.

Avner, the bachelor neighbor, suffered more than anyone else from the warm bundles of fur that surrounded Pnina-Mazal wherever she went. From the day he moved into a rented room in the building where she lived, and his eyes met hers, he made it a habit to drop in for coffee every afternoon, listening to the operas she played him on her gramophone, telling her about his plans for his retirement, and always pretending not to notice the stench. Sometimes they were to be seen holding hands in the Zion cinema, and afterward in the Nava café, gazing into each other's eyes over the steaming cups of tea on the marble table. The week he intended to go to Sara and ask her formally for her daughter's hand, the incident occurred.

Avner spent most of his time at the Main Post Office on Jaffa Road. He licked stamps, tied parcels, and sealed them with red sealing wax. In the evening, when he reached his room, he would put the cauldron on the gas ring, and when the water boiled he would wash his dirty shirt, starch it, and iron it with his steam iron. Anyone who didn't know him and who saw him in his immaculate ironed shirts was sure that he had a devoted wife at home, competing with her neighbors over the whiteness of her husband's shirts and the stiffness of their collars. Every morning he left his house in a freshly washed and ironed shirt, and even when the collars and cuffs began to fray, he would go on washing, starching, and ironing his shirts to death.

One evening, when he returned to his room with the sweet taste of the glue on the stamps he had been licking for eight hours on his tongue, he put the cauldron on the stove to boil as usual, and prepared to wash his best shirt, which he intended to wear the next day when he went to ask Sara for her daughter's hand. When he had finished washing it, he ironed some other shirts, and as he was putting them carefully away in the wardrobe, he heard a knock at the door. Glad to have his solitariness interrupted, he hurried to the door and opened it wide. But there was no visitor waiting on the doorstep. Disappointed, he closed the door behind him without noticing Pnina-Mazal's old striped cat stealing into the room. Its swollen belly and teats worn out by generations of sucking kittens dragged on the floor.

In the morning he got out of bed and with eyes bleary from sleep pulled a shirt from the top of the pile. Then a hairy paw armed with claws as sharp as spurs descended on his outstretched hand and left four bloody scratches on his skin. His hands groping wildly in the darkness of the wardrobe seized hold of the fur of the four-footed creature that was lying on his starched shirts, with the toothless pink gums of five tiny, softly purring kittens sticking to it like leeches. For the first time since he had started working at the Main Post Office on Jaffa Road, Avner did not show up for work that morning. After he had taken his courage in his hands and shaken the mother and her offspring off his shirts stained with blood, hairs, and flea droppings, he could not find a clean shirt to wear. Not even at the bottom of the pile.

Then he came to a decision. He left the house in a stained shirt full of wisps of fur and strode furiously in the direction of the Machane Yehuda market. He returned with kilos of chicken feet and heads packed in big cardboard orange boxes, which he dragged all the way home. Pnina-Mazal's fifty cats came out to meet him and followed him in single file up the stairs.

Like the Pied Piper of Hamelin leading the mice of the town to their deaths, Avner led the column of cats into his kitchen. And Avner was not the kind of man to let the cats eat raw meat. Till late at night he labored, cooking the chicken feet and heads in the great laundry cauldron on the gas ring. Then he dotted plates from his gold-rimmed china dinner service all round the house, and settled down to watch them enjoying their last supper. So he thought, at least, for on his way to the market he had stopped at Oppalteka's pharmacy at the entry to the Even Israel quarter. What he bought there nobody knows for sure, but it certainly included a sedative. After they had eaten their fill he gave the cats water to push the food into their stomachs, and in the water he sprinkled the pharmacist's powder.

And the cats slept. And how they slept, for they did not even feel him picking them up and squeezing them one on top of the other into the cardboard boxes that had previously held their food. He took them to the yard, where he had previously dug a pit, and threw them all into it, big and small; black, white, and striped; fat and thin; speckled and pied. After he had thrown them in he covered them with a pile of earth and danced on it for a long time like a Red Indian warrior.

*   *   *

What happened the next day nobody in the neighborhood will ever forget. The drama began when Pnina-Mazal burst into the street, her hair disheveled, claiming that she had been robbed. The neighbors who had gathered at the sound of her cries burst into relieved laughter when it transpired that the only thing she had been robbed of were her disgusting cats. The cat haters among them sniggered and swore that they had nothing to do with it, and that they wouldn't have stolen a single flea-bitten tail from her menagerie of wild animals, not even if their lives depended on it. Then they began to joke. They mentioned a certain Yerahmiel, a skinner who worked with Yehuda the tanner, and said that he might have stolen the cats to make a fur coat for the fat lady from the first floor, whose wardrobe was crammed with the furs of creatures that had long disappeared from the face of the earth. Every day, even on the hottest summer days, this woman would emerge from her house with her head held high, all her double chins wobbling, and her body, which resembled a stack of tires, wrapped in the fur of some anonymous hairy creature that had sacrificed its short life on the altar of her body. And when the fount of their jokes ran dry, they ran to protect Avner and his daring deed, refusing to hand him over to the furious Pnina-Mazal.

At that moment a terrible voice broke from the depths of the earth. And the voice grew louder and louder, as if dozens of devils were about to burst out of hell, scatter in all directions, and punish them all for their sins. As the faces of the neighbors clouded in anxiety, Pnina-Mazal's shrieks turned to shouts of joy: "That's my Sisi, that's my Mimi, my Yuki, my Ziva!" For they all had names and she knew them all and could recognize them by their voices, and many of her neighbors were ready to swear that they had heard her talking to them in their own language, and they answered her, and she did whatever they asked her to. And after she had recognized their voices she ran to the mound of freshly dug earth where the sound was coming from, and began scraping it away with her fingernails. Nobody went to help her. Only Avner, who was kindhearted by nature, and who loved her dearly, and who had only done what he did on the impulse of the moment, took a soup spoon from his kitchen and tried to help her break through the layer of earth.

One by one they emerged from the bowels of the earth, like soldiers in camouflage uniforms emerging from their trenches, the pupils of their eyes, which had grown accustomed to the darkness, contracting and narrowing to blind slits in the daylight. Tottering and stumbling they emerged on their four velvety paws, indistiguishable from one another, their coats stiff and clotted with dirt. And Pnina-Mazal greeted them joyfully, like a mother welcoming her long-lost children, hugging each of them as if it were the dearest to her heart, calling it by name, kissing its dusty ears, and sending it home with a light slap on the rear. And thus they emerged from the pit, all thirty, forty, or maybe fifty cats, down to the last one, safe and sound and hungry. And people say that there were even three more of them, for one of the cats who had been buried in the last stages of pregnancy had given birth in the darkness of the pit, and came out accompanied by her litter, gripping the napes of their necks between her teeth.

And the unfortunate Avner, who was a pure-hearted and honest man, could not look Pnina-Mazal in the eye, even though she never said a word to him about what had happened to her pets. His marriage plans were buried in the pit together with the cats.

That same week he carefully packed all his shining, stiff-collared shirts in tissue paper, after boiling and laundering them all over again, and moved to another neighborhood. Pnina-Mazal remained in her big house with her cats, and from that day on none of her neighbors dared to slander her pets, never mind kick one or another of them who happened to cross his path. For if they had emerged unscathed from the bowels of the earth, and even multiplied there, it could only mean that they were protected by hidden forces, and it was forbidden to touch them, speak ill of them, or even think bad thoughts about them.

Chapter Nineteen

 The many stories about the women of my family did not bring me any nearer to my father. When I despaired of finding him, my mother's comrades sent me to Sasha.

"Sasha knew your mother better than any of us," they told me. "He was the only one she was prepared to talk to, and not only about the problems of the Party."

I found him on Haj Adoniya Hacohen Street, in an old-age home in the Bukharan quarter. I asked a wrinkled, parchment-skinned old crone, dozing on a chair at the entrance to the building, where I could find him. Her reaction to his name was unexpected. The wrinkles on her face deepened in a broad smile, and with an agility surprising for her age she led me to him, skipping like a girl. With a childish gesture she pointed her finger at an old man seated in a fetal position in a wheelchair in the yard.

He seemed very merry and carefree as he sat there loudly cracking jokes to an admiring audience of his peers. The hard of hearing among them held their ears close to his roaring mouth, and the slanting rays of the afternoon sun reddened their transparent, blue-veined earlobes. He smiled as I approached him and I returned his smile. His eyes, traveling over my body with the appraising look of a man in his prime, brought an embarrassed blush to my cheeks.

"And what's a beauty like you doing in this vale of tears?" he asked, and caressed my breasts and legs with his eyes.

"I wanted to ask you a few questions," I replied, and the blush spread to my neck and chest.

"Go on, shoo." He waved his arms at the old folks surrounding him. "God has answered my prayers. She's come at last," he roared at them as they began shuffling off obediently in the direction of the building. "Don't disturb us. This is the girl of my dreams. Paradise couldn't be better."

I sat down on the chair vacated next to him. The seat was still warm from the buttocks of a little admirer who bore a pointed hump like a mark of Cain on her back. The beady black eyes glittering in her birdlike face fixed me with a malevolent look.

"Don't take any notice of her," he said, and waved his skinny arm dismissively at the little hunchback limping toward the door. "She's in love with me," he boasted. "And this is her chair. She curses anyone who sits on it. And she knows how to give the evil eye, too, so you'd better spit on the ground and make a hamsa at her back," he added with a mischievous smile.

For a moment I was tempted to do as he said. I looked at him again, and at the sight of the twinkle in his eye I clenched the fingers of my left hand, which had already begun to spread out in the five-fingered sign, into a fist.

"And now, my beauty, what can I do for you? As you see, I can't do you much good in the bed department," he said, and glanced at his loins.

"I wanted to ask you . . ."

"I knew you weren't going to drag me to bed." He sighed. "So what's the question?"

"Geula from the Party is my mother."

For a moment it seemed to me that his face froze and showed signs of embarrassment.

"I came to ask you if you ever met my father." I heroically succeeded in finishing the sentence.

The expression on his face changed again, and this time it grew grave. It seemed to me that another old man had taken his place on the chair. Deep lines netted the laughing expression I had previously seen on his face. He raised his eyes and looked at me, no longer with the look of an old lecher but that of a kindly grandfather whose beloved granddaughter has come to visit him.

From that moment on he began to talk about her without a pause. As if the mere mention of her name had pressed a hidden button and activated a machine that could not be stopped. He spoke for about an hour, and when he finished talking he fell immediately into a deep sleep, and did not reply when I said good-bye. As if the effort of remembering had drained the last vestiges of his strength.

What follows is the tape recording I made of his words.

"Of course I knew her. Who didn't know her in Jerusalem? She always stood out. She had the reddest hair I've ever seen. Not the usual ginger but red as blood. Her hair was stiff and unruly and stood out wildly round her head. She had pointed teeth, which gave her a cunning, foxy look. But that wasn't the only reason she stood out. She was always the cleverest and most extreme. She reached us very young, at the age of thirteen or fourteen, together with the Arab boy who jumped to attention at her every request. I think they came with an old Party member who later went back to Russia. Was he her teacher? I don't know. In short, as I said, she was very sharp and very extreme. She wanted us to plant bombs in the Jewish Agency offices and the British army headquarters. She incited us to engage in bloody campaigns against the Hagana, composed virulent leaflets calling for an all-Arab revolt against the British occupation and Jewish imperialism, and painted slogans on the walls. We didn't always agree with her. And when we didn't, she would send us hard, dark looks that gave us gooseflesh, even though they came from a mere child, and later on, a young girl. In spite of her youth, she succeeded in gathering a large following. Because of her, we almost split into two camps. The Arab boy, in his quiet way, was the only one who succeeded in restraining her. They spoke to each other in a strange, guttural language none of us could understand. It wasn't Arabic or Hebrew, or a combination of the two. Later on, when I met her mother, she told me that they had grown up together at the breasts of the same wet-nurse and invented a language of their own. The Arab boy worshiped her, and when she proposed her wild schemes, he would gently stroke her hand. When she got excited she was like a raging fire, lashing out indiscriminately in all directions. The Arab boy would pour water on the flames, not to put them out but to confine the fire and prevent it from spreading out of control and consuming everything it came into contact with. A romantic connection between them? I'm prepared to swear that there were no romantic or sexual ties between them. They loved each other very much, but like a brother and sister. Once I even asked her about it discreetly, and she looked at me with those flashing eyes and told me to mind my own business. Afterward, in a moment of grace, she opened up and told me that any such relationship with him was impossible, because it would be like incest. In short, she succeeded in twisting us all round her little finger. She received a lot of encouraging letters and praise from the Comintern. At a certain stage, when her opinions became so extreme that they endangered the Party, we tried to talk to her. But she stood her ground. She ignored all our warnings, and in all the Party debates she would repeat, 'In the end you'll see that I was right.' At that stage, when we began to oppose her ideas, she began to suspect her comrades in the Party of plotting against her, and she went into hiding. The Arab acted as a liaison between her and the Party, and she would send messages and instructions through him. When she saw that we weren't taking any notice, she gathered a handful of supporters around her and tried to operate independently of us. She printed pamphlets and held secret meetings. In those days bloody incidents took place. She knew that many of the comrades were so fed up with her that they wanted to hand her over to the authorities, in order, for once and for all, to get rid of this "red menace," as they called her. And so she stayed in hiding. Until she had a baby—in other words, you. Who was the father? She never told a soul. I'm sure it wasn't the Arab. A secret romance? As far as I know she never had one. Men were afraid of her, of her red hair, of her pointed teeth and her sharp tongue. She was always opinionated, extreme, and hard as nails. She looked like a man, she never showed any tenderness or exposed her feelings, and she walked around with a tough expression on her face, as if to say 'Don't come near me and don't touch me.' She dressed in a peculiar way too. She always wore men's clothes that were a few sizes too big for her, and tried to hide her figure. When she finally emerged from hiding we almost fell off our chairs. It was the last thing we expected to see. Never mind the fact that her hair was black with red roots and she was wearing dark glasses like a blind woman—all our eyes were fixed on her stomach. It was huge, and she was in the eighth month of her pregnancy. Apart from that, she was the same as usual: the extreme opinions, the tongue lashings, and the accusations of betrayal. She related to her pregnancy as if it had nothing to do with her, or to be exact, as if it didn't belong to her body. Nobody asked her who the father was. We were all afraid of her. Only that Arab of hers danced attendance on her and waited on her hand and foot. She exploited him. He would bring her delicacies during the siege of Jerusalem, clean her chair with his handkerchief before she sat down, and support her when she walked. Naturally we asked him who the father was. We were all bursting with curiosity. None of us could imagine her in a romantic context with a man, and speculations were rife. But the moment she approached with her huge belly, we would all fall silent and avert our eyes from her belly, afraid of her sharp tongue. In general, we would always shrink in her presence, and now, with her huge stomach, we were even more afraid of her than before. What did the Arab tell us? He said that he didn't know. He also stated firmly that he wasn't interested in what had happened, but only in the results. When we pushed him to the wall, he would shrug his shoulders, roll his black eyes to heaven, and say self-righteously that we should stop prying into her life, that he didn't care who the father was, and in any case, we could take his name off the list of suspects. Rumors? There were plenty of rumors. Since none of us were attracted to her, and even if anyone was he would be too frightened of her terrible character to do anything about it, we dismissed the possibility that the father was one of the comrades. At the time in question, let me remind you, she was living underground and hardly came into contact with anyone except for her followers, who revered her, were in awe of her, and obeyed her instructions blindly, never mind how dangerous and insane they were. It's hard to believe that any of her disciples made her pregnant. They worshiped her from afar, they worshiped the ground she walked on. But to get her pregnant? Not even in their wildest dreams. So I repeat: The chance that her daughter was the product of a romantic relationship is very slim indeed. I'm sorry to disappoint you. I don't believe anyone in the world knows the answer except for your mother herself. And maybe even she doesn't know. Rumors? There were plenty of those—like the rumors about the cruel gang rape that scandalized the town for months on end. The rumor spread because of a yeshiva student who participated in the rape, and afterward his conscience bothered him and he made the story public, thereby incriminating himself. The rabbis of the yeshiva, Hassidei

Tzaddikim I think it was called, denied the whole thing, issuing curses
and ostracisms against the impudent boy who had dared to besmirch the
reputations of their innocent and illustrious students. What happened to
him? Nobody knows. He vanished from the yeshiva after giving evidence at the police station. No doubt he couldn't cope with the pres-
sures exerted on him. They hushed the whole thing up very quickly,
especially because the victim, a man or a woman, never made a complaint to the police but disappeared, and the case was closed. I remember
that people speculated about it in secret, and even split their sides laughing at the thought that she had some little yeshiva student with earlocks
and a beard swimming in her womb. This thought was particularly
amusing to the comrades because she hated those yeshiva students so
much, she loathed and detested them. It's not certain she was raped, but
it's hard to ignore the coincidence, especially since she was living in the
ultra-Orthodox neighborhood of Meah Shearim at the time. No, I never
visited her there, but I was told that her room was right in the middle
of the neighborhood and right next door to the yeshiva from which the
rapists came. I'm sorry I told you. Why don't you ask her? She refuses
to talk? What about your grandmother? She doesn't know either? I'm
really sorry. I'm sure there isn't a person in the world who knows about
the circumstances of your birth, apart from your mother. Perhaps she
doesn't know either, and that's why she has nothing to tell you. One
thing I can tell you. That pregnancy softened her toward the end. We
sensed that she was truly happy about giving birth. She even began to
knit. Yes. Who would have believed it? At our meetings she was quiet
and soft-spoken, quite unlike her usual self, and her hands were busy
knitting little white bootees and baby jackets. And when you were born,
she brought you with her to the Party meetings. She would put you
down in a padded Jaffa orange crate, and glance at you lovingly from
time to time while she clattered her knitting needles. The noise of those
knitting needles drove everybody crazy, but we were afraid to ask her
to stop. And the Arab? He stuck to her like a Siamese twin, and he was
very proud of you. He would rock you in his arms as if he really was
your father, coo at you, and sing you songs in Arabic. Later on I heard
that she concluded her legal studies. She wanted to defend the perse-
cuted Arab minority, so she told us on one of her appearances at the
Party office; these became rarer and rarer, until she stopped coming
altogether, and disappeared together with her Arab. From then on I

never heard a thing about them until you suddenly showed up, as beautiful as the girl of my dreams. Promise me that you'll come back to visit me in my dreams, and give your mother my regards."

* * *

Thousands of women acompanied my great-grandmother Sara on her last journey. Young and old, barren and fertile, women in long, dark dresses with scarves bound tightly round their shining bald heads, others in tight-fitting jeans and platform heels, their eyes outlined in black. There were women of every community there: Jewesses, Arabs, Christians, Armenians, and even Druse in long white veils, who had come from the distant north to pay their last respects to their benefactress. They all walked in silence behind the stretcher, which gave off a scent of dying roses. In spite of the thousands of women gathered there in a medley of colors and tongues, there were no sounds of weeping or cries of grief, as if they were all resigned to her death and understood with the secret knowledge of the faithful that even after her death they would continue to receive her blessings.

When her light body was laid in its last resting place, and the undertakers asked her forgiveness and covered the pit gaping like a wound in the ground, the mourners were enveloped by a heavy scent of wilted roses. Not even the ritual washing of hands at the exit from the cemetery succeeded in ridding them of the flowery smell of death clinging to their bodies. And the smell stole up the steps of the buses waiting outside the cemetery, settled onto the padded seats, penetrated the air-conditioning systems, and traveled the length and breadth of the country in air-conditioned comfort, announcing the arrival of the mourning women.

* * *

About a year after her death I dared to enter her house. Actually I had no option, with both my mother and Pnina-Mazal pushing me to sell the house for them with the help of the Gates of Jerusalem real estate agency. At the office they warned me that it would be no easy job to sell the property, and that I would have to compromise on the price. The first to apply were a young couple who were looking for a house with a red-tiled roof, patterned floor tiles, and a small garden. Neither the general dilapidation of the neighborhood nor the increasingly ultra-Orthodox population deterred them from their determination to buy a house there. I led them through the narrow, winding lanes, which were inaccessible to motorcars. The narrower and more inaccessible to traffic the alleys became, the more their faces glowed with happiness. In a burst of uncontrollable enthusiasm the young woman whispered to her husband, loudly enough for me to hear, that when they had children they would never have to worry about them playing in the street and getting run over by motorcars. As soon as they saw the house and garden their eyes widened in delight, and with the frankness of people unpracticed in the art of commerce and bargaining, they enthusiastically informed me that this was the house of which they had always dreamed.

The iron door opened obediently to the turn of the key, releasing the strong smell of wilted roses that had been trapped inside the rooms for the past year. I walked round the house, opening the iron shutters with their little bars whose knobs were shaped like soldiers' heads adorned with fezzes. The house was flooded with sunlight. The rays of light breaking through the windows danced on the carpetlike floor tiles with their geometric patterns, touched the high whitewashed ceiling, and proudly displayed the rooms, which were gleaming with cleanliness, as if during all this time some hidden hand had been diligently cleaning the deserted house.

The young man took his wife by the waist and they began waltzing round the floor, humming a tune to themselves in unison. After they had danced through all the rooms they stood before me with flushed faces, tidying their hair and clothes, and announced that they were going to buy the house.

"It was built especially for us," they said to me.

I tried to show them the kitchen, to explain how to use the antiquated water pump and how to clean the water cistern underneath the house. They stubbornly refused to listen.

"There's no need," the young man said, dismissing my explanations. "I told you that the house is ours, and we'll find everything out ourselves."

I soon found myself leaning against the wall of the empty entrance hall, watching them arranging furniture in their imaginations, each in his or her chosen room. At those moments I felt like a voyeur spying on a scene not meant for my eyes. When they caught me looking they approached me in embarrassment and asked when they could sign the contract.

I led them, quivering with excitement, outside and showed them the garden and the mulberry tree sheltering the house with its branches. I looked up at the leafy crest and told them about the owner of the house, my great-grandmother Sara, who had planted the tree as soon as she moved in. They examined the tree from every side and saw the deep scar on its trunk. Then they heard the tale of the Turkish soldiers who had broken into my great-grandmother's garden and tried to chop the tree down for firewood. Once I had touched on the war, I told them about the other war and the siege of Jerusalem, the hunger and the scarcity, and how when the mallow leaves in the fields shriveled up in the summer my great-grandmother knew how to make delicacies from mulberry leaves stuffed with rice she bought on the black market, and how I could still taste their sour-sweet taste on my tongue.

I gladly offered them the recipe, explaining that the secret of success lay in picking the leaves at the right time. They had to be plucked from the tree before sunrise, when they were still drenched with the morning dew. Then you had to put them in a pot with a little water and steam them until they were soft. When they were soft enough they were stuffed with rice flavored with coriander and olive oil.

And then I told them about my mother, who liked to hide in the luxuriant foliage of the tree when she was a child, and, to the anxiety of those watching from below, to pluck the mulberries growing on the uppermost branches.

I told them about myself too, and what a coward I was, and how I would stand on a stool to pick the mulberries from the lowest branches, popping the juicy fruit carefully into my mouth lest the white blouse of my school uniform be stained with purple.

Nor did I forget to mention the flocks of sparrows twittering on the branches during the feasts they held there, or the swarms of black bats stealthily descending at night, and departing when the first rays of the sun appeared above the treetop, with their hairy bellies full of mulberries.

Carried away by my stories of the silkworm moths hovering over the tree, I failed to notice the clouds gathering on the faces of the young couple as they raised their eyes to the top of the tree. I followed their gaze with my eyes and I understood. In spite of the summer heat there was not a single mulberry on the tree.

"The neighborhood children must have picked the fruit and the birds and the bats must have finished the job," I said, trying to defend the tree without being asked.

"The tree doesn't bear fruit," the man said. "Look at the ground. There isn't a single stain and there are no birds in the branches."

"That's impossible," I said, and immediately realized the justice of his words. The mulberry tree, whose branches had always been full of cheeky sparrows greedily pecking at its fruit in the summer months, stood erect and bare of both fruit and birds, like an aristocrat stripped of his assets.

"Perhaps we should bring a gardener to explain the phenomenon?" I tried to reassure them. "Such a thing has never happened before. The tree has borne fruit every summer, it's never missed a single season."

The worried eyes of the husband strayed to the neighboring yard, where Esther had recently departed this world, and came to rest on the huge mulberry tree that was dying as it stood, its dry, leafless branches dwarfing the house at its feet.

"That's the cause," he said triumphantly. "The tree in that yard is dry."

"What's the connection?" his wife and I asked at once.

"Very simple," he said with a smile. "The mulberry tree is dioecious. They're divided like us into male and female. The pollen from the male blossoms is carried by the wind or various insects to the female blossoms, and it pollinates them. The dying tree in the yard next door is a male tree, and until we plant a new male tree our tree won't have any fruit. As you know"—he put his arm round his wife's waist and turned to me—"there can be no fertilization or reproduction without a male."

Silently I handed him the key, and named a date for the signing of the contract.

I left them standing arm in arm under the shade of the mulberry tree and went away with a heavy heart. That same day I went to the plant nursery of Avraham Farchi and Sons in the suburb of Talpiot and bought a fresh sapling of a male mulberry tree in an old pickle tin.

⁕ ⁕ ⁕

Once a month I would go up to the Mount of Olives with my son to visit my great-grandmother's grave. I began these visits straight after her death and I am still paying them today, by myself. In those early days I

would park my little Fiat at the foot of the hill, unstrap my son from
the baby seat in the car, take him in my arms, and make my way up a
crooked path between the thousands of crowded gravestones covering
the bare, rocky hill in an endless labyrinth.

Many times, as I made my way confidently toward her grave, I
would encounter people with giddy, confused expressions on their faces,
as if they had just stepped onto solid ground after a terrifying ride on a
roller coaster. They would seize my arm and beg me to help them find
the graves of their loved ones. I was never able to help them and I
would meet them again on my way down, after my visit was over,
wandering round the rocky graves in endless circles, with sad resignation
on their faces.

Unlike these hidden graves, concealing themselves among the
thousands of flat tombstones as if they were determined not to be visited,
the way to Sara's grave was distinct, familiar, and easy. A narrow path
beaten by the thousands of small, hopeful steps of women pleading for
their wombs to be visited, and retrodden by those coming to give thanks
for their bellies that had been filled and emptied again. People said that
you could also find Sara's grave by the smell, and that a scent of wilted
roses wafted into the air like a cloud from her grave and led the supplicants to it by their noses.

The source of the smell was the mound of plucked roses slowly
wilting next to her grave in the sun, which dried them and preserved
their scent. The blooms were brought by the women seeking her blessing, every supplicant laying a single rose on her grave as if they had
agreed among themselves beforehand to propitiate their benefactress
with roses.

In the course of time the smell was enhanced from an unexpected
quarter. Mussa, a quick-witted Arab boy whose nose was tickled by the
scent of the roses, smelled a chance to make a profit, and set up shop
at the foot of the stony hill, offering red roses for sale to the women
who had come without an offering. Underneath the umbrella that sheltered his dark skin from the sun he would smell out the supplicants, bar
their way to the grave, and like a stubborn suitor he would offer them
a single rose, holding the stem carefully by the tips of his fingers, as if
afraid the thorns would punish him for his exorbitant prices. With expressionless faces they would take out their purses and without batting
an eyelid they would pay him what he asked, even though they could

have bought a magnificent bunch of perfect roses in a fancy florist shop for the price he demanded for a single rose.

And the smell was enhanced from another quarter too. Early one morning, when I was sure that I would be alone with Sara and would not have to share her attention with the waiting women, I found crazy Dvora there. She was absorbed in her activities and did not hear the gravel crunching under my shoes. Muttering crazily to herself, she was intent on sprinkling the gravel with scented water from a bottle bearing a pink label on which was written in Hebrew and Arabic: "The Abu-Ali Distillery, Ramalla Rose Water." When I came up and stood next to her, she started violently, as if she had been somewhere else entirely, and told me without being asked, with an innocent look on her face, that she had come to freshen up the grave and quite by chance she had brought this old bottle, without noticing that it contained rose water.

Today the place can be recognized by the huge mulberry tree with its mighty boughs that shelter the grave in their shade. This tree, the only one growing on the bald hill, I planted myself on the first anniversary of her death. At first, the cemetery guards did not notice it. When it grew they tried to uproot it on the grounds that its strong roots were liable to penetrate the graves, crack the gravestones, raise them up, and disturb the dead. And even worse, the roots would latch onto the bodies of the departed seeking eternal rest, suck the marrow of their bones, and interfere with the work of the worms.

War to the bitter end was declared on the hill, the guards against the tree and the women against the guards. Whenever they came to chop down the tree the women defended it like wildcats and scratched their cheeks until they bled. For fear of the pink talons threatening their faces, and cowed by the determination of the women to save the tree that sheltered them from the burning summer sun, the guards surrendered and laid down their axes.

And the tree grew rapidly, striking roots into the dark, fertile soil filled with the humus of the decomposing bodies of the dead. And when it grew strong and tall, it pollinated the blossoms of the female mulberry tree that Mussa, his head swimming with figures and banknotes, planted at the foot of the hill. The juicy purple fruit he packed into paper bags and sold at an exorbitant price to the women visiting Sara's grave.

Instead of the customary stones, their offerings covered the gravestone. A little heap of plastic bracelets rose next to the mound of roses.

Pink and blue bracelets coiled together like snakes frozen in the middle of a mating dance. Every bracelet bore a woman's name and a date. These were the offerings of the women whose wombs had been visited. When they reached the place with their bellies emptied and their eyes full of the image of their newborn baby, they would remove the hospital bracelet, blue for a boy or pink for a girl, from their wrist, and lay it gratefully on the grave.

In the course of the years, as the gravestone was covered, they began to hang the bracelets on the branches of the mulberry tree, which shaded the grave with its decorated boughs. And in the winter, when it shed its leaves, the plastic bracelets would rattle on its naked braches.

Tourists who visited the site would take photographs of the Jerusalem Christmas tree with their pocket cameras. And when they showed the pictures to their families at home, they would tell them about the tree growing in the graveyard and the plastic bracelets that were a witness to the ancient biblical custom of making offerings to the dead. And there was even an article about the tree in *Science and Nature Magazine*. The anthropologist Bob Henrickson wrote about the custom of women who had given birth in Jerusalem to propitiate sacred trees planted in cemeteries.

I visited Sara's grave at all hours of the day and night, yet I never found myself alone with her. Late at night and early in the morning Dvora was there, as if she continued to count Sara's breaths at night and to wait for her to wake up so she could bring her a strong cup of coffee in the morning. And when she left, a long line of women swarmed from the foot of the hill to the grave. So I was obliged to share Sara's attention with the crowds of women who clustered round the black tombstone covering her, which at her request bore only the name Sara engraved on it in pink letters. And when the letters faded the women would take little bottles of pink nail polish from their makeup bags, and with the tiny brushes attached to the lids they would fill in the gaps in the letters with the shiny, metallic pink paint.

When I reached the grave I would put my son down far from the piles of dried roses, for fear of their thorns. The child would clamber gleefully onto the tombstone, seat himself on it as if it were his private playground, and sweep up the piles of bracelets with his chubby hands. Afterward I would seat him on my lap and show him how to attach the blue and pink strips of plastic to each other. Then I would join pink bracelet to blue bracelet in a long chain and hang it on the mulberry tree. And when my son tired of his games he would put the edge of a plastic bracelet in his mouth and chew it with his brand-new teeth.

And when the sun set opposite the hill, we would go down, making our way through a forest of deserted tombstones. Mussa would always be waiting for me at the foot of the hill, to give me the roses he had not succeeded in selling that day, fix his burning eyes on mine, tickle my son under the chin, and ask me to come and visit him the next day too.

At home, after the ritual of putting my son to bed, I would cram the roses, whose thorns Mussa had considerately clipped for me, into a vase. When the scent of the flowers spread and filled the room, I would open Sara's iron *sandouk* and spend a long time communing with her pictures. And when the weariness spread though my limbs, I would curl up on the brass bed and feel the rocking of the waves sending a thrill of sweet pleasure into every cell of my body. Sara illuminates the dark room with her radiant hair, lies next to me on the bed that was once hers and is now mine, and tells me stories all night long of roses, of sweet-smelling horse manure, and of the comet that cleaved the sky of Jerusalem.